The Wise Man Returns

Also By Kenny Kemp

I Hated Heaven

Dad Was a Carpenter

The Welcoming Door

The Carpenter of Galilee

City on a Hill

Oki's Island

Lightland

The Wise Man Returns

KENNY KEMP

SWEETWATER BOOKS
AN IMPRINT OF CEDAR FORT, INC.
SPRINGVILLE, UTAH

This is a work of fiction. The characters, names, incidents, places, and dialogue are products of the author's imagination and are not to be construed as real. The views expressed within this work are the sole responsibility of the author and do not necessarily reflect the position of Cedar Fort, Inc., or any other entity.

ISBN 13: 978-1-59955-496-9

Published by Sweetwater Books, an imprint of Cedar Fort, Inc.
2373 W. 700 S., Springville, UT, 84663
Distributed by Cedar Fort, Inc., www.cedarfort.com

LIBRARY OF CONGRESS CATALOGING-IN-PUBLICATION DATA

Kemp, Kenny, 1955- author.
  The wise man returns / Kenny Kemp.
    pages cm
  Summary: Thirty years after his first visit, Melchior, one of the three magi, returns to Judea to seek council from the King of the Jews, but does not encounter Jesus until he is standing at the foot of the cross.
  ISBN 978-1-59955-496-9
  1. Magi--Fiction. I. Title.

  PS3561.E39922W57 2011
  813'.54--dc22

                            2010051110

Cover design by Angela Olsen
Cover design © 2011 by Lyle Mortimer
Edited by Michelle Stoll
Interior illustrations courtesy of Bonnie Sheets

Printed in the United States of America

10 9 8 7 6 5 4 3 2 1

Superstition is cowardice in
the face of the Divine.

—Theophrastus
c. 300 BC

PROLOGUE

I take my stylus in hand and write. If I have properly hidden this scroll, I am to you as a voice from the dust. I do not know how many years separate us—it may be few or many. The city I lived in all my life—the world's greatest city in my day—may to you now be nothing more than crumbling rubble. But never mind. I have a story to tell that will echo down the corridor of time, not because it is my story, but because it is his.

You may wish to know the identity of your narrator, and in that you are not alone, for I have sought all my life to know my own heart, and only recently have I begun to see myself clearly. That is also his story, but when he tells it through me, it becomes mine. And I have no doubt he is at this very moment telling a story through you as well. It is his way.

So, though we will get to his story shortly, allow me to introduce myself. I have been called by many names: pontiff, counselor, magistrate, astrologer, oracle, sorcerer . . . even wise man—a dubious title, given what I am about to relate.

I was born Melkorios Alexandreus. My forbears hailed from the land the Romans call Græcus. In Rome I am known by Emperor Tiberius Caesar Augustus as Melchorus of Alexandria, the city that is the capital of the Ægyptus province. In Alexandria, I am greeted reverently in the Great Library, Museum, and on the marble steps of the Serapeum temple by my priestly name, Serapion. In Judea, a few remember me simply as Melchior.

And the reason I am known in Judea? Because I once brought a gift to their newborn king, which his mother received with grateful tears. It was a valuable gift, an almost prescient gift: an ebony chest containing myrrh,

1

the aromatic resin of the dindin tree, used not only to ease the pain of childbirth but in the anointing of the dead as well. It was so used at both extremes of the young king's eventful life.

And who was he? Like all of us in the Empire, he had names in many languages. In Aramaic, the common language of his people, he was called Jeshua. In the Hebrew of his kinsmen, Joshua. The Greeks, my own people, knew him by a name you may find familiar:

JESUS.

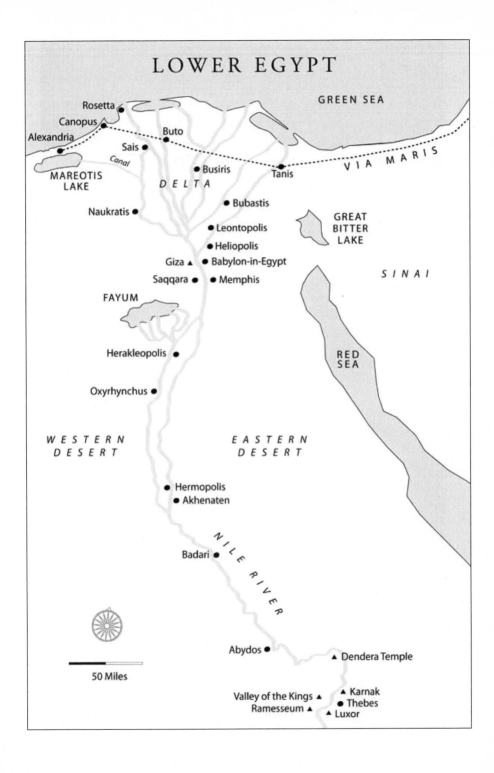

LOWER EGYPT

GREEN SEA

Rosetta
Canopus
Alexandria
Buto
Sais
VIA MARIS

MAREOTIS LAKE
Canal
DELTA
Busiris
Tanis

Naukratis
Bubastis
GREAT BITTER LAKE

Leontopolis
Heliopolis
Giza ▲ ● Babylon-in-Egypt
SINAI
Saqqara ● ● Memphis

FAYUM

Herakleopolis
RED SEA

Oxyrhynchus

WESTERN DESERT
EASTERN DESERT

Hermopolis
Akhenaten

NILE RIVER

Badari

50 Miles

Abydos
▲ Dendera Temple

Valley of the Kings ▲ ▲ Karnak
Ramesseum ▲ ● Thebes
▲ Luxor

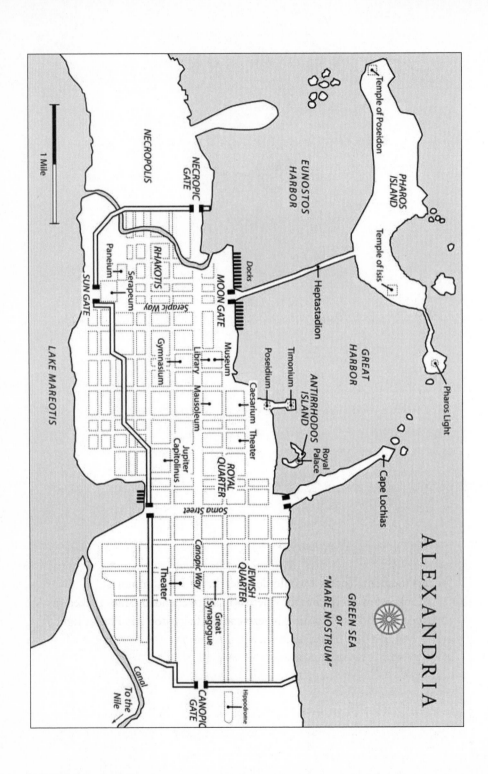

One

My story begins many years ago in Alexandria, where I write today, my fingers throbbing as they weakly grip the stylus, my remaining eye rheumy with age, and my back aching from my long journey home. I am bent over a table in the Great Library, surrounded by the world's most important books, yet my own small effort may dwarf them all. I say this not to boast but because it is a simple truth: others have seen the world as it is and have written about it; I have seen it as it will be, and you now hold my writings. You may judge which is of greater value.

More than thirty years ago, on a clear spring morning, I arose early, prayed before my fathers' death masks, had my head and face shaved by my servants, and stepped out of my villa onto Soma Street.

I had a long, curved knife with an ivory handle in my hand. Perfectly balanced and honed, it was a work of ancient art. I had waited a long time for this moment. Today, I would deal death, for I was immortal.

I looked toward the harbor where Soma Street ended. Ships rocked in their berths, and the morning breeze caught flags atop the Pharos light. The morning sun turned the Green Sea silver and white. A gaggle of albatross lifted off from the rocks. The air was chilly, but a brisk walk would take care of that. I smelled the sea, salt, and certainty. Today, I would fulfill my destiny.

I headed up the Soma: wide, marble-paved, and colonnaded. I felt my golden amulet bounce against my chest, a reminder of my limitless power.

I turned onto the Canopic Way, already thick with vendors, buyers, and slaves. I held the long knife loosely in my hand, swinging it back and forth as I walked, my face grim with purpose. Merchants saw me and fell to their knees, gesticulating. Children's eyes were covered by anxious mothers. A woman closed her shutters. I heard someone cry my name out from behind a closed door. I kept my eyes focused ahead and my chin raised. *I am Death*, I repeated inwardly. *All I do, I do for the glory of Serapis.*

I passed Alexander's red granite mausoleum, then turned onto the Serapic Way. Atop its acropolis, the brilliant white Serapeum came into view, its red tile roof commanding a view of all of Alexandria, from placid Lake Mareotis in the south to the rocky Pharos Island to the north; from the dusty City of the Dead in the west to the bustling eastern Jewish Quarter.

Tapering black granite pylons guarded the entrance to the square. As I passed, guards in crimson robes knelt, trembling hands clutching spears. I threaded my way across the forum between crowds of people, who fell to the earth when they saw me.

In two lines coursing down the steps, kneeling men demarcated an aisle. On the Temple porch stood twelve columns holding aloft the triangular pediment where Alexander leaned out of the stone, brandishing his sword, a copy of which I held in my hand.

As my feet touched the steps, everyone fell on their faces and began chanting. Some sobbed. As I climbed, I momentarily held my knife above the head of each penitent pontiff, measuring his worthiness. "Death comes," I hissed.

At the top of the steps, I turned and faced the forum. Hundreds of people lay prostrate, hands stretched out before them, chanting. The melody was nonexistent, just a rhythmic repetition of words, but words that were designed to appease *me*.

But I would not be appeased until I tasted blood.

The doors of the Temple stood open. I pulled the heavy curtain aside and entered. The cool darkness smelled of citron incense. I stood alone in the vastness of the adytum. In the dark, I saw movement. Kronion walked toward me with a torch. He knelt before me, extending the torch while I burnished the tip of my blade in the fire. Then I took the torch, ritually drawing my knife through the air in front of his neck, chest, and stomach. He fell to the ground, the first offering of the day.

I strode forward, holding the torch aloft. Column shadows rolled away as if in fear. My footsteps echoed on the marble. When I reached the rear of the hall, I lit a brazier atop a golden tripod. The hall filled with a dusky yellow light.

I looked up into the bearded face of Serapis, who sat on an immense marble throne. His eyes were hooded, and his thick hair fell in ringlets across his shoulders. He wore a great cylindrical crown and held a staff twined by two serpents. His right hand rested on the middle head of Cerberus, the three-headed guardian dog of the Underworld, who crouched at his knee.

I held the knife in both hands, raising it before Serapis. "Homage to you, O great god Khent, Amun-Tet, the Lord of Life forever, the renewed life of Ptah, Asar-Hapi, god of the Nile, the savior of Memphis, bull of the west, Askleios, Helios, son of Zeus. I come to assuage your anger and beg your benevolence."

I placed the knife on a swath of purple cloth draped over a gilded wooden box. Reaching down, I lifted a catch and opened a door. Inside, I grasped the lamb and lifted it out. It mewled weakly, and its spindly legs trembled. Smoothing its silky coat, I picked up the knife.

"Death is here," I said.

I emerged from the Temple, walked to the edge of the porch, and raised my blood-stained hands. The throng below, now numbering in the thousands, erupted into wild cheers.

All my life I have waited, I thought. *Today, I am Serapis!*

My patience had finally been rewarded. Just two weeks earlier, I had been appointed Supreme Pontiff. I had waited a long time for old Cheos to die or retire. I did nothing to hurry the former, but all I could to speed the latter. I was ambitious and, at thirty-six, well into middle age.

My assistant Kronion handed me the golden baton and placed the wreath upon my head. "Remember," he whispered, "you are human."

I turned to the forum and raised the baton. The multitude erupted in another burst of frenzied adulation. "Caesar! Caesar!" they chanted. People tore their clothing and threw themselves on the ground in ecstasy.

And today, I thought, *I am also Caesar Augustus.*

But I was not Caesar, whose golden baton was topped by an eagle, a reminder that while I represented him today at the Ides sacrifices, I most certainly was *not* the Emperor.

Nevertheless, I thought, *listen!*

"Long live Caesar!" they shouted. "Long live Serapion!"

The crowd undulated, swaying with the hypnotic chant. Women danced feverishly, men struck each other with joy, and children gamboled around their mothers' feet.

I nodded and the torch was again given me. I raised it, and the crowd fell silent. I walked toward the immense bronze brazier, shouting, "O great god Khent . . . ," and lit the oil-soaked wood, which exploded into flame, blasting smoke against the columns on either side. I continued the prayer but was drowned out as shouting people broke through the phalanx of guards at the foot of the steps. They raced toward us, holding their sacrifices out before them: a lamb, a goat, a bird, an ox shank—all to be consumed in the holy fire of Serapis.

I finished the prayer, but the sacrifices had already begun as people hurled their offerings into the fire, unable to wait for the pontiffs' blessing in their excitement.

I tossed the torch into the fire, recoiling at the animal screams. *At least they could wait until we cut the throats*, I thought in disgust, turning away. Kronion stood behind me, eyes bright with eagerness. He took my hands in his, relishing the still-sticky blood on them, and then wiped his hands proudly on his garments.

At the Temple entrance, I turned and looked back. The pontiffs were blessing sacrifices and throwing them into the fire. Smoke rose from the altar and boiled out from under the pediment eaves. Most offerings would be consumed in the brazier except for the choicest meat, which would fill the pontiffs' tables that night. The smoke would ascend to Olympus, and the smell of burning flesh would settle into the Underworld.

And the honor would go to Serapis, who bestrode both worlds in power and might.

Two

When the furor of the initial offerings died down, I took my place among the pontiffs at the brazier, blessing, killing, then tossing the carcasses into the fire.

By late afternoon, we were rushing to finish before nightfall. My voice finally gave out, and I waved a supplicant away. As I turned back to the Temple, I was surprised to see old Cornelius, the chief flamen of Jupiter Capitolinus. He had never so much as entered the Serapeum forum, yet here he stood on the Temple porch.

"I must talk to you," he said, motioning me to join him.

My surprise at seeing him was so complete that the remnants of my voice escaped me entirely. I merely nodded and joined him behind a column.

"You have been busy," he said, nodding toward the brazier, bloody with sacrifice, the half-consumed offerings strewn on the ground around it.

"Yes," I managed to croak.

"Too busy, I gather, to have heard the news."

"News?"

Cornelius leaned toward me, his toothless mouth working, spittle flying. "Today at dawn, in Babylon-in-Egypt, a bull was born."

I straightened with shock. "An Apis bull?"

"It bears the markings: a pure black coat with a white triangle on the forehead."

"And the vulture wing on the back?"

Cornelius nodded.

I leaned against the column, my knees suddenly weak. "And so near to Memphis!"

"How long has it been?" asked Cornelius.

"Five years," I said, "since we buried the old bull at Saqqara."

"You had begun to doubt," said Cornelius.

"Of course not," I said reflexively. "But why are *you* telling me this and not the pontiffs of Serapis at Memphis?"

Cornelius shrugged. "They too are sacrificing today. The flamens of Jupiter are delighted to share this good news with you. We all need good news when it comes to the gods." He turned away.

I grabbed his knobby shoulder, turning him back to me. "What does that mean?"

Cornelius looked up at me. He was no longer just old but tired as well. "Merely that the gods are not generous in these, the final days of the world."

"Final days!" I laughed. "Nonsense."

"Oh no?" said Cornelius. "Have you performed an augury recently?"

"I have seen no need." Yet I was getting nervous. Cornelius was not known to have an idle tongue.

"And you an astronomer!" he crowed. "Mark the omens!" he said, raising a bony finger and jabbing it skyward.

"What omens?"

He shook his head at my denseness, turned without speaking, and hobbled down the steps. I watched him go for a moment, then hurried to my chambers, excited beyond words. An Apis bull! Alive at Memphis, the storied city where the Nile river fans out into the delta. Memphis, City of Pharaohs, City of Light. Without an Apis bull, the world was out of balance. Unblemished black bulls were rare enough, but to find one with a diamond on its forehead, vulture wing markings on its shoulders, and the scarab mark under its tongue, was a miracle. Surely, Serapis had approved of my calling; hadn't Cornelius said the bull was born at dawn, prior to the beginning of our rites today? What other reason could there be? Old Cheos had offered daily pleas for the birth of a new bull for years, and his prayers had not been answered. But mine had.

I informed Kronion of the news and headed for the Island Palace to tell the Prefect as well. He received the notice with no more than a grunt, then turned away, leaving me standing on the ocean-side steps, confused and disappointed.

But later, as I trudged up the Soma toward home, I suddenly understood the Prefect's tepid reaction. Gaius Turranius would surely draw a connection between the bull's birth and my recent investiture as Supreme Pontiff. More importantly, the people of Alexandria would see the connection, and there would be no limit to the reverence I would receive; reverence perhaps even greater than they bestowed upon the Prefect himself. A sudden chill shook me. My power would increase.

"I must be careful," I whispered as I knocked on my door. *Careful indeed,* I thought. *The moment I return from Memphis, I must reinforce my loyalty to the Prefect. He must not become my enemy. Not yet.*

I tried to sleep but could not. I lay tossing and turning in my bed, visions of glory filling my fevered mind. Finally, a light, fitful sleep draped itself over me, and with it came a shocking dream. Cornelius stood before me on the Serapeum porch, growling, "Have you done an augury?"

I awoke in a panic. I had not.

I flew from my bed, dressed hurriedly, and raced along empty, dark streets. Above me, the River of Stars wound lazily in the blackness of eternity. On the eastern horizon, Scorpio was rising. I gulped back excitement. Cornelius was right. There would be omens.

I burst between the black pylons, startling the dozing guards. I bounded across the square and up the steps of the Serapeum, taking them three at a time. I pried open the great doors, swept through the heavy veil, and sprinted across the adytum, pausing for only an instant to kneel before Serapis, his stern visage now soft in the golden glow of the night braziers.

I burst into my offices, grabbed my *Star Almanac* codex from the shelf, and lit a candle with shaking hands. I cursed myself. Surely my failure to cast a natal chart immediately upon hearing the good news had erased any merit I had previously earned with Serapis today. To atone, I resolved to cast a flawless birth chart on behalf of the newborn calf. I dipped my stylus and held it poised over a sheet of vellum as I reflexively clutched my amulet and whispered a prayer.

Then, looking down, I stared at the blank parchment and reviewed the facts. Ptah created the world and controls the flooding of the Nile, and with it, mankind's destiny. His presence on earth is manifested through the Apis bull. There would be omens foreshadowing his coming. Again, I cursed myself; I hadn't marked any omens, so caught up was I in my own glory. Shaking my head, I vowed to honor Serapis more faithfully. My stylus touched the parchment, and I wrote: *Aprilis 17 of the 747th year of Rome and the 25th year of Augustus Caesar's rule.*

I then opened the *Almanac.*

THREE

The sun had risen by the time I stumbled from the Temple, all thoughts chased from my mind except those concerning the vellum I held in my trembling hand. I stood on the porch, blinded more by knowledge than the morning sun.

This was how Kronion found me, staring at the sky, my hands trembling. He pulled me back inside and guided me to my chambers, where he lay me on a couch and bathed my forehead with a moist towel. Suddenly, I came back to myself and jumped to my feet. "A king is born!"

"Yes, you told me yesterday," said Kronion. "Ptah returns in glory."

"Not Ptah!" I said, backing away. "Not Apis, not Osiris, not Serapis! Not any god of Mesopotamia, Egypt, Macedonia, Greece, Persia, or Rome!"

"What about Britannia?" asked Kronion, whose manner was to make jokes when he was afraid. And I was unnerving him with my behavior.

"Nor Britannia!" I shouted, thrusting the chart at him. "A king of the Jews!"

"The Jews have no king," he said, taking the chart without looking at it. "They have a prefect, just as we do, who rules at the pleasure of the Emperor."

"A king!" I shouted hoarsely.

"By the Black Stone, Serapion, what ails you?" Kronion backed away.

I pointed at the chart. "It is all there. I cast it last night. Look and see."

Kronion raised the chart, but before he could look at it, I snatched it away. I was afraid to let it out of my own hands. I was nearly mad with torment. I pushed everything off my desk, including my inkwell, spilling black ink onto the polished marble. Kronion moved to clean up the mess, but I grabbed his robe, hauling him toward the desk, where I smoothed the vellum flat. "It happened yesterday morning, in Aries," I said, my ruined voice no more than a whisper. "I visually confirmed it again this morning, just before dawn. *Every one* of the planets is in Aries. The Jupiter-Saturn-Moon conjunction is clear to the naked eye."

Kronion studied the chart. Among the wheel's twelve houses, all seven of the planets, including the sun and moon, were in the first, or rising, house. "This is unprecedented," he said, shaking his head.

I nodded.

"And whoever was born was born precisely at dawn?"

"Yes," I said. "In Aries."

Kronion smiled. "With Taurus following." He looked at me. "That connotes Apis."

"No," I croaked. "The birth has nothing to do with Apis." I pointed at the pie-shaped First House. "*Aries*. Its House of Self represents the head, or leadership. The conjunction of Jupiter and Saturn denotes kingship. And everything is ruled by the Sun—Ra himself. The newborn has male energy, cardinal quality, and the element of fire!"

"Aries *is* the symbol of new beginnings," offered Kronion.

"It is also the symbol of the Jews."

Kronion looked at me doubtfully. He knew as well as I that there were more than one hundred thousand Jews in Alexandria—crammed into their own squalid quarter, to be sure, but here nonetheless—and yet, unlike me, he knew few of them. Perhaps he was acquainted with a Jewish merchant or two, but he would never speak to them on the street. I, on the other hand, knew the Alexandrian Rabbi. He was a friend of mine and had instructed me about his people and their beliefs. "The first Jew was named Abram," I said. "He was a shepherd. His god Adonai appeared to him and commanded him to sacrifice his own son."

"Sounds like a Jewish god," muttered Kronion absently, still studying the chart.

"Or a Greek one," I countered. "Zeus murdered *everybody*—including many of his own children." I paused, collecting my disjointed thoughts. "Abram went to offer up his son, and was about to do so when an angel appeared and told him to stop."

"Changeable, these Jewish gods," laughed Kronion, recovering his sense of humor.

"Just one god," I said. "Which you know full well. Abram was glad Adonai had spared his son, but he was still under orders to sacrifice, so he looked about, and what do you think he found trapped in a nearby thicket?"

"A drachma?" laughed Kronion, mocking the Jews' legendary interest in money.

I pointed at the rising sign on the birth chart, the symbol ♈. "No, fool. Aries. A ram."

"So the rulers of Aries's triune—the sun, Jupiter, and Saturn—all appeared in the constellation yesterday morning at dawn?"

I nodded.

"And an Apis bull was born in Babylon-in-Egypt at that moment." He looked up at me. "So why do you think this is about the Jews?" he asked, tapping the birth chart.

"Just a feeling." I snatched the chart off the table. "To which I will soon add knowledge."

Rabbi Mesha ben Huz presided over the Grand Synagogue, which occupied nearly an entire square block in the Jewish Quarter. He was short, bald, and had intensely blue eyes.

And, in the fashion of all great storytellers, he was also a grand liar. I had sat many a time at his dinner table listening to him expound a fantastic story. But at the end, he would look around, find the keenest child, and ask him for the moral, of which there was always at least one.

In synagogue, of course, Mesha did not lie, but he did tell fantastic stories from the *Sefer Torah*, the Jewish scriptures, stories that seemed highly unlikely, to say the least. But such was the nature of his religion: it was strange, singular, and completely certain of itself.

Just like Mesha ben Huz.

When I found him, he was sitting in his courtyard, sipping his morning tea. He looked up as I burst in, nearly tripping over a servant. "Rabbi!" I said hoarsely. "You are home!"

"Where else would I be?"

"I looked for you at the Synagogue. You were not there," I said, taking the couch opposite him, completely out of breath.

"Your deductive powers are at their peak, Melkorios. Congratulations: you have tracked me down." He offered me a plate of dates and signaled the servant to bring more tea.

"I must talk to you," I said, my chest still heaving. I sat there, sweat streaming down my face, wondering why I was so excited. Then I remembered the chart and thrust it toward Mesha.

He leaned forward, squinted at it, then leaned back. "You know I don't hold with astrology."

"I know," I said, dropping it on the table and tapping it forcefully. "But you will."

"And why is that?"

"Because it has to do with *you*."

"Me? Is it *my* birth chart?"

"Of course not!" I looked around. None of the Rabbi's children were around. How many of them there actually were was unknown to me, but they seemed numberless—and always under foot.

Mesha, noting my anxiousness, said, "What is this about, Melkorios? You're acting the madman!"

"I *am* mad!" I said, surprising myself. "I have made a discovery, and though you do not believe it, in truth you *do*, for I will wager that this parchment," I tapped the chart again, "will change your life and that of your people forever."

Mesha, in spite of himself, snorted a laugh. "Bold words, sorcerer, bold words," he said. "And how will a natal chart do these marvelous things?"

"It tells of the birth of a king—a king of the Jews," I said.

Mesha laughed. "A king? Here in Alexandria?"

"Where did Abram sacrifice his son?"

"Mount Moriah," he said, "where the Jerusalem temple stands."

"Then that is where your king is born."

Mesha leaned back. "Unfortunately, the prophecy places his birth elsewhere."

Now it was my turn to be surprised. "Where?"

Mesha stood, tossing his napkin on the table. "I will show you."

FOUR

It has been said that if you have not seen the Grand Synagogue, you have not seen majesty in this world. It is an immense marble building with a double colonnade inside supporting three tiers of balconies overlooking the great central hall. It seats ten thousand men on the main floor and is so large that, during services, a man stands on the *bimah*, or dais, with a scarf. When the time comes to answer "Amen," he waves the scarf so those too far away to hear the prayer can join in the benediction. Gold and silver work and intricate carvings adorn every detail in the building. At the eastern end, in front of the bimah, are seventy-one golden thrones arranged in a semicircle, corresponding to the number of members of the Sanhedrin, the Jewish ruling council.

Mesha walked up the center aisle. I followed, a little nervous, as I always am in another god's temple. I hoped Serapis would not be offended. Then I stopped, realizing something. Mesha had already scaled the bimah steps, but noticed I was not behind him. "What is it, Melkorios?"

"It just struck me," I said, "that I am on an errand for a rival god. Perhaps Serapis will be offended."

Mesha was gentle. "Are you proselyting me?"

"No."

"Nor I you. We are not trying to change minds here. Nor are minds being changed."

I placed my hand on the railing. "Not yet," I said, attempting levity. I am not a naturally humorous man, and my skill at joking is paltry, but Mesha was a good friend and smiled anyway.

"That is right. Not yet."

I slowly scaled the steps. It felt like I was entering the adytum of the Serapeum. "Yes," I said hopefully. "We are merely sharing information. Not proselyting."

Mesha turned toward an ornate cabinet, the Aron Hakodesh, and opened two doors, revealing the *Sefer Torah*, the five books of Moshe, wrapped in a thick mantle of burgundy velvet. To one side were several other scrolls, and he withdrew one of the larger ones. "You're talking about the *Moshiach*, you know," he said, turning and placing the scroll on the podium.

"I am?"

"We Jews have had kings before, beginning with David a thousand years ago. But since then, we have been ruled by our own judges or client-kings appointed by slave masters. The current 'king' of Judea, Herod"—and with this, he made a spitting gesture—"is a vassal of Rome, a corruption and a viper—like his masters." He looked at me for contradiction. I gave him none.

Yet he well knew that his synagogue only survived because Rome was religiously liberal. Under any other master, it would long ago have been destroyed and the Jews scattered. I said nothing, thinking it best to not engage in an argument I had already won.

Mesha unrolled the scroll. "Prophets have foretold a day when the Moshiach—whom we also call the Anointed One—would free us from dominion. Perhaps the most prolific of these prophets was Isaiah."

He then expounded to me Isaiah's predictions, most of which I found obscure and confusing, like the spells in the Book of the Dead. So many vague references, so many possible explanations. But I gleaned this: Isaiah lived seven hundred years ago and counseled four Judean kings over a period of more than sixty years. I whistled. "Sixty years is a long time to serve a king and keep one's head."

"Yes, it is a long time," said Mesha. "Especially since his prophecies were usually critical of those he served."

Isaiah wrote at great length about the Moshiach. At the beginning of his book, Isaiah berates his people in the name of their god, Adonai. I have always marveled at the Jewish religion, which puts great emphasis on personal behavior. In this they are like the ancient Egyptians, who fretted over ethics, for how one fared in the afterlife was dependent upon how one behaved in this life. Greek and Roman gods, on the other hand, require little of men beyond the offering of sacrifice. Mesha calls our gods weak, unable to entice or compel men to do good. "A religion that does not require *ultimate* sacrifice—the sacrifice of pride—has no power to save the soul," he has said often, and some days I agree with him. Most days, however, I am glad I am not responsible for my people the way Rabbi Huz is for his. For my part, I bless their sacrifices, cast their horoscopes, and let them do as they wish. There is no doubt: mine is the easier job of the two.

Mesha laid out Isaiah's prophecies about the Moshiach: he would be born of a virgin and his name would be *Immanuel*, which means "God is with us."

"Is that his given name?" I asked, surprised at such a specific prediction.

"Who knows?" answered Mesha, rolling the scroll forward. "It is a common enough name. But I think it is more a title."

"Like 'rabbi,' " I said.

Mesha smiled. "I'm sure they will call him that as well, and he will earn the title. Here are a few of his other names: 'Wonderful, Counselor, the Mighty God, the Everlasting Father, the Prince of Peace.' "

I felt a shiver go down my spine. The natal chart suddenly felt hot in my hand. I laid it on the lectern, but a stern look from Mesha made me pick it up again. Still, it almost burned in my hand. Something strange was happening.

"It will be Adonai himself," said Mesha quietly. "Taking human form."

Like Ptah becoming the Apis bull, I thought, not daring to compare the Egyptian god to Mesha's god in his own sanctuary.

Mesha then began discussing Immanuel's kingdom, but I was only interested in the details of his birth—which, according to the vellum in my hand, had occurred *yesterday*!

"You said he would not be born in Jerusalem," I reminded Mesha.

"Ah, yes," he said, returning the scroll to the ark and retrieving another. "For that, we must consult Micaihu, who knew Isaiah. But if you think Isaiah was gloomy, listen to this . . ."

"Mesha," I said. "I live under Roman rule—I know of tribulation."

The Rabbi laughed. "Fair enough. But let's hear what Micaihu said anyway." He opened the scroll and read: " 'But thou, Beth-lehem Ephratah, though thou be little among the thousands of Judah, yet out of thee shall come forth unto me that is to be ruler in Israel; whose goings forth have been from old, from everlasting.' " Mesha looked at me.

"Beth-lehem," I repeated slowly. "That is a city, correct? Not Jerusalem?"

"Not Jerusalem, but nearby—five miles away."

My mouth dropped open. Five miles? I nearly crumpled the birth chart in my hand. It might as well have been on Mount Moriah itself! "Of this you are sure?"

"I didn't say *I* was sure," said Mesha. "Only that Isaiah and Micaihu were. But as prophets go, I always trust the doomsayers—they're right more often."

"But these prophecies are a ray of hope for you, are they not?" I asked.

Mesha rolled up the scroll, put it back in the Aron Hakodesh, closed the doors, and turned to me. "I haven't told you about the Moshiach's life yet. It will be full of darkness and difficulty. Do you want to hear about his kingdom?"

I nodded, the birth chart warm my palm. "Yes. Then I want to meet him."

FIVE

You want *me* to go to Memphis?" asked Kronion.

"Yes," I said, removing my heavy robe and hanging it up.

"But where are *you* going?"

I turned to him. "That is none of your business."

A shadow crossed his face. "Am I in trouble?"

"Should you be?" I asked. Not that Kronion was a dissembler, but I had learned from my predecessor Cheos to suspect everyone. Kronion shook his head a bit too fiercely. I gave him a withering look, just to let him know I was no fool. (I was a prideful man, and pride's handiest tool is petty tyranny.) My squinting at him and his blanching only convinced me that my eyes were getting weaker, as I had noticed when peering at the scroll Mesha showed me yesterday. *What next?* I mused. *Shall I also lose my mind? Or have I lost it already, going on this fool's errand?*

"Dominus?" asked Kronion. "What is it?"

I looked at him. He was much shorter than I, and portly—he always helped himself liberally to the sacrificial offerings. He was also a conniver and a political gamesman. Yes, should I not return, he would make a fine Supreme Pontiff. I decided I would recommend him in my will before I left. Not that I would tell *him* that, of course. "I know what you are up to, Kronion," I said imperiously. "Be careful what snares you lay."

"Snares?" he asked, trembling.

At which I knew of a certainty that he had none. Perhaps he would not make a good Supreme Pontiff after all. A man who desires power must trade part of himself in the bargain, and the man who has not lost some of himself will not use power as it is intended to be used: for serious reasons. I had always had such reasons.

As I headed down the Soma toward the Island Palace for the second time in two days, I was deep in thought. If I left Egypt, would I return? I had gone on many journeys; I had seen Rome itself. But as I walked past shops, baths, eateries, and temples, I was filled with sadness—I would miss Alexandria, the greatest city in the world.

The city was laid out on a grid, with stone-paved thoroughfares bordered by colorful canvas-covered colonnades, dozens of marble temples worshiping as many gods, scores of ornate marble fountains where women filled their jugs, public baths boasting hot running water, an immense hippodrome, and many theaters. Not to mention the Great Library and the Museum, centers of learning and wisdom unparalleled in the world.

But the true miracle of Alexandria is that all this grew from nothing. When Alexander arrived here three hundred years ago, Rhakotis was nothing more than a fishing village on a barren shore with a stinking swamp behind it. But the Oracle of the Siwa Oasis had declared him the Son of Horus, so to celebrate, Alexander commissioned a city. The shallow natural harbor would be dredged so that Greece's largest *triremes* could dock. On a rocky, guano-encrusted albatross perch offshore, a great lighthouse, or *Pharos*, would be built to guide those ships safely to shore. On a western promontory, a temple celebrating Alexander's newly-mined divinity would rise. And to the south, the foul Mareotis marsh would be dredged and a canal dug, linking Alexandria to the Nile delta, twenty miles away. The engineers remained behind when Alexander's army moved east. They were expected to have the city built by the time he returned from his conquests in the east. Fortunately for them (for something from nothing always takes time), Alexander died in Babylon just a few years later.

Standing at the foot of Soma Street, activity swirled around me. The docks bustled into the evening as stevedores loaded grain into ships bound for Ostia in Italia. When Rome commandeered Egypt, she improved upon Alexander's vision, building Alexandria into a city that equaled Rome in wealth and culture and exceeded her in cleanliness and climate.

As the ferry pulled from the dock, I noted with pleasure the bold outline of the Serapeum, the tallest building in the city. Cooking smoke diffused the rays of the setting sun, turning the city a dusky red. I sat in the bow and thought of what I would say to the Prefect.

Treading carefully with Gaius Turranius was a necessity because he was the *Praefectus Alexandriae et Aegypti*, hand-picked by the Emperor and charged with maintaining the grain shipments to Italia—the bread in "bread and circuses" that kept the citizenry quiescent. Turranius did his job well. Each year, Egypt shipped six million *artabas* of grain to Rome, filling the holds of hundreds of ships. He was one of the Emperor's closest friends and a shrewd politician whose secondary job was to see to it that no senator set foot upon Egyptian soil without Caesar's personal permission.

Our prefect was a true Roman—he knew his duty and was eager to have someone else perform it for him. Which is why I was only one of twenty-seven magistrates, or *viziers*, in his administration. The Prefect had viziers of taxation, public works, marketplaces, trade, liaisons with the military, education, health, festivals and games, budget, agriculture, courts, religion, and Jewish matters. Due to the banishment of a vizier for corruption, I oversaw two departments: Jewish liaison and temple construction, both unpaid honorifics. When I traveled upriver to Dendera to manage the refurbishing of the Sanctuary of Hathor, I took my own servants and hired my own boat and oarsmen.

Thinking about boats brought me back to my current plight. As I watched the backs of the rowers, I wondered again how I would excuse myself from my duties. Sea travel this time of year was difficult due to unpredictable winds. In addition, Turranius had not cleared the sea lanes of pirates, as he had been charged. This meant I would have to go overland on the Via Maris, which meant weeks on the road to Judea and back.

I needed a convincing reason for my absence. When the prow of the ferry touched the dock and I stepped ashore, I still had not conjured one.

Six

Ptolemy, one of Alexander's generals, was the true creator of Alexandria. After the young conqueror died in Babylon, Ptolemy stole the body and took it to Egypt, building a crystal sarcophagus for his childhood friend and enclosing it in a red granite temple. A master mythmaker, Ptolemy caused Alexander's image to be carved into temples as far south as the First Cataract of the Nile, ensuring that Egypt would deify his memory just as they had Cheops, Rameses II, and Tutmoses.

On Antirrhodos Island in the newly-dredged harbor, Ptolemy built the first of many palaces, this one shielded from his rival generals by water and an unscalable seawall. He waited and plotted, then battled and prevailed, retaking Judea and Syria from his former allies. His kingdom grew, his sons became pharaohs, and his distant granddaughter Cleopatra seduced Julius Caesar, securing Ptolemy's legacy forever.

The Island Palace, remodeled many times over the centuries, still favored Macedonian architecture: mosaic-tiled courtyards surrounded by broad, columned porches yielding astonishing views of Alexandria, a glistening white jewel balanced delicately between green sea and blue sky. As I climbed the hundred marble steps from the dock, I heard the squawking of seabirds and the crashing of water against the rocks. The sun had set, and the western sky glowed orange and red. I stopped to catch my breath and ponder the death of the sun-god, Amun-Ra. Even now, he was boarding the Sektet barque to begin his journey through the Twelve Hours of night. Tomorrow, he would be reborn and again make his transit across the sky in the Atet barque.

I looked up and my heart fell. There, at the top of the stairs, stood Polonius, the *exegetes*, or chief magistrate, outfitted in a sparkling white toga. His double chin and pug nose reminded me of Cerberus, the three-headed dog crouching at Serapis's knee.

"I heard you were coming," he said.

I scaled the steps and took his hand in fierce brotherhood. "A short journey," I said breezily, striding past him along the portico which had a relief carved into the wall depicting Ptolemy engaged in battle atop a racing chariot, lopping off the heads of his enemies ten at a time.

Polonius hurried after me. "The Prefect wants to know where you are going."

"He will know, soon enough," I responded. Then, thinking better of it, I stopped and turned. "It is nothing, just a tour of the eastern provinces." I held out my hand, which held the rolled-up birth chart, as a sort of proof.

Polonius eyed it closely. "An order? From whom?"

"Polonius, please," I abjured, "let me speak to the Prefect. It will take but a minute."

"You have your minute," came a voice, "but no more!"

I turned. There stood Turranius in a doorway. He was even shorter than Polonius and even broader around the middle. His chins had grown to three, but his demeanor did not remind me so much of Cerberus as of Poseidon himself, quick to anger and slow to forget. "What is this about a journey?" he asked, holding out the message I had sent earlier.

I turned to Polonius, silently begging him to leave. He simply smiled and stood his ground. I turned back to the Prefect. "I beg your pardon, your Excellency. I know my message was, to say the least . . . cryptic."

"Yes. Cryptic," echoed Polonius. He had a habit of repeating other people's words, which caused them to pile one sentence upon another before he could add his repetitive flourish. I smiled at him—a smile was all I ever permitted myself in response to his aggravating habit.

Turranius nodded at the paper in my hand. "What have you got there?"

"An order," said Polonius.

I shook my head. "I never said it was an order."

"What, then?" asked the Prefect. "Get to it, Melchorus. I'm a busy man."

I nodded, reminded of my lowly place in the Prefect's word. He knew the Emperor. He was a senator. His family had ruled in Rome for generations. Yet my forebears had served the Ptolemies for just as long. I was from a royal line. I had known Cleopatra herself, though I was just a child at the time. I wanted to say that all I wanted from him was to let me serve him as my fathers had served his predecessors. I began: "Your Honor, I am terribly sorry—"

"I long for Rome," he interjected, turning on his heel and entering the palace.

I stole a look at Polonius and caught him rolling his eyes. He reddened and turned, scurrying away. I followed Turranius under an archway and entered a garden-like courtyard tiled in luminescent green and blue mosaics. Slaves were rolling the canvas sunshades back, and the sky was beginning to glimmer with stars. Turranius flopped down on a striped couch and gestured for a slave to pour wine. He nodded at me and I assented, receiving a goblet as well. We silently toasted and drank. The silence lengthened, and then I had a marvelous idea. "Why do you not visit home?"

Turranius set his goblet down. "Rome? This time of year?"

"But it is always pleasant in Rome, is it not?"

"What do you know of Rome, Melchorus?"

"I have visited twice," I said, trying not to sound boastful. "I was young, but I remember it well. Very beautiful, smelling of rose and lavender."

"It stinks of slaves and Jews," said Turranius. (He was an egalitarian racist—to him, everyone but the senatorial class were dogs.)

A brilliant idea popped into my head. "Yes, there are many Jews."

"They multiply like locusts!" he grunted. "They fill the marketplaces and the games! You trip over them in the theater and feel their clotted press at the hippodrome!"

"Indeed," I said. "Rome is full of them."

"I wasn't talking about Rome!" shouted Turranius. "I was talking about *Alexandria*!"

I nodded my head gravely.

"The census vizier tells me they now number over a hundred thousand in Alexandria alone! They overflow their quarter!"

They did that forty years ago, I thought. *And your predecessor incited the people against them. Thousands were killed in the ensuing riots.* "What can be done?" I asked innocently.

The Prefect looked at me, frowning. I was his liaison to the Jewish community, primarily because of my friendship with Rabbi Mesha. Turranius relied upon me to keep him informed about Jewish plots against him. To satisfy his fears, I occasionally turned a young revolutionary over to him. Mesha and I had many talks about the delicate balance between the Jews, the Greeks, the Egyptians, and our Roman overlords. Yet, what we most discussed was how to manage our prefects.

I had to manage this one now. "I wish to go on a journey."

"You journeyed to the Synagogue yesterday," he said.

I shouldn't have been surprised; Turranius had even more spies than viziers. "Yes, I was talking with the Rabbi. We were discussing a possible, shall we say . . . *exodus*."

"That old wives' tale?" countered Turranius. "About them being slaves here, building the pyramids? There's absolutely no evidence they were ever slaves in Egypt! None!"

I nodded.

"The pyramids were built by volunteers performing their yearly liturgies, and then only when the Nile flooded and no farming could be done. Jews! Always the aggrieved party, always stirring things up!"

"Which is why I intend to go to Judea. I have an idea."

Turranius looked expectantly at me, and I took a moment to order my thoughts. If the natal chart I had cast was accurate, then the Jews would soon have a new king. If their god were as powerful as Mesha believed, Judea would soon be free of Roman dominance. Jews everywhere would want to return to Judea. But the thought gave me pause. I would miss Rabbi Mesha. I would miss the happy meals at his home with his family. And Alexandria would miss the Jews' productivity. Once the Jews left Egypt, Turranius would have only Greeks and Egyptians to oppress. Yet he would have the gratitude of Rome, because she would finally be free of the Jews, even if it meant losing Judea, which added little to Rome's coffers in any case. *Small price to pay*, I thought. I smiled. I had stumbled across the answer to several difficult questions.

"Melchorus?"

I had brought the natal chart, not to show Turranius, but because I didn't want to let it out of my sight. I was now pleased I had it with me. I spread it out on the low table between us.

He leaned forward. "It is a birth chart, yes?"

"Yes," I said. "The birth of an answer. For *us*."

❧ ❧ ❧

It was almost midnight, and we stood on the docks, stamping our feet in the cold. The Pharos beacon moved slowly across the dark sea, illuminating the whitecaps. The dock master's whistle had called the ferry, and we awaited its arrival.

"This could be trouble for Rome," whispered Turranius.

"Rome has bigger troubles," I said, "Britannia and Germania chief among them. Rome keeps Judea as a buffer zone against the Parthians. She doesn't really want Judea, or she would have formally annexed it years ago."

"And make Jews citizens? You joke, Melchorus."

I rarely joke, and gave the Prefect a humorless smile. "But knowledge is power, dominus. Your knowledge of such an event—the birth of a rival king—will strengthen your position with the Senate, not to mention with the Emperor."

"But such an event, if true, will not go unnoticed by Herod, who rules Judea. I knew him as a young man in Rome. He is as paranoid as he is brutal."

"Jews give no credence to astrology, Prefect."

"Yes, yes. They're devoted to their one god. Fools. Many gods mean many blessings."

And many appetites to satisfy, I thought. "As you know, I spoke to Rabbi ben Huz. He believes in the Moshiach, as they call him, but doesn't think the time is yet right. In addition, he does not believe Pax Romana to be as burdensome as his Judean kinsmen do. He is thoroughly Hellenized."

"You mean Romanized," said Turranius, frowning at the Grecian *chiton* drape I wore under my cloak.

"Exactly," I said, ignoring the insult. "So, if this newborn king exists, it will be years before he reaches his throne, and Rome will have ample time to stop him. If he prevails and obtains his kingdom, Egyptian Jews will certainly return to Judea, freeing us of them. And if he fails, you may still profit by having accurately predicted his existence."

"And if the chart is wrong and there is no king?" asked Turranius.

"Then I will pay for my journey."

Turranius looked hard at me. "Yes," he said thoughtfully. "You *will*."

I knew exactly what he meant.

SEVEN

For the next several days, I was busy making arrangements for my trip: purchasing a camel and provisions, obtaining letters of introduction, instructing the Temple staff. Kronion left for Memphis and would be gone for up to three weeks as the priests of our sister temple celebrated the birth of the new Apis bull. He was to be back here by the Ides of Maius, when the next cycle of sacrifices were to be offered to Serapis.

Before dawn on the morning I had set for my departure, I knelt before Serapis, my head bowed, my hands resting palms up on my knees in an attitude of prayer. Over the last day or so, I had started having doubts. I felt guilty about casting the birth chart, thus revealing the Jewish king's birth; guilty about giving credence to Jewish prophecies regarding Immanuel; and then, surprisingly, guilty about concocting the scenario of a Jewish exit from the Empire in my conversation with Turranius.

All this guilt! I looked up at the statue, lit only by the small terra cotta lamp on the floor by me. *O, Great God Serapis*, I thought, trying to find words, *I kneel before thee . . .*

But no words came. I had no vocabulary to plead my case; worship of Serapis was confined to ritual prayer and sacrifice. Yet I felt I should say *something* because the gods are notoriously jealous, especially the old gods, and Serapis was one of the oldest. Texts in the temple library attested that he had been worshipped two full millennia before the advent of Græcus and her famous Olympic pantheon.

And yet, Serapis's incarnation as the Apis bull coincided with the birth of the Jewish king. I was being pulled in two directions—one toward the familiar, the other toward the strange monotheism of Rabbi Mesha ben Huz.

"Melkorios?"

I raised my head and there stood—incredibly—Rabbi Huz. I scrambled to my feet. Jews had strict rules about entering pagan temples. Yet, there he stood inside the Serapeum, his hands clasped loosely in front of him, surveying his surroundings.

"Mesha!" I whispered. "What are you *doing* here?" I looked around to be certain none of the other pontiffs were present. If word of this got back to Mesha's people . . .

"So this is him?" said Mesha, nodding toward the statue. "Serapis?"

I took his arm, but he shrugged it off, taking a step forward and picking up the oil lamp, holding it high. The golden light illuminated Serapis' stern, bearded face.

"He looks a bit like Zeus," mused Mesha.

"What are you doing here?" I hissed, still looking around for watching eyes.

"I imagine Adonai sometimes looking like this, but without the . . . what *is* that atop his head? A grain measure?"

I grabbed his arm and turned him to face me. "You should not mock!"

Mesha jerked his arm free. "Nor should you." He shoved the lamp at me and strode toward the curtained Temple entrance.

I followed him. "Me? How so?"

He did not stop until he was out on the porch. To the west, a sliver of moon reclined on the roof of the Paneum. Mesha's face, almost invisible in shadow, was creased with anger as he turned and faced me. "You come to me," he said bitterly, "and ply me with questions about the Moshiach— the *Moshiach*!"

"I was sincere," I countered. "The birth chart—"

"Damn your sorcery!" hissed Mesha. "You enter the Synagogue, I unfold the scriptures to you, and then . . ." But he was too angry to finish. He turned and began descending the steps.

Confused by his anger, I followed, more penitent than I had been before Serapis himself. "Surely, this is a misunderstanding. I took all you said as truth—as you see it—"

He whirled around. "As *I* see it? Melkorios—or by which of your many names should I call you? Serapion? Vizier? *Viper*?"

My jaw dropped. I had never seen him angry before. He had always been the most even-tempered man I knew. I usually envied his peaceful demeanor, but now, when I should have been pleased to see a crack in his otherwise flawless character, I was hurt and more than a little afraid. To have that rare anger directed at me was terrible. I felt tears start behind my eyes, and I blinked them away, both in surprise and shame. "Mesha," I said plaintively. "If I have done—"

"What you've done, *sorcerer*," said Mesha, "was to betray a confidence!"

"What confidence?"

"You think we Jews sit in the Delta Quarter merely counting our children and our money? You think we are not aware of what goes on around us? You think we are so *stupid* that we don't know when others are plotting our ruin?"

"You heard of my visit to the Prefect," I said.

"I heard of the plan you are concocting using information I gave you—information about the *Moshiach*!" He glared at me, his fists knotted, chest heaving.

I raised my hands and took a step toward him. He held his ground. Such was the power of Mesha ben Huz, for I outweighed him and outstripped him in height. With his thin frame he was no match for me, but his anger was, and one step closer was all I dared. "Mesha, please," I said. "I needed a reason for my journey the Prefect would accept. I never believed it, and I was frankly amazed *he* believed it."

"It is an answer to his prayer!" hissed Mesha. "And you know as well as I do that if what you said to him about a king in Judea is correct, Rome will never allow it. She will crush him *and* his people—*my* people—and she will do it in every corner of the Empire! The streets of Alexandria will run with blood as punishment for a rebellion in Judea. Is this what you want?"

"Of course not," I said. I wanted to ask Mesha who his spy was in the Prefect's household, but I dared not. Suffice it to say, I had been caught telling a lie that might very well be a perverse truth. Then a greater truth revealed itself to me. "Mesha, don't you believe the prophecies?"

He sighed. "Of course I believe them. I just don't believe they're coming true *now*."

I sat down heavily on the Serapeum steps, pulling my robe around me. "But they *might* be coming true now. Moments ago, when you found me praying, I was trying to explain to Serapis why I was seeking after another god. And you know what he said?"

Mesha grunted. He would never believe a god other than his spoke to mankind.

"Nothing, because I *had* no good explanation. Only that I *believe*. *I*, Supreme Pontiff of Serapis, vizier to the Prefect, astrologist . . . and *sorcerer* . . . I believe—and you do not."

Mesha was touched, but he frowned. "You really are going?"

"I did not mean what I said to the Prefect," I said. "But I would have said *anything* to go on this journey. But I will not lie to *you*: I believe— and I put my soul in grave danger, saying this on these steps—that per- haps I go on this journey in the service of *your* god, and if that is so, then what have you to fear? For Adonai—"

"Do not speak his name," hissed Mesha, but I could tell the fire had gone out of his anger.

"If I am correct, then he is a powerful god. And besides, aren't you *his* chosen people?"

"Yes," he said, turning away. "And that has always frightened me." He walked slowly down the steps. I watched him until he disappeared, then lifted my eyes. There, on the eastern horizon, rose the constellation Aries.

I remembered then that the governing planet of Aries was Mars, the god of war.

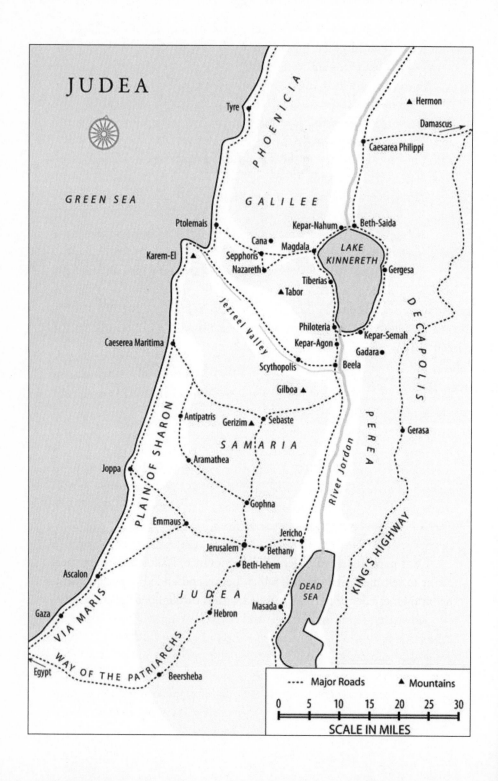

JUDEA

GREEN SEA

PHOENICIA

GALILEE

▲ Hermon

Damascus →

Tyre

Caesarea Philippi

Ptolemais

Kepar-Nahum ● Beth-Saida

Cana ●
Magdala

LAKE
KINNERETH

Karem-El ▲

Sepphoris

Gergesa

Nazareth ●

Tiberias ●

▲ Tabor

Philoteria

Kepar-Semah

Kepar-Agon

Gadara ●

Jezreel Valley

DECAPOLIS

Caeserea Maritima

Scythopolis

Beela

Gilboa ▲

Antipatris ●

Gerizim ▲ ● Sebaste

Gerasa ●

PLAIN OF SHARON

SAMARIA

PEREA

Joppa ●

Aramathea ●

River Jordan

Gophna ●

Emmaus ●

Jericho ●

Jerusalem ● ● Bethany

Beth-lehem ●

KING'S HIGHWAY

Ascalon ●

JUDEA

DEAD
SEA

Masada ●

Gaza ●

Hebron ●

VIA MARIS

WAY OF THE PATRIARCHS

Egypt

Beersheba ●

- - - Major Roads   ▲ Mountains

| 0 | 5 | 10 | 15 | 20 | 25 | 30 |

SCALE IN MILES

EIGHT

I will not tarry on the specifics of my journey to Judea, except to say that it was a long trip, even though I made good time. And it was long because I traveled by camel.

While camels are gifts of the gods, they are also the most recalcitrant, willful, and offensive creatures on earth. If you can get one to move, it will never stop, but plod along at a steady three miles an hour for days on end. If you can *not* get it to move, it will remain motionless for an eternity. The camel seems to say, "If you leave me alone, I will take you down this road. But if you goad me or in any way try to control me, I will fight you. I will growl, spit, and bite at you until you *do* leave me alone."

So you sit high atop this monster, swaying precariously as it trudges along, sick at the stench rising from its carcass, and survey the barren emptiness surrounding you. You pray your camel does not suddenly decide that it has gone far enough for one day, leaving you stranded miles from the next oasis. And thus the weeks of your journey pass in a nightmare.

I was particularly unlucky. In my ignorance, I allowed a sharp merchant to sell me a male camel, which began and ended our relationship by biting me. For my part, I quarreled with it throughout the entire journey, subjecting it to my diatribes and my willow goad. For its part, the camel generally denied me the satisfaction of a response, merely passing gas when I had made a particularly cogent point about its ancestry or the smell of its hide.

Aside from my camel, my journey across the Sinai was uneventful, both in landscape (the Green Sea ever on my left, barren hills on my right) and in company (no one seemed able to carry on a conversation about anything other than commerce).

But as I entered Judea, the landscape gradually changed. The road to Jerusalem branched from the seaside Via Maris and wound lazily up into the rising hills. Olive groves filled neat terraces. Occasionally, I detected the sweet fragrance of honeysuckle. After two blissful days ascending the green hills, I stopped at Hebron, a village perched on a hilltop surrounded by an evergreen forest. The innkeeper at the dusty inn seemed delighted to see me.

The festival of Pesach had ended two months before, and so the inn, situated as it was on the pilgrim road, was almost completely empty except for myself and a very old man with skin so dark I took him at first for a Nubian. He spoke no Greek, and I little Hebrew, but we discovered we could communicate in Aramaic. He was from the Negev desert, miles to the south.

"What brings you here?" I asked.

"Pesach," he said, gumming a piece of bread. "And the census."

"Census?"

"Caesar's census. So they can know how many of us they kill. Great record-keepers, the Romans—don't want to miss a single murder." He glared up at me fearlessly, even though I wore a Roman cloak. I turned to the innkeeper, who I assumed would contradict the old man.

He shrugged. "That's why the trade was especially strong this year," he said, filling my wine cup. "They come by the tens of thousands to Pesach anyway, but this year, because of the census, I heard that Jerusalem topped out at more than half a million people."

"A half million!" I exclaimed. "Indeed!"

"But they've all gone home now, except this old boy. What brings you to Jerusalem?"

I generally claimed to be on a business trip—after all, I was dressed the part. But now, as I neared Beth-lehem, just a few miles up the road, I wanted to cleanse my soul so I might recognize the newborn king when I saw him. I worried about this, because if the innkeeper was right about the recent throngs in Jerusalem, the newborns would number in the hundreds. I had noted many spring lambs cavorting on spindly legs in the pastures. If the people were as prolific as their flocks, I would need more than a little help to find this Immanuel.

"Actually, I am headed to Beth-lehem," I said.

"That dung pit?" laughed the innkeeper. "What in the world for?"

"To see the King," interjected the old man, staring into his cup.

The innkeeper rolled his eyes. "King David?" he laughed, turning away.

The old man sipped his wine thoughtfully.

"You have seen him?"

"Just like I'm seeing you." He looked up at me, his eyes cloudy with cataracts. "In a cave he was, with his mother. Gloriously beautiful, she was."

I leaned closer. "Did he have a name?"

"Didn't hear it. Too surprised, I was, with the angels and all."

I sat back. Perhaps the old man was touched.

"He is the Anointed One," said a voice behind me.

I turned, and saw a deeply tanned man wearing a blue turban and a purple cloak standing in the doorway, hands on his hips. His pronouncement hung in the air like a royal decree. His dark eyes were rimmed with kohl, and he wore rings on at least six fingers. But for all his darkness, his face lit up like a beacon when he smiled, and he extended his hand. "I've been waiting for you."

Balthazar had seen me in a dream he had while still in Babylon. As he helped himself to the innkeeper's wine, he told me of his journey, which paralleled mine in so many ways that I thought I might still be sleeping on the Sinai sands, dreaming.

But when he pulled out a birth chart drawn on fine white parchment, I came fully awake. Without a word, I produced my own, which was plain by comparison. Clearly, he had great skill in illuminating charts. His wheel was adorned with depictions of the animals of the zodiac: the crab, the bull, the ram, the fish, the lion, all in intricate detail. The planets congregated in the First House, just as they did in mine. We looked at each other, me in surprise, he in satisfaction. "I was about to go on without you," he said.

"I am Melkorios Alexandreus," I said, bowing. "I am sorry to make you wait—I have had no vision of you."

"Did you not?" asked Balthazar, puzzled. "Yet I saw you clearly, bent before an idol which was cloaked in darkness. Was it Yahweh, the Jewish god?"

Clearly, Balthazar knew little of Jewish beliefs. "They eschew idols," said I. "Their god's name is 'Adonai,' which means 'Lord,' but they do not use his name in discourse. Instead, they refer to him as 'Hashem,' which means 'the Name.' And no, I do not serve him, but another." I was embarrassed at this admission, and my face reddened.

"Until recently," said Balthazar, "I served the god of my people, Ahura Mazda."

"He is depicted on ruins in Egypt," I said. "A very old god and powerful as well."

"His power wanes. I learned of the Jewish king as I performed an extispicy."

"What did you find?"

"It was the singular form of the sheep's liver that alerted me, so I cast the chart and discovered the birth. Then, in a dream I saw a man praying before a statue in a temple, his hands lifted but his head bowed—a conflicted man of great belief but of equally great doubt."

"That is I," I said, recognizing myself, yet dismayed at the description.

"You honor your god, but he does not honor you," said Balthazar flatly.

"My heart is divided," I answered, pointing at my chart. "Because of this."

"You are being called by Adonai, ah, *Hashem*. The old gods are to be set aside. I have already done so. I renounced my faith and drew the knife."

I frowned. He wore a great curved dagger tucked into his waist sash, its hilt encrusted with jewels. "What do you mean?"

Balthazar set his jaw. "I have shorn myself of that which is unclean. I am now a Jew."

"You circumcised yourself?" I asked in horror. "But you have not even seen him yet."

"Nor could I, for I do not know where he is. Yet I have seen him in spirit. The flesh will be no more convincing. I saw you in spirit and knew you would be passing this inn, so I waited, knowing you would arrive. And when you did, I was no more sure of your identity than I had been when I saw you kneeling in my dream."

I looked at him in wonder. With his dark skin, long, oiled black hair, and a beard that extended almost to his belt, he was exotic, but not unlike many I had seen in Alexandria. His dark eyes burned with the fire of belief, a belief that had begun to warm even my cold and conflicted heart.

"I wish I had your faith," I said at last.

Balthazar touched the hilt of his blade. "I can help," he said, and then, at my startled reaction, he smiled. "You don't need help believing, Melkorios. Belief is what brought you here. But I can help you *act* on that belief."

I smiled, relaxing. There would be no blood spilt this day, at least. "We should be going."

"Did you not hear me?" said Balthazar. "I do not know where he is."

"Ah," said I, my purpose here finally realized, "but *I* do!"

Even as I said that, it was a revelation to me. Until that moment, I had been on the outside of unfolding events—an observer but not a participant. I suddenly realized that though Balthazar knew of the birth of the Moshiach, he did not know his name or the place of his birth. Of course, he would not; he probably had no one like Mesha ben Huz to open the secrets of the *Torah* to him. A shiver thrilled me, not unlike the one I felt in the moment I first heard the Rabbi read the names of the Moshiach, for now *I* was a part of the story! Of course, if Balthazar had inquired of enough people, he would have learned about the prophecy of Micaihu and the glorious city of Beth-lehem, birthplace of a king.

But he did not—he heard it from *me*. And the thought that a god— *any* god—knew who I was filled me with amazement. All the time I had served in the Serapeum I had never felt this. All those years, waiting for the sure knowledge old Cheos spoke of, and now this. It was a sure knowledge, but it was not *my* sure knowledge of the gods—it was their sure knowledge of *me*.

I gulped back the coppery taste of fear and led Balthazar out of the cool darkness of the inn and into the dappled sunlight of the Judean highlands.

Nine

"There is another," said Balthazar cryptically as we rode, he on his shining black horse and me on my spitting camel.

"Another?"

"Another magus," he said.

"Magus?"

"A visionary, wise man, or sorcerer."

Sorcerer, I thought. *Just as Mesha said*. "You have seen this other magus in a dream?"

Balthazar nodded.

"Who is he?"

"I don't know. I only know what he looks like."

"That is a help. Perhaps he is already in Beth-lehem," I said.

"He is not in Beth-lehem."

"Why not?" I asked. "That is where the Moshiach is!"

Balthazar did not break pace. "No, he is in Jerusalem as well, and when we meet the newborn king, our number must be three. That was my dream."

It was a long journey to Beth-lehem, and we arrived near dark. The village sat on a rocky ridge, and as we topped the hill, I could take in the entire town at one glance—a few dozen shabby, flat-roofed houses, and only two inns, both of which were nearly empty. This was no city of a king. It was, as the Hebron innkeeper had asserted, almost literally a dung heap. I was surprised and disappointed; still, its size would make finding the newborn easy.

By the time we retired to our musty-smelling rooms, I was so tired I simply fell into bed. Through the wall I could hear Balthazar praying. I thought to get out of my own bed and pray, but I was not a Jew—I quailed at the sacrifice required to become one—and Serapis did not hear prayers, especially prayers from a Supreme Pontiff who had compromised his faith. I closed my eyes. *Tomorrow*, I thought hazily. *Tomorrow we shall meet him.*

❧ ❧ ❧

By the time I dragged myself out of bed, Balthazar had already become fast friends with the innkeeper, and when I entered the room in a foul mood (the bed was not only hard, but it housed a horde of insects), Balthazar jumped to his feet and boomed, "Melkorios!"

I winced and sat down at a table. A slave poured me a cup of murky water. I frowned at it.

"He is not here!" said Balthazar.

"Who?"

"The third member of our party."

"What about," I said, leaning forward, "*him?*"

Balthazar took a loaf of bread and tore it like the neck of an enemy, shoving half toward me and wolfing down the other portion. As he chewed, he said, "I told you. He is in Jerusalem."

"Of course."

"But our host tells me there were stories a few weeks ago—on that extraordinary day you and I charted—that a light illuminated the other inn, and people heard voices raised in song."

"Where is the other inn?" I asked, finally risking a sip of the dirty water.

"Not far. When you've breakfasted, we will go."

I thought of my camel. "Can we walk there?"

❧ ❧ ❧

"Nonsense," said the woman. "Never heard such a thing." She closed the door, leaving Balthazar and me alone on the porch.

I looked at my companion. "You are sure this is the inn?"

"There is no other." He walked into the courtyard. "We still do not even know his name."

"An ancient Hebrew prophet foretold it as Immanuel—meaning 'God is with us.' "

Balthazar pursed his lips. "How did *you* know that?"

I was a perturbed at his condescension. "Just because I *dream* not does not mean I *know* naught," I said. Balthazar ignored me and walked out into the road. His horse was tethered to a tree, and he patted the animal on the withers. It nickered quietly to him. I glared at my camel, which stood a few paces away, glaring back at me.

I was about to speak when the bleating of sheep made me turn. A boy was driving a flock of sheep toward us. As they neared, my camel spit at them, scattering the flock. The sudden flight of the sheep struck us as funny, and we laughed as we ran to corral them. The boy stared at my camel in wonder.

"You have never seen a camel?" I asked, swatting at a sheep that was getting away.

"Not one that big," said the boy as he took a step forward, his gaze riveted on the silver studs adorning the leather harness. As he took another step, the camel growled and spit.

"Stop that now!" I shouted, raising my switch.

"Don't hit him," said the boy. "He means no harm."

"Oh, but he does," I said. "He means a *lot* of harm."

The boy reached out to the camel. I was about to warn him when the camel lowered his head and gently brought his muzzle up under the boy's hand. He stroked the camel's nose, cooing at it, all the while smiling innocently up at me.

"Do you want to buy a camel?" I asked.

"I don't have a lepton!" laughed the boy. "But if you're giving him away, I'll take him!"

Balthazar, having spent the last few minutes gathering the sheep, approached us. "We must be going," he said, barely noting the boy, whose eyes popped at Balthazar's appearance.

"You're kings!" exuded the boy.

"Merchants, son," I said. "Not kings."

"We are not merchants," said Balthazar.

"You *are* kings," repeated the boy.

I placed my switch over the camel's neck, a sign for him to kneel. He growled at me. "No," I said, tossing my bag up onto the saddle. "We are not."

"Then you've come to see the King," said the boy.

Balthazar knelt down before the child and asked, "Have *you* seen him?"

"Yes, sire. I saw the angels too."

"Where was this?" asked Balthazar.

The boy pointed. "They were on that hillside, there. Where we tend our flocks."

"But where did you see the *child*?" asked Balthazar.

"In the cave behind the inn," said the boy.

I frowned. The inn mistress had lied to us. "Show us," I said, nodding at the boy.

Without a word he gave a high whistle. The sheep followed him as he walked around the corner of the inn.

I looked at Balthazar. "Stranger things . . ."

He nodded and we followed the boy.

"Of course, that was weeks ago," said the boy, showing us the grotto dug into the barren hillside. "The town was full for Pesach. The ewes were birthing, so we slept out in the pastures to help them if they needed it."

"Tell us about the child," said Balthazar, still looking at the shallow rocky alcove, disgust on his face. The straw was filthy and the place stunk of dung.

The boy pointed. "His mother was there. His father stood behind her."

"He had a father?" I asked, remembering the prophecy about the mother being a virgin.

The boy nodded. "He was very small. The baby, I mean. He was wrinkly."

"Why were they here?" asked Balthazar, looking up to the rear wall of the inn above us. A doorway interrupted the stone wall, and a cascade of trash coursed down the hillside. The boy's sheep rooted through the refuse, stirring up the fetid smell.

"This is a stable," I said, noting the crude fence fronting the cave.

"The inn was full," said the boy. "My father let out our house, and we all slept in the fields. I guess they had to sleep here."

"You said you saw angels," said Balthazar.

The boy nodded. "They were dressed even finer than you, and their faces were so bright, I couldn't look at them. And they sang." He cocked an ear, almost as if he could hear them. "I can sing," he said proudly, "but I never heard singing like that before. Then they left, and we saw people coming down here, so we followed."

"Was there anything different about the child?" I asked, unable to restrain myself.

The boy looked back into the cave, thinking. "He cried. He cried a lot."

❧ ❧ ❧

"So he cried," said Balthazar. "So what?"

We rode along the road north of Beth-lehem, which wound along the hilltops between stands of evergreens and oaks. To the west, the rolling hills dropped away, lost in the afternoon haze.

"I do not know," I said, trying not to goad the camel, because he'd taken to stopping whenever I did so, and Balthazar, obviously impatient, had reined in his horse to wait for me.

When I drew alongside him, he said, "By Ahura, Melkorios, get a horse."

I shook my head. "That boy proved that this beast can be tamed. Besides, I will need him in the desert again." My camel continued forward as I spoke, and Balthazar nudged his horse into motion again. "I just thought," I said, "that the child might seem more kingly, especially to a small boy. After all, he thought *we* were kings."

"You're not married, are you?" asked Balthazar.

"No," I said. "You?"

"Twice. You know nothing of children."

"I know enough not to have any," I laughed.

"They are a blessing," said Balthazar, echoing a comment I had heard Rabbi Mesha say often, even as he swatted his children to punish them.

"Indeed," I said. "I have been busy."

"Yes," said Balthazar. "Your two masters."

"How much farther?" I asked, changing the subject.

Balthazar squinted into the distance, then pointed. I looked up. There, on the horizon, stood a city surrounded by a tall wall of white stone, glistening in the noonday sun.

Balthazar spurred his horse. "Jerusalem!"

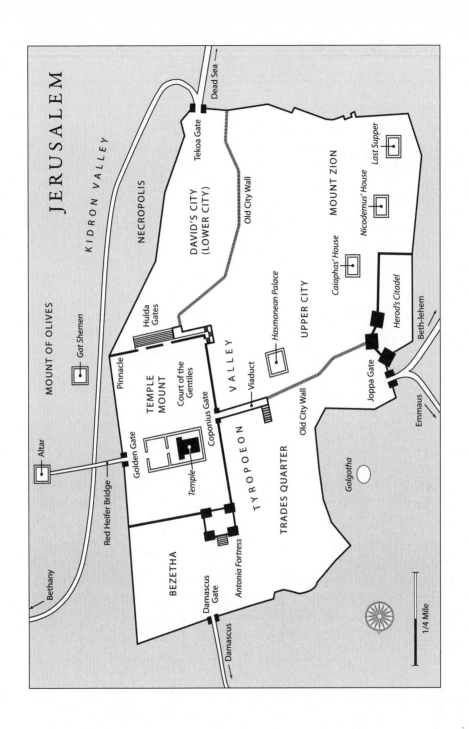

SECOND TEMPLE

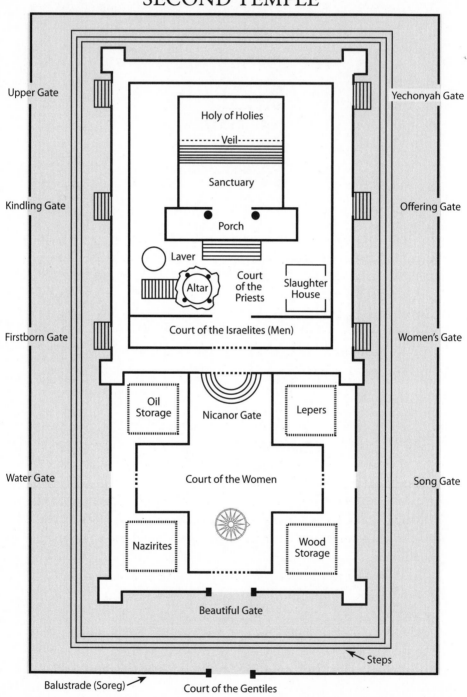

Upper Gate

Yechonyah Gate

Kindling Gate

Offering Gate

Firstborn Gate

Women's Gate

Water Gate

Song Gate

Holy of Holies

---------Veil---------

Sanctuary

Porch

Laver

Altar

Court of the Priests

Slaughter House

Court of the Israelites (Men)

Oil Storage

Nicanor Gate

Lepers

Court of the Women

Nazirites

Wood Storage

Beautiful Gate

Steps

Balustrade (Soreg)

Court of the Gentiles

Ten

On our way into Jerusalem, we passed the City of David, which coursed down a narrow shoulder of mountain at the southern end of the Temple Mount. It was walled with ancient, eroded battlements. Where David's City met the valley floor, the road split, the right fork heading up the Kidron Valley, the left ascending the Tyropoeon Valley, which bisected Jerusalem north to south as it passed along the western wall of the Temple.

High above us, we saw entrances to the Mount high above David's City. A few minutes later, as we entered the square at the foot of these tunnels, we noted baths enclosed in a simple but crisply designed building. Here we stopped to survey our surroundings.

Twenty broad steps led up to a columned porch running the width of the southern Mount, above which the limestone wall, decorated with pilasters and dozens of identical decorative arches, rose a hundred cubits into the air. The workmanship was astonishing; some of the wall blocks were as big as those in the pyramids of Giza! I made a mental note to ask where I might find the *tektons* who so precisely cut these stones—surely my architects at Dendera could use a few more good masons.

"Do we need to wash?" asked Balthazar, gesturing at the baths.

"At least our feet, I should think." I gave a drachma to a priest who led us to a shallow pool where people dangled their feet in the water. We did the same, smiling with pleasure at the water, which flowed past our tired feet like a cool stream.

When we emerged, our feet, hands, and faces washed, we scaled the steps and stood at the Huldah Gates, black squares in the base of the wall. I looked around. We were surrounded by a crowd, yet a sense of the sacred softened the footsteps and voices of everyone as they entered the right doors and exited the left ones. "I am strangely moved," I said. "Something beckons me."

Balthazar nodded. "Then let us heed the call. He is here."

I had grown tired of trying to figure out who Balthazar was referring to each time he said "he," whether it was the third member of our triad or the newborn king. So I merely nodded, and we followed a stream of people into the right-hand doorway. Soon we were walking up a sloping ramp in cool darkness. Far above us was a tiny square of light. Our sandal's echoes seemed loud; I tiptoed, trying to minimize the sound. Others crept forward as I did. I thought to take off my sandals, but realized that my feet would only get dirty again.

When we emerged into the Court of the Gentiles, I gaped in wonder. The Court was immense; a young man could run flat-out for two minutes and not reach the far end. A tall, double-colonnaded portico surrounded it, topped by a parapet where Roman legionnaires stood at regular intervals, their red cloaks fluttering in the breeze.

All this I took in from the corners of my eyes, for I could not take them from that which filled the center of the Court. It was the largest temple I had ever seen and appeared to be made solely of alabaster and gold. It was a stepped complex surrounded by a tall stone wall adorned with pilasters, arches, and doorways. The innermost building was easily a hundred cubits tall, its columns and pediments gilded. Topping the roof were large golden arrowheads meant to discourage the alighting of birds. Black smoke rose above the complex. A waist-high marble balustrade, or *soreg*, surrounded everything.

We picked our way through the throng which nearly filled the square, passing relatives greeting each other happily and long-lost friends having surprising reunions. Merchants worked the crowd, selling everything from prayer shawls to sacrificial animals.

As we approached, the Temple loomed over us, imposing its stillness upon our mouths, if not on our pounding hearts. The main entrance, or Beautiful Gate, was on the east side. White-robed priests guarded the doorway. Patrons ascended three steps and passed between two golden doors, which stood open, yielding an unobstructed view of the inner courts.

The first court—the Court of the Women—teemed with both men

and women. At the far end, a dozen curved steps led up to the next level and an even more ornate doorway, which also stood open—the Court of the Israelites. There we saw only men.

A low wall separated the Israelite Court from the innermost Court of the Priests, which contained the altar and behind it, the Sanctuary. While the Sanctuary was a marvel of intricate design and stunning craftsmanship, the altar was a great pile of unhewn stone. Four golden horns, each as tall as a man, encircled the shallow brazier on the summit. A phalanx of priests—their robes and hands stained crimson, their sweating faces and arms tanned black from the smoke and heat—tossed great chunks of meat into the blazing fire. Smoke billowed upward and was carried across the Mount, dulling the sun to a pale yellow disk and blanketing everything in an aromatic haze. Occasionally, a shout went up from the men: *Hosanna! Hosanna to the Highest!*

A shiver went up my spine. Though I was a distance from the ritual, its power reached me and brought tears to my eyes. I brushed them away, surprised—I had never felt such emotion at the Ides sacrifices at the Serapeum.

Eager to see more, Balthazar started forward, but I grabbed his arm. A legend had been carved into the stone balustrade surrounding the Temple. I translated the Greek for him:

No Gentile shall pass the barrier surrounding the Temple,
and whosoever is caught within shall be responsible for his own death.

Balthazar frowned. "I am permitted, for I am now a Jew."

The guards had noticed Balthazar's exotic clothing. They exchanged wary glances, and one put his hand on the haft of his sword.

"They do not know that," I whispered. "I think you will need someone to vouch for you."

"You could," said Balthazar.

"Not me. A Jew."

"But what if he's in there?"

"We will wait." I walked a few paces back. Balthazar remained at the entrance, watched by the guards. Eventually he came over to where I stood.

"This is hopeless," he said.

"When you saw him in your dream," I asked, "was he here?"

"It must have been here." He gestured at the pageantry around us.

"Where else would he be? We will come back later."

And with that, he marched toward the Huldah Gates. I followed.

We returned that evening, but the Mount was closed. Balthazar was in a foul mood; it seemed that when his dreams weren't realized in exactly the fashion he expected, he grew testy. "It's a big city," he growled. "We'll never find him. And time is passing; they will soon leave Jerusalem."

"How do you know?"

Balthazar shrugged, from which I gathered his belief was based on another dream.

"I recall," I said, "that a Jewish woman must wait forty days after childbirth before she is pronounced clean. She cannot travel until then."

"It's been more than that since the birth," said Balthazar.

"Then they may have gone home."

"And where is that?"

I pondered. "I thought it was Beth-lehem, but now I am not sure."

"As I said," scowled Balthazar, "it's hopeless."

"He is not the king yet," I said. "Herod's palace is not far. We might inquire of him."

"And what will he say when we tell him we're here to find a king who will dethrone him? Do you think he'll like that?"

"He is a Jew, is he not?"

Balthazar grunted.

"He might be happy to hear the news," I said. "Indeed, he may already *know*. Besides, he is as much a slave to Rome as his people are. He may be chafing at the bit as well."

Balthazar squinted at the Citadel, with its three ornate towers rising in the west. "If he is, he's chafing in style. All right, let's go see him." He stood.

"You will find our companion," I said amiably.

"How do you know?"

"You found me."

ELEVEN

❧

Herod's citadel stood at the highest point of the city. Its three distinctly designed towers were named after his brother Phasael, his friend Hippicus, and one of his wives, Miriamne. The spires also served as watchtowers against invading armies and his own people, who were not uniformly pleased with his governance. He was an adulterer and the murderer of his own children. In Rome, Herod was dismissed as a petty and flamboyant tyrant, but he kept the Jews in line, and for that Caesar was grateful enough to ignore all but his bloodiest excesses.

Despite his domestic troubles, Herod was no fool. He knew how to govern, having learned the art in Rome. Knowing that the Jews saw his mixed heritage as suspect, he went out of his way to curry their favor. He rebuilt the Temple, pouring millions of sestertii into its construction. This satisfied the *kohens*, or priests, as well as the rulers in the Sanhedrin. For the rest of the people, he inaugurated a building program to rival the Emperor's in Rome: dozens of aqueducts, hundreds of miles of paved roads, great cities throughout the province, amphitheaters, and hippodromes. These improvements kept the denizens of Jerusalem worshiping, working, and entertained, and so the priests and the rulers were satisfied, especially with the ample bribes he paid. To the people in the outlying villages, however, his name remained a curse, and he knew their disposition well enough to never leave Jerusalem without an armed escort.

As we waited outside the gate for admission, I whispered these things to Balthazar. My own experiences at court cautioned against coming here, but if we were to find the supposed third member of our party, we had to ask those who might know. I would rather have spoken to one of Herod's viziers, but we knew none of their names.

I warned Balthazar again about Herod: "You have never seen a family tree like his," I said, looking through the gate bars at the red-haired Gauls guarding the doorway. "He married two women named Miriamne, had them both killed, and then killed a half dozen of his own children, fearful of being dethroned."

"No wonder the Emperor likes him," said Balthazar, "he acts just like a Roman."

"So let us be careful," I said. "Let us be *prudent* in what we tell the king. Above all, let us get more information from him than he gets from *us*."

At that moment, the throne-room doors opened, and the guards stood aside. A young man wearing a toga strode across the courtyard toward us. "Your eminences." He bowed. "I am Archelaus," he said, opening the gate. "The King will see you now."

"It is his son," I whispered to Balthazar as Archelaus led us through the great golden doors. Past the nave, we entered the throne room. The walls were adorned with murals and tapestries. Couches and pillows littered the floor in an almost haphazard way—clearly, there had been a party there earlier in the evening. I glanced at the time candle on its stand near the door. It was the fifth hour of the night.

As we moved forward, a marble platform appeared, on top of which a heavy man slouched on a golden throne inset with onyx and ivory. The man himself, whom I took to be Herod, had gray eyes, short, curled gray hair, and a trimmed beard with no moustache. He wore a linen sleeping gown, over which he had donned a blue cloak, the hem of which he was examining. Thus occupied, he did not seem to notice us until Archelaus cleared his throat.

Herod shook the hem at us. "This stain will not come out, I know it." He fussed some more with the fabric, then scowled at us. "And what do these want?" he growled at Archelaus. "The evening ended an hour ago."

"I am Balthazar—"

"They are foreigners," interrupted Archelaus. "Here on a quest . . . to find a *king*."

"Tell them they've found one," he said, still bent on examining his cloak. "They can leave now."

"*Another* king," said Archelaus.

I stepped forward. "Your Highness, I am Melkorios Alexandreus."

I bowed low, and Balthazar, surprised at the court-seasoned tone in my voice, bowed as well. I remained in this position until Herod spoke, this time with genuine curiosity in his voice.

"Alexandria?" asked Herod. "Egypt?"

"I come here as a representative of the Egyptian Prefect," I said, counting my words, well aware that one too many or one too few with a man like this would be a fatal mistake. I waited.

Herod grunted.

"We are following a sign," I said. "An astrological sign."

Balthazar thrust his hand into his robe. Instantly, a dozen guards emerged from the shadows with swords drawn. Balthazar slowly removed his hand. It held the birth chart.

Archelaus gestured. The guards returned to the shadows. "There are plots against my father."

"A gift from Augustus himself," said Herod. "They were once Cleopatra's own personal guard, vicious and intractable, as are all Gauls."

I hazarded a look in the shadows, and sure enough, I recognized one of the guards from my youth in Alexandria. He had metal bands on his wrists, and his blonde hair was short. I could not remember his name, but I would never forget his smashed nose, as he was a pugilist. He had even sparred with me when I was a child. I tried to catch his eye, but he was attending to the king.

During this moment of recollection, Archelaus had taken the chart from Balthazar—very carefully and slowly, I might add, under the scowl of the Persian—and handed it to his father. Herod glanced at it, then tossed it away. It landed on the throne steps. None of us dared pick it up.

"Sorcery," said Herod.

That word again, I thought. *That proves he's at least partly Jewish.*

"The chart, my Lord, indicates a birth in your kingdom of a Jewish child," I ventured.

"Just one?" laughed Herod. "And I thought the Jews were *done* having children!"

"A king has been born," cried Balthazar. "The prophecy is fulfilled!"

Herod looked from Balthazar to me, trying to gauge our true motives.

I knew no way out of this. "A prophecy of Micaihu," I said flatly, hoping Herod was unfamiliar with the *Torah*.

"David's city," he snapped. "Beth-lehem."

Balthazar stepped forward. "But he is not—"

"He *may* be there," I interrupted. "We will inquire. We just wanted your permission."

"Well, I shall not live forever," said Herod, winking humorlessly at Archelaus. "And, notwithstanding my heirs who skulk around this palace with daggers in their hearts, if not in their hands, I am always interested in entertaining *other* candidates."

I heaved a sigh of relief; Herod was not taking us seriously. "We are seeking another who, like us, read these signs in the heavens. Perhaps he has been here."

"We have seen no one," said Archelaus.

"My friends," said Herod, "You may think I take such things lightly, but I do not. So, if in my lands you encounter this newborn 'king,' I ask you to do me the courtesy of informing me of it, for I too would worship him."

"Yes, your Highness," I said, bowing, then turning away. I hoped Balthazar would take the hint, but when I looked back, he had not moved. Archelaus picked up the birth chart and handed it to Balthazar, who was still looking up at the King, his jaw set. "He is the Anointed One," he said flatly. My heart dropped.

I turned. "Come, my friend," I said breezily. I bowed again. "Thank you, *King* Herod."

A servant led us across the gravel courtyard toward the gate. To our left, the darkness shifted, and a cloaked man emerged from the shadows. I raised my staff in defense, and Balthazar grabbed the hilt of his dagger. The man shooed the servant away and then pulled his hood back, revealing a blond head and a broken nose. "Melkie?" he asked. "Is it you?"

I suddenly remembered his name. "Paulos!"

We embraced, and Balthazar sheathed his blade. Paulos took my arm and led us toward the gate. "What are you doing here?" he whispered once we'd moved into the shadows, out of sight of the guards who patrolled the Citadel walls.

"As you heard," I said. "Nothing more."

"No intrigue? Nothing from the Egyptian Prefect?"

"Perhaps we are just chasing shadows." I shrugged.

Balthazar grunted disapprovingly.

Paulos shook his head. "Nothing here is as it seems. Be careful." He looked around, then leaned closer. "I have seen a man as you described. Dressed as your friend here."

Balthazar moved closer. "Where?"

"He was at the Palace and told the King the same story you did. When Herod pretended to know nothing, I knew you were in danger."

"What was the other man's name?" asked Balthazar.

Paulos shrugged. "He came here with a kohen, the same man who created quite a stir almost a year ago. Came out of the Temple Sanctuary claiming to have been struck dumb by an angel. Not that I believed it, but the rabble did, and the kohen was shouted about as a sign of the coming of the Messiah."

Balthazar and I exchanged looks. "What was his name?" I asked.

Paulos thought for a moment. "An old name. One of their prophets, I think . . ."

"It doesn't matter," I said, patting him on the shoulder.

"Zechariah!" said Paulos.

"The priest? Or the magus?" asked Balthazar.

"The priest," said Paulos. He placed his key in the lock, turning it. The iron gate swung inward, and we stepped back. "You've grown, Melkie. Your parents?"

I shook my head.

He nodded. "That's the way it is. I haven't been home in thirty years. Don't know if my wife is alive or dead."

"It is good to see you, Paulos," I said. "We shall meet again."

"Not here, I hope" he said, shaking his head. "Not here."

TWELVE

Finding this Zechariah was not a problem; he was a senior priest, and when we saw him exit the Beautiful Gate the next morning, I wondered what good it would do to ask questions if he was mute and unable to answer them. Yet when he cleared the balustrade, he said, "Shelama. I am Zechariah."

"You are not dumb?" I asked.

"No, young man," said the priest. "Not since the birth of my son."

Balthazar looked at me as if to ask, *Could this be the Anointed One's father?*

"Yes, I fathered a son," said Zechariah, anticipating our question. "He is almost a year old now." He looked at me closely, squinting from beneath shaggy white brows, noting my shaved head, silk chiton, and expensive cloak. "You are a priest," he said. "Pagan?"

"I am Supreme Pontiff of Serapis in Alexandria. We are looking for a man"—I glanced at Balthazar—"who shares our . . . errand."

"He is a magus, like us," said Balthazar proudly.

I winced.

Zechariah turned to Balthazar. "The man you seek hails from Antioch. He has your bold manner, my Persian friend."

"Where is he?" asked Balthazar.

"What do you want with him?" asked Zechariah.

"We are three, sent by God, to worship the newborn King," said Balthazar, a speech that sounded rehearsed. But it was a good speech nonetheless and had the merit of brevity.

"Which god?" asked Zechariah, fixing me with his piercing gray eyes.

"The one true God," said Balthazar. "Adonai."

Zechariah cocked his head at me for confirmation.

I nodded slowly. *Serapis, forgive me!*

Zechariah raised a finger to his lips. "We do not speak his name outside of prayer."

Balthazar nodded meekly.

Zechariah looked over Balthazar's shoulder. We turned. A portly man walked toward us, shorter than both Balthazar and I. He had black hair that was intricately braided at his neck, and his beard was closely trimmed. His eyes were rimmed with kohl, as were Balthazar's. Thrust into his waist sash was a curved dagger. He smiled and bowed low. "I am Caspar," he said.

"Well met!" said Balthazar, pulling Caspar into his arms and kissing him on both cheeks. I stood by uncomfortably at the display. I looked at Zechariah, who gazed at me placidly. "Now we are three!" exuded Balthazar, turning to me.

"Yes," was all I could think to say.

Zechariah put his hand on my shoulder. "I fear you are outnumbered."

I nodded. "That is nothing new."

We sat down to a meal of roast lamb, wheat cakes, cheese, grapes, citron, and syrupy pomegranate wine. As we ate, Caspar told us of himself. He was Persian by birth, but his parents had lived in Antioch most of his life. He had no memory of Persia and spoke little of the language, which greatly disappointed Balthazar. He wore a toga, but his accessories—his rings, earrings, and necklaces of gold and silver and precious stones—marked him as a proud and wealthy provincial.

"My family are merchants," said Caspar. "My father cared nothing for the gods because only a serpent knows how to barter!" His boisterous manner amused me, but Balthazar found him too jovial given our serious errand. "I am here at the behest of the Rabbi of Antioch," continued Caspar. "Levi ben Azem. He is wrapped up in the arcane prophecies—sorry, Zechariah—of his people. Always going on about the Anointed One."

"The *Moshiach*," said Balthazar, looking at Zechariah for approval.

The old priest nodded.

"So why did he send you?" I asked.

"I make regular journeys to Jerusalem. My trade is precious metals and stones. I came this time almost as a lark, to see if I could get old Levi to change the subject for once in his life." He looked around the table, saw none of us were laughing, and lowered his voice. "As I said, I was not raised to honor the gods—sorry, Zechariah, Adonai, er, *Hashem*—and so I knew nothing about them. I mean *him*. I studied at the Pergamum Library, learning Homer and the boys. I was destined to be a scholar, but my father died, and my older brother, who was supposed to take over the business, took to drink instead."

"You were telling us *why* you came," I said.

"Well," said Caspar, "I caught a ship from Antioch early this year and was in Jerusalem by Ianarius, and went straight to Beth-lehem—old Mic-aihu, you know," he said, winking at Zechariah. "But there was nothing there. Not a soul."

"Just a moment," said Balthazar. "You came here *before* the sign was given?"

"You refer to the birth chart you showed me?" asked Caspar. "I knew nothing about it. And Rabbi Levi certainly didn't. No, he just felt the time had arrived and that the Moshiach would be born soon."

Balthazar looked at me, wonder in his eyes. I then proceeded to produce my own chart.

Caspar looked it over quickly and gave it back. "None of that for old Levi. Straight from the top—sorry, Zechariah—is where he gets his information. Anyway, as I wandered around Jerusalem, I heard a story about Zechariah here, and I approached him about it."

"Accosted me is more like it," said Zechariah, chewing on a date.

"By then he had regained his lost voice—or at least the one he claimed to have lost!" Caspar laughed and continued. "And he told me about the circumstances of his son's birth. His wife is, what, sixty or so?"

Zechariah frowned at the familiarity, but it was hard to dislike Caspar. He was so friendly and matter-of-fact. Even when he was blaspheming, I sensed the gods would not fault his humor. "Not *that* old, Caspar," said Zechariah, bringing the tone of the table back to its proper pitch. "But she had been barren. An angel appeared to me and told me—"

"An angel?" I interrupted. "With wings?"

Zechariah pointed a finger at me. "Only in *your* religion are they winged, Melkorios. No, no wings, but an angel nonetheless. He said Elisheba would bear a son who would be the forerunner of the Moshiach.

I was doubtful, and so the angel gave me time to think about it—I was unable to utter a word for six months."

"What happened?" asked Balthazar.

"My son was born, and my tongue was loosed. Caspar was quite excited about the events and told me what his rabbi friend had said about the coming of the Moshiach. I confirmed the prophecy, and finally, when I had judged his inquiries as sincere, told him of Elisheba's young cousin Miriam."

There was silence at the table. I leaned in. "Her name is Miriam? Has she had the child?"

"Of course," said Zechariah. "Almost two months ago."

"On Aprilis 17, or Iyyar 1 in your calendar?"

The old priest nodded.

"What name have they given him?" I asked.

"They have named him Jeshua—Aramaic for *God is salvation*," said Zechariah.

"Immanuel," whispered Balthazar. "God is with us."

"The Anointed One," I said, marveling. "Christós."

It turned out that though Miriam's espoused husband Josef was of the house of David—hence his return to Beth-lehem for the census—in actuality, they were from Galilee, sixty miles to the north. But the moment Balthazar heard they were staying with Zechariah in Bethany, just three miles east of Jerusalem, he jumped up from the table. Zechariah and Caspar looked at him in surprise. "We must go, immediately!" said Balthazar.

"Why?" asked Caspar.

"*Why?*" bellowed Balthazar. "How long have you known this?"

Caspar thought. "About a month."

"Yet you've been here almost six!" said Balthazar.

Caspar nodded at Zechariah, who shrugged, saying, "I did not immediately trust Caspar—I told him only *part* of the story."

"I had been told by Rabbi Levi that there would be three gifts given the new king," said Caspar. "I came prepared to watch. But no one came for the longest time." And with this he leaned in and grew very serious. "I never imagined I would be one of the three. Never."

"Until your dream," added Zechariah, patting Caspar on the arm.

"Yes," said Caspar, nodding. "My dream."

"I consulted the commentaries," said Zechariah, "and sure enough, there is a reference to three visitors early in the life of the Moshiach—great kings who would honor his birth."

I leaned back. "But we are not kings," I said. I seemed to remember saying this before to someone. *Ah, the shepherd boy.*

"Nor are we great," added Balthazar.

"Nevertheless," said Zechariah. "Here you are."

"And you have come prepared?" asked Caspar.

"Prepared?" asked Balthazar.

"To honor him," said Caspar.

"What do you think?" said Balthazar. Yet confusion shone in his eyes.

"He wants to know about our gifts," I said.

"Gifts?" asked Balthazar. "I know of no gift!" He turned to me. "You have a gift?"

I nodded.

He turned to Caspar. "And you?"

"Yes."

Balthazar looked at Zechariah with great distress. Then he lowered his gaze and folded his hands on the table in front of him in thoughtful silence. His demeanor struck me as funny, and I began to chuckle, but Zechariah gave me a stern look, and I swallowed my laughter. He reached across the table and patted Balthazar's hands. "You'll think of something."

❧ ❧ ❧

The next afternoon we set out for Bethany. Zechariah had gone home the night before, having finished his Temple work for the week, to prepare the household for our arrival. We also needed time to help Balthazar pick out a proper gift. As we walked through the crowded Tyropoeon bazaar, Balthazar shook his head despairingly. "What was I thinking? No gift!"

"I am sure anything will be fine," I said. "Zechariah said they are quite poor."

Balthazar looked at me. "But *you* brought something."

"I serve in court and know the protocol. You cannot be blamed—"

"I *can* be blamed," he said, shoving a merchant out of his way.

"He's just a baby," helped Caspar. "He won't know the difference."

Balthazar turned to us. "You have greatly diminished my choices. You, Caspar, have brought gold, several talents' worth, so that solves their poverty."

"Not if they live like I do," joked Caspar.

"And you, Melkorios, you have brought a practical gift: myrrh. A profound gift."

"Why is that?" asked Caspar. "It's a pain reliever, isn't it? Good for toothaches and such?"

"Well," I said, nudging my companions forward. If we stopped, we would be deluged by hawkers. "Myrrh has many uses, such as in perfumes and as an analgesic. But it also has a spiritual purpose, according to *my* rabbi friend Mesha ben Huz. Tradition says that when the Hebrew Joseph was sold into slavery in Egypt, the caravan that took him there bore myrrh. When his father sent his other sons to Egypt for food during a famine, he told them to take along myrrh as a gift for the Pharaoh. So, it seemed proper to me that Egypt return the favor and bless the new king in a similar manner."

"See?" said Balthazar. "A gift with historical significance." He shook his head. "Well done, Melkorios. Very good." He was silent awhile.

"That only leaves one aspect of life," said Caspar as we walked among the stalls and barkers, each yelling to be heard above the other. "I bring gold, which you've pointed out can aid their poverty. Melkorios brings myrrh, which assuages pain, and pain symbolizes mortality. You, my kinsman, must bring something *spiritual*."

Balthazar trudged ahead. "Perhaps an icon from Melkorios's temple or one from the Jewish temple. Oh! I forgot: Jews don't *have* icons! No art, nothing to represent their god—"

"*Your* God," I put in quietly.

"Yes, and so what can I give him?" he asked, shaking his head hopelessly.

Caspar and I racked our brains, but nothing came. The apparel in the marketplace could be bought with Caspar's gold. The best perfumes and unguents could be produced from my myrrh. Balthazar answered his own question. "Whatever it is, it's not here," he said, trudging away.

Eager to be on our way, we prepared to leave the city, but Caspar had no mount. In a livestock pavilion in the City of David, he found a horse and was quite proud of his choice until Balthazar arrived on his own black gelding. Caspar was quite jealous until he saw my recalcitrant camel.

"I would offer you a ride," I said, "but he would probably take a hunk out of you."

"No, thank you," said Caspar from atop his mare. "Camels like me less than I like them."

"My camel doesn't like anyone," I said.

Balthazar sat on his horse, his jaw set. When he saw we were ready, he turned his horse and left the stables. He had still not found a suitable gift and was angry.

"We should keep looking in the city," called Caspar. "We won't find anything out here." At the forking, we turned north, keeping the city wall on our left. The Mount filled the horizon above us, golden in the afternoon sun. The road followed a brook at the foot of the Mount of Olives, a terraced hill of olive groves and vineyards opposite the Mount. Bethany lay on the other side of this rounded hill, though the road took the long way around, keeping to the valley floor.

At the foot of the southeast corner, or pinnacle, of the Mount, burbled the Gihon Spring. A number of merchandise stalls surrounded it. Balthazar dismounted and plodded over to the booths. Caspar and I remained behind, looking at each other. What could he possibly find here?

After a few minutes, he returned and, without a word, swung up on his horse and heeled it. We followed, me bringing up the rear, switching my slow-moving camel with a frustration that nearly matched Balthazar's.

THIRTEEN

Bethany was no larger than Beth-lehem, but it seemed much older. A natural spring gurgled in the town center. From this point, unpaved streets radiated in all directions, bounded by mud brick walls, inside of which were traditional two-story Jewish homes built above stables and kitchens. Suspicious eyes watched us as we watered our stock, but no one spoke to us. Caspar looked around at the inhospitable hamlet. "Zechariah said he would meet us here, at the spring."

"And we are on time," I said. "It is sunset."

Balthazar just sat on his horse, glowering.

The sky, moments before a brilliant red as the sun fell, quickly turned indigo. Down a lane I saw a figure walking toward us with a staff. Zechariah. At his side was a boy carrying a burlap sack over his shoulder. When they arrived, I took Zechariah's hand. "Shelama. Is all ready?"

Zechariah nodded, then looked up at Balthazar, still sitting glumly on his horse. "Will you join us, Balthazar? You are most welcome."

Balthazar grunted and slowly dismounted.

Caspar leaned toward Zechariah and whispered. "Were you successful?"

Zechariah nodded and approached Balthazar. Caspar winked at me. I looked at the boy's sack, wondering what it contained. "I understand you have no gift for the child," said Zechariah.

Balthazar nodded miserably. "I will give him my rings," he said. "They are valuable."

The golden rings on the Persian's fingers each featured a different precious stone: emerald, onyx, ruby, even what looked like a diamond.

This is generosity! I thought, noting that Balthazar's rings had to be worth many times the gold and myrrh Caspar and I had brought. I felt better for Balthazar—he had a gift after all.

Zechariah put his hand on Balthazar's arm. The boy set the sack on the ground. "That is a wonderful gesture," said Zechariah. "And it would be most welcome—and unexpected," he said, turning to the rest of us, "for none of you are asked to give more than your kind presence to the child. You know this, I trust?"

We all nodded. "The gifts are trifles," said Caspar, humbled by Zechariah's words, as was I. Suddenly, the idea of a gift seemed ludicrous—what gift could you give a child who might also be a god?

"We would like to give *something*," said Balthazar. "He *is* the Anointed One."

Zechariah gestured to the boy, who reached into the burlap sack and withdrew a small chest which was inlaid with ebony and mahogany. Zechariah took the chest. "You have been seeking a *spiritual* gift, I'm told," he said.

Balthazar glanced at Caspar, then nodded doubtfully.

Zechariah opened the chest. Inside, upon a bed of red velvet, were a dozen whitish rock-like nuggets, each about the size of a dove's egg.

Balthazar gaped in wonder. "Frankincense!"

I peered into the chest. "So much! Where did you get it?"

"I had hoped to rest today," said Zechariah, "but when I got Caspar's message, I returned to Jerusalem, where I obtained this."

I gasped. "You took this from the Temple?"

Zechariah gave the chest to Balthazar, who held it as tenderly as he would a tiny child. "Frankincense is burned in the *Kodesh Hakodashim*—the Holy of Holies—on Yom Kippur, the Day of Atonement," said Zechariah. "Its smoke represents the reconciliation between Hashem and mankind. Caspar felt, and I concurred, that there could be no greater gift for the Moshiach, the Great Reconciliator, than frankincense, which will be burned when he enters the Sanctuary as the newly-anointed King of Israel."

Balthazar's eyes filled with tears. He looked at Caspar. "This was *your* idea?" Caspar nodded. Balthazar tucked the chest under his arm and reached out to enclose both Zechariah and Caspar in an expansive hug. "This is *exactly* the gift I sought," he whispered. "Thank you, my friends. Thank you." He pulled back, eyes glistening. "Now we are ready to see the King."

❦ ❦ ❦

I expected that a priest of Zechariah's stature would live—as I did—in an estate with fluted marble columns surrounding courtyards filled with manicured shrubs and mosaic tile floors, but he did not. Instead, Zechariah and his wife Elisheba greeted us at the arched doorway of their small, mud-brick home. He held an oil lamp, and Elisheba had their toddler Johanan by the hand. He looked up at me inquisitively, and I—always self-conscious around children—took an involuntary step back. This somehow encouraged the child, and he took a halting step, his pudgy arms reaching for me, and his balance so precarious that I overcame my usual reticence and caught him, picking him up. He beamed at me.

"Johanan has another conquest," said Elisheba.

"Yes," I said, gently handing him back to Elisheba, "I am honored."

As he nestled into her arms, I took the liberty to look more closely at her. She was well beyond normal child-bearing years, as evidenced by the wrinkles around her eyes. She looked tired (as any new mother would be), and I wondered if she had a milk nurse for the child. Looking past her to the interior of her humble home, I knew the answer was no.

"Josef and Miriam are excited to see you," said Zechariah, beckoning us inside. Caspar entered first, and I followed. When Balthazar did not enter, I looked back. He stood, filling the doorway, his face ashen. I was about to speak when Elisheba crossed to the door with Johanan and handed the child to the Persian, tucking him into the crook of his arm. In his other arm, Balthazar held the small chest. Balthazar looked as uncomfortable holding the child as I probably did—which surprised me, as he had hinted before that he was the father of many. But then Johanan found Balthazar's beard, took a handful in his fist, and pulled.

"Ow!" yelled Balthazar, pulling the child away, but Johanan kept a tight hold. Hearing the man's yelp, the toddler chortled and reached out to snag another handful. Zechariah stepped forward and cooed in the child's ear. Soon the baby released Balthazar, whose face was red with embarrassment. Zechariah gently retrieved Johanan and handed him to Elisheba.

"Yet another conquest," I added, gesturing for Balthazar to join us. He nodded, then bowed to Zechariah and Elisheba and came inside, shutting the door behind him.

Caspar stood at the far end of the small room, which was furnished with rugs and pillows and an aged divan—the living and eating area, I surmised. A single oil lamp lighted the room. Elisheba excused herself and took the child with her. Zechariah bid us to sit, but I was too excited. The same was true of Balthazar. Only Caspar seemed able to bend his knees, and he sat down on the divan, holding his bag of golden coins in his lap, looking up at us with amusement.

"I'll go get them," said Zechariah.

"No!" whispered Balthazar. "We must come before them." He looked at me and Caspar for confirmation. I nodded, but Caspar shrugged.

"You have already come before them," corrected Zechariah. "And besides, their room is small. Even if you managed to squeeze in, Balthazar, I doubt you would ever get back out." He turned and left the three of us.

"Balthazar, sit," said Caspar, patting the divan. "Your journey is over. Be at peace."

Balthazar, however, did not sit. But I, unable to resist Caspar's good humor, joined him on the divan, placing my little black ebon chest between my feet. Suddenly it seemed wrong to be seated, and I moved the chest aside and got down on my knees. Balthazar joined me. Caspar looked at us in surprise, then he too knelt on the floor, clasping his hands in front of him.

No one spoke; we simply waited, looking down at the gifts we'd brought—the gold, the frankincense, the myrrh—each lost in his thoughts, each wondering why *he* was privileged to be here at this moment. I glanced at Balthazar, remembering what he said about serving two masters. For a fleeting moment, I felt an urge to escape and leave my offering behind. But before I could move, I heard footsteps.

Then, standing in the doorway, was a young man, no more than twenty. He was dressed in a simple striped tunic cinched at the waist by a leather belt. His hair was dark, as was his sparse beard. He wore a kerchief on his head. He seemed surprised to see three strangely-dressed men kneeling before him. He started forward, gesturing for us to rise, when we all heard: "Josef?"

He turned, and we strained to see beyond him into the darkness of the doorway. A candle was moving toward us. Josef met the bearer, took the candle, whispered something, and we heard a young woman's voice. Josef then led her into the room. She wore a dark dress and a red scarf. Her hair was thick and black. She was very small and very young—no more than fifteen. She cradled an infant in her arms. The light was dim, so it wasn't until she stood before us and lifted her face that I saw her unsurpassed beauty: her flawless skin was white as milk, and her eyes were a deep green.

She held her baby in her arms. Josef gestured for us to rise; surprisingly, I could not. On my right Balthazar kneeled, head bowed, as if the mere sight of the child would blind him. On my left, Caspar was on his feet, his face shining as he gazed upon the child. Zechariah and Elisheba stood behind Josef and Miriam, a sleepy Johanan in Elisheba's arms.

Josef, embarrassed at being unable to persuade Balthazar and myself to stand, touched Miriam's shoulder, indicating that she should kneel. Caspar thought quickly, placing two pillows on the ground as they knelt. Miriam's face was radiant, not just with the freshness of youth or the joy of motherhood, but with something else. Perfect innocence, I believe it was.

"I welcome you," said Josef, "though we have no home to welcome you to."

"You *are* home," said Zechariah.

Josef nodded and made to speak, but Balthazar touched his arm, gesturing that he should move the candle closer to the baby's face. Josef did so, and we all leaned forward to gaze upon the newborn King of the Jews.

I was too old to think there would be something remarkable about the baby's countenance—all infants are beautiful. In that I was correct. Jeshua slept, his round face sweetly passive. I glanced at Balthazar, whose eyes had filled with tears. Caspar was nodding slowly. But I, the skeptic of the three, asked, "On what day was he born?"

"Iyyar 1," said Miriam, her eyes never leaving the baby. "During Pesach."

"Aprilis 17," I confirmed, reaching into my robe to withdraw the chart.

Balthazar touched my arm. "We have no need of confirmation, Melchior. Faith is at an end, for our eyes have seen."

He was right. I tucked the chart back inside my cloak. The proof was before us, but it was not the child; it was his parents. Never before had I seen such sweetness between husband and wife. I was not a married man, but I was not unfamiliar with good marriages. Yet I had never seen a man look at his wife the way Josef looked at Miriam. Something had happened to these two young people. Their bond was more than a marriage—it was something holy and transcendent.

"We have long awaited your arrival," said Miriam. Her eyes rested upon me, and I felt an honor in them I did not deserve. "You are the first nobility to note his birth, outside of our family, of course." She looked at Zechariah and Elisheba, who looked at her like the proudest of parents.

"We are honored you would come," said Josef in a trembling voice. He looked down, and my heart was filled with compassion for him. Something in his eyes, just before he looked away, indicated the difficulty of the road he was traveling. And now he was grateful to find other travelers on that road as well. By the look of his rough hands, I knew he was a laborer, yet I also knew why I had knelt before him. Everyone in the room, except myself, was royalty—I did not belong there. I looked away, ashamed.

"Yes," said Miriam, drawing my eyes up to meet hers. "You are most welcome."

It was well after midnight when we finally left Zechariah's home. They invited us to stay the night, but we declined. Though I relished the luminance of Miriam and Josef, I found myself needing to step outside their circle of light to regain myself. As I knelt in that dark room, looking at the tiny child, I felt a desire to confess my sins to him. It was a deeply uncomfortable feeling, which did not leave me even after I left them. On the road back to Jerusalem, the feeling haunted me. At first I thought, *What sins?* but the lie lasted only an instant. I had a myriad of sins, no matter who judged me, be it Serapis or Hashem. But why did I feel such a need to unburden myself to an infant sound asleep in his mother's arms?

The faces of my friends shone with happiness; I hid mine under my hood. *My house is upside down*, I thought, though I knew the feeling was temporary. Soon, I would be myself again. I would seek no man's—or *infant's!*—approval; I would bare my soul to no one. After all, I was the Supreme Pontiff of Serapis. I was Melkorios Alexandreus.

Yet *that* is what I feared the most.

After many minutes of silent travel, Balthazar spoke. "We should not tell Herod of this."

"Yes," said Caspar. "I cannot bear the idea of that vulture in the same room with them."

"Zechariah says they are going north, to Galilee," I put in.

"Good," said Caspar. "Far from here."

"Yes," said Balthazar. "As *we* should be."

Fourteen

And so I found myself saying good-bye to my new friends the next day, each of us returning to our own land—compass points in equal arcs one from another, I pointed out. At that, Balthazar shook his head, which I took to mean, *Enough signs!*

But as I watched him ride away, I knew I would need these signs if what I had experienced was to remain in my mind as fact, and not as embellished memory. One of my many weaknesses is that I often retell my experiences better than they actually were, hoping the added bits would somehow impress the listener more than the bare story itself could. It is a sad tendency, the worst aspect of which is the sullying of my memories, which soon become unfamiliar, even to me.

Caspar pointed out that our spiritual journey was just beginning, then checked himself. "I'm sorry," he said. "As a pontiff, you are already acquainted with such matters. I know nothing of God other than what I've seen." He smiled. "But I have no excuse from this point on, do I?"

I put my hand on his shoulder. "None of us do."

"What will *you* do?" asked Caspar.

"I am not sure I understand *what* has happened," I said. "Balthazar and I charted the child's birth, and we both felt we should come here. He came most prepared, I think. Did you know he underwent circumcision?"

Caspar nodded, wincing. "His courage is even larger than he is."

"And you came at the behest of a friend—you yourself did not believe, correct?"

Caspar nodded.

"Yet you were not deterred when you visited Beth-lehem and found no one. You found Zechariah and prevailed upon him to tell you everything. You, Caspar, are a remarkable man: you have more faith, I believe, than Balthazar, and certainly more than I." I bowed. "I honor you."

Caspar chuckled. "Perhaps you have been in the temple too long, Melkorios. We all tend to discount things constantly before our eyes. With my new sight, I see before me a man who serves with all his might, who seeks knowledge, and who follows his heart. Balthazar would say that these are the makings of a magus."

"Or a sorcerer, as my friend Rabbi Mesha would say."

Caspar laughed. "Oh, well, rabbis." He shrugged. "What can you do?"

"You must do what they say," I said, "or you will never hear the end of it!"

"What I mean," said Caspar, "is that you have within you the seed of greatness. You will yet accomplish much in your life. And now it will be according to the new sight you have been given. We all benefitted by the exchange of gifts last night—nothing can match what we received. As a merchant, I'd say it was a profitable journey."

"I see greater profit in your future, Caspar."

"Hashem willing!" he said. "That is what Rabbi Lev always says. Wait until he hears *me* say it!"

"We *are* lucky in our friends, are we not?" I said. "Safe travels, Caspar."

Caspar headed through the marketplace, and I turned toward the stables. The smile left my lips—my camel awaited me there.

I was about halfway through the Sinai when my camel decided it had traveled far enough for one day and simply stopped. In the slanting afternoon light, I looked about. To my right, rolling dunes separated me from the Green Sea. To my left, mesas stepped upward to cloud-shrouded highlands.

Nearer, two palms nosed above the red rock. I looked back at the camel. He was a nasty traveling companion, but he knew where the water was. I took my skin with me as I dismounted. Two standing stones, thrown up eons ago, marked the oasis entrance. A muddy pool of water was surrounded by a few dusty palms. There was a fire ring of blackened stone but no ashes. The oasis was obviously rarely used, hidden as it was by a shoulder of sandy hill. I had raisins, dates, flat bread, and a flask of wine. I also had a hare I bought from a vendor this morning at the last oasis, along with a brace of wormwood.

As the hare cooked, I looked up at the darkening sky. With no city lights or cooking fires to sully the air, the darkness came quickly once the sun set. Soon, all that was left of day was a red slash across the horizon. Stars twinkled in the dome of the sky where the archer Chiron was feasting; smoke from his cooking fire wafted northward, forming the River of Stars.

Aquarius rose in the east. I removed the natal chart from my satchel and flattened it over my knee, remembering what Balthazar had said about no longer needing proof. Yet holding the chart somehow made it more real, solidifying my memory of Miriam, Josef, and Jeshua—the tiny child whose name promised that *God is with us.*

I felt my amulet dangling against my chest. I pulled it out and examined it in the firelight. On one side of the golden disk was Serapis seated on his throne, Cerberus at his knee. On the other, an incantation: *O Serapis, renewed life of Ptah, let my ears never be deaf to the Truth.*

I looked from the amulet to the birth chart. Two masters indeed.

I awoke, shaking. It was after midnight—the sixth hour: Taurus had just cleared the eastern horizon. The camel, no more than a silhouette beyond the upright stones, was looking at me, its eyes reflecting starlight. I must have cried out and awakened it. I looked around, struggling to remember what had terrified me. A foreboding filled my heart, but my mind was empty. *Oh, that I had Balthazar's gift!* I lamented. *Or Caspar's intuition!*

There was no moon. Only starlight glimmered, land indistinguishable from sky. I was in a cradle of darkness, and I imagined snakes—offspring of Apep, who swallowed the souls of those who do not merit rebirth at dawn—slithering across the ground, their hoods flaring, drawn by the smell of my fear. I clutched my amulet, then cried out—the disk was burning hot. I dropped it, but not before it branded the embossed image of Serapis into my palm. I scrambled off my bedroll, looking about wildly for shapes moving toward me, eyes slitted with malice, fangs bared.

To my left, the red eyes of a serpent glowed dully. I found a piece of wood and hurled it. The eyes exploded as the fire coals ignited. In the renewed light, I sighed relief when I saw no attacking serpents. Apep was still below in the Underworld, devouring souls there—my unworthy soul would not be consumed tonight. I looked around. Where had I dropped the amulet? Then I realized it was still around my neck.

What dream had startled me? What Underworld evil had brought me face to face with the destroyer Apep? I wanted to touch the birth chart again, but resisted. I was too superstitious. I knew too many incantations and saw too many omens, yet I knew too few unassailable *truths*—the ones I had pledged Serapis I would hear. Fear held me in its cold claws. My heartbeat filled my ears. There was no one here, yet the immediacy of danger was palpable.

Suddenly, my fear arced into the sky like a bow-shot arrow. I expected to see its tail feather glowing red in the darkness as it raced eastward. And in that instant I knew the source of my paralyzing anxiety.

King Herod was going to kill Jeshua.

IFTEEN

To say I flew back to Judea is to say birds have wings. I drove my camel so hard I feared he would drop before we reached Gaza. I left him there and bought a horse. I raced inland toward Beer-sheba, climbing the rising green hills, cruelly flailing at my mount.

At Hebron, I stopped to water the horse before speeding on, forgetting to feed myself. By the time I got to Beth-lehem, I was falling out of the saddle, for I had been traveling five days with no sleep or food. The horse was covered with foam. When the stable master saw him, he would not let go of the reins. "You're killing him," he said flatly. "He cannot go on."

I climbed off and said, "Then get me another," and fainted dead away.

Once again, the snake-fear was upon me. I awoke, shouting, "Apep! Apep!"

The innkeeper stumbled in with a lamp, calming me in a strange language. I babbled as he shook his head. Finally, I found my tongue and spoke in Aramaic. "Where am I?"

"Beth-lehem, sir," said the innkeeper, relieved I was not possessed.

"How long?"

"Two days."

"Two days!" I shouted. "My horse!"

He sat on the edge of the bed. "We had to put him down—your haste destroyed him."

"My satchel!" I shouted.

He turned to the foot of the bed and picked up my bag. I snatched it from him and searched the contents, finding the natal chart at last. I held it to my chest, relieved. Then something occurred to me. I pressed a palm against my chest. "My amulet?"

"What?" asked the innkeeper.

"You have stolen it!"

"No, dominus!" He reached into his apron, withdrawing the amulet. I snatched it away from him. "Safekeeping only," he said. "We knew not who you were."

"Yet you knew the value of gold," I barked.

He bowed his head.

"I need another horse," I said, rummaging through my satchel. "I have money . . . I think."

The innkeeper again reached into his apron and produced a handful of coins, holding them out sheepishly.

"More safekeeping?" I frowned. "What else of mine are you keeping *safe*?"

He shook his head.

"What hour is it?" I asked, getting to my feet.

"The third watch," he said, steadying me as I stumbled. I was still weak. Hadn't they fed me? *Of course not*, I thought. *I've been unconscious.*

I raised myself to my full height, towering over the innkeeper. "Prepare a meal and get me a fast horse. I leave within the hour."

"Where are you going, dominus?"

"Bethany." I turned away and began packing my things.

It was only seven miles to Bethany and I made it there shortly after sunrise. I reined to a stop in front of Zechariah's home and rapped loudly on the door. As I waited, I looked around. Heavy dew hung on everything and the clouds promised rain. A peephole slid open and I saw Elisheba's surprised eyes. "Shelama!" she said and slid the bolt aside, opening the door.

"Are they still here?"

"Josef and Miriam? Why, no, they left last night."

"Your husband, is he home?"

"He went with them," she said. "Oh, Melchior, what is it? Are you all right?"

"I am afraid," I said, stepping inside and closing the door behind me. "They are in danger."

"Yes. Josef had a foreboding dream several nights ago."

"Where did they go?"

"Jerusalem, but I do not know where they will go from there." She looked at my worried expression. "You had the same dream."

I opened the door. "No," I said. "A worse one, I am afraid."

As soon as the gates to the Mount opened, I sprinted up the tunnel and emerged onto the Court. Under the surrounding porticoes, merchants were opening their stalls. I crossed the expanse quickly and leapt over the stone balustrade, ignoring the chiseled warning, bounding up to the Beautiful Gate. The two gold doors were shut fast. I banged once, twice, three times. Then I turned.

Everyone on the Mount was looking at me. I stepped back, imagining the anger of the priest who was at this moment striding toward the doors. I heard a latch slide and one of the doors opened. A wiry old man stood before me wearing a blue turban and cloak. He had on a breastplate that was divided into twelve squares, each embedded with a colorful stone. I recognized the regalia; today he was officiating as the High Priest. "Yes?" he said mildly.

"I am sorry for knocking. It is just—"

"You wanted into the Lord's House," said the old man, "as we all do, my son."

"Well, no," I said. "I came to see Zechariah."

"Which Zechariah?"

"Of Bethany."

"That doesn't help much," said the priest. "His father's name? His tribe?"

I shook my head.

Suddenly, the other door flew open and there were the two guards, still cinching their sashes tight, death on their faces. One of them reached for me, and I stumbled back, falling down the steps and landing on the pavement, striking my head. The guards grabbed me and hauled me to my feet.

"Leave him, please!" said the priest.

They stepped aside as he descended the steps. "He has already received his punishment, thank you," he said, taking my arm. His grasp was firm as he led me outside the balustrade.

The fall had shaken something loose in my head. "Elisheba," I said. "His wife's name is Elisheba."

"Oh," said the High Priest. "You mean Zechariah of the Abijah course. He is inside. May I tell him who calls?"

"Tell him Melkorios—Melchior—of Alexandria."

The High Priest looked at me standing there, blood staining my cloak at the elbow. Seeing I was a greater danger to myself than I could be to Zechariah, he nodded and turned away.

I waited as the two guards surveyed me under furrowed brows.

"We did not know what to do," whispered Zechariah as we walked briskly toward the western gate. "It is not safe in Judea. Talk of the events surrounding the birth has faded, but Josef now fears that news of your visit will reinforce the prophecies."

I scowled. "We should have been more discreet."

We had exited the Mount and were crossing an arched viaduct that led to the Upper City. "It is not your fault," said Zechariah. "People talk . . ."

"And Herod hears," I said. "Where are they now?"

"With friends, preparing for travel. They may go to Phoenicia—we have relatives in Tyre. But I fear it is not far enough away."

For the first time in days, I saw light. "I know of a place that is."

$\mathscr{S}$IXTEEN

I rode behind them. Josef walked, leading Miriam and the child on the camel. The couple spoke little, just an occasional whisper, and they rarely looked back at me. I wondered if they trusted me. I wondered what I was doing.

Once again, I found myself halfway across the Sinai. My presence would guarantee this young family's passage into Egypt. In Alexandria, Rabbi ben Huz would help them—wouldn't he? If I told him of Zechariah's visitation, of Elisheba's remarkable pregnancy, of angels singing *Hosanna!* on the night of Jeshua's birth, would he still be skeptical that this child was the Anointed One? I found it hard to believe myself; how much harder would it be for Mesha?

Another unanswered question still nagged at me, so I spurred my camel forward. Miriam smiled. She rarely spoke to me, preferring instead to whisper to her husband. I found this rather tedious, yet Josef assured me she was too shy to speak to a great man such as I. I let that pass.

"I was wondering," I said to Josef, "if you might share your dream— the one that warned you to leave Judea."

"It was like yours, I suppose."

I grunted, doubting that was the case.

Josef took this as a yes. "Gabriel appeared to me."

"The same angel who appeared to Zechariah?"

"He seems to be responsible for this family," said Josef, looking up at Miriam. "He appeared to Elisheba, then to Miriam, and finally to me."

I nodded. If this was not true, they all had remarkably similar imaginations.

"But I'm not sure if it was a dream or a vision," said Josef.

"How so?" I asked. I had never had a waking vision or a prophetic dream, so I was keen on the distinction.

"You know how it is, Melkorios,"—it flattered me that he used my Greek name—"in such a state, you forget all except the glory of the messenger and his words. Everything else seems to simply . . . fade from sight."

I reflected on my own experience. At the oasis, I had awakened from a nightmare. Once I realized Apep was not about to devour me, my thoughts shifted toward the defenseless newborn child in Bethany and the great evil Herod would undoubtedly inflict upon him once he knew of his existence. It was logic alone that drove me back to Jerusalem; I did *not* receive a visit from Gabriel or any other heavenly messenger.

Josef, misconstruing my thoughts for reflection on my own encounter with Gabriel, continued, "He looked just as he did the first time, when he told me that Miriam was with child by the power of the Holy Spirit."

"Holy Spirit?"

Miriam looked up at me, then bent to Josef, whispering. He listened, then spoke: "You do not know of the Holy Spirit?" I shook my head. "Perhaps you know of it by another name?"

I knew many spirits: the *ba*, or soul of man; the *ka*, his life essence; the *akh*, when the ba and the ka unite to dwell in the Field of Reeds. But these were the spirits of dead men, not of living gods. I shook my head.

"The Holy Spirit *is* Hashem as he speaks to our souls," said Josef. "If we listen and obey, we will be led back to him, like a sheep to its shepherd."

Just one god, I mused. *One god who speaks directly to man.* Well, why more than one god anyway? What need did we have of Atum, Anubis, Osiris, Isis, Ra, Horus, Hathor, Amun, Ptah, Khons, Mut, Thoth, Ma'at, Khnum, and Bes? One god should suffice. But which one?

The one you've already chosen, came a voice from inside me.

Suddenly, I was filled with fear. Was that Hashem whispering to me? Or was it Serapis?

Two masters, said Balthazar's voice.

"Melkorios?" Josef was saying.

"Yes?" I answered dully. "What is it?"

"Your vision, how did it seem to you?"

I felt my amulet against my chest. "Dark," I said, spurring my horse ahead.

As we approached Alexandria, I watched my companions, eager to see their reaction. I was not disappointed. Josef's mouth hung open in frank astonishment and Miriam, in one of her rare moments of unguarded speech, said, "Oh, it's incredible! Look how it shines!" She turned to me. "And you are the king of Alexandria?"

We were in a boat crossing Lake Mareotis, south of the city. "No, my dear," I said. "I am sorry if I ever gave you that impression. I merely *serve* the Prefect of Egypt."

"But you are also a pontiff—a priest," said Miriam. "A high priest, no?"

I looked up. On the hill above the lakeshore, I saw the sparkling marble of the Serapeum. And yet a sight that had on every other occasion filled me with pride now seemed to pale in comparison to the Jerusalem Temple, not just because the Serapeum was smaller (which, alas, it was), but because I now knew one of the priests of that Temple, Zechariah, and knew him to be a better man than was the Supreme Pontiff of the Serapeum. Josef followed my gaze and guessed my secret. "Is that your Temple?"

I nodded.

"It is beautiful, Melkorios," he said. "Is it proper for us to call you that here?"

"Call me what?" I was still comparing the temples in my mind.

"Melkorios. Or do you have a title?"

"I would be happy if you called me Melkorios. That is my given name."

"What is your title in the Temple?" Josef asked.

"Serapion."

"And your title in the city?"

"Melkorios Alexandreus," I said, "but—"

"We are in your country, now," he said. "We will use your proper titles."

"If that is your wish," I said, embarrassed.

"But to us," said Miriam, "you will always be the *magus*—the wise man." I smiled wanly. *Yes*, I thought bleakly, *wise man . . . and sorcerer.*

On a trip lasting several weeks, one has ample time to consider the journey's end, and I had pondered the various scenarios to exhaustion.

One thing is certain, I thought as our boat slowed for docking: *I will lie to the Prefect.*

For generations, Ptolemy and his heirs had battled their rivals, the Seleucids in Syria and the Antigonids in Macedonia, for the lands bordering the eastern shore of the Green Sea. Judea, unfortunately situated, had been the nexus of many battles and campaigns. So, to stir up a revolution in Judea by bringing a pretender to the Jewish throne to Egypt, as I was doing, was more than a bad idea—it was insane and possibly traitorous. Strange how that calculus never entered my mind when I was convincing Josef and Miriam to accompany me to Alexandria.

No, the Prefect should not know about this. And so I would pay the costs of my "failed" expedition. *Small price*, I thought, glancing back at my charges as our boat glided into its slip, the slaves lifting their oars as one.

We walked up the stone steps. Before us stood the twin pylons of the Gate of the Sun, the one on the left inscribed with a relief of Cleopatra VII, lover of Caesar and the last queen of Egypt. On the right pylon was her consort, Marcus Antonius, with whom she died rather than surrender to Octavian, now our estimable Emperor Augustus. Both figures were dressed and posed in the Egyptian style: feet striding to the right, the body facing forward, the faces in dramatic profile, Cleopatra wearing the crowns of upper and lower Egypt, Antonius wearing the blue and gold striped headdress.

"The pylons represent the banks of the Nile," I said. I had often given visitors tours of Alexandria, though none of them exhibited the delight of my two young friends. Jeshua, awoken by our disembarkation, goggled about, blinking.

We passed between the pylons, symbolically entering of the land of the pharaohs, and continued up the Soma, roofed arcades on either side supported by numberless columns. Above the porticoes rose buildings up to three stories tall. The smell of the city filled our noses: baking bread, roasting meat, dust, dung, and humanity. Josef looked behind us, noting the porters carrying our belongings. "Where are we going, Melkorios—er, Melchior, I mean Sera—?"

"To introduce you to a friend."

While his wife Dinah entertained Josef and Miriam, Mesha took the opportunity to pull me aside. Several of his children were gathered around the young couple, whispering to tiny Jeshua, who babbled happily. We stood at the other end of the courtyard, beyond a splashing fountain. "So that's them," he said flatly. "And the particulars of the prophecy?"

I shrugged. "Close enough."

He raised his chin. "Close *enough?*"

"He was born on the day the chart predicted, at sunrise, in Bethlehem. His father is of the tribe of David—Isaiah predicted this, remember?—and his kinsman, Zechariah, is a priest in the Temple . . ." At this point I saw Mesha's attention wander.

"But why bring them *here?*"

"They feared for their lives in Judea."

"Why?"

"Josef and Zechariah had dreams."

"Oh, well. *Dreams.*" He shook his head. "And you?"

I looked at Josef and Miriam, struggling to communicate in Aramaic and Hebrew to people who spoke only Latin and Greek, but still feeling the love and connection of kin. I turned back to Mesha. "No dream, a nightmare."

"And so on the strength of their dreams and your nightmare, you take them hundreds of miles from their home and bring them *my* house! What am I to do with them?"

"He is a tekton," I said. "A carpenter. And I hear a competent one."

"Did his wife tell you that?" asked Mesha.

"If you cannot help, just say so. I thought that since you were both Jewish, you might—"

"There are well over a hundred thousand Jews in Alexandria, Melkorios. And we are crammed into just one tiny quarter." He looked up at the scene beyond the fountain. "Look at them. These are simple country children, not sophisticated urbanites. Alexandria will crush them. They speak no Greek, Latin, or Egyptian! How will they survive?"

"As we all do, Rabbi," I said firmly. "With help from the gods."

$\mathcal{S}$EVENTEEN

$\mathcal{R}$abbi Mesha was reticent, but I knew his heart: once his misgivings were aired, he would do all he could for Josef and Miriam. And he did. I was present at the Grand Synagogue when he introduced them to the congregation. Josef was greeted warmly by the members of his guild, so noted by the chips of wood tucked behind their ears, and I saw him smile up at his wife and child who were seated above in the women's balcony.

From the bimah, Mesha gave me a resigned look. Though he was pleased to see Josef accepted into fellowship, the family still had no place to live. In addition, he told me at the conclusion of the service, it was *my* responsibility to find work for Josef. "You brought them here," he said as we stepped out into the warm evening. "You must find work for him."

"I could place him as a stone mason on the Dendera temple, but that is almost four hundred miles to the south," I said. "Too far for a young man to be from his wife."

"I doubt he will work on a pagan temple," said Mesha. "But there's other work, isn't there?"

"They have no papers. I brought them here under my own auspices."

"So use your auspices. Turranius might help."

"Turranius is the last person I want to know they're here. I will find Josef something—as I am sure you will find them a place to stay."

Mesha sighed. "Dinah has already fallen in love with the child—I fear we shall have guests at our table in perpetuity."

"I have also been a guest at your table," I said. "Do you regret that?"

Mesha frowned. "Sometimes."

"Why should our lives be easy, my friend?"

Mesha scowled. "Because we wish them so! Why else?"

I knew he'd finally forgiven me. It was easy for him to forgive because he did not believe the child crawling on the rug was the Anointed One. Watching Jeshua fuss and squall, as children do, made me doubt as well. I longed to be home at my villa, where the birth chart lay hidden in my library, to touch it so I might know once again of its verity. Already, my recollection of Caspar was fading, though Balthazar's image remained crisp in my memory, along with his harsh statements about my divided loyalties.

I shook the Rabbi's hand and bid him farewell.

"And your expedition? How did you fare?" asked Turranius, fingers laced across his stomach.

I shrugged. "An expensive vacation."

"Did you see Herod?"

Now it gets interesting, I thought. "Yes, for a moment. I realized the absurdity of my quest when I heard myself repeat it out loud to him."

"And yet you felt no such embarrassment with me," said Turranius.

"I suppose it was the length of the journey. Lots of time to think. He knew nothing of a birth, though as a half-Jew, he was somewhat familiar with the prophecies."

Turranius let out a percussive laugh. "Dis! *I'm* as much a Jew as he is! He probably had a good laugh at the Egyptian Prefect's vizier. Well done, Melchorus, well done."

I knew our talk would come to this—Turranius turned every conversation to its impact upon *him*. "Yes, sire, probably so, but I think he found me more amusing than incompetent. That was my impression, anyway. Do you know him well?"

"I have precious little to do with anyone else in the Empire. Augustus keeps me on a short leash—which I should do with you, by the way. But now you're back to business again?"

"Yes," I said, relieved. "The Apis bull was as reported: perfect in every way. I shall be going to Memphis next week for a conclave."

Turranius was already bored. "And what did you bring back from Judea?"

I was startled. Had he heard? My mind raced and my mouth went dry. I coughed, buying time as my I searched for an answer. I could think of nothing.

"The gift!" said Turranius. "If there was no king, then you could not deliver the gift. You never told me what it was."

"Oh, it was just a trifle. A bit of myrrh, that's all."

"Myrrh? You mean the stuff they smear on mummies?"

This man, I thought, *knows* nothing *of Egypt!* "Yes, what they smear on mummies."

"Why in the world would you give a gift like that to a baby?"

I looked at the Prefect and wondered the same thing.

I had been back in Alexandria for five days and had still not gone to the Serapeum. I told no one I had returned, but word soon got out. Kronion stood at my door, his head bowed.

"Kronion," I said, "do come in."

He hesitated. I never invited junior pontiffs to my villa, preferring to keep our relationship formal. He looked around, taking in the colorful Egyptian religious scenes adorning the entry walls. "They are . . . *beautiful,*" he said.

"I had the artisans from Dendera paint them," I said.

"Yes," said Kronion, "I can see their resemblance. They are scenes from . . . ?"

"*The Book of Breathings,*" I said, leading him along the corridor. Where it ended, we walked down the steps to the courtyard with its fountains and plants. On all sides, behind columns, the murals continued: representations of the journey after death, the passage through the hall of the twofold Ma'at, the weighing of the heart by Anubis, the presentation of the deceased before Osiris, and the glorious rise of the soul in Light Land.

"Splendid," said Kronion. Then he turned to face me. "We are wondering if you are ill?"

"Ill?"

"You have not returned to the Temple, yet you have been back almost a week."

"I have been busy," I said. "I was planning to go back tomorrow. I trust all is well?"

"Yes. You saw the message I left about the Apis bull?"

"Yes," I said, pointing to a table upon which were several scrolls. "Wonderful news."

"The anointing went well," said Kronion. "The bull answered every question put to him, including that of his own life span."

"And?"

"He nodded, indicating he would live at least ten years."

"That *is* notable," I said.

"Thousands attended the ceremony at Saqqara. I wish you had been there. Theon sends his best wishes. How was your journey?"

"Uneventful," I said lightly. "Would you like any refreshment? Wine, perhaps?"

Kronion waved the offer away. "I have to get home. We will see you tomorrow, then?"

I led him to the door. "Yes, later in the day. I will be purifying myself in the morning. If there is any business, please take care of it."

"I would be honored, Serapion. Though I missed your presence, I must admit I enjoyed officiating at the Ides rituals while you were gone."

"I cannot see why that must stop now that I'm back," I said.

"Really?"

"Certainly. I think it is time to give you a larger role."

I thought Kronion would hug me with gratitude.

Contrary to what I told Kronion, I went to the Serapeum that night, just after the second watch. I walked across the echoing adytum without a candle, sensing rather than seeing the columns arrayed around the perimeter like Serapis's own Praetorian Guard. I continued past the statue without stopping; I did not want to see his face just yet, so I strode purposefully toward my chambers.

After closing the door, I lit a candle and removed the birth chart from my cloak, flattening it gently between two leaves of a large codex, and returning the book to a high shelf. Then I walked through the rear door to my private baths. I did not light a lamp but left the room in darkness, lit only by a small window high above through which starlight shone. I disrobed and entered the warm water. At the end of the font was a golden ankh set into the wall just above the water's surface. I wet my fingers and touched the circle-headed cross, then touched my forehead, lips, eyelids, and ears, symbolic of my thinking, speaking, seeing, and hearing the words of life. Then I buried myself in the water. Below the surface, I saw nothing but phantom sparkles dancing in the liquid blackness. I sat cross-legged at the bottom of the pool.

Over the years, I had learned to hold my breath for a full three minutes. Soon the ripples of my entry had spent themselves, and I looked up at the undisturbed surface, which was like a window of thick glass, the ceiling and high window unmoving silver ghosts. I felt balanced between life and death in my watery cocoon.

When my lungs burned, I lunged up, gasping. I got out of the pool, leaving the stack of towels untouched. I left my offices and entered the adytum, stopping before Serapis, who was lit only by the faint night braziers. I knelt, palms up on my thighs in an attitude of prayer, naked before my god.

Water pooled around me on the floor. My eyes slowly adjusted to the many shades of black. Serapis glared down at me. The wand in his right hand, symbolic of Ptah's renewed life, had changed into Poseidon's triton, its three barbed tines glistening with blood. At his knee, Cerberus studied me with six malevolent yellow eyes. Then the hand on Cerberus's head moved, and I fell back in fear. *What have you done?* asked Serapis in a voice like a sarcophagus lid sliding aside. *What have you done?*

You know, I answered miserably. *Nothing is hidden.*

Yes. Nothing is hidden. The fetid breath of Apep chilled my spine. I was stricken with fear and could not turn. I prostrated myself, hands out before me, palms resting on the cold marble. At any moment Serapis would snatch my ka, leaving my empty corpse to wither like a lotus petal in the desert sun. Apep would chew my desiccated carcass like a papyrus leaf. I could feel Serapis's eyes upon me. *Nothing is hidden.*

I stumbled down the Canopic Way, toward home, shivering under my robes. It was well past midnight, so no one heard me muttering to myself. I had been found out. Serapis had discerned my heart and exposed its blackness. I could not go back there. I was a fraud. I had betrayed him, and now my life was forfeit. I would never officiate in the Serapeum again. I was through.

And yet, when I awoke the next morning my heart was still beating. The sun shone in the heavens. I opened the shutters and a cool, clean sea breeze greeted me. I looked down at the busy streets. Nothing had changed;

people still went about their business, unaware of the end of my world.

And when I got out of the divan at the foot of the Temple steps, all thirty-six pontiffs stood on the porch to greet me. Each one bowed his head as I passed, and Kronion offered me the scepter of office. I touched it, and my hand did not wither. I entered the Temple and still drew breath. I stood before Serapis and did not die.

God was merciful.

EIGHTEEN

It was not long before Mesha found a place for Josef and Miriam to live, on the third floor of an apartment building just three blocks from his own home. The best living quarters were, of course, at street level, but Miriam said she did not mind the stairs; they would give her a chance to meet her neighbors. As soon as they were settled in, I received a message inviting me over for dinner. Being a bachelor, I accepted, even though my own cook rarely disappointed in the table he set. What he could not provide was the fellowship I would receive in Josef's home. I would soon see this as a two-edged sword.

The evening came around, and I struggled for almost an hour to pick attire that would be dignified yet not ostentatious. When I arrived, promptly at sunset, I dismissed my litter bearers and told them I would walk home. They were surprised; to be this far inside the Delta Quarter without a guard or bearers was foolishness, but they did not argue with Serapion and instead bade me good evening and beat a hasty retreat down the cobbled street.

As I arrived at the third floor, I saw a group of people clustered by a doorway. From their surprised looks, I knew my arrival was unexpected. Only Miriam moved, a shout of happiness bursting from her, and she ran toward me, reaching for my hand as if to kiss it. But I withdrew it and took hers, whispering, "Not you, my dear."

Undeterred, she hugged me. I stood there, flummoxed, as the people surveyed the unlikely situation: a Jewish woman embracing the Supreme Pontiff? Josef appeared in the doorway and came toward me, taking my hand and leading me to the group, which parted for us. I could feel their eyes upon me, especially upon my silk chiton.

"Welcome Melkorios Alexandreus," said Josef. "We are affixing the mezuzah." He held up a hollowed-out piece of wood with a tiny piece of parchment inside. "We are commanded to place it on the door post of our home. It contains verses reminding us to serve Hashem with all our heart and soul." Josef nodded to his friends. "Melchior, these are our neighbors. They have come to share this event with us."

"Shelama," I said, nodding uncomfortably. I did not know I would be attending a Jewish religious ceremony—and so shortly after begging forgiveness from Serapis for my recent betrayals. I shook the thought away.

He withdrew a nail and, with a swift and accurate tap of a hammer, affixed the mezuzah to the door post. "Time is held between memory and hope," he said. "The mezuzah is a reminder that we have come a long way, but our voyage does not end here. We continue our journey."

I was perplexed. They had just moved in and were talking about moving on?

"We are strangers in a strange land," said Josef "We are visitors in this life, travelers moving toward an unknown destination. We are nomads," said Josef, "and we will never be home until we are in the presence of the Master of the Universe."

"Amen," said the group, and they all left. In moments, I stood alone with Josef and Miriam.

"He has been practicing that speech all day," she said.

"I was impressed," I said. "It was yours?"

Josef's eyes crinkled proudly. "A Jew must also be a scholar. If he isn't, he will be shamed at synagogue when he takes his turn reading *Torah*."

"Will you do that, in the Grand Synagogue?" I asked. That would be daunting, even for me, reciting scripture and answering questions in front of ten thousand men.

"Perhaps some day," he said. "If I study hard."

Miriam beamed up at him. "Look at my husband," she said, having already spoken more during the last five minutes that I had heard on the entire journey from Judea, "the head of the household and still humble." She squeezed his arm. "Please come in, Melkorios."

Dinner was passable. Young women are rarely great cooks; it is a skill that takes years to master, and many of the herbs and oils Miriam usually cooked with in Judea were unavailable in Alexandria. I was spoiled, I have to admit, but as I said before, I came for the company, not the food.

We had finished and were leaning back on the pillows—gifts from neighbors—in one of the two rooms of their tiny home. To one side, Jeshua slept in a cradle—new, from the look of the freshly sawn wood. I asked if it was Josef's creation. Pleased I had noticed it, he said, "It needs more work, but the baby needed it *now*."

I looked down at the perfect little slumbering face. "He thinks it is just fine." I reached out to touch his tiny hand. Reflexively, his fingers closed around my forefinger.

"Why are you not married?" asked Miriam suddenly.

In my circle, such questions are not asked, and so I had no ready answer.

"Miriam!" said Josef. "Such a question!"

"But a good one," she said, looking up at me.

Josef sighed and said, "You may prefer her when she's shy. I do." And with that they exchanged a look that was so intimate I was embarrassed to witness it. I extracted my finger from Jeshua's grasp.

"It is not against your religion, is it?" asked Miriam, undeterred. "Marriage?"

"No," I said. "It is encouraged, but I have never . . ."

"You never found a woman who wanted to be as happy as you would make her?"

We laughed and the baby stirred. "Uh oh," I said, "we have awakened the baby."

"Good," said Miriam. "Perhaps you'll answer him, if not me."

"Miriam!" said Josef.

I waved his concern away. After all, the question *was* a good one. "You have some advice for a bachelor, I take it?"

"Only that you need a wife," said Miriam. "All men do, you know."

As if on cue, both Josef and I nodded, which made us both laugh.

"It's true," she affirmed. "And you would be a good father."

"I am not sure about that," I said. "I am not the man I should be."

Miriam smiled. "Neither was Adam, which is why God made Eve!"

❧ ❧ ❧

A few days later, Josef and I were walking along the Canopic Way, past shops and markets, baths and restaurants. People swirled around us, carts laden with fabric, hides, food, jingling cookware, and exotic caged birds. "You must forgive my wife," he said without preamble.

"Miriam? Why?"

"At our house, after dinner, when she spoke about marriage."

I laughed. "I too have told myself I should marry but never quite so *bluntly*."

"She means well," said Josef.

I could tell he wanted desperately for me to think highly of him. It was touching, this humble soul who had taken upon himself one of the greatest burdens a man can carry—to raise another's child as your own and never speak a word about it.

And he wanted *my* respect.

The morning sun stretched our shadows out before us as we walked. It was a glorious day, and I was not going to squander it feeling peevish about an uncomfortable yet accurate assessment of my life. "Everybody *means* well, yet look," I said, pointing at a policeman surveying the passing crowd. "Not everyone *does* well, which is why that man has a job."

"So you don't mind her views?"

"Mind them? Josef, I *relish* them."

And with that we moved on ahead, carried along by the surge of humanity, few of whom, I knew, could boast the honest friendship of people like Josef and Miriam.

Nineteen

"Well," I said, sweeping my arm about, "here it is!" We stood before the Great Library, a structure of classic Greek design squatting above many marble steps. Its triangular pediment was supported by fluted columns rising from a deep porch. The square fronting the Library was bounded on two sides by shops and on the third by the broad Canopic Way. We ascended the steps. "Is it true," asked Josef, "that Titus Livius is in Alexandria?"

"Yes," I said. "Last night there was a dinner given in his honor at the Island Palace, celebrating the completion of the one hundredth volume of his *History*."

"One hundred volumes!" said Josef. "And all about Rome?"

"He complained that there are still another hundred volumes yet to be written."

At the top of the steps we turned. Below us, the square was full of people. On the other side of the Canopic Way was the Gymnasium, the heralded school for boys. Beyond that, atop the city's backbone, was the red roof of the Serapeum. I was about to point it out when Josef said, "Can a Jew attend Gymnasium?"

"A few now and then. Philo did. I am sure there have been others."

Josef set his jaw. "I would like Jeshua to attend, if possible."

I looked at him out of the corner of my eye. Surely, his short time in Alexandria had taught him one basic truth: anyone can be accepted anywhere if he is rich. Josef was not.

"We have money," said Josef. "What Caspar gave to us."

Caspar had indeed given them money—six golden talents, in fact; enough to live in style in Alexandria for several years. But would it be enough to admit them to the society that would determine whether Jeshua could be admitted to Gymnasium? That I doubted. Yet, I heard myself say, "I will do what I can."

"He needs whatever we can give him," said Josef. "He must be prepared for his destiny."

The main doors of the Library were two stories tall. I gave a drachma to the guard, and we entered the *pronaos*, or foyer. All around us, inscribed on the granite walls in bas-relief, were scenes of scholarship: philosophers engaged in discussion, teachers lecturing students, and—my favorite—a man holding a spherical contraption in one hand and gesturing to the sky with the other.

"Aristarchus of Samos," I said, gesturing at the relief. "The greatest mind in his time and one of the Library's first chief librarians, over three hundred years ago."

"What is that he holding?"

"An orrery—a device that shows his theory of the solar system: the planets, including earth, orbit the sun, not the other way around. It was a divisive idea in his time . . . it still is."

"The Jews have never believed in an earth-centered universe," said Josef.

"Really?" I asked. Mesha had never mentioned this to me.

"It goes against reason. Hashem created the universe, and so everything necessarily revolves around him—the planets and our sun, along with the other stars."

"Other stars?"

"Our sun is a star," said Josef. "It's just very close to us, so it is much bigger."

"That is what Pythagoras said!"

Josef smiled. "Did he also say that those stars are suns to the people on the planets that orbit them?"

"People?" I said. People on other planets orbiting distant stars? I found a bench and sat. Not even Eratosthenes had envisioned such a thing. The coolness of the pronaos could not lower the temperature in my suddenly feverish mind. I looked at Josef, who still gazed up at the relief. He wore a threadbare gray tunic and shabby sandals. His weathered tool box sat at his feet. So far as I knew, he had no education outside of synagogue, yet he had just clearly explained a concept that scholars in the Museum next door were probably debating at this very moment.

Josef pointed at a Greek inscription at the foot of the relief. "What does that say?"

I quoted from memory: "Superstition is cowardice in the face of the Divine."

Josef looked around, smiling. "I think I will like it here."

I was hoping to secure Josef work in the Library; several Egyptian artisans had been fired for plotting to deface a number of irreplaceable literary works they considered heretical. Fortunately, their scheme was exposed, and they were apprehended and jailed.

We stood on the second-story balcony overlooking the *naos*, the Library's immense interior open space, which was filled with benches and tables, which in turn were filled with men reading and knots of teachers and students conversing. At the far end was a giant statue of Alexander wearing the crowns of Upper and Lower Egypt and holding the crook and flail, the symbol of the ancient pharaohs.

We turned from the balustrade, and I gestured at a bank of wooden shelves built in wine-rack fashion and filled with scrolls, loose parchments, and vellum books. Two librarians were emptying the shelves. Assistant librarian Hermias, a thin man with close-cropped white hair, approached us. "Serapion," he said, bowing, "is this he?" He fixed his watery gray eyes on Josef.

"Yes," I said. "Josef of Jerusalem, newly arrived in Alexandria."

Hermias turned to Josef, "You're a tekton?"

Josef nodded, pointing to the wood chip tucked behind his ear.

"Not some religious zealot, I hope. We've had enough of those."

I stepped in, unsure of how Josef would take that remark. "He is a devout Jew, which as you know, means he honors knowledge and wisdom."

Hermias grunted. "So say all who desire to work here."

Ignoring our debate, Josef walked toward the now empty shelving. "I see your problem," he said. "This is constructed of Aleppo pine, is it not?"

Hermias shrugged. "Is it?"

"Aleppo grain, while beautiful, is too long to support the weight you're imposing upon it, as seen by the cracks at the crossing points."

"That is why we are emptying them," grunted Hermias. "Because they are cracking."

"But if you are planning simply to reinforce the junctions, you might want to reconsider."

"Is that right?"

"The problem is the wood itself; Aleppo is not strong enough for this design."

"I suppose you would recommend cedar," said Hermias. "As if we were made of money."

"This *is* the Great Library, isn't it?" asked Josef.

Hermias turned to me. "I will give him a try." Then he turned to Josef. "For now, just repair the old shelving. I want to see if your hands work as well as your mouth."

❧ ❧ ❧

I left the Library in a good mood. Josef had handled grumpy old Hermias deftly. It seems Mesha's fears about this country boy's ability to fit into our urban world were unfounded. I just hoped Miriam would adapt as well as her husband did.

I spotted my litter on the avenue. As I walked toward it, I was mindful of the respectful looks directed at me. Unlike most days, however, I paid my audience little mind. I had found Josef a job, Mesha had found them a place to stay, and Jeshua was safe from harm.

One of the bearers pulled aside the curtain, and I entered the litter, seating myself on the cushion. I took a plum from a glass bowl and examined it. It was purple and perfectly ripe. I bit into it, savoring its sweetness. "The Serapeum," I said, and the litter began to move. I closed the curtains and leaned back in the darkness, closing my eyes. It was good to be home.

WENTY

Though much has undoubtedly changed from my time to yours, one thing I am sure has remained the same: time slips by, years eclipsing days in the blink of a distracted eye. Busy with our labors, we forget our most cherished hopes and our darkest fears. But in the dark watches of the night, when we join Ra in the Sektet boat as it glides along the *Keku Samu*, or River of Death, each remaining breath is held so precious that we recoil at the notion of letting a single minute pass by unheralded, uncomprehended, and unlived. But though our bodies, along with Ra, are reborn in the morning, our souls often remain comatose, dead to their true purpose.

Which is simply an admission that life slipped by me as well. It wasn't long before many months had passed and my visits with Josef and Miriam became fewer and farther between.

One day, I saw Miriam in the Royal Quarter. I was on my way to see the Prefect. She was on her way home from the market, having purchased food for a special meal celebrating Jeshua's first birthday. My mouth dropped open in surprise. Had it really been a year? Had I forgotten the most singular event of my life? I begged her forgiveness, which she gave, laughing, saying it was nothing. When we parted, I promised to visit soon.

Later that night, in my offices, I looked at Jeshua's birth chart for the first time in many months. It seemed foreign, as if drawn by someone else. I promised myself—as we all do at night—that tomorrow I would visit his family. But the next day, Temple affairs took precedence, and I did not think of Josef's family until I received a message from Dinah, Mesha's wife.

Mesha ben Huz was dying.

❦ ❦ ❦

"Mesha, my friend," I said softly. His breathing was ragged and uneven. His breath was foul, and on it I smelled the bitter tang of death. I clutched my amulet through my chiton, my heart aching.

"Melkorios," he managed. "How are you?"

"Mesha, what can I do?"

His eyes were still clear, even as he approached the dark door. "You can make something of yourself," he chuckled. "It is not too late."

"I am trying, Rabbi."

"Oh, that I *were* your rabbi. I would charge you with apostasy before the Sanhedrin!" He laughed, which turned into cough. When he lowered his hand, it was stained with blood.

"I warned you about the necropolis," I said. "There is plague there, and you are always carting bones about."

"Making room for new arrivals," said Mesha. "The Romans will not give us more land, and Jews die every day."

"We *all* die every day."

"Make something of yourself," he repeated, reaching out for my hand. I am proud to say I did not pull away, even though I feared the touch of a man condemned to death by the gods.

"What would you have me do?" I asked. "If it is in my command, I shall do it."

"Be a man," said the Rabbi. "Get married. Have a family. Learn what life is really about. Get out of that crypt you live in."

"My villa is not a crypt," I said, knowing he was referring to the Serapeum.

"Do this," he said weakly. "Pretend, just this once, that I *am* your rabbi. My wish for you is to begin living a life of *your* choosing, not the life you were given." He waved his hand weakly, as if to dismiss the possibility that I would listen to him.

"I am afraid, Mesha."

"We all fear. Brave men act anyway."

I nodded. I was not brave.

"One more thing," he said. "Jeshua, son of Josef."

"I will look in on them."

"No!" he said. "They do not need you to 'look in on them'! They need your protection!"

I stiffened. "Do you now believe he is the . . . ?"

Mesha shrugged. "There is . . . *something* about him. But more than that; when I *think* about him, my heart fills with . . ." He paused. "What did the chart say?"

"Mesha, you do not believe—"

"What did it say?"

"That his life will be hard," I said. "I looked it over again, and I think I have misinterpreted it. He may not be destined to be a king."

"Then what?"

"A teacher, perhaps."

Mesha closed his eyes. "Judaism has enough teachers. We need a *king*."

"And you hope he will be that king?"

"Hope," said Mesha, "is the last refuge of the conquered. Yes, I have hope—that is what fills my heart when I hear his name: I hope he will free us."

"You always said freedom of the heart is what matters."

"I was wrong. Freedom to *act* is the only real freedom." He looked heavenward. "I would have liked to see the Anointed One." He looked at me. "But perhaps I have. And if that is true, then I should ask him to protect *you*."

"Me?"

"You are the one who sees but doubts. A precarious position for a believer."

"I have done my best," I said.

"Have you, Melkorios? Have you?"

At the time of his death, Rabbi Mesha ben Huz was thirty-five, almost ten years younger than I. His eldest son Apollos was just ten years old and not yet ready to take his father's place in synagogue. The Sanhedrin chose a man named Elizur as his successor. Elizur means "my God is a rock," and he was as hard as his name. He had no interest in good relations with Greeks or Egyptians or Romans, all of whom he saw as oppressors, evil-doers, and slave-masters. Needless to say, I was not welcome in the Delta Quarter once he began presiding at the Grand Synagogue.

I stood at a distance in the Necropolis as they placed Mesha's linen-wrapped body inside the sepulcher. I wondered if I would meet my friend again. Would he face Osiris in the Underworld, or would he fly to the center of the universe to dwell with Adonai?

As the masons removed the stone box containing the bones of the previous inhabitant for burial elsewhere, I walked away. A multitude had turned out to witness the interment, but I did not see Josef or his family. Dinah stood stoically, clutching young Apollos's hand tightly, her face veiled. I grieved for her and her large family, now without their father.

As I left the Necropolis, I pondered Mesha's advice, which had not left my mind since he gave it to me a week ago. I knew he was right, and my own heart told me it was past time.

It was time to fill my life with life.

Twenty-one

Yes, I got married. As I write this, I am alone again, a widower of many years. The pain of loss still sears my heart so deeply that I can barely make my hand move across the papyrus. I will try, however, for the sake of her blessed memory, to tell you about my beloved wife.

Thaesis was the eldest daughter of Decimus Macrimus, the administrator of the Gymnasium. I met her when I went to secure five-year-old Jeshua a place there, armed with a letter from Turranius (which I wrested from him before his long-awaited return to Rome) as well as one from the Jewish philosopher Philo, who, at twenty, was already establishing himself at the Museum as a gifted thinker. Macrimus read the two letters, along with my own missive, as I sat in his office, waiting.

It was then that I saw her, standing in the doorway, a slender woman with unruly red hair, not beautiful (her weak chin prevented that), but striking in the intensity of her eyes, which were fixed upon her father. I coughed, and Macrimus looked up. From his expression, I knew she was his daughter, and he delighted in her.

She was in the office just long enough to hand him a message, but her expressive face was burned into my memory, and for the remainder of the interview I thought only of her.

"This boy, Jeshua, is he extraordinary?" asked Macrimus.

"Yes," I said, wondering how to turn the conversation to his daughter.

Macrimus sorted through the letters. "Can his family afford the expense?"

I had already debated this with Josef, informing him that I would pay the tuition. He had handed me one of Caspar's golden talents. I took it only because he threatened to knock me down if I did not take it, but I silently vowed to return it to him one day, when he needed it most.

"Serapion?" asked Macrimus.

"There is an account at the Temple bank," I said. "You may draw upon it as needed. His family is not to be contacted regarding the costs of his education here."

Macrimus smiled at me like a conspirator. "I understand."

"You understand *what*?" I asked. I knew he thought I must be the boy's actual father, the Supreme Pontiff dabbling in the flesh of the Jewish Quarter.

Macrimus nodded. My anger had not persuaded him. "Nothing. It will be done."

I saw no purpose in disabusing him of his perverse notions. "Then see to it," I said, still wondering how I might meet his daughter. Suddenly, she appeared in the doorway again.

"Thaesis!" said Macrimus. "Do come in. This is his Excellency, Melkorios Alexandreus."

Thaesis. What a glorious name! It was a variant on Theoris, which was Egyptian for Athena: the Greek goddess of wisdom and purity. I got to my feet numbly, unable to speak, I was so taken by her. She nodded without meeting my eyes, slipped another missive into her father's hand, and exited. I was devastated. She had not even noticed me.

"Poor Thaesis," said Macrimus, reading the note. "She has two younger sisters who wish to be married, but Thaesis thus far accepts none of the men I've chosen for her."

Serapis be praised! I thought. "Why do they not suit her?"

Macrimus just shook his head and sighed. "The Jewish boy will be admitted for the coming term. But he will have to work hard, no matter whose son he is."

I ignored the insult, still focused on Thaesis. "Why is your daughter unwilling to marry?"

"Oh, she's not unwilling, she's simply unconvinced." He smiled. "Like you, I suppose."

I was used to being teased about marriage. Most of my acquaintances had married and put away one or more wives, yet I remained the celibate bachelor, and though they assumed I visited the prostitutes at the temple of Aphrodite down by the sea shore, I did not. But if I were to explain my life to anyone, it would not be to Decimus Macrimus. "I too have been . . . *unconvinced*."

"Perhaps you two should meet!" laughed Macrimus, not knowing that was exactly what I intended to do the moment I left his office.

Thaesis. The very name is a welcome and a warning. Athena, sprung completely grown from Zeus's head, was the ablest of her father's many children. She was a goddess of war, weaving, and crafts. She never took a consort but helped many heroes such as Heracles, Jason, and Odysseus in their trials. Thus was Thaesis, whose heart I never fully mined but whose trust, once obtained, was a precious gem. When I escaped Macrimus's office, I saw her walking across the large courtyard. I ran to catch up with her, and as I approached, she heard my footfalls and turned. Surprise lit her face. At that moment I became a fool. "You are Thaesis?"

She nodded.

"I am Melkorios."

She nodded again. "Yes."

"I wanted to meet you."

"We just met."

"Yes, but we did not speak. I mean, *I* did not . . ."

. . . and so on. I felt like Sisyphus, endlessly hauling the stone to the mountaintop. It was excruciating, even as it was exhilarating. During our short conversation, I stuttered like a fool, entirely forgetting that she was an uneducated woman and I was the Supreme Pontiff of Serapis.

In matters of the heart, there are only two castes: the worshipper and the adored.

The details of one's romance are rarely interesting to others, so I will not share them. Suffice it to say that we began and ended our relationship clumsily; each ached to know the other's heart, yet each lacked the necessary skills. Once, after we had been married two years, I was droning on about the difficulties I was having with the Temple acolytes' lack of interest in the grander elements of the cult. I looked up and saw disappointment on her face. I broke off speaking.

"Go on," she said.

"You are not interested," I countered.

"No, I'm not."

"So why go on?"

"Because you *need* to, Melkorios."

"But I need to because I need *you* to hear."

"Can I solve your problems at the temple?"

I shook my head. "Probably not."

"Then *why* must I hear?"

"Because . . ."

"You *need* me to." She sighed. "Very well, then."

Many of our conversations went that way. We were both so clumsy with intimacy that we barely knew where to begin. Yet, if there was a practical problem, we could easily put our heads together and find a solution. She oversaw our household with great skill, just as I ably administered the Serapeum. But when it came time to be quietly together, to whisper as lovers whisper, words hid from us. I'm sure she ached for the key to my heart, but I had not that key myself. So we spent our years together as best we could, and I think neither of us ever knew how much we meant to the other until we were separated. I am certain that was my case.

After a year of marriage, it became apparent that Thaesis was barren. We comforted ourselves by asserting to each other that our lives were too busy for children anyway, but it was a terrible blow, especially to her.

Then one day our servant Senteph returned from his weekly trip to the city dump with hopeful news. Some Egyptian servants had recovered a female infant from the refuse pile that day, discarded because of clubfeet. Senteph said it was a Greek baby, and I shook my head at the callousness of my race. Egyptians and Jews, who abhorred the practice, often rescued these babies. We bribed the servants, and they brought the child to our villa. When Thaesis saw the baby, so perfect except for her tiny misshapen feet, she wept, gently holding the tiny newborn out to me. I took her carefully. I had not held an infant since the birth of Jeshua. I looked at the child's deformity, then pleaded silently with Thaesis to be reasonable.

"You will not deny me this," she said, taking the baby from me.

Thaesis was the ablest woman I knew, but she was not strong enough to raise a deformed child. "I would deny you nothing," I said, "but—"

"You have denied me your heart. Let me have someone who will give me hers."

"I do my best," I said quietly. "But this child—"

"What did your rabbi friend say?" Thaesis knew what a tender subject

Mesha was, but she was not being cruel—she was merely making a point. I lowered my eyes, bowing to her logic. "You need to start living," she whispered, handing the baby back to me. "You *have* held a baby before, haven't you?" she asked. I nodded. "How did it feel?"

The tiny child looked up at me, her dark eyes meeting mine. "It was . . . life-changing."

❦   ❦   ❦

We named her Athena. Her legs would not carry her about with quiet, measured dignity, so she instead shook the villa walls with shrieks of joy as she was pushed about in a wheeled chair built by my dear friend, the great inventor Hero. Wooden ramps were constructed so steps were no impediment. Her chair's wheels ran over my bare toes so many times that I asked Hero if he could do something to lessen the pain. He suggested I wear boots, then set to work gluing leather strips to the wooden wheel rims, which not only allowed my toes to heal but quieted the races as well.

Thaesis, never separated from her daughter, proudly took Athena and her remarkable rolling chair with her wherever she went. On the other hand, I was ashamed of Athena's disability, thinking it best that the child remain out of the public eye.

Thaesis would have none of it. "Absolutely not," she said. "She is not a cripple."

"If you mean she has not been slowed by her deformity, I agree. But it is not *proper*."

"Perhaps not in the Serapeum, but in the streets of the city she is admired for her courage."

"She is too young to have courage. She is simply bold, as you have taught her to be."

"And you have neither courage nor boldness," said Thaesis flatly, leaving the room.

But I gave in, as always, for I could not deny Athena any happiness, and her face was radiant as the slaves wheeled her out into the street to accompany her mother to market. As I closed the door behind them, I hoped Athena would be strong enough to bear the hurtful whispers she would inevitably hear. I could not help but wonder what people would think of Serapion allowing his lame daughter to flaunt her imperfection in public. I hated myself for being so petty, wondering when the word "family" would mean more than daily compromise to me.

As I reread the last few sentences, I am reduced to tears, because both my precious Athena and my lovely wife Thaesis are now gone. I wish I was better able to describe what an impact they had on my life, how they softened my heart even though I was often irritated with their noise and distractions. Thaesis used to say we are stones rolling down a hill, getting our edges knocked off until we become smooth and round. I used to say I was the pillar at the bottom of the hill that was destroyed when those smooth, round stones collided with it.

"A pillar holding up . . . what?" asked Thaesis.

"Nothing, probably. Just standing there."

And yet with my wife and daughter, I began to feel like perhaps I *was* holding something up: a house built not of granite or marble but of connections and purpose.

I held little Athena in my arms the night she died. She was just five years old. She had caught a cold that quickly filled her lungs. The sniffles turned into racking coughs, and soon her appetite failed. She lay in her bed, surrounded by crying servants and her mother, unable to raise her head off the pillow. The doctors stood outside the door, unable to help her beyond herbal teas and poultices. She was slipping away, and there was nothing we could do.

Earlier that day, I had sacrificed on her behalf at the Serapeum. But a bad omen appeared when I noticed a serpent coiled around Serapis's feet. I blinked and the serpent changed into a harmless coil of rope, Cerberus's leash. I was reminded of my nightmare in the Sinai, eight years before, of Apep's sharp fangs, ready to devour the unworthy souls that dared navigate the Keku Samu. When I returned home, my heart was heavy. Thaesis met me at the door, eager to know how the sacrifice went. I shook my head.

"Then you must go to see Josef," she said.

"Josef?" I said, surprised. "Why?" She merely looked intently at me. "You think Adonai can heal Athena?" I asked. She was an even more devout follower of Serapis than I was.

"Can Serapis?"

I took her hand. "But would it not be as offensive to Adonai for us to suddenly beg his help as it would be to Serapis for us to suddenly eschew his?"

Thaesis's eyes were full of tears. "I don't care what they think! One of them can heal her!" She paused, then said, "I sacrificed at Jupiter Capitolinus today."

I was horrified.

"And at the Caesarium." She lowered her head.

"Thaesis!" I said, shocked.

"And at the temple of Isis."

My mouth hung open. It was not improper to worship at the temple of one favored deity, but to sacrifice at several at once! And she, the wife of the Supreme Pontiff! I was speechless.

Thaesis touched my sleeve. "Ask Josef to talk to the angel—the one who cares for his family."

I guided her to a low bench, were we sat. "There is no time. The doctors said so."

"Doctors!" said Thaesis, shaking her head, tears flying. "What do they know?"

"And the gods?" I asked gently.

"I knew your faith was weak, Melkorios, but I didn't know it was nonexistent."

"It is not," I said, trying to find the words. "It is just that I never really dared to hope I would have you and Athena for very long." I looked away. "I have never merited such happiness," I said.

Thaesis, ever pragmatic, said, "Now, listen to me: our lives may be up to the gods, but our happiness is most certainly *not*. If we choose to be happy—in spite of calamity—they cannot—they *would* not—prevent that."

"But what if our happiness is dependent upon the lives of those we love?"

She put her hand on my cheek. "Then we are in trouble."

As we returned to the sick room where Athena lay, my heart was full of foreboding. I knew the truth of all Thaesis had said. And I would have sent a message asking Josef to come running had Athena lived through the night. But she did not.

Two days later, we placed Athena on the pyre on the steps of the Serapeum and watched as her body was consumed by fire. My seven-pointed star diadem was on my head, and Thaesis was dressed in a white mourning shroud with a body-length veil. We grieved silently for two weeks, often passing rooms where the other sat staring blankly into space, face contorted with pain, but neither of us said anything. What could we say? So great was our grief that if we voiced it, we feared it would expand and fill the whole world.

Then one night I came to her chambers and saw Thaesis sitting at the foot of her bed, her cheeks glistening with tears.

"What is it?" I asked from the doorway.

"She is happy. Athena is happy."

I sat next to her, taking her hands in mine. "How do you know this?"

"I just do," she said. "And she can run, Melkie! Swift and graceful as a fawn!"

I tried to imagine Athena running but could not. "Was it a dream?"

"No. A waking view of Elysium. She is happy there, and she runs—as fast as Hermes! She is surrounded by light and holds a star in her hand." Tears fell from her cheeks onto our clasped hands. "She lives among them now, Melkie. And they love her, more than we ever could." Then she broke down, and my own tears spilled onto my cheeks. My precious Athena, finally whole.

❧ ❧ ❧

Many days later, when I was sitting in the caldarium at the public baths on the Canopic Way, I realized that Athena was no longer subject to the imperfections of her parents. She was loved by the gods themselves, who showered her with gifts of stars. Thaesis's feelings of inadequacy as a mother and my guilt for my weaknesses dissipated as we realized that Athena was now being loved as she truly deserved. Freed from us, she had finally found true joy.

And then another insight came. I realized that in my overwhelming grief, I had somehow finally given *all* my heart to Thaesis. The final dam of self had burst, and I was drowning in a fullness of feeling for her. I jumped to my feet and ran across the slippery tile, almost falling, rushing to the dressing room. When I got home, I discovered she had gone to the dockside markets. I ran to the piers, searching for her. I found her in front of a fish stand. I grabbed her arm, whirled her around, and kissed her on the mouth. She was so surprised she dropped her bag. I heard the tinkling of breaking glass. When I released her, she looked about, astonished. Everyone around us was frozen, watching us. I ignored their stares and kissed her again.

"Melkie!" she exclaimed, pushing me away. "What is this?"

"I love you!" I shouted, and a peal of laughter arose near us. We were the center of attention on the crowded docks. I put my arms around her. "I love you," I whispered.

"And I love you," she said doubtfully.

"Louder," I pleaded.

She looked around, aware of the many eyes upon Serapion and his wife. "I love you."

"Louder!" I shouted, throwing my arms up.

She furrowed her brow. Then I think she realized that although I might be mad, it was a pleasing sort of madness. "I love you!" she cried, embracing me. Someone in the crowd laughed.

"Yes!" I exclaimed, whirling her in a circle. "I love you!"

"Prove it, Serapion!" shouted a stevedore.

"No! Not here!" came a woman's voice, and the whole market laughed, then someone clapped and soon there was scattered applause all along the docks.

I held Thaesis close and whispered "Athena turned the key. My heart . . . is finally open."

Thaesis hugged me tightly. "I love you, Melkorios," she whispered. "And you love me?"

"Yes, yes, yes," I said. "I love you."

Twenty-Two

Although Thaesis's vision of Athena running through the Elysium fields gave us both great peace, the emptiness of our home was a sadness only those who have lost a child can comprehend. Every corner you turn, you expect to see your child; every unexpected noise you hope to be a precursor of her gay arrival; every curtain-lifting breeze you hope will carry her fresh smell. And every time you are disappointed. You turn the corner and find nothing but an empty room; the clatter in the kitchen was a dropped pan; the breeze carries only the scent of the sea. Your home is an empty stage, the main player absent, and you, as the audience, await the beginning of a next act that never comes.

And then someone reminds you that it is *your* life that must take the stage now, or there will be no play. For me, it was Josef of Judea, who arrived at my doorway one morning, and with him, the most surprising person I ever knew: little Jeshua.

"Did you get my message last night?" asked Josef, entering the vestibule.

"I was at the Serapeum until late," I said. "What is it?"

"Nothing," said Josef. "It's just that—"

"We're going to hear a speech," interrupted Jeshua excitedly.

I looked down at him. He was almost eight and growing into a healthy boy. He had curly hair, a fair complexion, and brown eyes that looked up at me expectantly. A tiny wood chip was tucked behind his ear, like his father. I had seen them together at synagogue, sitting with the other tektons, their prayer shawls over their heads, moving rhythmically as the cantor melodically recited scripture. I had never seen a child take such interest in religion. His father declared him a prodigy: the boy had memorized hundreds of *Torah* verses at synagogue, even as he had memorized entire chapters of Homer's works at Gymnasium. I bent toward the boy. "Who is speaking?"

"Rabbi Philo," said Jeshua proudly.

"He's not a rabbi, yet," corrected Josef. "But he will be one day. It's his first speech at the Museum, and it has to do with an invention he brought back from Rhodes."

"I heard about this," I said, "but I had forgotten about it. I have been to Dendera and just got back last night."

"If you're too tired . . ." said Josef.

"Please come!" said Jeshua, tugging on my chiton. "Rabbi Philo is a great speaker. I've heard him in synagogue. And now he's at the Museum!" The boy's enthusiasm made me smile. I was tired and would have rather spent the morning in the baths, but I could not say no to Jeshua.

"I would honored to hear Philo," I said, ushering my guests out the door. "Let us go. We do not want to be late."

"Yes!" said Jeshua. "We want good seats!"

The Museum was connected to the rear of the Great Library by a roofed colonnade a furlong in length. On either side was a park with many fountains, trees, and meandering paths where teachers walked with their students, lecturing in the Socratic style of questions and answers.

We passed through the Library, the main floor full of people gathered under Alexander's placid gaze. I noted my friend Hero, the inventor, who smiled at me. Across the room I recognized Seneca, the great rhetorician, recently arrived from Rome to winter in Alexandria.

As we walked under the colonnade toward the Museum, Jeshua saw one of his classmates and ran ahead to talk to him. We also saw Rabbi Mesha's son Apollos, who was accompanied by his guardian. It was still a good half hour before the lecture, but the crowd gathering at the Museum doorway was thick. I was glad Josef had thought to invite me. "So, what is this invention?" I asked.

"I'm not sure," said Josef. "But we've been hearing of it in the Library for days. The name Geminus has been mentioned."

"The great astronomer," I said. "But he has been dead almost fifty years."

"Yes," said Josef, "but he built something before he died, something like the orrery Aristarchus holds in the relief—the one that so fascinated me the day I first entered the Library."

I looked at Josef. "Has it really been eight years?"

He nodded. "Eight good years. Except for Hermias." He laughed and we nodded, aware of the demanding head of Library maintenance.

"What are you working on these days?" I asked.

"As always: shelves," said Josef. "It seems the Chief Librarian is intent upon expanding until we're double the size of the Pergamum Library. He's talked of using the Serapeum library for the overflow. Is that true?"

"Like all scholars, Zeno talks," I said. "But I told him we are already at capacity. In addition to being the 'daughter library,' the Serapeum is also a bank and a court of law, and now Kronion is pressing me to open a beer parlor for the plebs. A far cry from the Jerusalem Temple."

"They buy and sell there too," said Josef. "We have the same problem in the Leontopolis temple in the delta. It's much smaller than the Jerusalem temple, so those selling sacrificial offerings do business in the inner courts. The Pharisees are angry about it."

"I imagine Mesha would be too," I said, "but things change. And today I believe we are going to witness change on a grand scale: Geminus was the greatest mind of his generation."

We had arrived at the Museum, which stood three stories tall with great black-painted columns out front, topped by colorful capitals carved to look like spiky acanthus leaves. The floor of the inner hall, surrounded by balconies supported by more black columns, was filled with benches. Around the walls stood immense marble statues of the nine muses, looking down upon us with noble hauteur. There was an open bench near Urania, the muse of astronomy, which I took as a good sign. We seated ourselves. Chief Librarian Zeno and his counterpart, Ammonios Paternos, head of the Museum, stood on a raised dais, surrounded by green and yellow bunting. Paternos was a fat man who had recently shaved his head. Josef leaned over. "Paternos was ill and lost most of his hair."

"I should give him my remedy," I said. "Ointment of laudanum and myrtle steeped in dry wine, plus a bit of maidenhair fern." I smiled, rubbing my head. "My own hair remains thick, even though I shave it. Life is unfair."

The crowd grew quiet, and we turned. Striding up the aisle was a young man with thinning chestnut hair and a full beard. Philo's arms were full of scrolls, and his brow was sheened with sweat. Slaves followed him, bearing by litter something the size of a stone building block but covered with a silk drape. They set it upon the dais and withdrew. Philo stood to one side, looking out across the sea of men. I knew he was looking for Jewish faces, but I saw by his expression that few of his fellow tribesmen were present. However, the Greeks and Romans of Alexandria had turned out to see what he had brought back from Rhodes.

Paternos stood behind the lectern. "Salve, citizens!" he said in a bleating voice. "Philo Judaeus has obtained a treasure that will be displayed at the Library, to be studied by all of Alexandria, but especially, I think, by our most prominent inventor."

There was applause, and Hero, seated near the front, stood. "Should it prove worthy," he said, and everyone laughed as he took his seat again.

Paternos smiled. "Perhaps more worthy than your steam engine," he said, at which several whistles and catcalls were heard, ribbings from Hero's friends and competitors.

"We acknowledge the presence of Alexandria's most learned," said Paternos. "I note Strabo is present." Strabo, the unparalleled geographer, stood to thundering applause. Josef leaned toward me. "He intends to discover the source of the Nile."

"Known already," I said in return. "It issues from the mouth of the god Khnum."

"Yet Herodotus says it began in a place he called the 'Mountains of the Moon.'"

It was my turn to smile. He obviously spent more time reading at the Library than he did repairing shelving. "As an astronomer," I concurred, "I find that argument persuasive."

Paternos continued recognizing the various dignitaries. Each stood in turn, and each received great applause. I looked past Josef to Jeshua, who sat down the row next to his young friend, whispering, both their eyes focused on the cloth-shrouded object on the dais.

Paternos finally ceded the stage to Philo, who looked out across the large hall. "Fellow Alexandrians! I have returned from Rome." A smattering of applause. "The Senate inquired as to our welfare, to which I replied, 'Overtaxed!'" A cheer went up. I looked to the dais, seeing our new Prefect, who had just entered the hall by a rear door. He scowled as he took a seat next to Paternos.

Philo continued, "Rome sends her greatest affection—"

"And her legions!" came a shout. Around the hall's perimeter were many Egyptians, few of which had risen beyond the status of the low-level civil servant. They did not react to the comment but simply looked on with blank expressions. *Very politic*, I thought. *They will outlast us all.*

"On my way home, I stopped at Rhodes," said Philo. "They send their kindest regards." A cheer went up from the Greek contingent. "While there, I saw something I believed would be a marvelous addition to the Library." We all looked at the shrouded object on the dais. "We've all admired the bas-relief of Aristarchus at the Library entrance," said Philo. "As you know, his orrery represents the structure of the solar system."

"The *theoretical* structure!" someone shouted. Others cheered their agreement.

"Yes, *theoretical*," continued Philo, "but it is *plausible*, given Archimedes's—"

"Murdered by Rome!" shouted someone.

Paternos raised his hands. "This is a scientific lecture, not a political rally. Pay heed and keep silence!"

Philo continued, "Whose ideas were improved upon by the incomparable Eratosthenes."

Jeshua was whispering in Josef's ear, and Josef turned to me, "Jeshua thinks he knows what's under the coverlet."

Did he? I certainly did not.

"And the great Geminus of Rhodes added his own contribution," exclaimed Philo. "Thus!" And he whisked off the shroud to reveal a wooden box three cubits tall, two cubits wide, and a cubit thick, almost as large as a sarcophagus. On the front panel was a bronze dial with six concentric rings surrounding a golden circle in the center. The sun, I supposed. Three arrows of different sizes and positions were anchored at the sun's center. Around the outermost ring were twelve divisions bearing the signs of the zodiac. Philo nodded, and two slaves turned the heavy box around, revealing the rear panel which contained two more large dials, each with pointers like the front. "Perhaps you cannot see from where you are," said Philo, "but—"

"I can see fine," said Hero, leaning forward. "But I still don't see what it *does*."

I smiled at Hero's pragmatism. In his opinion, if a theory didn't result in a practical mechanism, it was a waste of precious time.

"Man has always been a prisoner of time," said Philo, winking at Hero, knowing his mind. "Subject to the seasons, the rising of the sun—"

"Praise the Sungod! Praise Ra!" shouted someone, probably an Egyptian.

Philo nodded. "In his mystical Atet barque, the Sungod transits the twelve hours of the day and then boards the Sektet ship to sail through the twelve hours of the night. Twenty-four hours for each day. Ten days in a week, thirty-six weeks in a year, and five festival days. Time, but time measured by the earth. What about celestial time—time measured by the stars?" He looked up for effect, and I found myself looking up as well, to see the mural on the ceiling far above. The goddess Nut's long slender body stretched from one end of the vaulted ceiling to the other, her hands grasping the western horizon, her feet touching the birthplace of the sun. Behind her, stars blazed against a blue background. The mural design had been borrowed from the ceilings of several Egyptian temples.

"This is a solar clock," said Philo, pointing to the box. The slaves obediently turned it so the front faced forward. "It measures time *outside* the Earth. Look!" He reached and opened the front panel, which swung away on a hinge. Inside the box were a dizzying array of interlocking gears. He removed a zeta-shaped bronze object from his pocket, holding it high. "This is the key." He shut the front panel and placed the key in a hole in the side of the box and turned it slowly. The hands on the dial began to move. Like everyone else, I leaned forward, fascinated. "The outer circles represent the orbits of the planets, including our own, around the sun. Around Ra." He continued turning the crank, and tiny orbs on each of the six concentric circles moved steadily along their arcs around the sun, though at differing rates. "Yes," said Philo proudly, "as Aristarchus believed, the Earth is a planet just like our neighbors—tiny Mercury; ever-present Venus; red-faced Mars; ringed Saturn; and mighty Jupiter, king of all planets."

I thought of Jeshua's birth chart, long unexamined, pressed between the leaves of a book in my office. I stole a look at Jeshua, whose eyes were wide with interest.

"We orbit the sun," continued Philo, "and this clock moves the planets through their orbits in their precise time, as I'm sure master astronomer Serapion will, upon examination, confirm."

Jolted by the mention of my name, I looked up and saw many people looking at me. "Upon examination," I replied vaguely. Hero was looking at me with an expression equal parts humor and skepticism.

"Even the movement of our own moon and its phases is represented, as are the rising and setting of each of the twelve constellations of the zodiac." Again, Philo nodded to the slaves, who turned the mechanism around so its rear panel again faced the audience. People had begun to strain forward for a better look. "On the rear panel, the two dials show—with perfect accuracy—the *true* length of a year, using the Metonic Cycle of 235 lunar months."

Historically, the difficulty in fixing calendars—crucial for an agricultural society—was in the troubling difference between the lunar month of twenty-eight days and the solar year of 365 days, which difference, in just a few short years, results in a calendar at odds with the seasons. If Philo's solar clock was accurate, then that problem had been solved. And if it accurately traced the movements of the planets and stars, my astrological almanac had just been rendered moot—all one had to do was turn the bronze crank to find a date and then note the positions of the planets, stars, and constellations.

My head was beginning to hurt.

"Wasn't that marvelous!" exclaimed Josef as we exited the hall. Following Philo's presentation, the press of people had been too great for us to get a closer look at the clock, but I had no doubt that, after today, it would be available to me whenever I wished. I felt like an oarsman who sees his first ship with sails. We wandered through the park between the Museum and the Library. I found a bench and sat, my mind whirling. Josef sat by me, lost in his own thoughts.

"Melchior," he finally said. I looked at him, and he nodded at Jeshua, who was sorting through a bed of decorative stones. "I want you to hear something," Josef said.

"I have heard enough today," I said, shaking my head. "Remarkable."

"So is this," said Josef. "Jeshua!" he called. Jeshua came and stood before us. I looked at his fist, inside of which I knew was a stone projectile.

"You are not going to throw that, are you?" I asked.

Jeshua blushed and opened his hand. "Look," he said. "It's round—like the clock."

"Jeshua," said Josef. "Tell Master Melchior about Eratosthenes."

Jeshua straightened and put his hands behind his back, as they are taught in Gymnasium. "About the stick and the well?"

"Yes," said Josef. "And the size the earth."

"Yes, sir," said Jeshua. He was only eight, but I could not help but see him sitting on Herod's ivory and onyx throne, preparing to speak to his subjects.

"Eratosthenes was smart," began Jeshua, "but he was lazy."

"Lazy?" I laughed. "Was not he the ablest of all?"

"They called him 'Beta' because he was the second best at everything in the world."

"Including finding perfect stones?" I asked.

"Jeshua is best at that," said Josef, laughing. Jeshua blushed and the perfectly round stone dropped to the pavement behind him.

"Go on," said Josef.

"Eratosthenes wanted to know how big the world was," said Jeshua. "When he stood on top of the Pharos lighthouse, he saw the sails of ships coming into port first, then their hulls, so he knew the earth was round, like a sphere. But he didn't want to walk all around the earth to prove it."

"So, is that why he was lazy?" I asked.

"No," said Jeshua. "He was lazy later. He heard stories about a well far up the Nile . . ."

"Near Syrene," added Josef.

"A deep well, where the sun reflects in the water at the bottom just once a year."

"The summer solstice," I put in helpfully.

"He thought if the world were really flat, like others said, then there would be a well in Alexandria where the sun reflected in the water on the same day, just like it did in Syrene."

"Hmm," I said.

"But it wasn't flat," said Jeshua, turning around and picking up the stone he'd dropped. "And to prove it, he had the royal pacers measure the distance between Syrene and Alexandria. It was almost five hundred miles."

"So he made others walk it for him," I said. "Is *that* why he was lazy?"

"Not yet. The next year, on the same day, Eratosthenes was ready to test his theory. If the sun reflected in both wells on the same day, then the earth was flat, but if it didn't, the earth was curved because sun's rays would enter the well in Alexandria at an angle and would not hit the bottom."

I was beginning to see why Josef wanted me to hear this. The story was a familiar one, every child in Alexandria learned it, but to tell it so well and to understand it so completely was a rarity, especially for an eight-year-old. I leaned forward. "So why was he lazy?"

"Because he couldn't find a deep enough well in Alexandria. So he drove a stick into the ground. If the stick cast a shadow, then he would know the earth was curved."

"Did it cast a shadow?" I asked helpfully.

"Yes," said Jeshua, as proud as if he himself had made the discovery. "Eratosthenes measured the length of the shadow and figured the angle. It was about seven degrees."

"Then what?" I asked.

"Using the distance to Syrene and the angle, he calculated the earth's circumference."

"And?" asked Josef.

"Twenty-four thousand, six hundred and sixty-two miles," said Jeshua proudly.

I lifted my eyebrows. "That is big."

"Thank you, Jeshua," said Josef.

"Father?" asked Jeshua, revealing the stone in his outstretched hand. "We know how big the earth is, but how big is the universe?"

"That we don't know."

Jeshua looked at his stone. "I think if the earth were the size of this stone, this would be the size of the universe." And with that, he hurled the stone. It landed on the Library's tile roof with a loud clatter. Josef and I cringed.

"Don't do that," said Josef. "You might hit someone."

Jeshua bowed his head. "Sorry."

"You can go now," said Josef, and Jeshua ran off. Josef turned to me expectantly.

"You are right," I said. "He should not throw stones."

"No, what do you *think*?"

"He is doing well at Gymnasium, I see."

"He is bored. I think he needs a tutor."

"Then I will have Macrimus hire one."

"That is most generous," said Josef. "But I was hoping *you* would tutor him."

"Me?" I asked. "I do not have the time—"

Josef knew that since the death of little Athena, I had nothing *but* time. "Not regular studies," he said, "but things he might not get in Gymnasium, or in Synagogue, or in our home."

"I doubt there is anything worth knowing that he does not get in one of those three places," I said. "Especially the last one."

Josef blushed. "He is getting knowledge, but knowledge is not wisdom."

"I have precious little of that myself. He should tutor *me*."

"Please, Melkorios," said Josef. "He needs experience. Places and people. Ideas."

"Is he ready?" I asked, then stopped myself. Of course he was ready. He had just explained the most controversial idea since Aristarchus told us the earth revolved around the sun. "I will do what I can," I said. "You want him to tag along with me now and then?"

Josef nodded. "Yes! Just answer his questions. I cannot. I barely understood the story he just told us. But you knew it already."

"I was raised here, Josef," I said, immediately regretting how arrogant that sounded.

"I know," he said, looking down at his rough hands. "He needs more than I can give him."

I shook my head. "He will not get it from me, then."

Josef raised his head, his eyes pleading.

"But I will give him what I have," I said.

Twenty-three

In the months that followed, I took Jeshua places I'm ashamed to say I never took my own daughter because of her deformity. We visited the homes of wealthy scholars, and Jeshua listened with rapt attention while they recited poetry or discussed philosophy. When his opinion was asked, he gave surprisingly thoughtful answers. Once, when Hero asked if Jeshua had any ideas for new inventions, Jeshua looked around the workshop and asked, "Where are your children?" Hero waved the question away, but Jeshua pressed, "Aren't they your best inventions?"

The old scientist scowled at me. He'd been divorced twice and fathered many children, but none lived with him. Stung by Jeshua's innocent question, he dismissed us, claiming he had work to do. Outside, Jeshua said, "He is unhappy. You should invite him to come with us on our visits. He needs to be around me."

"Why?"

"Because he misses his children, though he doesn't know it. If he's around me, he'll remember and call for them. Then he will be happy."

We did just that. When I took Jeshua to the Pharos for the first time, Hero accompanied us, and though he was vexed with Jeshua's constant questions, he clearly relished being a teacher. I noted that Jeshua, who often took my hand when we walked, now took Hero's, and soon they were fast friends.

One day, Jeshua shared his lunch with Hero, saying his mother always packed more than enough. When Hero accepted the offering, Jeshua added, "She feeds me food, but you're feeding me ideas." He patted his stomach. "I'm getting full."

Hero looked at me with such joy that I almost said something, but Jeshua gave me a glance that cautioned silence. In the still moments that followed, Hero asked, "How old are you, Jeshua?"

"I'm nine," said the boy.

"I have a son who is ten," said Hero.

No more was said, but the next time we went out—this time to see the boats in the harbor and go aboard a *trireme*, a tremendous ship with three tiers of oars—a boy named Marcus came with us. At first, Marcus was tentative, but after a while, Jeshua took the boy's hand and placed it in Hero's just as simply as you please. After an uncomfortable moment, Hero pointed at the trireme's sail and began talking about the advantages of the square sail over the triangular sail as Marcus looked up at him hopefully. I also noted that Jeshua took pains to see to it that Marcus was always standing between himself and Hero, so the old inventor's eyes fell upon his son when Jeshua asked a question.

During the second month of Akhet, when the Nile flooding was at its peak, I asked Josef if I could take Jeshua upriver with me to the Opet Festival.

"Isn't that a pagan celebration?" asked Miriam.

"I will not indoctrinate him."

"Nor could you," said Joseph. "He will indoctrinate *you*."

"Which you have no qualms about, I suppose," I chuckled.

"How long will you be gone?" asked Miriam.

"A month."

"A whole month?" asked Miriam.

I nodded, looking around. She had three more little children at her feet now: Judah, nearly six; his younger brother Simeon, five; and little Salome, three. "Do you *want* another child underfoot, now that Gymnasium is closed for the summer?"

She gave me a look only a mother can give. "They're not underfoot, Melkorios."

"I just thought you might need a rest, that's all."

"Not from my children!" she said.

"We are happy to let Jeshua go," said Josef. "He will love the adventure."

"We will stop at Giza to see the pyramids, as well as your temple at Babylon-in-Egypt. You have not been there, have you?" They shook their heads. "It compares with the Jerusalem temple in grandeur, if not in size. I will introduce him to the Kohen Gadol, an old acquaintance of mine. Then we will travel up river to Thebes, where Jeshua will see the greatest celebration of his life."

I also invited Hero and Marcus, but Hero could not go; he was in the midst of another invention and would not take the time off. I was pleased, however, to see that Marcus was at the workshop when I stopped by, as well as an older boy, whom I took to be another of Hero's many sons. They seemed too busy to even consider my offer, and I left feeling pleased, not only that Hero was happily among his sons, but that I would have Jeshua all to myself.

The pyramids of Giza, built by the fourth-dynasty king Khufu and his sons Khafre and Menkaure, stood in geometric grandeur, separated from the Nile by a fertile strip of palms and papyrus. A canal connected the complex with the river, and the slaves rowed our barge into the harbor at the foot of the Sphinx. Atop the sandy plateau stood the three pyramids, encroaching dunes pressing against their western flanks.

"How old are they?" asked Jeshua.

"Twenty-five hundred years," I said. "Look." I pointed at Khufu, the largest pyramid. "Though it is now a ruin, it was once sheathed in white limestone, blinding in the sun. But over time, the stone was scavenged for other buildings."

"What is it for?" asked Jeshua as we walked toward it.

"It is a tomb. Deep inside are burial chambers."

"Were they afraid of death?"

"Why do you ask?"

Jeshua shrugged like any small boy, and I let it go. We stood in the afternoon shadow of the Khufu, gazing upward. Only the casing near the pinnacle remained unplundered. "Do you know how tall the pyramid is?" I asked.

Jeshua nodded. "We learned this in Gymnasium. Six hundred years ago, Thales used a stick to figure the pyramid's height."

I knew that story well. "How did he do it?"

"At the same time of day, he measured the shadow lengths of the pyramid and a stick he drove into the sand. Since it was easy to measure the height of the stick, he simply compared the shadow lengths, then used Pythagoras to calculate the height of the pyramid." He bent and drew an equation in the sand. I nodded approvingly. He looked up at me. "It's interesting, but it's not very important. No matter how tall they are, the pyramids could not bring the pharaohs closer to God. That had already been proven."

I had not heard of that. "Who proved it?"

"In the *Torah*," said Jeshua. "In Babylon, they built a tower to reach heaven."

I had also heard this story, from Rabbi Mesha himself, in fact. "Were they successful?"

"No. Hashem confused their tongues to punish them, which is why there are so many languages." He turned and looked at the pyramids, the largest man-made structures of all, stripped of their shiny skin, crumbling to dust, slowly being buried by the inexorable sand of the desert. "Just as he punished the Egyptians."

I thought about the columns and spires of Alexandria and the immense Serapeum. "Man hopes to commune with eternity, so he builds towers and pyramids."

"And temples," said Jeshua, turning to face the Nile, which flowed slowly past, red with mud from the spring rains, far away, in the south. "Even my people think the Temple is Hashem's home, but his home is not on this earth."

"It is symbolic," I said.

"We are passengers on a boat floating down a river," said Jeshua. "Nothing on the shore matters, only our destination. We are travelers, like Odysseus, and we are far from home, so we are unhappy, as he was."

"Do you think we are meant to be happy?" I asked.

"I think we are meant to be *good*, which makes us happy," he said, looking up at me. "Are you happy, dominus?"

I shrugged. "Happy enough, I suppose."

For a long time Jeshua looked up at me, saying nothing. Then, "She awaits you."

"Who?"

"Athena."

My eyes stung, and I looked away.

Jeshua said, "You will join her, but not soon."

"No?" I asked, blinking back a tear. "I wish it were soon."

"You still have important things to do."

I looked down at the boy, his face so clear of worry and age, yet his eyes so deep and wise. I sighed. "To continue *our* journey, we go south— to Thebes."

TWENTY-FOUR

The temples of Karnak and Luxor; the great mausoleums of Rameses II, Thutmoses III, and Queen Hatshepsut (the only woman to rule all of Egypt until Cleopatra); the colossal twin statues of Amenhotep III; the funerary Valley of the Kings—are all on a short stretch of the river near Thebes and all are surrounded by endless desert on every side.

As our barge docked, we heard drums, pipes, and horns. I pointed at several obelisks that towered above the palms lining the river bank. "The Prefect is here," I said to Jeshua. "During Opet, he represents the Emperor, whose coronation is reenacted." I pointed south, where a temple rose above the river bank greenery. "That is Luxor, where the procession ends, but it starts here in Karnak. Come, the music means it is about to begin!"

I donned my star diadem as we climbed up the embankment steps and the immense walls of the Karnak temple complex came into view. It was the largest sacred city in Egypt, begun fourteen hundred years ago by Amenhotep III. Since then, a dozen pharaohs have expanded upon it. Continuing tradition, Emperor Augustus even had a relief depicting his adoptive father Julius Caesar and Cleopatra making offerings to Osiris carved on one of the many Karnak walls.

During the floods, the Nile filled the great lagoon at the Temple entrance. Hundreds of miniature reed boats floated in the lagoon, symbolizing the journey of Amun-Ra, his wife Mut, and their son Khonsu to their shrine at Luxor, two miles south. Anciently, the procession went by river but in the distant past had been shifted to a more predictable land route—a broad, paved avenue between Karnak and Luxor which was lined with hundreds of solemn stone sphinxes.

Red banners waved atop the pylons at the Temple entrance where thousands of people thronged. I hoped my diadem would secure us ease of passage, and indeed, most people respectfully moved aside when they saw me. We passed musicians clanging cymbals and pounding drums, and vendors hawking alabaster icons of the Theban triad.

At the pylons, which soared fifty cubits into the air, we stopped in front of a line of Nubian guards, their hands on their swords. I showed them my diadem and robes and they parted. I said to Jeshua, "We now enter the land of the Nile. The pylons are its banks, and we are the river."

We entered a hall filled to overflowing with priests, who stood with their hands raised, chanting in a rhythmic murmur among a great forest of columns painted to resemble papyrus stalks. It would take ten men with outstretched arms to encircle the base of each column. Their capitals, dim in the darkness above, supported spans of wooden roof beams. Swallows swooped and dove between the columns.

At the far end of the hall was another doorway, bounded by two more pylons. I took Jeshua's hand, and we walked slowly between the priests. As we passed through the doorway, we once again found ourselves outside. On either side of us were two tall obelisks, each made of a single piece of pink granite. Jeshua gaped up at them. "They represent the petrified rays of Aten, the Sungod," I said.

Before us was another building fronted by another set of pylons. The exterior was carved and painted with historical scenes: great conquests, pharaohs making offerings to the gods, and even prosaic renderings of ancient daily life—bakers kneading bread, masons carving stone, hunters stalking lions. In addition, high up on the walls, row after row of gods were represented along with their names inscribed in hieroglyphics above their heads.

Inside the open doorway, an even thicker crowd of priests stood. I bent to Jeshua and whispered, "The Temple of Karnak." We entered, slipping between the priests, who all had shaven heads and faces like mine. Unlike the exterior temple walls, the interior was not gaudily painted but was carved with religious symbols. When we had moved forward as much as we could, I lifted Jeshua in my arms so he could see. At the rear of the building, lit only by oil lamps, was the Chamber of the Divine King, a building within a building, rising atop a stepped platform, its slanting door jambs echoing the familiar Nile pylon motif. On the porch was an almost life-size ship made of bound river rushes, with a golden pavilion on the deck. "That's the solar barque," I whispered, "where the statues of Amun-Ra, Mut, and their son Khonsu will be placed for their journey upriver to the Luxor Temple."

"Where are the statues now?" asked Jeshua

"They are inside the Chamber," I said. I looked around, recognizing many of the priests. A number of them would bear the solar barque this day, a once-in-a-lifetime privilege. I had borne it almost a decade ago, before my visit to Jerusalem. I thought then about Zechariah, who had been privileged just once in his life to enter the Holy of Holies of the Jerusalem Temple, where he met Hashem's messenger Gabriel, who told him of the miracle of his wife Elisheba's pregnancy and cursed him with silence for his doubts until she gave birth. Yet he also told him about the Moshiach, who, if Jewish prophecies (and my natal chart) could be credited, was now sitting in the crook of my arm, goggling about as any child would.

As if on cue, the priests began chanting, low at first, then rising in intensity and volume: "Amun! Amun! Amun!" The doors of the Chamber opened, revealing the statues, which were lit by hundreds of candles, making them shine like the sun itself. Drums pounded, punctuated by shouts, and a long blast of horns erupted. Jeshua squirmed in my arms, and I let him down. He looked up at me, a confused expression on his face.

Suddenly, I was ashamed to be standing there, wearing the star diadem on my head. I turned away. Jeshua tugged at my sleeve. I turned back. There were tears in his eyes, which I interpreted as fear. I scooped him up and made my way out of the Temple. Behind us came a shout, and I knew the statues had been removed from the Chamber and placed upon the barque.

Outside, we found ourselves facing another temple. I turned left through a doorway, and we were on a sun-drenched plaza dominated by a shallow, rectangular pool of water. A multitude stood around it, waiting in silence. In a few minutes, the barque would be transported across the pool on the priests' shoulders, its hull not allowed to touch the water. The procession would pass through the temples of Rameses II and Mut and would finally turn toward Luxor, where Prefect Gaius Isidorus would pretend to be Octavian Augustus Caesar—even as I had at the Ides celebrations in the Serapeum.

We left the Temple complex. On the Avenue of the Sphinxes, we again found ourselves in the crowd, overwhelmed by the music, tinkling and thundering by turns, accompanied by nearly naked Nubian dancers. Priests stood between the flanking sphinxes and chanted in unison.

We walked south along the Avenue. Gradually, the crowd thinned. It would take hours for the solar barque to be carried the two miles to Luxor. Along the way, it would stop six times, and people in the crowd (chosen in advance) would ask questions of the statues. A priest would place his ear next to the statue's mouth and listen, and the throng would hold its breath, awaiting the answer. Then the priest would turn, raise his hands, and give the god's answer: "Yes, the harvest will be bountiful!" "Yes, the Emperor will live many more years!" "Yes, no enemy will disrupt the peace of Egypt!" It was all a charade, of course, but everyone enjoyed the hopeful messages.

But I did not wish to see the play unfold; I had to make my presence known to the Prefect, who was in Luxor. I took Jeshua's hand, and we hurried down the palm-lined Avenue.

Twenty-five

When we arrived at the Luxor Temple, there was almost no one around except scurrying priests. Flanking the pylons were six colossal statues, three on a side.

"Who are they?" asked Jeshua.

"They are *all* Rameses," I said. "As you know, he reigned thirteen hundred years ago. Egyptians call him the 'Great Ancestor.' We Greeks call him 'Ozymandias,' but I call him a bore."

Jeshua laughed. "Why?"

"Because of this," I said, gesturing at the statues. "No matter whose temple it is, he managed to place a statue of himself in front of it." I pointed across the river at another immense complex of stone buildings. "That's his Ramesseum, which he dedicated to himself."

Jeshua squinted at the buildings and frowned. "But it's just a ruin now."

"Yes," I said flatly. "Serves him right."

We entered the enclosed temple courtyard. Two rows of columns carved to mimic papyrus stalks formed the perimeter. At the far end were two statues of Rameses, this time seated. On our right was the chapel of Serapis, a small shrine set into the wall, fronted by a four-columned porch. To my disgust, the chapel was empty; the pontiffs were in Karnak, celebrating another god.

"These will all be ruins one day," said Jeshua when I turned back to him.

Knowing he also included the Serapis shrine in that comment, I took his hand roughly, and we walked across the courtyard, entering a long colonnade of twelve columns, each representing an hour of the day. I asked a priest about the Prefect. He pointed into the gloom. I left Jeshua examining a statue of Amun-Ra and went to the Prefect, who was talking to a priest in the Sanctuary.

"Gaius Isidorus," I said as I approached. "How wonderful you look!"

The Prefect scowled at me. "This?" He tugged at the pleated skirt he wore below his bare belly. "I would feel like a fool," he said, "if not for this." He held up a golden baton like the one I used at the Serapeum, though his was capped by an eagle. My mouth dropped open.

"Yes, it is the Emperor's," said Isidorus. "He loaned it to me when he was here two weeks ago."

"The Emperor was in Alexandria?" I asked. "I did not know."

"No one did," said Isidorus. "He just showed up to examine the books, then boarded his galleon and sailed off."

"Close call," I said before thinking.

"For whom?" asked Isidorus. "What have you been up to, Serapion? Temple intrigue? The fleshpots of the Delta Quarter? Turranius told me you were fascinated by Jewesses."

Nothing I could say would make a difference. In fact, if Isidorus thought I was a mortal like himself with equally mortal failings, his respect for me would probably increase, so I held silence.

Satisfied, he nodded toward the entrance. "How soon?"

"Hours yet," I said. "They're probably still crossing the reflecting pool."

"I'm actually surprised to see you," said Isidorus. "Kronion has been officiating in the Serapeum these days. Getting tired of it, are you?"

"Not tired of it," I said, grimacing, "just tired."

"Time to step down?"

"When Serapis calls me home," I said wearily, "but perhaps not before then."

Isidorus smiled. "You're a politician, Serapion: never a straight answer."

Just then a priest entered our line of sight and motioned at the Prefect, who left without another word.

I shook my head at the Prefect's receding back. I was standing next to the statue of Amun-Ra in the colonnade. I looked around. Where was Jeshua? "Jeshua!" I hissed.

I walked into the courtyard and asked a priest if he'd seen a boy. He shook his head. I turned and headed back into the darker precincts of the Temple. "Jeshua!" I called in a low voice. "Jeshua!"

I continued into the darkness. Passing through the Sanctuary, I entered the Barque Shrine, which was lit by a single brazier. Alexander himself had placed a small solar barque replica here, which mimicked the life-sized one now approaching us on the Avenue.

"Jeshua!" I whispered. Only the Offering Room lay beyond and only the Temple priests were permitted in there. I took a step toward it. The drape was parted and I drew close. Inside, a candle burned on a broad stone table. I heard a whimper behind me and turned, seeing a narrow doorway to my right.

I entered the small anteroom, which was filled with columns. Another doorway opened to my left, this one so narrow I had to turn sideways to pass through it. The chamber was a duplicate of the previous one, filled with columns and lit by a slit window high on the wall. Niches in that wall held animal-headed icons, the pantheon of Egypt. I moved past a column, listening.

Then I saw him. Jeshua stood with his back against a column. Tears tracked down his cheeks as he stared raptly at a relief on the wall in front of him.

I knelt by him. "Jeshua! What is it?"

He stared up at the relief.

"What is it?" I repeated.

"I'm afraid."

I took him in my arms and he collapsed against me, sobbing, clutching at my clothing. When his tears subsided, I pulled back and asked, "Why are you afraid?"

He stared right through me. "It's me," he said, his voice breaking. "It's me."

I guided Jeshua out of the Sanctuary. He trudged silently at my side, his eyes unfocused. In the courtyard, we passed the Prefect, whose face broadened into a sardonic smile when he saw the Jewish boy with me. I cursed under my breath and took Jeshua out into the blinding day of the late spring afternoon. In the distance, the barque was moving slowly toward us down the Avenue, surrounded by people. We turned left, plunging through a hedge between two sphinxes.

On the other side of the hedge was a tilled field bordering the river. I pulled off my diadem and let it fall to the ground. Jeshua continued walking across the furrows toward the brown river. We should not have come.

This trip had been a terrible mistake. And it was my fault because I knew what he had seen in the Temple.

At the riverbank, Jeshua stopped at a low bluff. Below him, the flooding brown Nile rushed by. The wind lifted his hair. Suddenly, fear gripped me. What if he threw himself in? I stumbled across the furrows, calling his name. He did not turn. I reached him and folded him into my arms, hugging him fiercely, but his body did not bend toward me this time; he was lost inside his mind.

I was intent upon returning to Alexandria that very afternoon, but I despaired of turning Jeshua over to his mother in his condition.

We were staying with the pontiffs of Serapis in Thebes. I had rehearsed a scathing verbal bruising I would give them for abandoning the Luxor shrine, but my concern about Jeshua pushed it from my mind. I asked for dinner, and the cook broiled mutton, which went uneaten by both of us. I picked at a cluster of grapes and watched Jeshua, who sat at the table, eyes downcast, hands in his lap, saying nothing and eating less.

I suggested that we go to bed, though it was barely dark. The boy got up and waited to be led to a sleeping chamber. I shook my head in mad grief. What had happened? Had Amun-Ra cursed him, robbing him of his ba?

I led him to a straw sleeping pallet in our quarters. He sat down listlessly, and I knelt before him and began unbuckling his sandals. Then, his hand was on my shoulder. I looked up. He was looking past me, at the night sky through the window.

I turned. A purple band on the west horizon was all that was left of the sunset. Venus glistened above the jagged mountains. Suddenly, I knew what to do. I scooped Jeshua up and carried him into the main eating room.

"I need a horse!" I called out.

It was past the sixth hour of night when we arrived at the mountains. Jeshua had said nothing as we crossed the plain west of the Nile, but his eyes gradually awoke to the concourse of stars above us. I pointed out constellations. There was Heracles, swinging his club, and there, Cassiopeia reclining on her couch, conversing with her husband Cepheus. Orion was hunting, his bow taut, his sword at his waist. I felt sure Jeshua was listening, but he said nothing.

We stood now at the entrance of a broad, shallow canyon. I helped Jeshua off the horse and let the reins drop. I hoped the horse would not wander far.

I gestured before us. "The Valley of the Kings." A dirt path climbed the canyon walls around eroded shoulders of barren earth. We followed it and soon we were high on a rocky slope, looking down at a faint network of paths, many terminating at shale-strewn slopes. As we walked, I pointed to a three-sided peak brooding over the valley. "That summit represents the Mound of Creation out of which Atum arose," I said. "Its shape was the inspiration for the pyramids."

Uncomfortable with the ensuing silence, I continued. "The pyramids were plundered, so they began burying the pharaohs here in unmarked tombs, now hidden by the sands of time. Thieves still find them now and then; it is hard to protect a body when it is buried in a gold coffin."

We sat on a large boulder. Jeshua stared across the emptiness. I wondered if I had imagined him listening as we rode to the Valley. I sighed. "It is quiet here."

"Yes," he said.

I started with surprise. Had he spoken?

"The dead *are* quiet," I encouraged, hoping for more.

Jeshua looked up just as a shooting star arced across the sky. "But their souls fill the universe with song." I leaned forward to better see his face, lit by the full moon. His eyes still had a faraway look. "You believe too much in death," he said flatly, without looking at me. "All of you do."

"Yes," I whispered. It was true.

"But death is only a short sleep. Every soul will awaken."

"You mean the righteous. The wicked are condemned to eternal coma."

"No," said Jeshua, fixing his eyes on me for the first time, "Everyone."

I blinked at him, not understanding.

"Even you."

Twenty-six

The next morning we boarded my boat, and the slaves rowed us down river. Jeshua was not quite himself yet, but at least he was not catatonic. He spoke little, sitting on the prow of the boat, watching the passing shore.

Three days later, his mother met us at the docks by the Gate of the Sun and swept him into her arms. I returned home. Thaesis attempted to draw me out; she'd never seen me return from Opet in a dark mood, but I could not speak of what had happened. Not yet.

Over the next few days, I tended to Temple business. Then, one evening, as I left the Serapeum, I saw Josef standing at the foot of the steps, waiting for me. I hurried down to him.

"Josef," I said. "What is it?"

Josef turned and started toward the square entrance. I followed him, my heart pounding. Something bad had happened.

It wasn't until we were on the Serapic Way that he spoke. "Something happened to Jeshua." He wouldn't meet my eyes; it was hard for him to reproach me. Notwithstanding my many weaknesses, he still somehow respected me. Knowing that made me feel even worse.

"At the festival," he continued.

I stopped and he took a step or two before turning back. "Yes," I said. "Something happened."

Josef came toward me, his hands open. "What was it? He's not himself."

I nodded. "That is the question. Who *is* he?"

Joseph shook his head. "I don't know what you mean."

I had been thinking about this. The Opet Festival had indeed changed Jeshua, or should I say, had *revealed* Jeshua to himself. I took Josef's arm and led him under a portico for privacy. It was quite dark and the street was empty. "What have you told Jeshua about his destiny?"

Josef straightened. "We've told him truth as befits his age."

"What truth is that?"

"That Gabriel announced his birth. That angels sang in the heavens. That wise men from distant lands brought gifts."

"And his father?" I asked. "What did you tell Jeshua about him?"

"Nothing. We've been unsure what that knowledge would do to him."

I sighed. "Well, he knows now."

"*You* told him?"

"No. We were in the Luxor Temple, and he found his way into the Birth Room."

"You took him *inside* a pagan temple?" asked Josef.

"I was on an errand. It was just for a minute."

Josef said nothing. I remembered that he had waited for me at the foot of the Serapeum steps rather than touch them. Josef was even more devout than Rabbi ben Huz, who had once entered the Temple adytum itself. I looked at the ground, ashamed.

"What happened in this room?" asked Josef.

"He saw a relief, perhaps two thousand years old, depicting his life."

"What?"

"Well, the artists thought they were carving various events in the life of Ra, the Sungod."

"What events?"

"The relief is four panels," I said. I had been in the Birth Room many times; a tiny image of Serapis filled a niche there, and I always left an offering before it at the Festival. But I had never given the relief on the opposite wall much thought until I saw Jeshua standing before it. "The first shows the virgin Neith being visited by Thoth, messenger of the gods, who informs her that she will become pregnant, though not by a mortal man." I paused.

"Go on," said Josef warily.

"The second scene shows the gods Kneph and Hathor impregnating Neith by holding the ankh symbol up before her mouth. In the third panel, she gives birth to Ra, and in the final panel, the infant is worshiped by gods and mortals."

Josef looked at me. "Did you see yourself in that relief?"

"Many cultures share similar myths, such as stories of a garden of creation or a great flood."

"But *this* story, Melchior, is no myth—you and I were there." When I did not dispute this, he continued: "That's why he's so withdrawn—he has just discovered his destiny."

I touched Josef's shoulder. "Fear not. The last panel of the carving shows Ra being worshiped as the Son of the Morning. If this truly foreshadows Jeshua's life, then rejoice, for his reign will bring peace and prosperity."

Josef shook his head. "If Ra represents Jeshua, then I *am* afraid. I've read the *Amduat*—the journey Ra takes each night through the Underworld. He travels the River of Death, battling all manner of evil, including the great snake, the soul eater Apep. Though he is born again each dawn, half of his life is spent in combat with the enemies of light. His life is a terrible conflict between light and dark. As a father—even a stepfather—my heart aches for the trials he will face."

He turned and walked away, down the dark Alexandrian street, his shoulders slumped with concern. As I watched him go, I promised myself I would renew my efforts to do my part to prepare this boy to be a king, if that was his destiny.

Twenty-seven

As time passed, the startling image of the Luxor relief faded for all of us, even Jeshua; he was, after all, still a boy. I encouraged him in school, and, to my delight, he become a gluttonous learner, and when he visited his father at the Library, he pestered everyone with endless questions.

"You know what he asked me?" said Hero one day when we met on the street. "He asked me what made me happier—my family or my inventions."

"And what did you say?"

"I said they were different kinds of happiness—they were not mutually exclusive!"

"And what did *he* say?"

"He engaged me in an hour-long dialogue about values. Socrates, Plato, and Aristotle together couldn't answer his questions! How he taxed me!"

"But are you sure he wanted an answer?"

"Why else would he ask?" And with that, Hero walked away, shaking his head.

But Jeshua's his most endearing facet was his gentleness—he was never cruel, even when sorely vexed. In the harsh world of children, instead of giving blow for blow, he would simply turn away, leaving the offender to ponder his unacceptable behavior. I saw this on two occasions and was impressed by his reaction. When he returned to play after a suitable absence, his presence had been so missed that the other children were on their best behavior for the rest of the day. He was, simply put, the most remarkable child I had ever met.

And yet our association was destined to end before he fully healed me of the loss of my own daughter. Just a few months after our return from Karnak, I found myself on the docks, saying good-bye to Jeshua and his family. Though I had a long discussion the night before with Josef, I tried once more to convince him not to go.

"We miss our families," he said simply.

"Then bring them *here*. There are more Jews in Alexandria than there are in Jerusalem!"

"They won't leave Judea," said Miriam. "It's their home. It's *our* home too."

"We will miss you," said Thaesis, resigned to their departure.

"Remember the dream!" I begged. "The danger!"

"It is past now," said Josef simply. "I told you."

"Gabriel could be wrong."

Josef smiled. "He's not wrong. It's time for Jeshua to return to Judea."

"He is just a boy," I said. "Let him be one! He has only five years at Gymnasium—he's barely begun his education!"

"We will educate him."

I snorted my opinion of Judean schools. "Josef, you are a master tekton at the Library! In a few years you will be a member of the Sanhedrin— a ruler among your people! You are safe here. And"—and with my next words I looked at Thaesis—"you are loved."

"Melchior," he said, "all that you say is true. We will miss many things about Alexandria, but mostly we will miss your friendship and wisdom."

I grunted my reaction to that characterization.

"Wisdom," continued Josef, "that has guided us every day since we first met. But you have a blind spot, my friend: you doubt the signs—and you, an astrologer!"

"There are signs in heaven and there are signs on earth," I said. "I trust the latter."

"And yet you look to the heavens for them."

"Don't we all?" I asked, giving up.

Josef grasped my arm. "For all the greatness you've achieved, Melchior, more is in your future." He looked to the heavens. "At least that's what Hashem tells me."

I shook my head. "He has ever been silent with me, Josef."

"That may change."

I did not believe in change; I had seen little of it in my own life. And yet, in the ten years I had known Josef, he had changed into a confident, competent, and faithful provider for his family.

"I won't change," said Jeshua, who appeared from behind Josef, giving me that direct look of his. "I will always love you."

I bent toward him. "Do not forget your uncle."

"I won't," he said, kissing my cheek.

I straightened and blinked away a tear.

"May you have peace, grace, kindness, mercy, and a long life," said Josef, quoting the *Kaddish* prayer.

"It was probably inevitable," I said. "The *Shema* says, 'I am Adonai, your God, who led you from the land of Egypt.'"

Josef smiled. "Come with us, Melchior—you are almost a Jew!"

When their ship left the dock, I kissed Thaesis good-bye and walked along the waterfront to the *heptastadion*, the mile-long causeway that connected the mainland with Pharos Island. I wanted to scale the Pharos to see the ship's sails disappear below the horizon as Eratosthenes did two hundred years before. When he looked out to sea, he realized that the earth was a sphere; I was about to realize a loneliness I had never felt before.

As I walked along the causeway, I recalled that the last time I visited the lighthouse was when Athena was alive. It had been a cool winter evening. The setting sun had painted a rainbow on the horizon, which quickly faded to indigo. Stars peeked out from behind a scrim of high clouds. I pushed Athena in her wheeled chair along the causeway and was only vaguely aware of the stares of those we passed, both at her marvelous chair and her sad deformity.

At the foot of the lighthouse steps, I placed her on my back, her arms tight around my neck. We scaled the steps two at a time, and I felt her excited breathing against my neck. At the top of the short flight of stairs, under the colonnaded porch, we looked back at Alexandria, where ten thousand windows glowed with reflected golden light.

"Are you ready?" I asked.

"Yes," she said in her childish lisp. "Take me to the stars, Father!"

I faced the tower. It was sheathed in sparkling white marble and consisted of three stages: the first was square and squat with many small windows;

the second was tall and eight-sided; and the third was a squat cylinder topped by a columns and a cupola, underneath which an immense bronze mirror focused light from the fire out to sea. Poseidon stood atop the cupola, a warning and a guide for mariners approaching the rocky shoals of the African coast.

Twin ramps curved around the interior of the first stage, where donkeys plodded slowly upward, laden with bundles of wood for the fire. At the top of this tower, we walked out onto a great porch and stood behind a tall stone balustrade, looking again at Alexandria, which glowed duskily with a million oil lamps, it seemed.

Inside the octagonal second stage, the ramp became a narrow staircase jutting from the interior wall. In the open center, an ingenious system of pulleys lifted the wood to the upper section. As we ascended the stairs, all thoughts fled from my mind except my next step.

We finally arrived at the top and found ourselves on a landing just below the cylindrical tower. I placed Athena on a bench and opened the tower door. A slave was transferring wood from the lower lift to a smaller one, which would carry the fuel up to the beacon fire. We were not permitted to go higher, so I pointed toward the cupola above us. "See the mirror?"

"Yes," she said. "The fire is in it!"

"Just the reflection, dear," I said. "Can you feel the heat?"

She nodded. Just then, we heard the sound of great metal disks grinding against each other. The bronze mirror began to turn slowly, its beam moving steadily across the dark sea. It was magical. Mariners said they could see the light thirty miles from the shore. Though I had been to the lighthouse before, I had never been there at night, and I was glad we had come. I carried Athena over to the balustrade, and we both caught our breath. The city lay far below us, a strip of lights between dark Lake Mareotis and the harbor. I pointed at the Royal Quarter, where we lived, picking out our villa. Athena was delighted to see it.

"What is that?" she asked, pointing to the western gate of the city.

"The Gate of the Moon," I answered.

"And that?" she pointed again.

"The Stadium."

"And that?"

"The Island Palace."

And so on, until I was too tired to hold her any more and set her down.

❧ ❧ ❧

Now, I scaled the steps, sadly unburdened, and within a short time I was on the Pharos pinnacle. Josef's ship cleared the breakwater, and its square sails unfurled. They snapped and luffed, but finally caught the wind, and the Phoenician trader soon passed out of sight, the hull slipping first into the sea, just as Eratosthenes had observed.

I looked back at the sparkling city. The Necropolis lay beyond the western city wall; to the east, the oval Hippodrome stood in its incomparable majesty just outside the Canopic Gate. In between were the five city quarters. I focused on the dark roof of the Grand Synagogue in the Delta Quarter. It seemed smaller—with Josef's departure it had just lost a leader as well as the right to call itself the synagogue of the future Jewish king. Alexandria, undisputed as the greatest city in the world, was also diminished

As was I.

TWENTY-EIGHT

hose memories are painful, but they pale in comparison with what I am now about to relate. My hand is shaking; I am so overcome with emotion that you no doubt find my writing nearly illegible. Grief pierces my skin, seeps through my muscles, and washes through my veins like a sickness, filling my heart with despair, for Thaesis is dead.

I killed her.

Yes, I killed my beloved wife. It had been twenty years since Josef's family returned to Judea. Their ship's captain had returned to Alexandria a few months later with a report of their safe arrival in Ptolemais. I wrote them twice but did not receive an answer. I could only assume my letters did not reach them. I was in my sixty-fourth year; Thaesis, her forty-sixth.

That winter we traveled to Dendera to see the progress of the rebuilding of the Sanctuary of Hathor, the cow-headed goddess of motherhood and music. Dendera is an immense complex, much of it in ruins. Because Hathor was the protector of Osiris in the Underworld, she was greatly revered, and her face was carved into the capitals atop each massive column fronting her block-shaped Sanctuary. Tiberias Caesar himself had ordered the restoration.

Thaesis and I stood inside the hypostyle hall, surrounded by columns and darkness. "This is it," I said, taking her hand and leading her to another smaller chamber at the rear of the hall. I held up a clay lamp, lighting our way.

"Where is it?" asked Thaesis. "The inscription?"

A stone table stood in the center of the smaller room. Above the door, pictograms marched along the lintel. I traced them with my finger, reading, "The Hall of the Child in His Cradle." Then I turned to the opposite wall where something was carved into the sandstone in bas-relief. As I moved the lamp nearer, the shadows of the incisions grew and the picture suddenly sprang to life.

Thaesis gasped.

Proud to be the steward of my wife's discovery, I said, "Here is Hathor on the birth stool, holding her son Horus. Above his head is his cartouche, which reads, 'Child of Light and Savior by Water.' Her nursemaids are at her feet."

Thaesis traced the outlines of the mother's face with her finger. "I know you'll think I'm foolish, but I think she *looks* like Miriam."

I had also seen the similarity in the profile, and yet it was chiseled three hundred years ago by Nectanebo II, the last of the native pharaohs.

Thaesis moved closer to the glyph, but I dropped the lamp, thrusting us into darkness. She laughed. "End of tour?"

"I suppose," I said, brushing the spilled oil from my cloak. "Sorry. Let us go."

As I guided her out of the chamber, I looked back at the lower right portion of the relief, now in complete darkness. I had long ago memorized it: three figures knelt facing Hathor and Horus, each one with his arms stretched overhead, hands cupped, one bearing a feather, another an ankh, the third a lotus flower, the symbol of the sun.

The figure holding the flower looked remarkably like the current Supreme Pontiff of Serapis.

We left the darkness of the Sanctuary and entered the sun-drenched forecourt. Among the forest of columns, dozens of workers chiseled stone, troweled plaster onto walls, and painted murals with the primary colors of red, yellow, and blue. I saw the chief builder across the way and grabbed Thaesis's elbow, steering her sharply toward him. She stumbled over a tekton, who dropped his bronze chisel. She stepped on it, deeply slicing the ball of her foot.

Back at the barge, the doctor stitched up the cut, but within a day it was swollen and tender. Poultices and potions had no effect, nor did prayers or the burning of incense. The doctor said her foot was infected and would need to be amputated. Thaesis was willing to suffer the loss—if little Athena could do without two feet, she could do without one, she said bravely.

I opposed it, saying we should trust the gods; she might recover. But Thaesis was adamant, and I finally yielded. That night, the doctor amputated her foot. I paced the deck of the barge, sick with anguish as she cried out, but doubly terrified when she fainted from the pain. The next day she seemed better, but on the third day the vessels on her leg began to turn black, and the doctor shook his head sadly.

My beloved Thaesis died three hundred miles from her home in Alexandria. We wrapped her body in a linen shroud and burned it in the Dendera temple courtyard under a moonless sky, her pyre smoke rising to Elysium. Too devastated for prayer, I simply hoped that Thaesis would find Athena there, and together they would run in the Field of Reeds.

In the months that followed, I withdrew. Athena had been gone almost twenty years, and yet a day did not go by that I did not ache to hear the screech of her chair wheels on the villa's floors. I often found myself sitting in the *lararium*, holding her waxen mask and that of her mother, running my fingers down Thaesis's strong, aquiline nose and Athena's little, upturned one.

I soon turned most of my temple duties over to Kronion, who was a much better Supreme Pontiff than I had ever been. He was at the Temple each day at dawn, supervising the Rising of Ra ritual, and took great pride in the Ides ceremonies, standing on the porch long after sunset, suffering the blood and stench of the sacrifices without complaint. He was also a better politician than I, as evidenced by his regular invitations to the Island Palace.

With little to do, I wandered the streets of the city. I often found myself atop the ramparts of the western wall at sunset, gazing across the Necropolis, its whitewashed crypts poking up out of the brown hills like scattered teeth. I wondered where Mesha's bones had been placed once they had been removed from the sepulcher. I would have to ask his son, Apollos.

Then it struck me: Mesha ben Huz, my old friend, was gone. Josef and Miriam and Jeshua, gone. My joyful Athena, gone. My beloved Thaesis, gone. My position at the Prefect's court, gone. My authority at the Serapeum, gone. Time, accident, and illness had taken childhood playmates, youthful friends, elder confidants, and my only island of hope— my family. All gone.

Only I remained, and I wondered why.

Twenty-nine

For many years, there had been talk in the Greek *boulé*—the governing council—about expanding the Serapeum library. Licinius, the chief librarian at the Great Library, sorting his collection due to its increasing size, had sent all religious manuscripts to the Serapeum while keeping control of scientific, literary, and philosophic texts. This created no small conflict, as many pontiffs—as well as many Alexandrians—saw philosophy and religion as twins, much like Apollo and Diana, whose rightful place was to be together.

But five hundred years of naturalistic Greek thought had made a unified family difficult. Scientists such as Democritus (who believed life arose from primeval ooze) had long disputed the gods' existence, though their doubts did little to discourage believers in the *anima*, or soul. Thus, an ever-widening gap yawned between science and religion and many scholars were glad to see the Great Library emptied of all religious texts. Hence, Serapeum library shelves became so full that scrolls rolled off onto the floor and had to be stacked like firewood against the walls. When that space disappeared, they were placed in boxes and stored in the Temple catacombs, a rather unfitting place for sacred texts.

So an expansion of the Serapeum temple library was long overdue, and with the ascension of Augustus's adopted son Tiberius to the throne in the year 767 (or twenty years after my initial visit to Jerusalem), the wheels of progress finally began to turn in distant Rome. Tiberius, eager to emulate his father's aggressive building programs, was quite willing to pay more for Egyptian grain if we would earmark a portion of the profits to the expansion of the Great Library. This meant that many more scrolls, codices, and manuscripts would be moved to the sister library in the Serapeum. And if we needed a larger space for our own collection, so be it. Thus our own expansion program began apace, and one day, nearly thirteen years after the initial proposal, I received a message from our new Prefect Cestius Galerius, notifying me that funds had been allocated to the Serapeum library project.

During one of my rare visits to the Serapeum, I asked Kronion to find the architectural plans, which had been collecting dust on a shelf for years. In my offices (I had not yet moved entirely out), we examined the plans and discovered that the design was as appropriate on that day as it had been when they were drawn up many years before. In short order, I confirmed our funds at the Treasury and ordered Kronion to begin the removal of the books from the Temple library in order to prepare for the expansion.

In the Empire, when money is made available, it is amazing how fast things move. Soon, the original architect, old Varius Lagunas, reviewed his plans, pronounced them "timeless," and set to work like a man half his age. Tektons began removing the roof at the rear of the Serapeum, and giant cranes were brought in to move supporting columns. The expansion of the Temple was to the rear, facing Lake Mareotis, which would not inhibit our daily Temple rituals, nor would it conflict with the income generated by the Ides sacrifices.

One day, Kronion and I watched as the crane moved a lintel from a pair of tall columns. On the ropes, dozens of sweating slaves moved the granite block inch by inch, lowering it slowly. It finally came to rest with a jarring *thud!*, shaking the Temple foundation. We looked up, hoping the building would not come down upon our heads. Lagunas cursed the workers and shared his energetic but angry disposition with us as well, until we cut short our audience and retreated into my quarters, where slaves brought us bread and wine, and we reclined on the couches, jumping every time another lintel was set on the ground. Kronion, now nearly my equal in management of the Temple and senior officiator in all things in my absence, said, "You know, Serapion, you ought to think about expanding your offices."

"You mean *your* offices," I snorted.

Kronion smiled. "All right, you ought to think about expanding *my* offices."

I looked around, noting the furniture, the statues, the floor mosaics, and the colorful mural depicting Serapis being worshiped by Ptolemy Soter, the first Greek pharoah of Egypt. I shrugged. "It is sufficient as it is, Kronion. But what would *you* advise me to do . . . for the benefit of *future* tenants?"

Kronion looked around. The room was airy because its high windows caught the onshore breezes. "The offices are not large enough, to begin with," he said. "You cannot entertain more than a couple of people in here at a time."

"Why would I want to?" I said. "More guests means more intrigue. If I am found dead in here, I want there to be no doubt as to who my murderer was."

"So that's why you have so few visitors," laughed Kronion. "I thought it was because you were unpopular."

"As well," I said. "But popular or not, I only allow one killer in my chambers at a time."

Kronion made a "who, me?" gesture, and we laughed. "No, really, your offices need expansion," he said. "And look at this." He arose and stood in the narrow doorway to my little private library, where shelves jammed with books and scrolls filled every available inch of wall space. A single skylight far above was the only light source, hence the numerous candlesticks on the overflowing table in the center. "It's too small." He peered into the room. "What a mess. Are all these books yours?"

"They belong to whomever is Supreme Pontiff," I said. "And do not criticize. I do not want the cleaners in there; I like it the way it is."

"Then you've achieved your goal," said Kronion, bending to pick up a scrap of parchment that had fallen to the floor. He placed it back on the table. "But since we're raising so much dust already, you should take advantage."

I shrugged. Such things did not interest me. I was just making conversation with Kronion, whose tone therein was all but commanding me to retire.

We both jumped as another stone block struck the ground. I got to my feet. "That is enough commotion for one day. I am going home."

"I'll keep watch," said Kronion, picking up a pear from a bowl and examining it.

"I know you will," I said.

THIRTY

It was three weeks before I returned to the Serapeum. I wanted to avoid the dirt, the shouting of the tektons, and the banging of tools on granite. But without Thaesis, my villa was too depressing, and after I had visited every other place of interest in Alexandria, I decided to stroll past the Serapeum one morning to see how they were progressing. I was astonished. The entire rear of the building, the great peristyle porch, had been entirely removed. Tumbles of broken stone lay everywhere, as if an earthquake had cast them down.

I walked up what remained of the rear steps, now being dismantled by hundreds of busy Nubian slaves, in preparation for expanding the foundation. I had not really looked that closely at the architect's plans, but now it was clear he intended to double the size of the Serapeum and to devote nearly half the expansion to the Temple library. As I entered the building, dodging dirty workmen and blanching at their prolific curses, I feared the worst for my private chambers.

Kronion was nowhere to be found. A junior pontiff indicated that he had gone to visit the Prefect. Generally, Kronion informed me of his visits to the Palace, but he had not done so this time. Only Dis knew how many times he had gone to see the Prefect without my knowledge.

When I entered my chambers, I heaved a sigh of relief. Nothing had been disturbed, though everything was covered with a thin layer of stone dust. I noted a wooden box bristling with scrolls by the divan, another nearby, and three more stacked against a wall. I turned into the doorway of my tiny library alcove and was shocked. Most of the shelves had been emptied; a slave was removing scrolls from a lower shelf and placing them in a wooden box.

"What in the name of Nemesis are you doing?" I shouted.

The old man, stripped to the waist, almost fell over with fright. He cowered on the floor, his hands raised, his eyes wide with fear.

"Speak up!" I commanded.

"Kronion ordered it, d-d-dominus," stuttered the slave.

"Ordered it? Why?"

"New library," he said, getting to his knees.

"Not *my* library, fool," I said, jerking a thumb over my shoulder. "Out *there*. Not in *here*."

"D-dominus, p-please forgive, but he told me—"

"Get out!" I shouted.

The slave scrambled to his feet and stumbled out of the room, stepping on several scrolls as he did so. "Watch what—!" I yelled. "And put some clothes on! This is the Serapeum, not the baths!" But he had disappeared.

I sat down on the divan and looked around. My library was in a shambles. I racked my brain for a reason for this and finally recalled the conversation weeks before when Kronion had hinted that I should remodel my offices. "I swear on the Black Stone," I muttered, "he will regret this." All the work! The time I would have to spend reshelving and reordering! It made little difference that I had never organized the library in the more than thirty years I had been Supreme Pontiff; it had never required organization before.

But now it did. I looked at the table in the center of the circular room, piled high with scrolls and manuscripts. Yellowed parchments of decrees affecting the Temple. Leather-bound codices of incantations. Ancient scrolls containing copies of the Pyramid Texts of the Fifth Dynasty, twenty-five hundred years old, priceless works, not only of religious belief, but of unparalleled illumination, with hieroglyphics painstakingly painted in red ochre and outlined in gold. Fortunately, nothing seemed to be missing. I relaxed.

Then, suddenly, my blood froze. Jeshua's birth chart! I began searching for the red cover of my *Star Almanac*. It was not on a shelf, nor on the table. I sorted through boxes of scrolls, then went out into the main office, where I canvassed the contents of each box there. It was nowhere to be found. "Thieves!" I shouted. "By Dis, I swear *excruciating* punishment!" I went back into the tiny library and began my search anew, this time more slowly. I went through everything, until sweat ran down my back and dripped off my nose.

Then I saw it. The *Almanac* leaned against the foot of a bookcase, coated with dust, its red cover now a dirty brown. I knelt, praying the chart was still pressed between the leaves. I opened the codex and smelled its mustiness. I turned the brittle pages slowly. How many years had it been since I had looked at Jeshua's birth chart? Before Thaesis died, that was certain. Probably since before Josef and Miriam left for Judea. How long ago was that? More than twenty years? I turned a page and let out a relieved sigh. There it was. I sat on the floor and carefully unfolded the chart. It was stained with my own sweat from my journey to Judea more than thirty years ago.

Nothing about it had changed; the planets still congregated in the First House, in Aries. The sun still ruled, signaling new beginnings, energy in pursuit of goals, idealism, and imagination. The moon still indicated a balance between the obvious and the hidden.

I remembered Jeshua: our visit to the Pharos; his insights into the inventor, Hero, now dead many years; the conclave where young Philo— now almost forty—had unveiled the solar clock, making half the astronomy texts in my library obsolete. But most of all I remembered that night in the Valley of the Kings, when he finally spoke after his alarming encounter with prophecy in the Luxor Temple. His words about a universal afterlife had filled my heart with joy yet chilled me as well.

Mars, the planet of unstoppable action, was still in the First House, overriding everything, even self-preservation. A chill coursed down my spine, and I was suddenly afraid for Jeshua, even though he was no longer a boy, but a grown man. He *must* be ruling his kingdom by now. Yet I had heard nothing about it. My sporadic letters over the years had gone unanswered. More importantly, I had not read his name in any Empire communiqué, which I would have if he had any power in Judea. I tried to remember who was ruling in Judea at the moment. No name came to mind. But *was* Jeshua ruling his country? Or was he just a rabbi or a member of a small town Sanhedrin? I felt a stirring urge to know.

I folded the natal chart and replaced it in the *Almanac*. I was about to put it back on the wooden shelf when something caught my eye. There, behind the shelf, usually hidden by scrolls and texts, was a seam running up the wall, halving several stone blocks. I got to my knees, removing a stack of papyrus leaves from the next higher shelf. The seam continued. The third shelf, the same. By now I was standing, sliding texts aside. The seam was gone. I examined the shelf just below it. There, the seam had turned to the left to form a horizontal line. After two cubits, it turned sharply again toward the floor. I stepped back

It was a door.

In my time in the Temple, I had never moved the shelving; I had no reason to. If my predecessor Cheos knew of the door, he never told me. I tried pulling on the right side of the shelving, but could not get my fingers behind it for leverage. I was about to call for help, but realized it would be rash to include others in my discovery until I knew what I had found. I looked at my private library with new eyes, finally understanding why there were so many shelves packed into such a small room.

I walked out into my office and picked up a large basalt statue of jackal-headed Anubis, hefting its substantial weight. It would suffice.

Not stopping to consider the blasphemy of using a holy relic as a pry-bar, I positioned Anubis's large upraised ears between the shelf and the wall. I leaned into it, and the oak shelving moved an inch. I stuck my fingers into the crack and pulled with all my might, my joints popping and pain radiating up my arms. The shelving moved some more. Now I could get my shoulder behind it. I pushed and the shelving screeched loudly, moving enough to allow access to the hidden door. I pressed my hand against the seam in the wall. The stone door, hinged on the inside, opened with surprising ease and utter silence. The interior was black as night and musty-smelling. I lit a candle and got down on my hands and knees, squeezing through entrance, thrusting the candle before me. I heard the scuttling of tiny feet. Rats.

Or something worse, I thought. Perhaps Apep was angry at me for misusing Anubis and was poised to strike. I held the candle up, but the flame illuminated little. The ground was springy and soft. I lowered the candle. The floor was littered with the remnants of chewed manuscripts. The rats cowered in the corner, but then made quickly for the exit I had just opened to them. I stood and raised the candle. The chamber was small, just two strides across, also a kind of library, though it had no shelves. Instead, manuscripts and scrolls were stuffed into wall niches. Picking up a bit of chewed papyrus, I guessed the rats only recently found a way in when the demolition work opened a crack in the foundation. Most of the chewed manuscripts were in the lower niches; the upper ones were as yet untouched.

I turned around, taking in the room. The Serapeum was almost two hundred and fifty years old. This room had been part of the original design, yet knowledge of its existence had been lost.

I retrieved a bound set of papyrus leaves from a high shelf. The Greek letters on the cover were too faded to read. I opened it gently and tiny scraps of dusty parchment wafted down upon my sandaled feet. I replaced it on its shelf and noted another, larger volume nearby. Though it seemed equally as old, it was in better condition and quite heavy. I turned it over in my hands, noting its fine craftsmanship. I tucked it under my arm and ducked out of the room. I placed the codex on the table and reached for the little door, tugging it toward me. It closed easily. I put my shoulder against the shelving and pushed it back into place, knowing that tomorrow I would ache like a stevedore for my efforts.

I turned to the table. In full light, the codex's quality was even more impressive. The papyrus leaf edges were straight and true. The black leather of the cover glistened once I wiped off the dust. Why it, along with dozens of other manuscripts, was hidden in a secret room was a fascinating question, the answer to which might very likely be found inside a cover bearing an equally fascinating title: *The Great Secret.*

Thirty-One

I clutched the codex to my chest and bustled down the street. It was near midnight, and there was just a sliver of moon. With every dark corner, I grew more fearful. Alexandria had many thousands of law-abiding people, but it was also home to more than a few cutpurses and murderers.

I lived in the Royal Quarter, which was relatively safe, but I had to pass through the dangerous Egyptian Quarter to get there. I had wrapped the codex in linen and tucked it inside my cloak. My sandals slapped on the cobblestones, and my wheezing breath was loud in my ears as I hurried along. Most of the houses were dark; these I did not fear. But my heart jumped when I passed a tavern with a group of men conversing outside. Their talk trailed off as I approached. I kept my head down, hoping all they saw was an old man limping home after a long day.

Alexandrian men carried the *khopesh*, a small curved knife, using it for everything from slicing fruit to slitting the throat of an enemy. I carried no weapon—it was contrary to my vows to arm myself. My safety was in the hands of the Fates, but tonight I feared that no god would help me because of the heretical text tucked inside my cloak. It was foolish to be walking alone at this hour, but I had no choice; I had read enough of *The Great Secret* to know it could not remain in the Serapeum one more night.

When I finally arrived home, I banged on the door. After a minute, Senteph opened the peep hole. "I thought perhaps you were staying the night," he said, opening the door.

I took his lamp. "No. I am home," I said. "Now go to bed."

Senteph left, perplexed at my curtness. I hurried into the lararium and placed the codex on a table near a divan. I lit the candles behind the face masks of my ancestors in their alcoves. Soon, the room was filled with a golden light from the wax *imagines*. I sat down, placing the linen-wrapped bundle on my knees and removed the codex from its wraps.

In gold leaf on the cover was depiction of an ibis. This was Tchehuti—Thoth, as we Greeks call him—the god who invented writing. He often appears as a man with an ibis head in the *Book of Breathings*, standing next to the judgment scales, holding a stylus poised over a tablet, recording the events of the final judgment while the crocodile-headed creature Ammit waits to devour the heart of the wicked, should it overbalance the scales.

Below Thoth were characters in hieratic script, a cursive language few can read, it having been eclipsed by demotic Egyptian. The characters gave the name of the book: *The Great Secret*.

I knew the secret now, and my mind was racing. In the hour it took to walk home, I had tried to convince myself that what I had spent the evening reading was merely a humorless joke or perhaps a heretical outrage that had been secreted inside the inner vault to prevent it from poisoning the minds of the faithful. But in my heart I knew it was neither.

I opened the codex. The first page was empty except for a single name. Manetho.

This was certainly Manetho of Heliopolis, the great historian who lived three hundred years ago during the reign of Ptolemy I, the same general that stole the corpse of Alexander and brought it to Alexandria. After he'd wrested Egypt from his Macedonian rivals, Ptolemy had himself crowned pharaoh at the Opet Festival. Manetho, who had been an Egyptian priest of Amun-Ra, sensing the winds of inevitable change, aligned himself with the new monarch and rapidly became his most trusted advisor. It was Manetho who took Ptolemy to the Siwa Oasis and had him pronounced a "Son of Ra," like Alexander had been. Then, from the court of the new pharaoh, Manetho began his life's work: the creation of the authoritative list of the thirty dynasties of Egyptian pharaohs, reaching as far back as Narmer himself, more than three thousand years ago.

He also wrote *Ægyptica*, the definitive Egyptian history, and became the most respected mortal in Egypt since Imhotep, the architect of the Saqqara pyramid—the first true pyramid—who was deified shortly after his death. Manetho was equally revered, though not deified, unless you count the vast number of texts mentioning him in the Great Library.

And now here was another text written by him, unseen perhaps in hundreds of years, yet I doubted it would ever be displayed in any library in the Empire.

Why? Because it contained a secret that would not only shake the foundations of Egypt, but of Rome as well.

The Egyptian language is unexpressive, using pictographs, which, even in the stylized hieratic form, are not words per se, but representations of things. In other words, as I noted above, the ibis can represent the god Thoth, as well as writing, wisdom, and record keeping. It can also represent a sound or a letter, whatever the context requires, which is sometimes hard to ascertain. Therefore, it can be difficult not only to read Egyptian but to understand what you are reading. So I will not attempt to quote Manetho directly from his book, but will instead give you the essence of what he said in my own words.

Much of what I read in the codex I had heard elsewhere before, but the events and stories I heard had been given different meanings than what actually transpired. This was, shockingly, all according to plan. What made *The Great Secret* so dangerous was that if it truly *were* written by Manetho, then the religion I had believed in all my life was nothing more than a bald, cynical fabrication.

In my conversation with Josef when we discussed the Birth Room relief that upset Jeshua in Luxor, I attempted to dismiss the similarities between the relief and Jeshua's life by saying that all cultures had similar stories; that we all shared a kind of common mythology. Josef reminded me that he and I had been there during the making of the "myth" that surrounded Jeshua's birth, and we both knew the events we had experienced were real and true.

The same could be said about Manetho. But he was not only present at the unfolding facts which would become a famous story, he was the architect thereof. When Alexander conquered Egypt, he was greeted by the Egyptians as a liberator, for they hated the Persians who had dominated them for decades. And when Alexander assured them that he had no interest in imposing Greek religion upon them, they reciprocated by elevating him to the status of deity, inscribing his image on many temples. Ptolemy did his mentor one better: he married Egyptian and Greek belief into a single religion, thus ensuring the loyalty of the populace forever. And he did it with the help of his co-conspirator, Manetho. This was the subject of *The Great Secret*.

Egyptians take few things more seriously than the cycles of the Nile. Spring floods are evidence that the gods are satisfied, for they promise a bountiful harvest in the fall. But when the Nile does not flood, famine ensues, and thousands die. Ptolemy knew that Egypt would always be a target for conquest because of her prodigious harvests. He also knew that no one who had conquered her grain fields had ever conquered her populace; the Egyptian peasant was as ungovernable as the Nile itself and just as unpredictable. No, the people of fair Ægyptus had to be coaxed into servility, not beaten into submission. But how could they be convinced to serve when no Parthian, Hyksos, Nubian, or Persian master had ever achieved it?

Here was where Manetho provided his invaluable services. Noting that both Egypt and Greece worshiped a pantheon of gods, might there not be someone in that great crowd who could mollify the people of Egypt and unify both countries? Ptolemy reminded the priest that no Greek would ever worship a bull or a dog or a cat.

Manetho agreed. "What I proposed," he wrote in his manuscript, "was a unity of both worlds: the unrivaled power of the Egyptian gods as demonstrated by the Nile floods, combined with the personal involvement in human affairs as manifest by Zeus and his Olympic heirs. But first, who was the greatest Egyptian god? Osiris, of course, for he was the first man to overcome death and be resurrected. Or so they say."

At this point, I glared at the ceiling. Manetho, the greatest priest in five hundred years, talking about the gods like so many fungible game pieces!

Manetho continued:

I asked Ptolemy who was the greatest of the Olympians. Without hesitation, he said Zeus, but then, correcting himself, said, "but the favorite among the people is certainly Apollo, son of Zeus and Leto."

"What are Apollo's traits?"

"He is a great archer, musician, and healer. He is also the patron of the Oracle at Delphi."

"Healer?" I asked.

Ptolemy nodded. "He is also associated with the sun and in that capacity is called Apollos Helios."

I was delighted, for Ptolemy had just described two of the chief characteristics of Osiris, the Egyptian god of the Underworld, a healer of souls, so to speak, who took the ba of the righteous with him in his barque as he traveled the River of Death, sending them on their renewed way at dawn with Ra, the Sungod.

We pondered the possibility of combining the attributes of Osiris and Apollo, and I asked the Pharaoh if there was a representation of Apollo that I might see.

I shut the manuscript, outraged. Manetho was baking a cake. More to the point, he was creating the deity I had served all my life. But Serapis was an old god, older than both Ptolemy and Manetho. Or so I had always thought.

Unable to stop, I opened the codex again. Manetho continued, unconcerned about how he was turning my world upside down.

When Ptolemy produced a scroll with a depiction of Apollo, I was disappointed, for he was a beardless youth. But as I examined the picture, the Pharaoh said the world was a balance between the chaos of Dionysus and the order of Apollo.

"Show me this Dionysus," I asked, and he did. And in that pleasant, bearded face, I knew we had found an acceptable representation. "This is the opposite of Apollo?" I asked.

"Yes," said the Pharaoh.

"Opposites, like Osiris and his brother Seth," I responded.

"Tell me about them," Ptolemy requested.

I obliged and proceeded to lay out to Ptolemy the most famous story in Egyptian cosmology: King Osiris was killed by his brother Seth in a fit of jealous rage. Seth then cut Osiris into a hundred pieces and cast them into the sea. Osiris's grieving sister-wife Isis, with the help of her son Anubis, found the pieces washed ashore on Byblos. They put Osiris back together, and he returned to life. But he was no longer mortal, so he could not rule the living again. So Amun-Ra granted him the Underworld kingdom. Thereafter, Osiris was always portrayed as a mummy, a reminder of the limits of his domain.

"Byblos has long been a Greek protectorate," said Ptolemy, pleased.

For months, we two conspirators compared notes on Apollo/Dionysus and Osiris/Seth. I gloried in our good fortune. I became convinced that this Dionysus would be the best physical candidate for our new god. I then set to work to discover this god's name.

That was when I slammed the codex shut and came home. Later, seated in the dusky light in my lararium, I opened it again and read, my heart pounding in my chest.

Ptolemy and I considered an appropriate name for our concoction. Clearly, a name similar "Osiris" was in order. The closest form was Osirapis, which was what the deceased Apis bull of Memphis was called. Osirapis, like all hearth gods, was very old. I also told Ptolemy that there was an ancient stone marker in Saqqara that termed Apis the "Life of Osiris, the Lord of Heaven."

The simple connection between the Apis bull and Osiris overjoyed Ptolemy. He asked me to continue.

At this point, I unrolled one of my scrolls to check whether Manetho was accurate in his description of Osirapis. When I compared the two, I was heartsick. Manetho was a damnable charlatan but a solid historian, at least as far as the true Egyptian gods went. He wrote that fifteen hundred years ago, in the Eighteenth Dynasty, Osiris and Apis had been formally joined by the priests of Memphis into one, whom they called Osirapis. Even then, Apis was called the "renewed life of Ptah" (the Creator), so combining the bull with the god of the Underworld, the resurrected or renewed Osiris, was a simple step.

In addition, wrote Manetho, *I told the Pharaoh of common current references to Osiris as the Bull of the West. So the syncretism we sought to perfect had already started hundreds of years ago.*

I am sure you know that syncretism is an attempt to reconcile contradictory beliefs. My mind was rejecting everything Manetho had written in his wicked manuscript, yet I believed every word he wrote. *That's* syncretism. After all, *The Great Secret* was obviously designed to be seen by only one person, hidden as it was in the private library of the Supreme Pontiff. And I will wager the first Supreme Pontiff was hand-picked by Manetho.

I shall not belabor this much more. My stylus hand is again shaking, not from grief, but the bitter anger of the betrayed. Suffice it to relate one last event, the most evil and calculated of all. After the details of their creation had been clarified, Ptolemy pretended to have a dream about this new god, whom he called *Serapis*, saying that the god's colossal image was being held hostage in a distant country, but it desired to return to Egypt. Many couriers were sent in search of the statue. Finally, Ptolemy himself found the god in Sinope, a city on the shore of the Black Sea. (Of course Ptolemy had been to Sinope before, during a campaign with Alexander. Manetho did not mention this; I knew it from my own education. Sinope was the site of a battle between Alexander and the Persians.)

In Sinope, Ptolemy "found" a majestic white marble statue of Serapis. In truth, he had commissioned the statue two years before: a seated, bearded man with a corn measure on his head denoting fertility (Osiris was originally a fertility god), the dog Cerberus at his knee (Cerberus was Hades's guard-dog and one of his three heads was that of a jackal, like

Anubis—how convenient!), holding a staff entwined by a serpent (*exactly like the healing staff of Asclepius, which signified Apollo's medicinal aspects*) . . . and on and on.

Ptolemy's men "stole" the statue from the startled Sinopians (no doubt after a magnificent mock battle) and transported it to Alexandria. The Pharaoh stood on the steps of the new Serapeum and told the throng that in Sinope, the statue had entered his ship of its own accord, certain it would be greeted in Egypt with accolades befitting its long absence. Sure enough, a great celebration ensued—weeks of sacrificing and debauchery. The statue was placed in the Temple where, three hundred years later, I had bowed myself before it three times a day for most of my life.

But the most remarkable thing, I thought as I closed the codex near dawn, *is that the worship of Apis, Apollo, Osiris, and even Osirapis still continues!* But what was one more god to the Greeks and the Egyptians? We two peoples were so much alike, it is no wonder we have found peace together—a sort of perverse syncretism—here in Egypt.

In short, because Serapis was depicted as a man, he was acceptable to the Greeks. For the Egyptians, his name and the presence of Cerberus tied him to Osiris, god of the Underworld, which was full of bizarre creatures like the three-headed dog. And the snakes that curled around Serapis's staff not only represented the Underworld but Apollo's healing power as well.

And I must not forget one more serpent: my old nemesis, Apep, whom I wished at that moment would break the bonds of night, enter daylight, devour me, and extinguish my soul.

Thirty-Two

The coming of day brought no light to my mind. I dismissed Senteph and the rest of my slaves, retired to my room, and buried my aching head in my pillow. My mind spun around Serapis like the planets of Geminus's clockwork solar system. I dared not believe it. I could not believe it. Yet I *did* believe it.

Late in the afternoon, I arose and stared out an upper window. It was a gray day, and a curtain of rain fell out over the ocean. Low clouds obscured the Pharos. Only a dull, lifeless glow therein indicated the guide light. No ships would approach Alexandria today; the rocks were too treacherous, and the clouds would give way to a dense fog by nightfall.

I walked the rooms of my villa, noting each religious icon, statue, relief, mural, and *imago*. A lifetime spent serving Serapis, only to discover that he was a calculated fiction concocted by a cynical priest and a cunning tyrant! I looked at my star diadem in despair, felt the offensive heaviness of my amulet, and realized that I could no longer serve in the Serapeum.

Nor could I align myself with Jupiter, Isis, Vesta, Cybele—for they had all, once upon a time, been Greek gods before the Romans appropriated them. Who knew their antecedents? And the Egyptian gods Atum, Amun, Aten—all of them were once hearth gods of Heliopolis, Thebes, or Amarna respectively, who rose to prominence when a conquering pharaoh made that city the country's capital. They were probably all manifestations of the same ancient god—and yet how the nations had gone to war over the differences!

Fifteen hundred years ago, Pharaoh Amenhotep IV became disillusioned with the chief-god Amun and so lifted the god Aten to supremacy, banishing the powerful priests of Amun at Karnak. He changed his name to Akhenaten ("Spirit of Aten"), moved the capital from Memphis south to Amarna, and ordered all statues of Amun to be destroyed, all reliefs defaced, and the Temple of Karnak closed—the same temple I visited yearly for the Opet Festival. But when Akhenaten died, the priests of Amun restored themselves—and their god—to power. Soon it was the statues, reliefs, and inscriptions of Aten that were destroyed, defaced, and forgotten.

All this I had known from my youth, but I never understood it as I did now. All these gods! Were they nothing more than cruel hoaxes designed to obtain obedience to the pharaoh and taxes for the priests—men like myself—who lived in fine villas like the one I was rattling about in?

I threw myself onto my bed again, feeling like a fraud and a dupe at the same time. On my nightstand was my golden star diadem, where I had set it upon returning to my bedchamber. I crumpled it into a ball and hurled it into the corner.

I stayed that way, unable to sleep, my thoughts returning again and again to the pointlessness of my life, until many hours later, when I heard a knock at the front door. I ignored it, but the knocking continued, and soon the visitor began shouting my name—the most hateful name in all the world: "Serapion! Serapion! *Serapion!*"

I crawled off my bed, went to the window, and threw the drapes aside. Below me, vague in the fog of night, stood Kronion, shivering. "Salve, dominus!" he called. "Are you well?"

I glared at him.

"Can you take a visitor?"

I shook my head and reached for the drapes.

"I heard about what happened in your chambers. Bentu told me."

I looked down at him. Kronion was the very picture of a pontiff of Serapis. His head was shaved and anointed with unguents I could smell from the second story. His fingernails were manicured, and the robe under his cloak was of the finest Indus silk, bordered in blue. Even his sandals were spotless; tradition required pontiffs to wear new, clean sandals every day.

"Told you what?" I asked.

"You are upset," said Kronion. "I am sorry. I thought it would be a nice surprise."

"Oh," I said, "it was a surprise all right."

"Please open the door," pleaded Kronion. "It's not proper to make me stand out here and shout up at you." He fidgeted, looking around. I was filled with disgust. Suddenly everything and everyone having to do with Serapis seemed an abomination, if any true judgment still remained in a universe of invented gods, lying priests, and wicked rulers.

"Please!"

"Oh, all right," I said, closing the drapes and trudging downstairs.

I opened the door and he burst inside, shaking the dew from his cloak. We retired to the main living area, not the lararium, where we usually met. Since I had finished reading Manetho's abomination, I could not bring myself to enter the shrine to even look at the book. Even the masks of my ancestors seemed foolish now. My loved ones did not await me in the Field of Reeds or Elysium or Paradise or whatever they called it; they were surely as dead as Akhenaten. I sat down on a couch. Kronion sat opposite me. "Are you all right?" he asked gently.

"What do you want?"

"I came to apologize. The slave said you were angry. I told him it was my idea, but he won't go back into your library."

"I do not care," I said. "Go ahead and remodel your offices, Kronion."

Kronion blanched. "You mean *your* offices, Serapion."

"Do not call me that!"

"But that is your title!"

"Not any more. I have just resigned. You are now Supreme Pontiff." I looked at Kronion's surprised face and saw, after the initial shock receded, a trace of surprised pleasure.

"Do you mean it?" he asked.

I nodded. "It is yours, young man. Squeeze the lemon until it squeaks."

He looked at me in surprise. "What?"

"Say," I said, changing the subject, "in your administration of the Serapeum library, have you run into any manuscripts that . . . *surprised* you?"

"Surprised me?" asked Kronion. "Surprised me how?"

I shrugged as nonchalantly as I could, trying to keep the tension out of my shoulders and the anger out of my voice. "Oh, just anything that cast a different light upon things—our cult, in particular. You know, interesting revelations and all that."

"Well, in moving the texts, we found a scroll that filled in the blanks between the Anaxadorus and Heliander administrations—the three missing Supreme Pontiffs of last century."

"That is delightful," I said sourly. "Now we have a complete genealogy of the perpetrators."

"Perpetrators?" he asked. "Serapion, are you all right?"

"I just told you," I said, gritting my teeth, "not to call me that. Here is my seal." I pulled the heavy golden ring from my finger and handed it to him. "I would give you my diadem, but it is being polished. I will send it over in a couple of days with Senteph, who will clear my things out of your offices." I looked around the room, filled with tapestries and murals, which now filled me with anger. "If you like, you can even have the villa—I will be moving out soon."

"Dominus, what is the matter?"

I stood. "I am old, and you have been waiting a long time for me to retire, have you not?"

"But, dominus," said Kronion, but then he said no more.

"Exactly," I said. "Good luck with your renovations. I am sure you will find nothing during the reconstruction that will impede your progress."

"*My* progress?"

I gestured toward the entry, and we walked to it. I opened the front door and turned. "The Serapeum, of course. May it change your life as it changed mine."

"Praise Serapis," said Kronion doubtfully as he exited.

"Oh, certainly," I said flatly. "Praise all of them, from Jove to Bes. They are, after all, exactly what we bargained for."

And with that I shut the door, leaving a confused Kronion standing on the porch.

THIRTY-THREE

"I got your message," said Rabbi Apollos, approaching me. "I came as soon as I could."

The young rabbi, eldest son of my old friend Mesha, was now a man—though his sparse beard was mostly on his chin and his cheeks were still smooth. I said, "Thank you, Rabbi."

"I am not your rabbi, Serapion, though my father often said *he* was, though in jest, I think. I am, I hope, a friend."

"You are," I said, nodding. "And I am no longer Serapion."

"You've retired?"

"It appears so," I said. "Given it all up: the robes, the villa, the wealth, the prestige." I pinched a piece of my chiton drape, not a beggar's rag by any means, but not silk either. "I shall be living like the rest now."

"Are you ill?" asked Apollos.

"In my heart only," I said. "Which is why I sent the message. I did not think you would have time to come to the Necropolis yourself. I apologize for the inconvenience."

Apollos waved it away. "We hear from you so seldom, I wanted to come, especially given the nature of your request." He led the way under the arch and we entered the City of the Dead. "My father's remains are not far," he said.

"I did not know where they were," I said. "I saw the sepulcher where his body was laid, but I know your people move the bodies later."

Apollos nodded as he walked. "After decomposition, we put the bones in a *loculus*, a stone sarcophagus that is placed in a family mausoleum—

160

rather like the way we live in our quarter—one on top of the other and squeezed in side by side."

"I may join you there," I said, wondering where I would stay after I moved from my villa.

Apollos stopped and turned. "Here it is."

The mausoleum looked much like a sepulcher, but there was no rounded stone barring the entrance. It was a limestone-walled building set into the hillside, a flight of steps going down toward an open doorway. It had no defining writing or symbols etched upon it. Apollos stooped under the low lintel; I followed. The interior was dark and narrow, and on either side were small cubicles, some openings plastered over, others open. A stone bench sat between the facing walls, and Apollos seated himself, gesturing for me to join him. Then he pointed, and I looked up. There, in Greek script on one of the tiny compartments, was his father's name: Mesha ben Huz. Nothing more; no titles, no laudatory inscriptions or hopeful incantations, just his name, which filled me with sadness. *My old friend!* I whispered in my heart. *Oh, that I could speak to you today!*

"I sometimes come here to ask him questions, though he doesn't answer me directly," said Apollos.

I do not doubt that at all, I thought, marveling at how quickly I had become cynical. Mesha and I used to have vigorous arguments about the nature of Hashem and his relationship to man but never about his existence; yet right now, his existence—or lack thereof—was foremost on my mind. At the moment, all I saw around me was a cave full of bones, the only proof that these people had ever lived.

"I am glad it gives you peace," I finally said.

"Oh," said Apollos, "he does more than that. He visits me in dreams. He once asked about you, but I could tell him nothing, for I had not seen you in many years."

"Probably almost two decades," I added.

"Since Jeshua's family left Alexandria," said Apollos.

I nodded. A long silence followed, and I could feel Apollos looking at me. I looked down at my clasped hands and shrugged. "I have wanted to visit your father many times. He always had, if not the answer, at least an opinion that in his mind qualified as one."

Apollos laughed. "That is the Judaic curse! Our beliefs must trump all others, don't you see? We are the chosen people. But Father used to wonder what we were chosen for: to suffer, to be a hiss and a byword, or merely to irritate our non-Jewish neighbors."

I could not help myself—I laughed. "Perhaps all three."

We both looked at Mesha's plastered cubicle for another minute, and then I stood to go, ducking low so I would not open my skull on the ceiling—which would be a just dessert, Mesha would say, for coming to visit the dead with no faith in my heart. Outside, I turned to Apollos again. "Thank you for showing me the location. May I come visit on my own?"

"Of course." Then, "What is it you meant to ask my father? Perhaps I might help, or if not, perhaps I can pray about it, and he'll advise me."

I shook my head. "My questions are too big, even for your father."

"Then perhaps you should ask Hashem."

I shook my head again. "Adonai. Jupiter. Serapis. None of them have the answer, for my questions concern their very existence."

Apollos drew back. "Is it that bad, Melchior?"

I looked away. "It is that bad."

"You've lost much," he said. "Your vocation, your friends, your family. Now your faith. I feel to bless you, if I may."

I shrugged. "It would not help."

But Apollos, so much like his father, would brook no argument. He simply took my hand and lowered me to my knees. He knelt in front of me and reached up, placing a hand on my head. At his touch I felt tears start in my eyes. *Old fool!* I thought in dismay. *Still hoping that all this nonsense might mean something! Fool!*

Yet I let him, and he bowed his head and closed his eyes. "Adonai, look down upon us with compassion. As thou hast taken, so please give. This man, thy servant"—and I blanched at the notion of me serving *any* god at this point—"seeks comfort, for thou has taken all from him, and he is in darkness. Illuminate him. Speak to his heart during the day and through dreams at night. Do not extend his sorrow, but bring peace to his soul."

He removed his hand, and my head tingled where he had touched me. I rose, turning away to collect myself. The prayer was sincere, but it revealed far more about the kind of man Apollos was than it did about my own troubles. Nevertheless, I turned to thank him and discovered that he was already ten paces down the path, heading back to the city. I watched him until he disappeared, then turned to the mausoleum where Mesha's bones lay. "He is not as wise as you were," I said, "but he is just as kind. So you bested me again, Mesha. Unlike me, you were as good a father as you were a priest."

And now I am neither.

Thirty-Four

Not many days later, I was wandering around the city, my feet and thoughts equally lost, when I found myself in the forum fronting the Great Library. It was a stiflingly muggy afternoon, and as I had no bearers, I was sweaty and tired. The cool darkness of the Library's interior beckoned, and I trudged up the steps, stopping on the porch, winded.

I looked back. The city was suffocating in a haze of heat, cooking fire smoke, and black plumes rising from the Ides sacrifices at the various temples. I had forgotten all about the Ides sacrifices. I had so quietly slipped from sight that no one had even noticed, not even I. My friends had disappeared, taking my withdrawal from the Serapeum as a sign that I had fallen out of favor. Kronion was now the keeper of the knife, the augurer to the wealthy, and advisor to the Prefect. All I had left was my oversight of the Dendera Temple reconstruction, which I could not bring myself to visit, as it was the site of the death of my beloved Thaesis.

As her name entered my mind, I felt depression press down heavily on my shoulders, and anyone looking at me at that moment would have seen an actual darkening of my countenance. I had become a pathetic sight: my head and face bristled with unruly gray hair, and I must have looked like a beggar in my sweat-stained chiton.

As I had promised Kronion, I sent Senteph to the Serapeum to retrieve my personal effects, but not until I had a competent jeweler repair the diadem I had crushed in my despair. I asked Senteph to retrieve just one book from my private library there: the old, red-covered *Star Almanac*. But it wasn't until he handed it to me and I found Jeshua's birth chart between the leaves that I even remembered the chart. I shook my head and placed the volume on a shelf in my home library, wondering where all these old manuscripts and scrolls would go when I moved out of the villa, for Kronion had sent a message with Senteph asking me if I truly intended to vacate my residence. He averred that he had no personal interest in the villa, but it *was* the residence of the Supreme Pontiff, after all. Perhaps I might sell it to him?

I crumpled the note and threw it in the fire. *If he wants the house,* I thought bitterly, *then he can ask me in person, not in some cursed letter!*

And yet, I harbored no real resentment for Kronion. I had no aversion to giving the villa to him—I had effectively said as much to him that night weeks ago—but since then I had become angry at the way he had taken me at my word and moved ahead, acting like the Supreme Pontiff even though he would not be officially ordained until the fall conclave at Saqqara.

I laughed. *You old fool. You give offense but expect kindness in return. You torture Kronion by living too long, then you are angry that he expects to take your place when you go. Just because you did not have the sense to die!*

Looking out across the crowded forum—where street vendors vied, crowing for business, and children played hoops between classes at the Gymnasium across the street—I realized I *had* lived too long. I ought to follow the example of Eratosthenes, who went blind and, not wishing to be a burden, starved himself to death. If I had any gumption, that is what I would do.

I set my jaw. *Maybe I would,* I thought. *Maybe I could make one last, unforgettable gesture.*

I walked past the giant gilded doors and entered the Library. The coolness was refreshing, and my overheated thoughts of noble suicide soon receded. Lining the entry walls were the reliefs of Thales, who deduced the height of the Khufu pyramid using the shadow of a stick; of Pythagoras, who first said the earth is a sphere revolving around the sun; of Eratosthenes, who calculated the earth's circumference; and of Aristarchus, who held his revolutionary heliocentric solar system model in the crook of his arm, the legend below him reading, "Superstition is cowardice in the face of the Divine."

"He did not say that," I muttered as I passed.

"What was that?" asked someone.

I glanced over and dismissed the speaker as an uncouth youth.

"Theophrastus said it." I said harshly. "And it is untrue, at any rate."

The man laughed, whether at my wit or at me, I did not know. I glared at him.

Suddenly, he blinked and said, "Serapion?"

"No," I said, turning away. "He is at the Temple, sacrificing. Why are you not?"

Laughter, again.

"I am glad I amuse you," I said, walking away.

A hand grasped my sleeve, and I turned. At a close range, he was older than I had initially thought. "Melkorios?" he said, "Do you not remember me?"

I glared at him.

"Philo!" said the man.

"Young Philo?" I asked.

"Young?" laughed the man. "I'm past fifty! Not much younger than you!"

"Bah!" I said. "Everyone is younger than I." I turned away.

Philo joined me as I walked toward the naos. He was an important man in Alexandria, one of the few Jews to be accepted at the Museum. His writings filled many shelves in the Library. His father had been a friend of mine. But like Rabbi Mesha, Philo's father was dead many years, as I would be, if I had any moral fiber left.

"Why aren't you at the Temple?" asked Philo, pity in his voice, which angered me.

"Same reason you are not," I snapped.

"I doubt that. Unless you've converted to Judaism."

I laughed bitterly. "The study of the gods is a waste of time given the brevity of life."

"Protagoras," said Philo.

"Congratulations," I said. "You know what dead men say. What do you know about *life*?"

Philo took my arm, and for some strange reason (especially given how angry I was with him), I allowed him to lead me to a bench. "What bothers you, my friend?" he asked.

"Friend?" I queried. "When have we been friends? Have you been to my home? Have you visited me at my temple? Have you invited me to the celebrations of your people?"

He blanched. "I never thought you'd come. I didn't think you cared for me, to be honest."

"Oh, be honest," I said, glaring into the distance. "By all means."

"Dominus, you are a busy man. I never thought you'd be interested in me."

"False modesty is a distorted mirror," I quoted.

"Who said that?"

"I did!" I exclaimed. "Must I beg your consideration? Your simple, unalloyed kindness?"

Philo looked at me, and I could feel him wanting to leave me alone with my anger. Yet I did not want him to leave. I wanted to talk with someone—anyone—and here I had stumbled upon one of the greatest minds in Alexandria, and I was being unforgivably rude. But you see, my pride was another other possession I was finding it hard to part with, along with my life.

Fortunately, Philo had been taught to be respectful of his elders. "I beg your forgiveness. I just remembered that, in the time I had Geminus's clockwork mechanism here in Alexandria, I never brought it to you for your examination."

I never expected him to, but I lied anyway. "I was offended."

"I am sorry. But you eventually got a look at it?"

I pointed to the hall. "It was displayed right over there for months. Of course I saw it."

"I am glad," said Philo. "It was a pity Rome wanted it."

"Yes," I said. "Because it should have remained here as a reminder that the universe *is* a clock, a mindless machine that grinds everything to dust."

"But the clock has a maker," said Philo.

I grunted my opinion.

"You disagree?" asked Philo. "You doubt the gods?"

"Why not?" I said, staring ahead. "You doubt all of them except one."

Philo laughed. "But that one *is* the clockmaker."

"Believe that if it gives you peace," I said.

"It does," said Philo. "All of this," he said, gesturing around, "is nothing compared to my faith. All the knowledge in the world—and most of it is here in this building—is nothing compared to Hashem. He gives us knowledge a little at a time, and thus reveals himself a little at a time, a slow unveiling of his wisdom."

"A faithful philosopher," I said. "Your father would have been proud."

"I hope so," said Philo, and I noticed he was now looking at the floor thoughtfully.

"He has been dead, what, twenty-five years?" I asked.

Philo nodded.

"Before you came into your own," I said. My own anger was subsiding, and I thought about Philo's father Lysimachus, as good a man as I had ever known. Indeed, most of the good men I had known were Jews. Suddenly I was reminded of Josef of Judea and Jeshua. "Philo," I said, "what news from Jerusalem?"

"News?" he asked, still thinking about his father.

"Who rules?"

"Senatus Populesque Romanus—the Senate and the People of Rome."

"No," I said, "who is the vassal king?"

He shrugged. "You mean the Kohen Gadol of the Temple?"

"Is he considered the king?"

Another shrug. "Melkorios, I really don't follow events in Judea. The Jews there are hopelessly backward. I admire their independent spirit—there is much about the Empire to gainsay—but their reticence to accept the good things: security, education, roads, culture—"

"Taxes," I interjected.

"Civilization costs money," said Philo, "and they've rejected what those taxes buy! Constant insurrections, a never-ending succession of charlatans posing as the Moshiach—"

"Moshiach?"

Philo looked at me. "A deliverer. A hopelessly childish fiction, if you ask me."

I looked at Philo. His eyes were dark, as was his skin, tanned by a lifetime in the Egyptian sun. He wore the Roman toga, not a belted Greek chiton or even a Jewish tunic. His toga was made of white linen with a green stripe, the symbol of his office (he was a magistrate, as I had been). His hair was cut short in the Roman style, and he had no beard or side curls, as most Jewish men had. I wondered how he was received in the Grand Synagogue, looking so irredeemably Roman. Yet he wrote about the *Septuagint*, the translation of the five books of Moshe into Greek, and the idea that Jewish thought had inspired thinkers like Socrates, Plato, and Aristotle—concepts that were controversial in the Museum but applauded in the Delta Quarter.

"You think it's nonsense," said Philo, taking my woolgathering for disdain.

"So you know nothing of the king?"

"Tiberius Claudius Nero is the king," said Philo. "Our worthy Emperor."

"But what of Jeshua, son of Josef and Miriam?"

"Jeshua?" asked Philo. "The tekton's son?"

I nodded.

"He knew my younger brother," said Philo. "I'm closer to your age than I am to his."

"I just wondered if your brother had heard anything from him or his family."

"I shouldn't think so," said Philo. "They kept to themselves, though I do remember seeing Jeshua with you quite often. I heard you got him admitted into Gymnasium."

I nodded.

"How did he do there?"

"Well. An active mind. Wonderful questions. And some surprising insights."

"And they took him back to Judea," said Philo, shaking his head. "To be schooled by shepherds, tanners, and dung collectors. Such a waste."

"Some drown in the fleshpots of Egypt," I said, quoting a Roman saying.

"Then one must learn to swim."

"As you have?"

"But I swim alone. A 'voice crying in the wilderness' as they say. Too little time, too little help from my own, and too many who would like to see me drown. Indeed," he said, "you're one of the few Romans who's ever been civil to the Jews. Why is that?"

I let the "Roman" insult pass. "I have known Jewish men of merit," I said. "And I have begun to appreciate your conundrum: trapped in a world not of your own making. What does one do in that case?"

Philo stood and looked down at me. "One fights to escape."

"Like your brethren in Judea?"

Philo grunted. "Perhaps. But you cannot defeat Rome with arms. You must do it here," he said, pointing to his head, "by learning the truth— from whatever source—before declaring war. If not, you'll end up dead, and what's worse, you may have died for the wrong reason."

He stood in a rhetorical pose, one hand tucked inside his toga, the other lifted to the heavens. I could not help but admire his intellect. And, as an old man, I also admired his posture.

I got to my feet. "We all die. Perhaps all we can hope for is to have not lived in vain."

Philo nodded. "To truth, then—may we find it before it finds us."

THIRTY-FIVE

I had not arrived home before I had made up my mind: I would go to Judea to see Jeshua bar Josef. I called Senteph to my sleeping chamber, where I was hurriedly throwing clothing into a shapeless bag. "You are to dismiss the household," I said.

Senteph looked around at the room, which in just five minutes I had reduced to a shambles. "Where are you going?"

"Away. Give everyone their due and send them away."

"There is no one, dominus, just myself."

I stopped packing and looked at him. "Really? I had not noticed."

"You had not noticed," he confirmed.

"Then you too are dismissed. Freed."

"Freed?"

I turned to him. "Yes! I free you! I will draft the document. Is that not what you want?"

Senteph, a slave his entire life, stood there, his knees almost knocking with fear. Seeing his distress, I invited him to sit. He would not, but I did. "Look. I am going away," I said evenly. "Maybe forever. Regardless, there will not be a 'household' when I get back. Kronion is taking the villa."

"Kronion?" asked Senteph, at sea with all these changes.

"If he wants help, I will recommend you, though I do not think you will like him much."

Senteph shook his head. "Don't free me, dominus."

"What is this?" I asked. "You do not want the one thing all slaves desire?"

1 6 9

Senteph looked toward the door, then at the ground.

"I understand your fear. I am venturing into the unknown myself."

"You venture with money," said Senteph.

"If that is all you fear," I said, opening my purse, "here is a talent—a few more of these, and you can buy yourself a senatorship in Rome." His hand shook as he took the golden coin. Tears filled his eyes. "Now, if you are going to cry," I said.

He fell at my feet, weeping.

"Too late," I said. He was kissing my feet, and if I had not just come from the baths I would have prevented him. After a while, he looked up. "I should have done this years ago," I said, lifting him to his feet. "I have been a poor master. Now that you are free, I apologize to you."

"To me?" asked Senteph, sniffling, still holding the coin tightly.

"Yes. You are a good man. With a wife and three children."

"Four," he said, looking at me directly, which he had never done before. "And twelve grandchildren."

"You see?" I said. "I do not even know your family. And you have been with me how many years?"

"Thirty-seven," he said.

"Thirty-seven," I repeated, shaking my head. "And a slave all that time." I was suddenly struck by the inequities of life, inequities which I had endorsed and added to. "I am sorry, Senteph."

"My real name is Senteptah," he said.

"After the god?"

He nodded.

"And I did not respect that name, I fear."

Senteph shook his head. "No! You respect *all* the gods, dominus! It's just that my given name is sacred, to be used only on holy occasions."

"I see," I said. "Well, Senteptah, this is a holy occasion: the moment of your freedom. You are a wealthy man now and can live as you choose. What will you do?"

Senteph shook his head. Clearly, he had never considered it. Such is the life of a slave: hard but simple. "I might buy a house in the Rhakotis Quarter, with my people."

"Will it be a fine house?"

He shrugged, allowing himself a smile. "I will have to decide." He looked at the coin.

"A free man has many decisions," I said. "But first, will you help me prepare for travel?"

"Where are you going, dominus?"

"Melkorios," I said. "I am no longer your master, nor am I Serapion. I am just an old man who has less than you have." Senteph looked at me strangely. I continued, "You have a family, and a man who has a family is never just a slave but also a father and a husband. I have no family, and so I remain a slave to my poor choices, to that coin I just gave you, and to much more." I shrugged. "But I intend to escape from slavery. And, as you pointed out, I am rich, so I have had no excuse for my fears." I looked at the clothing on the bed, then back at Senteph. "All I need is a cloak and a decent tunic, right?"

Senteph looked at my belongings. "And a good pair of shoes."

I laughed. "You see? Even a slave knows more about what is important than I do."

Senteph smiled. "That will change, domin—Melkorios," he said, bowing his head at my name. "No matter what you say, you were a good master, and if you feel yourself a slave, then you were a good slave as well. I believe you will also be a good freeman."

"High praise, Senteptah. Thank you."

I had already consulted with the harbor master and learned that travel by ship to the east was not advisable yet. Winter was ending, but the winds had not yet changed, and there were dangerous sea storms this time of year.

So I bought my second camel in my life—this time a docile, agreeable female—and set out eastward along the Canopic Way. As I left the Royal Quarter, my hood over my head, I marveled at the anonymity I had so quickly achieved. Wearing a tunic and a cloak, I passed unnoticed through the crowd, just another old man limping along with a camel trailing behind him.

The Canopic Way transited the Jewish Quarter, and I took a hard look at the Grand Synagogue as I passed. Its marble walls glistened in the morning light, the golden porch columns sparkling in the sun. Streams of people, mostly men, were entering the building. It was the Sabbath. The men inside would consider it a sin to travel on this day, but I had committed so many sins in my life that one more was nothing to me.

"Melchior?" came a voice. I turned. Rabbi Apollos strode toward me, arms outstretched. "I thought that was you!" He wore his striped prayer shawl and held his phylactery boxes in one hand, the leather ribbons trailing. "What's this?" he said. "A journey?"

I nodded. "Shelama, Rabbi. Yes, a journey."

Apollos nodded toward the city gate. "You're going east—I'm guessing to visit friends."

"If they are still alive . . . and if they are still friends."

Apollos cocked his head. "You have changed, Melchior. You almost look like a Jew now: hairy and disheveled!" He laughed.

I rubbed my beard. "The better to pass unnoticed."

"If my father could see you now," said Apollos, "he would be amazed." "Why?"

"You must make an offering on his behalf in Jerusalem. Two turtle doves will suffice. Will you do that?"

"Will they let me?"

"You must have someone enter the Temple for you, but if you stand at the gate, I'm told, you can see right into the Sanctuary when the doors are open. The altar is visible then."

"Yes, I know."

"That's right! You have been there! You also know a Temple kohen, if I recall correctly."

"*Knew* one—Zechariah—but I am sure he is dead. He was old thirty years ago."

"But you also know a young man who lives there?"

"I hope so," I said. "And it is my greatest hope that he still knows me."

Apollos looked at the Synagogue. Two men were closing the doors. "I have to go, but my blessing still applies: may Hashem guide you."

"A nice thought," I said doubtfully.

"And bring me word of the King!" he shouted as he trotted toward the Synagogue.

I smiled. There were no secrets from Mesha ben Huz or his son Apollos ben Mesha. I waved after him but said nothing. If I returned, I would bring word. If I did not, no one would notice.

Thirty-six

At the delta, the Nile separates into seven branches that empty into what the Romans imperiously call the *Mare Nostrum*—Our Sea. Before sunset, I arrived in Canopus, fifteen miles east of Alexandria, where I found lodging in a room overlooking a papyrus field. That evening I walked around the roof parapet. It had been a cool day—the kind of day Egypt rarely sees—and the night sky would be spectacular, if the clouds on the horizon kept their distance.

I ate on a veranda overlooking the town with other travelers. I recognized a minor official in the restaurant, but he did not recognize me. Musicians set up in front of the inn, and I was treated to the sounds of lyre, flute, tambourine, and drum, all in the thrumming, rhythmic Egyptian style. As they played, women trailing long, colorful ribbons danced before us, moving sinuously to the music.

Although Canopus was one of Egypt's largest cities, it had a small-town feel to it. Many years ago I rented a villa here for several weeks while I dedicated a new Serapeum. For an instant, I considered visiting the Temple but decided against it. I was Serapion no longer and had no business to conduct there. None of the pontiffs would grovel at my feet now, and no one would try to bribe me for favors I could no longer dispense.

An old woman approached carrying a tray of wooden icons: Anubis, Nephthys, Ammit, and various others. She held out an image of a woman suckling a baby: Hathor and her son Horus. I handled the figurine, thinking about Dendera and, of course, Thaesis. I gave it back to the woman. She then showed me a carving of Osiris. I shook my head. Not to be deterred, she produced an icon of a bearded man on a throne, a serpent-entwined staff in his left hand, and a three-headed dog crouching at his knee.

I frowned at the statue. The old woman was about to put it away when I handed her a denarius, twice the value of the little statue. She snatched up the coin and left.

For the remainder of my meal, I dined with Serapis, looking now and then at the statuette on the table. Reduced to this size, he was a toy: a bearded man relaxing in his favorite chair with his bizarre dog at his side. He was not a god; he was not even a man. He was a trifle for children, and when they reached adulthood they would lock him away in a chest, forgotten, with their other toys. I smiled as an idea came into my mind.

Over the next few days, I made good progress across the delta. Caravansaries were situated about ten miles apart along the Via Maris, so one could generally find a bed under a roof at the end of a day. There were few merchants on the Via, which meant the economy was bad. It also meant there would be robbers, who tended to grow more numerous as tax burdens became untenable. In response, some men left their homes to become brigands, stealing from others so they could pay their taxes and return to their lands and families. Thus, wise travelers carried little money.

I did not leave all of my money in Alexandria. Against the risk of robbery, I had several gold talents sewn into my saddle. My Serapis amulet—also gold—hung on a chain around my neck. If a robber wanted it, he could have it, along with the bitter dreams it engendered.

Serapis was said to bless his followers with dreams. When the pontiffs discussed their dreams, I always listened with despair. Balthazar was led by dreams in which he had seen Josef and Miriam and even Caspar and me. Josef dreamed of Herod's threat to the newborn child. Everyone had insightful dreams except me. Even my dear Thaesis had an epiphany: a vision of Athena running happily through fields of flowers in Elysium.

But I had only one sort of dream—a nightmare—and it was always the same. Sometimes I felt the serpent Apep's fetid breath upon me in the dark watches of the night. I shivered, recalling the Sinai many years ago. While Josef and Zechariah were being shielded by Hashem from Herod in Jerusalem, I was on the Sektet barque on the Keku Samu, awaiting the appearance of the dreaded serpent. If that was the only sort of dream the gods would send me, I would gladly forego them altogether.

Then why are you going to Judea? a voice asked. *Do you think he will give you the answer you seek?*

Rushes towered overhead on either side. There was no sound but the steady *clop* of the camel's feet on the dirt-packed road. Leaden clouds hung low. Humidity soaked my clothing. I wanted to forget. I wanted to forget Thaesis and Athena; forget Kronion and the Serapeum; forget the Great Harbor and the Pharos light; forget the Library and the Museum; forget the Birth Room at Luxor and the Hathor mural at Dendera. Forget it all and sleep a dreamless sleep through a night from which I would not awake.

For a week, I traveled across the delta in this state, barely awake during the day, dreamlessly dozing at night. The heat and emptiness slowly burned the anger out of me. My sense of betrayal seemed pointless. As the miles fell to the implacable plodding of my camel, so also did my bitterness. It belonged in Alexandria. I was more than a hundred miles from there now, and not even hate can fly that far on a single thought.

As I was ferried across the final Nile branch, I saw the Sinai plateau in the far distance, a great broken slope rising to barren, cloud-shrouded highlands. White wings beat the air overhead. "Storks, returning from wintering in Ethiopia," said the ferryman. "A good sign. The floods are coming."

"Have you been to Ethiopia?" I asked, making idle conversation.

"Yes. Nubia too," he said.

"Ah," I said. "Did you find gold there?"

"No, so I wonder why they call it that," he said. "I saw only starving people."

"Have you ever wished to return?"

"What for?" he said. "We have starving people here, don't we?" This brought a laugh from the slaves poling us across the river. "Where are you headed?" asked the ferryman.

"Phoenicia."

"Why didn't you wait a month and go by sea?"

"I am in a hurry."

"Emergency, eh?" said the ferryman.

"Of a sort," I replied.

"By the Black Stone," he said, kissing a ring on his finger. "Bad luck."

"Bad luck," repeated a poleman, and the rest grew silent.

"But a beautiful day, nevertheless," I said.

"Always how it is," said the ferryman, making a warding-off gesture. "There's always a pretty sunset just before nightfall."

I looked behind us. The sun hovered above the reed fields, the unvaried flatness of the delta a tabletop behind which the sun would disappear in another hour.

"Lodging ahead?" I asked.

The ferryman nodded. "Aye, and that's bad luck too. You won't find a decent inn now that you've left civilization behind."

Good, I thought. *It is civilization that has nearly killed me.*

THIRTY-SEVEN

I joined a caravan to cross the Sinai. We were fortunate—we encountered no brigands, but there was a rumor that they had struck another merchant train and killed someone. The drovers that brought us the news looked little better than brigands themselves, and some among our number questioned whether they were those of whom they had spoken.

Our caravan chief, a swarthy Spaniard, pulled out his sword and began to methodically sharpen it. When he'd honed it sufficiently, he swung up onto his horse and rode off, raising a cloud of dust. We all looked at each other, wondering what would happen next.

In a few minutes, he returned and nodded at his lead man. The caravan, loaded with Egyptian faience jewelry and ivory, started moving again. I did not doubt the Spaniard's ability to protect us, but I worried that our merchandise might be too tempting for desperate thieves to resist. I decided once we were past this dangerous stretch, I would strike out on my own.

We were more than halfway across the Sinai. The closer we came to the Judean border, the less likely it was that we would be attacked. At our midday rest stop, I moved on ahead on the wide plain, happy to be leaving the caravan smell behind. I called my camel Nefer, after Nefertem, the Egyptian god of the fragrant lotus flower, not because she did not stink, but because she did not stink as much as the last camel I rode across this desert. Solitude was also needed to formulate a plan for when I arrived in Judea.

After several hours off the beaten path, Nefer turned toward a jumble of sandstone boulders at the base of a mountain spur. It was not until we passed between two upright, squarish stones that I remembered camping here long ago. This was where I had the nightmare of Apep and the foreboding fear for Jeshua's safety.

I dismounted and went to the shallow pool and filled a bowl. I took it to the camel and she drank it, so I knew it was safe. I scooped a handful of water into my mouth. It tasted like iron.

I built a fire and cooked a piece of fish. The sun had set, yet the sky was still full of light. I watched the stars come out. Venus sparkled on the horizon; Virgo rose in the east; Orion was overhead, as he always was in late Februaris. Aries hunted near the western horizon.

I reached inside my tunic and withdrew Jeshua's natal chart. The ink had faded, but I could still make out the unity of planets in the First House. I shook my head at my foolishness. There were only twelve houses, which meant there were only twelve kinds of people in the world, which was false on its face. Long ago, I had done birth charts for twins, a brother and sister, who lived entirely different lives. He became a doctor who drowned at sea while still a single man. She married three times, had many children, and was still alive. There was nothing similar about their lives, and yet they had the same birth chart.

Another case in point was my own daughter Athena. Because she was a foundling, we did not know her birth date, without which casting a natal chart was impossible. I tried many times, and came up with different charts on each occasion.

I looked at Jeshua's chart. Its once-in-a-lifetime conjunction of planets had led me to him. Balthazar's identical chart did the same, but what of that? Astrological almanacs were the same the world over. Evidences that were so compelling years ago now seemed laughably coincidental.

Yet, I *had* seen wonders. Zechariah's tongue-tying and Elisheba's pregnancy. Josef and Miriam and their remarkable son. But I did not *know* whether Elisheba actually bore Johanan. I did not hear angels singing at Jeshua's birth. Hashem's messenger Gabriel never visited *me*.

Years before my first journey to Jerusalem, at an after-supper discussion in my villa with Heliphon, the famous astronomer, I asked him to explain the Great Circle, something he had written about, which I could not understand.

"It is a circle the stars *seem* to inscribe around the North Pole."

"Meaning?" I asked.

"Five hundred years ago, Anaxagoras told us that stars are *not* pin-holes in the bowl of sky surrounding earth that allow the light of the cosmos through."

"That's true," one of my other guests interjected. "He said stars are actually fiery stones."

"Yes," said Heliphon. "Like our sun, as confirmed three centuries later by Eratosthenes."

"But what does this have to do with the Grand Circle?" I asked.

"Who said, 'There are two things: science and opinion. The former begets knowledge; the latter ignorance'?"

"Hippocrates of Cos," I said. "So cure my ignorance! What *is* the Grand Circle?"

"The earth spins on its axis, like a top," said another guest. "The stars seem to move around us as we turn, but it is we who move, not them." He leaned back, pleased with himself.

Heliphon smiled. "Ah, but the stars *do* move. They move from year to year, not just from season to season. Two hundred years ago, Hipparchus observed that the earth *wobbles* as it spins on its axis, like a dreidel slowing down. He called this movement *precession*. Thus, the axis of earth—its true north—points to different stars over time. When Khufu built his pyramid, he pointed it at what was the pole star in his day: Thuban, in Draco. Yet now, twenty-five hundred years later, the pyramid is aligned with empty sky, because true north has moved along the arc of a circle. In two thousand years, a star in the tail of Ursa Minor will be the pole star, and then another, and so on, until we return to Thuban again. *That* is the Great Circle, and it takes twenty-six thousand years to complete."

"So how can the stars affect us," I asked, "if they are constantly moving?"

"*Everything* is constantly moving," corrected Heliphon. He looked at my guests, cleared his throat, then finally looked at me. "But, as far as affecting us . . . the scientific answer is that they cannot."

The evening ended soon after. We were all polite, of course—he was a visiting dignitary, after all—but he had said something so heretical, so outrageous, so . . .

"True," I said to my campfire under the stars. "I just couldn't accept it for thirty years."

But it *was* true. Astrology was an attempt to reconcile the vagaries of human behavior with the apparent unchangeability of the heavens. Everything returned to the same starting point each year. Yet Hipparchus had shown even that to be false. The stars were not unchangeable. The problem was we did not live long enough to see the changes; our perspective was flawed. We were blind men steering a ship in the ocean by the feel of the breeze in our faces.

I crumpled Jeshua's chart and tossed it into the fire, then lay back on my bedroll, closing my eyes. I was more than halfway to Jerusalem. Though the answers I had hoped to gain in Judea were dwindling, there were even fewer in Egypt. Besides, I simply wanted to see Jeshua and wish him well. I needed no astrological chart to convince me that seeing him once more would make my journey worthwhile.

I stumbled about in the darkness, not knowing where I was. The dark stone walls on either side of me were inscribed with reliefs, and the only light came from the eyes of the carved figures in the reliefs: gods and goddesses, captives and slaves, pharaohs and queens. They followed me as I ran from room to room. There was no ceiling; the tops of the walls disappeared into the darkness above.

I slammed my knee against something. I hobbled backward, rubbing my knee. I had run into the base of a bronze column. There were two columns, one plain and one covered with carved vines, standing a man's height apart. Hung between them was a drapery with the Eye of Horus on it. The pupil of the eye was a white sun.

I grabbed at the curtain but was unable to find the seam. Then suddenly, I was beyond it, inside some kind of temple. The cloying smell of frankincense made me cough. Smoke rose from the floor, lapping like water at my knees. I staggered forward. The sky goddess Nut's long, thin body was recreated in mosaic tile under my feet, her upper body and head disappearing ahead of me. Stars covered her body, and the frog-like symbols of *heka*, or secret magical knowledge, surrounded her.

I heard a sound and peered into the dark, smoky distance, my ears pricked. I heard chanting: drawn-out syllables, ending abruptly with a strangled howl, then a repeat. The smoke had risen to my waist, obscuring the sky-floor, and I moved forward with my hands extended, squinting into the darkness. Soon I saw a number of kneeling hooded figures, the

Eye of Horus painted on the back of their white robes. They seemed to be floating just above the ground.

As I drew nearer, the object of their devotion emerged from the rising smoke. It was an immense, seated figure carved from stone, and it was slowly moving toward me. The head turned regularly from side to side, its mouth opening and closing, accompanied by a machine-like sound. The statue's eyes found me, and the head stopped turning. I heard a low growl and turned. Behind me was Cerberus, as large as a man, his three mouths dripping steaming saliva. No collar restrained him.

Then I heard a hissing and turned back to the statue. Serapis sat motionless, but towering behind him was Apep, its immense emerald cowl wider than a man's outstretched arms, its red eyes fixed upon me. Cerberus growled, and I again turned. It had moved forward, shoulders hunched, ready to attack.

Then suddenly, Apep struck, knocking me aside. The serpent sunk its fangs into Cerberus's jackal head. Cerberus howled, and his great claws swiped at the air, knocking me down.

As the two beasts battled, I scrambled backward. The kneeling figures had not moved, and their faces were still mostly in shadow, yet one I recognized—it was Athena. Her eyes were twin suns, but no expression lit her face. Inching closer, I touched her cheek, but it was as cold and hard as stone. I whispered her name, trying to make her sun-shot eyes meet mine, even if it meant my own blindness. I wept, cupping her face in my hands, as the bloody contest between Cerberus and Apep occurred just over my shoulder.

Then I was in my home, kneeling before the family shrine, holding Athena's imago in my hands. The mask was warm from the candle that lit it in its alcove. I had squeezed it so tightly that the thick wax had distorted. Her face was now elongated, and a crack had opened on the bridge of the nose. I stared at it for a long time, still hearing the distant barking, hissing, and striking sounds of the battle, the disembodied chanting that accompanied the arrival of Serapis, and the grating sound of the statue's mouth opening and closing like one of Hero's steam contraptions.

I awoke in the desert oasis, blinking and looking around wildly. An egret that had been perched on one of the palms lifted off, startled. Egrets are harbingers of doom. The fire embers were barely glowing. I shivered and pulled my blanket around me. I lay back, looking up at the sky. Orion was gone; it was the fifth watch, and morning was near.

I reached inside my tunic, removing my Serapis amulet. I could still hear the distant, echoing sounds of Apep and Cerberus clashing, the clanking of Serapis's jaw, and the meaningless, repetitive chanting of the robed figures. I turned the amulet over and over in my hand, then suddenly yanked it free and hurled it into the fire, sending sparks flying. I fed wood into the blaze, which was soon crackling and spitting like Hades's forge.

Then I remembered the icon I had purchased at Canopus. I dug it out of my bag and stood before the blazing fire. "Lies!" I shouted. "Lies! Lies!" I threw it into the fire and stumbled back, tripping over my bedroll, falling clumsily on my rump. Soon I was crying, cursing, and shouting insults to every god I could name: Serapis, Horus, Nephthys, Hapi, Apis, Khensu, Anubis, Ammit, Amun, Ra, Zeus, Jupiter, Saturn, Apollo, the Furies, the Muses, all of Olympus, even at Ptah himself. I even railed against Osiris' false promise of resurrection.

The only one I did not curse was Sobek, the crocodile-headed god who represented the destroying power of the sun. Topping his tall crown were the two feathers of justice. When my voice failed me, my chest heaving and my brow glistening with sweat, I silently implored Sobek to mete out justice to an unjust universe, beginning with man. Everything was a lie and ought to be destroyed.

Sobek, I thought bitterly, *I deny your existence. Prove me unjust and take my life.*

HIRTY-EIGHT

I almost believed, then, for when I awoke the next morning, I was sick with fever. My boiling pulse pounded in my temples, and my eyes felt as if they would burst. I expected my forehead to blister. I spent the day huddled under a blanket, shivering in the blazing sun. As the afternoon dragged on, I thought, *It is fitting that I should die; that is what cursing the gods gets you.*

But sickness is not death, and I laughed, for there were no gods to offend; the clock had no maker. The meaninglessness of existence gave me a sort of sour pleasure, releasing me from the need for the gods that had made my life a pathetic plea, one day for mercy, the next for justice. But with no judge at the bar, I feared no punishment beyond the heat of day and cold of night. If I stayed away from poison and blades, I would live until the clock stopped. And after?

I did not care.

By late afternoon on the second day, I had recovered my faculties somewhat and laughed at my ordeal. After all those years of spiritual famine, as the sun burned my skin and the fever cooked my mind, I was inundated with dreams and visions. In my delirium, I saw ominous figures in black, flocks of geese in the southwest quadrant, abnormal dog entrails, and evanescent images in smoke. The egret returned, filling me with fear, but it was frightened off by a vulture—a good omen.

Near sunset, I arose and prepared to leave. I was weak as slave tea but decided to die elsewhere on another day, not there and not then. The vulture watched as I packed, and my camel, who had barely moved while I was sick, promptly got to her feet when commanded. We headed east as the sun was setting in the west. We traveled all night, arriving at the Judean border at dawn, the legionnaires slumbering at their posts. When Nefer snorted our arrival, they jumped to their feet and pointed their *gladii* at me. But when they saw nothing more than a sunburned old man, they waved me through, not even looking at my papers. After all, I was leaving Egypt, which was undoubtedly pleased to be rid of a vagabond such as I, and Judea . . . well, who cared who entered Judea?

My spirits lifted when I arrived in Ascalon, a seaside town surrounded by ancient earthworks. It was market day, and the agora was full of fish mongers, perfumists, vegetable farmers, bakers, and butchers. Suddenly famished, I bought food, ate, and basked in the bustle. I found an inn, where I retired and slept uninterrupted through the night for the first time in months.

After a satisfying breakfast of melon and fruit juice, I regretted my desert despondence. Bitterness toward the gods was pointless. If they existed, they would punish me for my insolence; if they did not, why bother cursing them? In the morning breeze, with the sun peeking over the green eastern hills, it was pointless to consider the gods at all. It was no more than three days to Jerusalem, where I would be greeted by King Jeshua and dine in splendor at his palace.

I bought two loaves of cinnamon bread, consuming one almost before leaving the shop. I was feeling better and asked the baker about Judean politics. "Where are you from?" he asked, noting my accent.

"Alexandria," I mumbled between mouthfuls.

"Don't they have bread there?" he chuckled.

"Not like this," I said. "Wonderful!"

"What's your interest in local politics?"

I shrugged. "I just wanted to know who reigned. I have not been here in thirty years."

"Herod's sons are sucking the bones now."

"Who?"

"Herod the Great. His sons." He looked at me like I was a dolt.

I shrugged. Playing the fool was easier than trying to appear wise, and since I *was* a fool, it also had the benefit of honesty.

"They divided the country between themselves when the old adulterer died."

"They?"

"Philip and Antipas up north," said the baker. "Archelaus used to torture us down here, but Tiberias banished him. Now there's a prefect in Jerusalem."

"His name?"

"I have no idea," said the baker.

I congratulated him on his ignorance of government and left Ascalon. There were no trees in the town, but on the hills to the east I saw oak, myrtle, and olive. The sun was pleasant on my face, and I shut my eyes, hearing nothing but the squawk of a plover gliding overhead in the cloudless sky.

The coastal plain tilted up to the highlands. Between vineyards and pastures fenced with limestone, I saw many tidy homes. It was not yet Martius, yet the trees were budding lavender and white. The hillsides were dotted with yellow lilies, pink hollyhocks, and red everlasting, a shrub said to have sprung out of the ground from blood shed by the Maccabeans in their rebellion against Rome a hundred years ago.

The clean air, the riot of hillside color, the fragrant blooms, and a full belly lifted my spirits to a height I had not felt since before Thaesis died. I wondered if Jeshua's kingly blessing powers extended even to nature.

Just outside of Emmaus, I stopped and fed white crocus petals to Nefer, and she, much delighted, decided we'd traveled enough that day and hunkered down in the middle of the road, much to my frustration. It was only after holding a bunch of Veronica blossoms in front of her snout that she finally rose and ambled off the road. I let her munch a mouthful of the blue petals and finally succeeded in getting her on the move again.

I stayed the night in Emmaus at a caravansary with rooms above the stables. Though the pallet was hard, I slept well after a meal of vegetable porridge, wine, and the last of my cinnamon loaf. Tomorrow I would be in Jerusalem, my spirit healed by the Judean spring, my heart again open to receive the friendship I so desperately missed. As I drifted off to sleep, I wondered how Jeshua had changed. Did he look like his father: muscular, with dark eyes? Or would he favor his mother: fair-skinned and slender? No matter; he would look regal seated on his throne, and I would be welcomed as a friend in his court. I might even offer my services to him. Though I doubted his people would appreciate my astrological gifts, my auguring skill would undoubtedly be of great value when Jeshua pondered the future. I would no longer be Serapion or Melkorios Alexandreus. Instead, I would be simply "Melchior, Advisor and Friend to the King of the Jews."

The title gave me a shiver of happiness. After so many years in the desert, I was finally entering a garden where comfortable cushions, stimulating conversation, and bountiful banquets awaited, as well as the greatest pleasure of all: the company of a fine young man who wanted nothing more than to rule with equanimity and justice.

Suddenly, I believed in heaven again, even if it were only on earth.

From Emmaus, the mountains become more rugged. When the road disappeared into a stand of evergreens, I stopped. If there were bandits in Judea, they would be there. I reached for my amulet and for a startled moment was unable to find it. Then I remembered I had thrown it into the fire in the Sinai. I realized I was now free to be afraid without a talisman to protect me. I was also free to find my own destiny. And if that destiny was to be murdered, so be it. With the confidence only an old man who has had a long, safe life has, I continued into the forest.

Jerusalem sits on the spine of Judea. I had heard there were days in which you could see the Green Sea to the west and the Dead Sea to the east. As I approached the city, I knew that would not be the case today—low clouds blanketed the highlands. When I first saw Jerusalem thirty years ago, she was a beautiful young bride, her walls sparkling white in the morning sun. Today, she brooded like an old crone, tired and wrinkled. Billowing smoke from the Mount mingled with the rain-heavy clouds, suffusing everything with a depressing gray light.

Her foreboding aspect was but one reason I skirted the city and headed east, to Bethany. Zechariah was almost certainly dead, but I had to be sure. The clouds seemed so close I could wring water from them. On my left, David's City climbed the flank of Moriah. On my right was the Mount of Olives. Little had changed since my last time here.

At Bethany, I dismounted at the center of town. Rain was falling, and a chill wind blew my cloak around my bare legs. No one was on the street, and windows were shuttered. I could not remember where Zechariah's home had been. Nothing looked familiar. I left the camel and walked down a cobbled street. The rain came down more heavily and soon water was cascading off the roofs. I took refuge under a porch and knocked on a battered door. A slide opened, revealing a leathery face. "No boarders," said the old woman in a gravely voice.

"Shelama, madam," I said. "I seek Zechariah, a kohen at the Temple."

She peered at me. "Dead," she said, and closed the shutter. I knocked again, and from the other side of the door, I heard, "What?"

"Where did he live?"

The shutter opened again and she glared at me. "Here, you old fool. This was his home."

"*Here?*" The woman tried to close the shutter again, but I stuck my hand through the opening first. "What about Elisheba?" I asked. "What about their son, Johanan?"

"Dead. All dead," she said. "Dead fools, all of them." She slammed the shutter against my hand, pinching it. I yelped and withdrew it. The shutter slid home.

I looked around. The rain came down in sheets and the street ran like a river. I banged on the door again but she would not answer. How could I be certain we were talking about the same Zechariah? Yet the woman was as old as they would have been—well into her eighties. I had expected them to be dead anyway. But what happened to Johanan? He was just six months older than Jeshua. Why was *he* dead?

I slogged back, falling twice, slamming my knee onto the cobbles the first time and nearly breaking my elbow the second. I was too old for this sort of adventure. As I limped toward the fountain, I realized in horror that Nefer was gone! I whirled around, my heart thumping, a victim of a crime. But then I saw her, intelligently standing under the low-hanging branches of a tree across the square, out of the rain. As I should have been.

I found no lodging in Jerusalem. It was well into the second watch, and everything was shut as tight as Bethany had been. But I found a stable, and the keeper let me sleep in the stall with Nefer. I was grateful; I just wanted to be out of the rain. I bedded down, throwing a canvas tarp over me, which caught most of the water dripping through the leaky roof. I had nothing to eat or drink but a mouthful of brackish water from the trough. I lay against my saddle, shivering, and wished for the arid climate of Alexandria—few died of pneumonia there.

Except my Athena. And with that depressing thought, I closed my eyes. If the gods would forgive my many blasphemies, with luck, I would join her and her mother in Elysium before morning. But I knew the gods—I had served them all my life. They would forgive me only after painful penance. Perhaps I was beginning my penance now, in this muddy land, far from home, preparing for my final sufferings.

Thirty-nine

I was awakened by a cacophony of sound. Animals, living according to nature's clock, awaken at dawn, and the city seemed full of crowing roosters and barking dogs. Nefer sat quietly, her haunches a cushion for my head. When I moved, it was with great pain. Every joint complained, and I could not bend my knee or move my elbow without agony. After trying to get to my feet and failing, I leaned back against my camel, sweat standing on my brow. I renewed my complaints to the Furies: if they wanted me, take me, but let me at least walk to my own execution!

I must have fallen asleep, for when the innkeeper roused me, the midmorning sun glared in my eyes. He was angry at first, but when he saw I could not stand by myself, he helped me up and led me indoors. His wife brought me a bowl of porridge, and I warmed my hands on the bowl, hoping the steam would clear my sinuses. I coughed and sneezed. The innkeeper and his wife stood by, probably wondering if I was going to die before I paid them.

Seeing their concern, I reached into my tunic, half expecting to find the natal chart—I had burned that too in a moment of rage—and found my purse. I extracted a couple of assarions, more than enough for my accommodations. Their faces lit up, and the scurrying of a busy kitchen resumed. I was forgotten as I ate, my head pounding every time a dish clattered against another. I finished quickly and hobbled outdoors. The day was bright and dry, though mud puddles were everywhere. A stable boy had saddled Nefer.

"I have business in the city," I said, waving him away. "I will be back later."

"Do you want me to unsaddle her?"

I nodded and was about to go when the boy ran into the shed, returning with a rubbed-wood staff. "It was old Jacob's, but he's dead now." He handed it to me.

"Thank you," I said and gave the boy a prutah. I walked out into the street, which was full of people dressed in the Jewish style: women covered their heads and many wore veils. Men, hatless, wore striped cloaks over dun-colored tunics. Few women wore wigs, and most men had greasy hair and untrimmed beards. The overall impression was one of poverty and slovenliness.

As I navigated the muddy, winding streets, I longed for the broad avenues of Alexandria and the hot Etesian winds that scoured the city of the stink of humanity. In Jerusalem, the rain released odors that had been baked into the ground by the sun. The stench was overwhelming, and as I turned a corner, I discovered why. I had spent the night in the trades quarter, where tanners, copper smelters, and undertakers did their work. The result was an odor that made the eyes water.

I covered my nose and headed east. The Temple rose high above the mud-brick city. A viaduct spanned the Tyropoeon Valley, connecting the Upper City with the Mount. At a *mikvah*, I washed my feet, then walked barefoot up the viaduct steps, carrying my sandals. The viaduct itself was crowded, and I had to shoulder my way past merchants and beggars as I approached the Mount ramparts. I passed through the Coponius Gate and entered the Court of the Gentiles. Directly before me was the rear of the Temple complex, the Sanctuary rising high above the alabaster walls surrounding it. I followed the crowd, which fanned out toward moneychangers and animal vendors, whose stalls crowded the shaded colonnades on the Court's perimeter.

As always, two white-robed priests guarded the Temple entrance. Suddenly, they snapped to attention. I looked around. A group of men approached from the south, one wearing a white gown covered with a long blue robe. On his head was a blue turban with a golden band. He was tall, with white hair and a beard that flowed over a large brooch on his chest, inset with a dozen colorful gemstones. If this wasn't the High Priest, then I had never been one myself.

I walked resolutely toward the advancing group. Oh, how I wished for my own vestments! Instead, I would have to rely upon my experience. As they approached, I bowed. "Shelama," I said in Hebrew. "I am Melkorios Alexandreus."

The High Priest stopped and surveyed me silently.

"He is the Kohen Gadol of Hashem, the One True God," said a priest. "And you're blocking his way." He pushed me, and I fell to the ground.

I looked up. "But I am Supreme Pontiff of Serapis in Egypt."

Another priest laughed. "Get off the Mount, dog worshiper."

As the High Priest passed me, I said, "Zechariah of Bethany was my friend. He would never have treated me this way."

The High Priest stopped and turned. "Your friend is dead."

"I seek a cousin of his by marriage," I said, getting to my feet. "Her name is Miriam and she has a son named Jeshua." I paused. "He was destined to be your king."

"Tiberius Caesar is our king, as an Egyptian should know better than anyone."

"I am not Egyptian," I said. "But no matter. Jeshua bar Josef is your king. I seek him."

The High Priest smiled. "Then you have made a long journey for nothing, Melkorios Alexandreus, Supreme Pontiff of Serapis. We do not recognize your position or your gods in Jerusalem, and we certainly do not recognize the king of which you speak." He leaned closer. "And I wouldn't go around Jerusalem talking about a 'king' or you're likely to wind up there." He nodded toward the Antonia Fortress, which towered over the northwestern corner of the Mount.

He walked briskly away. I watched as his retinue scaled the steps to the Gate Beautiful, disappearing inside the Temple complex.

A man picked up my staff and handed it to me. "Be careful," he said.

I took the staff. "What is his name?"

"Caiaphas," he said. "Josef ben Caiaphas."

I walked back to the Coponius Gate. As I walked along the viaduct, I looked to where the three towers of Herod's Citadel rose above the western city wall. If Jeshua was in power, even by another name, he would be there.

It took me an hour of slow shambling through crowded streets to get to the Citadel. I did not pass a public bath the entire way. With each plodding step, I grew angrier. How I hated this filthy city! No baths, no sewers, and apparently no running water! Just yesterday I hailed Judea as a gift of the gods. Today this same land was a hellish Tartarus. Yet nothing had changed except my outlook. I wondered if Hashem was chastening me before allowing me to find Jeshua, who, if he met me this moment, would turn away in disgust at my deplorable disposition.

I resolved to have a better attitude. It was still spring. The rain had passed and the sun shone. I was lame, but my camel was not, and I still had money sewn into my saddle. A bath could be found, eventually. Food was for sale and sleep required only that I lie down. I had not broken any bones in my falls and would probably heal. I still had almost half of my teeth and most of my sight. In other words, I had little to complain about.

So when I knocked on the Citadel gate, I straightened to my full height, determined to be cordial and polite. The inner door opened and only a barred gate stood between me and a young soldier. His fair features reminded me of my old friend Paulos, the snub-nosed Gaul who warned us of Herod the Great in this very courtyard so many years ago.

"What do you want?" asked the guard.

"Salve, citizen," I said. "I seek your master."

"He's in Caesarea."

"Herod?" I asked.

The young man laughed. "He is in the Herodium mausoleum, fifty miles that way." He pointed south.

I considered thrusting my staff through the bars and knocking him down for his insolence. Instead, I smiled. "What is your master's name?"

"What is *your* name, citizen?"

"I am Melkorios of Alexandria, Vizier to Prefect Cestius—"

He slammed the door in my face! I was outraged. I had experienced more disrespect in one day in this miserable city than I had in my entire life in Alexandria! Me, Melkorios, friend of emperors, pontiff to the gods, chart-caster to . . .

I hung my head and turned away .

FORTY

It was sixty miles to Caesarea Maritima, a seaside fortress built by Herod and named after his patron, Julius Caesar. The journey took me almost a week, for I was sick with a miserable cold and an interminable headache. By the time I reached Aramathea, on the Sharon plain, I had to stop and recover, for I had begun coughing up bloody phlegm.

I found an inn, and the innkeeper, a woman named Ducalia, cared for me like one of her own. Her husband had died two years before, leaving her with four children, but she had been fortunate; the inn was prosperous. I called her my "dark angel," because I feared her healing arts as I suffered under her stinking poultices and choked down her bitter potions.

As I recovered, I had time to ponder. Jeshua was not king of Judea—that much was clear. The province was administered by a prefect, one Pontius Pilatus, a Roman from the sound of his name. So one of two things must be true: Jeshua currently reigned in some obscure area of Judea, or he had not yet come to power. As for where he might be, all I knew was that when his parents left Alexandria, they were headed back to Galilee, a province sixty miles north of Jerusalem. The problem was Samaria, which stood between the two. I was advised to avoid Samaria because they were a bloody, violent, and cruel people. *More so than the Jews?* I asked myself.

Caesarea Maritima was on the coast, west of Samaria. Two days' ride north of Caesarea was Ptolemais. Inland from Ptolemais lay Galilee. I could avoid Samaria by this route and arrive safely in Galilee within a week. I then hoped to find Josef in his hometown, though I could not remember its name.

I asked Ducalia for a map of Galilee. She asked me why, when only bandits, turncoats, and criminals lived there. She added if I insisted on going there, all her attempts to restore my health would come to naught, for I would soon be as dead as Homer.

By this I knew there were no maps of Galilee and thanked her. If Galilee was as rural and sparsely populated as I had heard was, it should not be too hard to find Josef and Miriam, not to mention their son Jeshua. So it was only a matter of time.

Besides, I relished the chance to visit Caesarea, which was famous throughout the Empire. A colossal statue of Poseidon guarded the entrance of its man-made harbor, and it boasted a hippodrome nearly as large as Rome's, as well as a theater that seated four thousand people. The Augustus Deified temple rivaled the one in Rome. After the dirt and disrespect of Jerusalem, I was ready for civilization again. I was also ready to be greeted by a fellow Roman who would be respectful of my office.

When I had recovered enough to travel, I set out for Antipatris. It was built, as everything seemed to be in this country, by Herod, but Antipatris, named after his father, was really nothing more than a crossroads town surrounded by unhealthy swamps.

Two days later, I saw Caesarea glistening like an abalone shell against the Green Sea. It was as I had been told: a walled city with marble buildings lining broad avenues. The Cardo so reminded me of Alexandria's Canopic Way that I got homesick as I led my camel up the main avenue. There was a forum fronting the Caesareum and a great domed basilica where legal matters were judged. And to my great delight, there were spotlessly clean public baths.

So, after weeks on the road, I indulged myself, easing my aching bones into the *caldarium* and luxuriating in the hot water. After a long, satisfying soak, I cooled off in the *tepidarium*, then finally I lay naked on a cool marble slab in the *sudatorium*, breathing sweet sage vapors as a masseuse kneaded my aching muscles. The cost was high: a silver denarius, but it seemed a bargain to me.

During my day in the baths, I had my clothing washed, and so by the time I was walking down the Cardo again, my soul was restored, and my body was also. I walked to the Prefect's palace, breathing the tangy sea air, my cold beaten back almost to a stand-still. I looked out to sea. In another hour the sun would set, promising glorious colors.

The harbor was bursting with Phoenician frigates and Roman triremes. Sniffing the sea air, I again remembered Alexandria, and a wave of nostalgia washed over me. I was a sentimental old man pining for that which I did not have, or for places where I was not. Young men think of the future; old men of the past. And yet, here I was on a quest like the foolish youth I had been thirty years before, searching for a nightshade.

But perhaps I would find instead a young man ready to take his throne—a young man who might desire the wisdom and experience of an older man.

Well, at least the experience.

Forty-one

His Excellency will see you now," said the chief steward, bowing and exiting. The foyer walls were painted with murals. Overhead, the ceiling had been painted to resemble a blue sky.

I turned at a sound. A man with a horseshoe of graying hair approached. He was clean-shaven and wore a silk toga with a blue stripe, the symbol of his equestrian rank. He raised his hand in familiar Roman benediction, speaking in Aramaic. "Welcome to Caesarea."

I answered in Latin: "I am Melkorios Alexandreus, Vizier to the Praefectus Alexandriae et Aegypti, Cestius Galerius."

Pilatus bowed and responded in Latin as well: "Pontius Pilatus, your humble servant." We walked down the entry hall, I examining the statuary (some of it rivaling pieces I had seen in Rome) and Pilatus examining me. We stopped outside two large doors. "Throne room," said Pilatus, shrugging. "I never go in there. Doesn't seem right, you know."

I nodded my agreement.

Pilatus pointed to a courtyard visible through a doorway. "Why don't we visit out here?" We took our places on facing divans. "I haven't eaten yet," he said. "I hope you'll join me."

"Thank you, Prefect. It would be an honor."

A servant filled two goblets with wine. We toasted one another, and I prepared myself for an exotic taste. I was surprised; it was a familiar vintage. I smiled. "Tuscan?"

Pilatus grinned. "You *are* a Roman!"

"One really misses the little things," I said, "when one is far from home."

"As you are, Vizier," said Pilatus, raising his goblet to me.

"Yes," I said. "I am on sabbatical."

"A tourist? From Egypt?" laughed Pilatus. "But isn't Egypt itself a tourist destination?"

"Have you been there?"

He shook his head, then finished his second goblet of wine in the time it had taken me to swallow two mouthfuls of my own. "I've been busy scaling the *cursus honorum*—putting time in here, for example. Can't wait to get home. Four more years—and I *despise* it."

"Why is that?" I asked. "I find it rather . . . *quaint*."

"That's one way to put it," said Pilatus. 'Dirty and backward' is another. And that's just the *place*! Don't get me started on the people! Slovenly yet proud, they are the most—"

"I am seeking a man," I interrupted, asserting myself over this commoner who seemed stupidly oblivious to his enviable position and equally careless with his tongue. His Latin was atrocious and his manner coarse. I judged from his name that he was from Pontus, near the Black Sea. If there ever was a slovenly yet proud people, it was his.

"I thought you were on vacation," said Pilatus, reeling from my commanding tone.

"A social call. I have not seen him in many years. With his gifts, by now he would be a leader, a magistrate, or perhaps even *more*."

Pilatus knew what I meant.

Dinner came then, and there was inconsequential talk as we sampled the roast bird and almond and walnut salad. Pilatus continued draining his glass, and I continued sipping at mine. Soon two of his friends entered and seated themselves. Lacking any polite curiosity about my presence, they merely filled their bellies with food and howled as they exchanged off-color jokes. Their Latin, so poor they could not maintain it, soon gave way to equally crude Aramaic. I was growing tired and was no closer to getting answers now than I had been hours ago when their arrival effectively cut off all intelligent conversation. During a brief lull between bawdy stories related by Helvius, the more portly of the two, I repeated my inquiry to Pilatus.

"What was this man's name?" asked Pilatus.

"Jeshua," I said, "from Galilee. His mother was Miriam and his father, Josef."

"Well," said Helvius, "*that* narrows it down!"

Pilatus leaned forward. "Melkorios, my friend—if I may call you that—I wonder if you understand the politics of our little province."

I shrugged. I thought I did, but was interested to see how Pilatus understood them.

"I am the prefect," he began.

"Salve, Prefect!" shouted Helvius, raising his goblet, accompanied by his friend.

Pilatus waved them to be quiet. "My power is limited to collection of tribute and some judicial matters. Lucius Vitellius is the Syrian governor and has more commerce with the Jews than I do—he appoints the High Priest, after all."

"Caiaphas," I said flatly. "Yes, I have met him. A very disagreeable fellow."

"As they all are," said Helvius.

"In addition," said Pilatus. "Vitellius is a senator. To be truthful, I'm just a figurehead."

"But you strike a good figure," said Helvius, raising his goblet.

"Also, Herod had a batch of sons," said Pilatus, "three of whom are currently vying for favor with Rome. Philip rules northwest of Lake Tiberias, Antipas rules Galilee and Perea, and the unfortunate Archelaus, who used to rule here in Caesarea, now governs some hamlet in Gaul. With him gone, Antipas and Philip are in constant conflict as each seeks to undermine the other and regain the kingship of their father. I spend my time quelling petty quarrels; I'm more of a schoolmaster than a prefect." He leaned back. "So you see, I have little power but great responsibility."

"Not a good combination," I agreed.

"So I'm afraid one more pretender to power is of little consequence to me. He can get in line behind the others or, better yet, disappear into the wilderness with the Essenes."

I raised an eyebrow.

"Followers of an offshoot of Judaism. Communal living, vegetarianism, and poring over religious texts all day. Celibacy."

"*That* is as anti-Roman as you can get," laughed Helvius.

"Who is their leader?" I asked.

Pilatus looked at his companions, his brow furrowed. "What was his name?"

The other two, now sodden with wine, looked stupidly at each other.

"No matter," said Pilatus. "He's dead. Antipas killed him for sport."

"Barbarians," said Helvius.

"Yes," I said bitterly, "just like the gladiatorial games."

"Now that *is* fun!" said Helvius's companion, a fellow whose name I had not caught.

Pilatus placed his hands on his knees. "I've got a busy day tomorrow. Court, you know."

"Here's to the death penalty," said Helvius, raising his cup.

"Stay the night, Melkorios," said Pilatus. "Enjoy a good breakfast before you start tomorrow for Galilee."

I nodded my thanks.

"I hope you find your friend," said Pilatus. "What was his name again?"

I looked up at him, never more aware of the clockwork of deceit whirring in another man's head. "Jeshua," I said lightly. "No matter; it is a trifle. Thank you for your hospitality." I stood and bowed. Pilatus swept from the room, followed by several servants. Through the doorway, I saw him turn left and enter the throne room, where he did not feel *comfortable*, no doubt.

I turned to Helvius and his friend. "I bid you good night."

"Stay a bit longer," pleaded Helvius. "There's another amphora that needs emptying, and we need help doing it. You're not in a hurry. Sleep in tomorrow, rest from your travels. Caesarea is a fine place to enjoy fine things. You *do* enjoy fine things?"

I smirked a smile. "Since I was younger than you."

Helvius clapped his hands, and more wine was served. Musicians appeared and female dancers paraded before us as my companions stamped their feet like low-born Germans. We emptied the other amphora, but I kept my wits about me. Helvius and his friend Baltanius (I had to have him spell it for me, finally, to get it right) had obviously been instructed to discover what kind of intrigue I represented. I had frequented palaces all my life and knew that when a person of rank visited, there was always more on his mind than sightseeing. But in the many years and hundreds of banquets I had attended, I had also learned the value of drinking little, saying less, and listening much. As the wine loosened their tongues, Helvius and Baltanius began to tell *me* the true state of affairs in Judea.

Strictly speaking, Pilatus had been honest. His position was precarious, and so he filled the country with spies seeking out plots against him. Even the palace was not safe; he suspected everyone of treachery. His paranoia got so bad that his wife returned to Rome with their children, leaving Pilatus behind with his slave girls and sodden friends. He was looking, Helvius noted in a breathless whisper, for a way *out*. Soon.

"How will he do that?" I asked innocently. "His term is just begun."

Baltanius said, "You know what a scapegoat is?"

I nodded.

"He's looking for one. Has his eye on the Syrian military command."

"Becoming a Dux requires senatorial rank," I said.

"Aye," said Helvius. "He's working on that. He'll have to put down an uprising or something of that sort. Prove his mettle, kill some prosperous revolutionaries, and then increase the tribute to Rome when their property escheats to the state."

"Most of all, he wants control over the Jerusalem Temple," said Baltanius.

"What about Vitellius in Syria?" I said.

Helvius nodded, touching his temple. "Aye," was all he said.

My boorish companions talked well into the night. I asked a servant if there was another amphora of wine, and she nodded. By the time it was gone, I knew my own life was in danger. I left them snoring on their couches and placed a shekel into the palm of the senior steward, a dark-skinned man from the Indus. He had been present all evening and I was certain he had overheard enough that without his acquiescence I would not leave the palace unharmed. He bit into the coin. "To the stables?" he asked.

I nodded. "And five more if you get me out of here safely and quietly."

Within minutes I was leading Nefer out of the palace. I left Caesarea by night with a full belly, a headache (one cannot entirely pretend to drink and be believed), but at least my head was still connected to my neck. Tomorrow, should Pilatus send riders, I wanted to be in Phoenicia, where the information I had gleaned might ensure a welcome reception by the Syrian Governor.

I was pleased. Palace intrigue in Judea was child's play compared to Alexandria, where I had successfully navigated its murky waters my whole life. But my heart was heavy. I did not know Jeshua as an adult; I did not know his inclinations, whether they leaned toward the opulence of palace life or the austerity of a desert community. If he was the one Antipas had killed, my hopes were dashed. Yet I *did* know Jeshua well enough to know him as careful. I could not imagine him stirring up revolution, but neither could I see him running from one. In my mind he was becoming complex, and I realized I now knew nothing about him beyond his name. Was he a peaceful ascetic, living in the desert, discussing religion? Was he a desperate fighter, leading skirmishes against the Tetrarch's army? Was he a simple carpenter in some forgotten village in the Galilean hills? Or was he dead, along with his sweet mother and loving father?

If that final possibility was the truth, I felt sure I would not live much longer myself.

FORTY-TWO

I rode through the night, expecting to hear hooves pounding behind me at any moment. I could not say what I would be arrested for, but I was sure Pilatus would think of something. My head ached, my cold had resurfaced, and I felt terrible. Plus, it was raining.

When dawn arrived, the mountain of Karem El ("Vineyard of El") revealed its forested flanks, its summit lost in the dripping clouds. A road wound along the seaside slope above sheer cliffs that ended in a rocky jumble far below.

Mesha once told me a story about the priests of Ba'al and Hashem's prophet Eliyahu and a great battle that took place on the summit of Karem El. Of course, Hashem prevailed, and the pagan priests were put to death. After finishing, he smiled as if to say, "So watch your step!"

I laughed then, but I was in no mood to laugh now.

By noon of the next day, I rounded the promontory that formed an arm of the Bay of Akre. Ptolemais lay at the northern end of the bay, boasting a fine harbor. The Hebrews knew the town as Acco. It was one of the few cities they were unable to subdue when they swept into Canaan fifteen hundred years before. But Alexander conquered it and renamed it after his friend Ptolemy, the despised inventor of Serapis.

I arrived in Ptolemais well after sundown. After stabling my camel, I retired, exhausted and feverish. But before putting out the lamp, I consulted a map I had purchased. Galilee began where the wet coastal plains rose into the drier highlands. I scanned the village names, but none seemed familiar. Holding the lamp closer, I was dismayed at how many towns there were, far more than I could reasonably visit. Tzippori was underlined, which meant it was notable for some reason. It was about halfway to Lake Tiberias, the eastern border of the Galilee. I would go there first. If there were trade-guild offices, I might be able to find Josef or his son through them.

I lay back, trying to breathe shallowly so as not to excite my cough, musing about the ships in port. One of them was surely bound for Alexandria. The salt air would clear my sinuses, and I would recuperate. Back home, I could purchase a small villa and a slave or two. Maybe even litter bearers. I would find something to do with my time as I waited for it to run out.

What lunacy had taken me from such a comfortable life in the first place?

I was awakened when the innkeeper looked in my room to see if I was still there. It was almost midday. Seeing me in bed, he apologized and shut the door. I sat up stiffly, slowly rotating my sore knee and feeling my neck crack as I turned my head. My hands were practically useless after my long ride yesterday, though my arthritis was always bad in the mornings.

I finally made my way downstairs and into the dining area. I thought it was empty, but then I heard a familiar voice: "Serapion? Is that you?"

I turned, and there was a man about my height but three times my girth, his arms open, his dark eyes flashing. He hugged me fiercely. "Balthazar?" I asked.

The man pulled back. "Who? Don't you remember your old friend Honorius? Poseidon's navigator and kraken slayer!"

"Honorius?" I asked. "What are you doing here?"

"This is a *port*, Melkorios! The better question is, what are *you* doing here?"

"I am traveling," I said, finding a seat at a table.

Honorius snapped his fingers. "More food!" Then, to me, "Are you all right?"

"I have a cold, that is all. And I am old."

"You're not ten years older than I," said Honorius, sitting down opposite me.

"Yes, but those last ten years . . ."

"I'll avoid them," he laughed. "Now, by Dio's beard, what brings you here?"

I was so used to hiding my true intentions that I found it difficult to reveal them to anyone, which was ridiculous, for I had known Honorius for forty years. "Friends," I said. "A tekton I knew in Alexandria who hailed from Galilee. I am here to visit him."

"A laborer?" said Honorius doubtfully. "Where does he live?"

"I do not know."

Honorius looked at me blankly. "Then he will be hard to find."

"He left Alexandria years ago, and I wanted to renew our acquaintance before I . . ."

"Became emperor?"

I ignored the joke and continued. "His name was Josef, and he had a son named Jeshua. The boy had the most astonishing natal chart I had ever cast."

Honorius raised his eyebrows, for he was, like most Romans, deeply superstitious, and being a sailor, doubly so. However, his superstition had the salutary effect of making him a merry fellow, for if one's destiny truly is in the hands of the gods—as every sailor feels his is—worrying was thus a waste of time. "You cast my chart years ago," he said. "Dead accurate. Except for the part about money—I'm still poor as Diogenes." (You will recall that Diogenes was the Greek philosopher who had no personal property, preferring to drink from the hollow of his hands rather than possess a bowl.)

"You are still alive, my friend," I said, giving him the answer I always gave the poor.

"I might ask the Teacher," he mused. "Maybe he can teach me how to be rich."

"The Teacher?"

"That's right, you wouldn't know about him," said Honorius. "An Essene fellow wandering about the countryside, casting out devils and curing the sick. Maybe I'll get him to cast a chart for me." He smiled and so I knew he wasn't serious.

But I was. "What is his name?"

"The Jews call him 'Rabbi.' "

"Was he not killed by Antipas?"

"Who's he?"

"Tetrarch of Galilee, son of Herod the Great."

"Oh, you mean the old sod they call 'the Adulterer'? Well, it would be a pity if the Rabbi's dead. I need a chart."

"I will cast your chart in exchange for passage home," I said, surprising myself.

"I'm not going home. I'm headed to Sidon, then Byblos, then Athens. *Then* home."

"That will be fine."

"It will have to be a spectacular chart," said Honorius.

"It will be," I answered. "When do you sail?"

"Tomorrow morning at the changing of the tide." He shook my hand fiercely. "Let's dine tonight. Right now, I must oversee the loading—we are taking horses up to Sidon. I have not yet arranged a cargo from there, but you know me, I'm a lucky one." He lifted his eyes heavenward. "By Poseidon's fork!" he said, standing and striding out of the inn.

❧ ❧ ❧

I did not dine with Honorius that evening, because his work at the docks went long. He sent word, however, that he would be sailing the next morning before the second hour. If I was going, I would have to be at the docks by then.

I arose early the next day, a part of me still dismayed as to why I was leaving when I was so close to achieving my purpose. But my purpose was foolishness. I had no idea where Josef and Miriam lived, or if they were even alive. Jeshua might be this wandering Teacher, or he might not be. And even if he were, he was likely dead.

By the time I reached the stables, my mind had sealed the argument. My whole life had been a fool's errand, believing in the unbelievable. *That is why I should go home*, I reasoned. *Be done with these childish superstitions once and for all. Grow up and be a man.*

While the stable boy went to fetch Nefer, I asked a groomsman if there was a market for camels in Ptolemais. He trotted off for his master. The old fellow arrived with a ledger book under his arm, just as the stable boy arrived with Nefer, saddled and ready to go.

He gave Nefer a cursory look. "I don't have much call for camels."

That was an untruth. I had seen caravans from Gaza to Ptolemais. "Pity," I said. "She is very strong. Though I rode her all the way from Alexandria, and she is still in fine condition."

The stable master examined the camel's toes, then straightened. "Twenty denarii."

"I paid forty," I said, "but I will take thirty."

"Just because you got cheated, do not expect to cheat me. She is too small for burdens."

"She is best for passengers."

"Yes, but the caravans around here carry cargo. People ride horses."

I frowned at him, but then thought, *What do I care? Ten denarii are nothing.* I nodded and the old fellow opened his tablet and withdrew a piece of parchment. "Need a receipt?"

I shook my head. "Coin will suffice." He withdrew the money from his purse, handed it to me, then walked away. Suddenly, I heard myself ask, "Have you lived here long?"

He turned. "All my life."

"So you know Galilee?"

"As well as you know you just made a good deal," he said.

"I am looking for someone," I said, shaking my head at my foolish hope. "He is a tekton, nearing fifty by now, by the name of Josef."

"From where?"

"Galilee, is all I know."

The old fellow pinched his cheek. "His father wouldn't happen to be old Heli, would he?"

"I do not know his father's name."

"Heli was a good old boy. When I was young, he and his brothers built a house in Cana for relatives of mine. We children would play nearby, sneaking a few timbers here and there to build a playhouse of our own. He caught us, but instead of whipping us, he built us a little cottage, complete with a plaster roof and a window. Even made a door out of an old table."

"From where did he hail?"

"Nazareth."

I remembered Nazareth from my map. It was not far from Tzippori, where I had been heading anyway. "How big is Nazareth?"

The stable master laughed. "Smaller than its name—a few houses."

I thought hard as the stable master looked at me. I had not decided what to do until he said, "You will be needing a horse."

FORTY-THREE

At the docks, Honorius was dismayed at my decision. He queried me at length about what I was expecting to accomplish, but I told him little and promised I would cast him a chart when I returned to Alexandria. Satisfied, he shook my hand and bade me farewell.

I returned to the stable, got my new horse, threw my belongings over its flanks, and set out toward the Galilee highlands. It was eighteen miles to Sepphoris, an Aramaic translation of the Hebrew Tzippori, which means "bird perch" because it sits on a hillock amidst the rolling farmland of the Beth Netofa Valley. When Herod died, there was an insurrection in Galilee. As punishment, Sepphoris had been burned to the ground. When Antipas received his portion of his father's kingdom, he rebuilt the city, naming it Autocratis ("Imperator") after Caesar. But my map carried the old name: Tzippori.

It was cool and cloudy as I climbed into the highlands. In sharp contrast to the dry and rocky south, the hills of Galilee were green and smooth. Red anemones and yellow tulips were bunched on the hillsides. I soon found myself in the Beth Netofa, a shallow valley running east to west. In the distance was Sepphoris, perched on her hill. At a crossroads north of town was a Roman garrison, from the looks of the earthworks.

By late afternoon, when I turned south at the crossroads, Sepphoris had fully revealed her beauty. She was a white crown nestled on a green head. Columned buildings dominated the summit and amphitheater arches filled the western slope. An aqueduct ran into the southern hills. As I entered the city, the sun was setting, and the sky was turning from orange to scarlet.

After stabling my horse, I found a tavern. It was crowded, and the barman was rude, but a patron overheard me questioning him and came over. "You won't find the king here," he said, motioning for the barman to fill his cup, then nodding at me to pay. I put two quadrans on the counter. The barman took it, and my new companion emptied his cup.

"Which king?" I asked in Aramaic.

"Your pronunciation gives you away. Your native tongue is Latin."

It was not, but no matter. I switched tongues and repeated, "Which king?"

"Antipater, of course. We call him Antipas. What king were you looking for?"

I wondered if it was safe to talk openly of Jeshua. The fellow to whom I spoke, a beefy man with small eyes, was prosperous enough to know Latin but cheap enough to exact payment for a conversation. I did not trust him. "There are so many," I said. "I cannot keep them straight."

"From the looks of you, you know which way the road turns," he said, taking a fold of my cloak sleeve between his fingers. "What's this material?" I pulled my arm away. "What brings you to Sepphoris, friend?" he asked.

"Visiting friends, *friend*," I said. I was irritated by his familiarity. I had already bought him two drinks, and he had yet to tell me anything worth knowing.

"Oh," he said. "What are their names? Maybe I know them."

"I doubt it, but you *could* tell me the name of the Sepphoris ethnarch."

"That's Neri, but he's licking Antipas's boots in Tiberias. If you want information, I'm your man." He held out his cup, but I ignored it, determined to get something for my trouble this time.

"Is there a tradesmen's guild here?"

"I wouldn't know," he shrugged. "I'm a merchant."

"How about a civil register—public records and the like?"

"You could check at the new basilica, where the Cardo meets the Decumanus."

"The Cardo was colonnaded, right?" I asked.

"So is the Decumanus," said the man, setting his empty cup down hard on the table.

I ignored his demand. "How far is it?"

He simply looked into his cup, smiling.

I left the tavern and walked up the Cardo. The close-set buildings on either side were shops with residences above. As I approached the city center, a square opened up before me. On my right was the amphitheater I had seen from afar. I heard shouts and the sound of swordplay as a drama unfolded inside. Fronting the theater was a fountain of Diana pouring water from a pitcher. Surrounding it were carts of food vendors. To my left was a new basilica, its white columns above many steps showing no weather stains.

I found the doors locked. I returned to the square and bought a piece of flatbread topped with a garlicky meat from a vendor, then sat on the fountain edge, considering my options.

"Are you enjoying our town?" asked someone.

I turned. Before me was a man in a dark cloak. He had a narrow face and a sharp nose and wore a striped prayer shawl over wiry, graying hair. He leaned on a staff.

I got to my feet and bowed. "Shelama. I am Melkorios."

"Welcome to Judea," said the man. He sat next to me, leaning on his staff between his knees. "I am Rabbi Sadoc. That is my synagogue." He nodded at a dilapidated two-story wooden building wedged uncomfortably between the amphitheater and the basilica. "You are far from home, citizen."

"And I thought my clothes drew no attention," I said.

"What is your destination? Not Sepphoris, I'd wager."

A gambling rabbi, I thought. *Not Mesha's sect, certainly.* "What makes you say that?"

"I saw you exit the tavern. If you had friends here, they would have advised you against patronizing that particular establishment."

"I am going to Nazareth."

"Nazareth," said Sadoc. He said it as if the word itself pained him.

"Do you know a tekton there named Josef? His father's name might have been Heli."

Sadoc stiffened. If I hadn't been looking at him, I would have missed it. He knew I had seen his reaction, so he could not dissemble. "I knew him. His sons worked on the basilica you see before you."

My heart raced. "What were his son's names?"

Sadoc shrugged. "I cannot recall. They did not attend my synagogue."

"Was one named Jeshua?"

Sadoc, undoubtedly prepared for this, did not flinch, which told me all I needed to know. I pressed my advantage. "You knew him."

Sadoc pursed his lips. Just then a great shout came from inside the amphitheater and the crowd cheered. "That might have been his name. As I said, I didn't know them well."

"I have heard he was dead. Killed," I said.

"That doesn't surprise me," said Sadoc. "He was always in some sort of trouble—little respect for tradition." He looked at me. "You believe in tradition, don't you, Serapion?"

It was my turn to flinch. "What?"

"I've heard your name before, uttered in the halls of power."

I was not sure whether to believe him or not.

Sadoc continued. "I don't know about Jeshua, but his father has been dead a number of years. An accident, I believe."

"What about his mother, Miriam?"

"Sorry," said Sadoc, rising. "I really couldn't tell you. You are far from home. I hope you find your way back safely."

He walked across the square, his staff clicking on the pavement. An actual *darkness* seemed to surround him, or maybe it was just his haughty manner. A few moments after he entered his synagogue, a lamp was lit upstairs. There was movement behind half-closed shutters. I wondered if he was watching me.

Most of my meal was uneaten, but I had lost my appetite. I decided to think of more pleasant things. I wondered what play was being presented inside the theater. A tragedy by Euripides? Or perhaps one of Aristophanes's marvelous comedies?

I would soon find out, for at that moment a great fanfare blew, and people began streaming out of the amphitheater. Most wore togas, though a few wore chitons. Still others wore the tunics and striped cloaks favored by Jews.

I spied a young man exiting the theater with an older rotund man. They wore fine togas, but the fat man's bore the gamma design, a symbol of rank. He got into a sedan chair. I threaded my way through the crowd, reaching the younger man just as the litter disappeared down a dark street. "Who was that?" I asked.

"Neri, the Ethnarch. Why?"

I muttered a low curse. *That* was the man I needed to see.

"You have business with him?" asked the man. His head came only to my chest.

"Tomorrow will do," I said, turning away.

"He's going to Jerusalem tomorrow."

I turned back. "Who is in charge when he is gone?"

"He has assistants."

"Are you one of them?"

"Me?" laughed the man. "No, I'm merely a farmer."

"Yet you are friends with the Ethnarch," I said, noting that the quality of his silk toga rivaled many of mine.

"I would be friends with all men," he said. "Salve, citizen. I am Naaman of Cana."

"Melchior," I said curtly. Naaman smiled up at me. "What are you smiling at?" I asked.

Naaman's smile opened into a broad grin. "You are a great man, Melchior."

"How do you know?"

"Because of the way you treat people."

I blanched. I wasn't treating him all that well at the moment. My encounter with the rabbi and my disappointment at missing the Ethnarch had made me forget my manners.

Naaman went on, "I have learned to treat people not as they are, or even as they think of themselves, but as they *could* be. And when I do, they rarely disappoint."

I sniffed. "And if the man you are treating so well is a thief and a liar?"

"Then he will reveal himself anon, but I nevertheless try to give better than he gives me."

"And you have tested this risky philosophy?"

"Yes. And lest you think me a fool, know this: For most of my life, I treated people as they deserved and got *exactly* what I expected in return—mistreatment and misery."

I smiled at his frank admission and felt I could trust him. "Then treat me better than I deserve, Naaman. Perhaps you can help me find someone, a man from Nazareth."

Naaman's face brightened. "I know some—"

"Though I fear he is dead," I added.

Naaman's face drained of color. I led him to the fountain and sat him down. He seemed unable to speak. Finally, after a time, he found his voice. "Jeshua!"

I was stunned. "You knew him?"

"He is my most valued friend! Dead, you say?"

"It is just a rumor—"

"It cannot be! I saw him in Cana two weeks ago!"

"Perhaps this is a different Jeshua," I said. "It is a common enough—"

"His father is Josef, his mother Miriam," blurted Naaman. "His brothers are Judah, Simeon, and James." He looked at me in despair. "Who killed him?"

"I have been told it was the Tetrarch."

Naaman shook his head. "No. Antipas wouldn't kill him. Jeshua saved his life, right over there." He pointed at the basilica. "A wall collapsed during construction, and Jeshua pushed Antipas out of the way."

"Are his parents alive? They would know, would they not?"

"His father is dead, but his mother sometimes travels with him."

"Travels? Where? Doing what?"

"Why, he's the Rabbi, of course. Spreading his logos to all who will hear."

Logos. The Greek word with a dozen meanings: reason, thought, speech, logic—it even meant the matter from which the universe was created.

"What is his logos?" I asked.

But Naaman was too upset. "He can't be dead!" he lamented. "It cannot be true!"

I put my hand on his arm. "I am not even sure it was the same person."

"It cannot be!" he said, jumping up. "I must tell Neri!" He ran off, leaving me at the fountain in the now empty forum. I thought to follow, but he was young and swift and soon disappeared. Tomorrow, if this was the Jeshua I was seeking, and he *was* the Rabbi, news of his death would fill the city. Others would then confirm what I now only suspected.

I rose and trudged back to the inn. I looked to see if any birds flew in the southwest quadrant. I saw none, but it was night, and birds do not often fly at night.

But what if evil comes at night? I wondered. *What augurs can the darkness bear?*

A sliver of moon was hazy behind a scrim of clouds, but no stars were visible—another bad omen. I pulled my cloak around me. I was reaching the end of my journey, and what seemed to be waiting for me were not rest and peace, but death and disappointment.

FORTY-FOUR

When I rose the next morning, I expected the city to be abuzz with news of Jeshua's death, but it was not. On the street, I inquired about the Rabbi, but few knew much about him. He was not known to visit Roman cities like Sepphoris, Ptolemais, or Tiberias in his travels. Yet these were the largest cities in Galilee. Where else *would* he go?

Nazareth was a half hour's ride south, in the range of hills separating the Netofa from the Jezreel Valley. Cyprus and evergreens lined the ridge top. The hamlet of Nazareth was nested on the summit, surrounded by rocky hills. I looked for Miriam in a line of women at the spring just outside of the village. I did not see her, and no one gave a start of recognition when I pulled down my hood and showed my face.

I looked for craftsmen's shops. There was a tanner, a dyer, two smiths, but only one carpenter's shop. There did not appear to be any public buildings. At the far end of town, I got off my horse and noticed an old woman standing a few paces back, a water jug on her hip.

"Peace be unto you," I said in Aramaic, bowing.

She said nothing.

"Salve, domina," I said in Latin.

Nothing.

"Shelama," I ventured in Hebrew.

She strode toward me. I almost took a step back, because though she was barely half my height, she seemed quite angry. "What do you want here?" she barked in Aramaic.

"I am seeking someone," I said.

She glared at me.

"May I help you with your water?"

"I don't need your help."

"But I would like to," I said. "In exchange for information, perhaps."

"Follow me, then," she said, and marched off, leaving her amphora on the ground.

I picked up the jug, amazed at its weight, and led my horse down the narrow street after her. I marveled at how easily she had carried it on her bony old hip. I trudged along, moving the jar from one arm to another, never taking my eyes off her. She was soon far ahead. At the edge of town, she passed through a gate. I saw a stone barn. Next to it was a home with a thatched roof.

She pointed at the barn. I stepped through the doorway. Men were working a press, and the smell of crushed olives filled the air. A man took the jug from me, thanking me in a language I did not understand. I walked outside. The woman faced me, still angry. "What is it you want?" she growled.

"I am looking for a family I once knew. A tekton named Josef and his wife."

"Miriam," said the woman.

"Yes," I said, elated. "They lived here?"

"He died five years ago."

"I am Melchior—"

She looked at me as if I had just emerged from a sealed tomb. "You're him!"

Finally, my fame had preceded me, if only in Nazareth. I bowed. "What is your name?"

"Esther," she managed. "You're the magus, just as Miriam described! She said you were very tall and regal." She peered closer at me. "But she said you were always clean-shaven, which is why I didn't know you."

"How is Miriam, and where can I find her?"

Esther glanced at a low stone wall at the rear of her property. The wall was whitewashed, indicative of a necropolis. "She's with her son."

Without another word, I set off toward the cemetery. I did not look back. I had caused the poor woman enough distress for one morning, and I was too sad to talk anyway. I had lost three of my best friends in one day and I needed to grieve.

Unlike the well-tended City of the Dead in Alexandria, unkempt grass clotted the small Nazareth graveyard, hiding many sepulchers. As I walked from one tomb to another, looking for familiar names, my heart thumped. All three, dead! I lamented a world that let an old fraud like me live and took all the good people. I thought of Thaesis and Athena, whose ashes had been thrown into the Nile; of Mesha's bones in their cubbyhole; of the funeral pyres of my parents and two sisters, long dead in various accidents of age, illness, child-bearing, and disease.

Yet I still walked the earth, unwelcome in either the darkness of the Duat or the light of Elysium, where Thaesis and Athena ran among fragrant flowers. Was I sentenced to remain alive, like Prometheus, to have my liver torn out daily by the eagle of regret, only to have it grow back each night to be tortured again tomorrow?

I could not find the sepulcher and sat on a hump of grass, my sadness too deep for tears. I was astonished at the pointlessness of it all. Thoth did not record the deeds of men. Anubis did not weigh their hearts. Ammit did not devour the wicked. Osiris did not welcome the worthy into his presence or condemn the wicked to eternal coma. The earth simply revolved on its wobbling axis around a star. The sun's warmth was a lie. When the harvest was reaped, no matter what we had sown, we would be as chaff, lifted into the mindless wind. The earth abided, but man did not.

"Dominus?" came Esther's voice.

I did not turn. "What?"

"Did you find him?"

"No. It does not matter."

"He is here."

I turned. She was pointing at a grave marker at her feet. I got up. "Who is it?"

"Josef."

I walked over to her. The marker was a featureless basalt slab, its edges overgrown. Esther knelt and began pulling the grass. "I was here last week," she said, "but it comes back so fast."

I joined her, my knees popping as I knelt, and began pulling a creeper, bright with tiny white flowers, making its way across the surface of the stone. "They are all here?"

"Josef, and one of Miriam's babies, dead at birth," said Esther.

"Where is Jeshua's body?"

Esther sat back on her haunches. "He is not dead!"

"I was told that a man—an Essene, they said—had been killed by the Tetrarch. In Sepphoris, I learned he was called the Rabbi."

"Those are two different men," said Esther. "The Essene was Johanan, Jeshua's cousin."

"Johanan?" I exclaimed. "Son of Zechariah and Elisheba?"

"Yes," said Esther. "He had quite a following until Jeshua began teaching. Johanan gave way, disappearing into the desert for a time."

"And so Jeshua is the one they call the Rabbi? And he is all right?"

"For now," said Esther. "But there are those who would like his fate to follow Johanan's."

She went on to explain how Antipas's second wife Herodias—"His brother's wife!" she exclaimed bitterly—and her daughter Salome had conspired to have Johanan killed, tricking the Tetrarch, who was too much in love with Herodias to deny her anything, even if it meant killing Hashem's prophet.

"But Jeshua is all right?" I repeated, just to be sure.

"Yes!" said Esther. "But he is in danger—his teachings offend people. Powerful people."

"Like Antipas?"

"Certainly, but he's a greater threat to the Jewish rulers. The Sadducees in Jerusalem—they run the Temple and the Sanhedrin—hate him because he's too conservative. And the Pharisees, who hold sway out here in the countryside, dislike him because he's too liberal."

"So when you said his mother was with him—"

"When I saw you enter the cemetery, I knew you had taken my meaning wrong," she said. "At present, Jeshua and Miriam are somewhere to the east. He often stays in Kepar Nahum, a fishing village on Lake Kinnereth, what you Romans call Tiberias. But he has followers everywhere, though few walk the halls of power."

"A man who challenges the powerful needs powerful friends," I said.

Esther smiled at me. "Then it is fortunate you've come."

Esther took me to Miriam's home. Her youngest daughter Hannah lived in the walled compound with her husband and family. As we entered, Hannah, with the dark hair and pale complexion of her mother, came down the steps from the living quarters, holding an infant in her arms.

When we had been introduced, she said, "You're just as I imagined you," and gave me a kiss on the cheek, surprising me. "I'm sorry to be so forward," she said, "but I've heard so much about you, I think of you as family." And with that she handed me her baby, swaddled in a blanket. I rocked him uncomfortably for a moment and gave him back.

"Will you stay for dinner?" she asked.

She was so much as I remembered her mother that I was speechless. I did not deserve the honor she was prepared to bestow upon me.

Esther saw my discomfort and made an excuse, saying I was in a hurry to find Jeshua. Hannah took my hand in hers, holding it to her cheek and closing her eyes. "I wish I had seen Alexandria. Jeshua always says it was the most wonderful place."

I nodded. My hand burned in hers, and I felt a compulsion to escape. Esther took my arm and said, "He will return after he has visited your mother and brother."

When we were back on the street, I was silent. Seeing Hannah, such a similitude of her mother, reminded me of how many times over the years I had ached to see Miriam again.

We were nearly to Esther's home before I finally found my voice. Unfortunately, all I could speak of was an irrelevancy: "Josef worked in the Great Library," I said. "I introduced him to Hero, the inventor."

"He never spoke of it," said Esther.

"He was so curious! Whenever I saw him at the Library, he was talking to a scholar."

"Hmm," said Esther.

"He could have been a scholar himself," I said.

"He was a carpenter," said Esther, "which is far more useful."

When we arrived at her house, I used her story against her. "I must go," I said. "I am eager to catch up to Jeshua and Miriam."

"Roll that carpet out under the sycamore," she said, heading inside. "I'll be back."

I did as I was told. She soon returned with two bowls of lentil stew. She filled my cup with water and went back inside for bread and apples. When she returned, we ate in silence for a time. I looked up at the heart-shaped sycamore leaves.

"You have no idea what you've done, do you?" said Esther.

"Oh," I said ruefully, "I know full well what I have done."

"You worship the wrong god."

"I regret worshiping any god at all." I glanced at her. She seemed unfazed.

"Remember what the Siwa Oracle said to Alexander? 'The son of God has come!' "

I was surprised. This woman from a village in a frontier province had just quoted Strabo. "Yes," I said, "and look what happened to him: dead at thirty-three."

"Yet he was great."

"Was he?" I asked idly. Her point, whatever it was, did not interest me. I munched an apple and watched as the workmen inside the barn slowly turned the olive press.

"Greatness is not only knowing what *should* be done, but overcoming fear and *doing* it. All great men have done so: David, Alexander, Caesar, Jeshua bar Josef."

I began to be interested. "What does Jeshua fear?"

"Sometimes he fears his destiny," said Esther. "And you?"

I shrugged. Not much, anymore.

"You have a destiny too, Melkorios."

I nodded. "My destiny, as yours, is to die," I said, as if it were an indisputable fact.

"Your destiny," said Esther, "is to serve Hashem! He led you to Jeshua. He guided you back to Egypt, saving the lives of Josef, Miriam, and the Moshiach! Why do you doubt?"

"Perhaps because I have seen too much."

"Seen too much and learned too little! You confuse knowledge with wisdom."

"I always thought knowledge *was* the path to wisdom."

"*Truth* is the path to wisdom," she said. "Find Jeshua. He will teach you."

"Teach me what?"

Esther fixed me with her gray eyes. "To be unafraid."

ORTY-FIVE

I stood on the Nazareth summit looking out over the Beth Netofa Valley. The day was cool, the sky was clear, and the valley floor rolled like a peaceful green sea. The island of Sepphoris glittered like a gem in the afternoon sun. The road descended from the overlook, one branch dropping steeply toward Sepphoris, the other sloping gently toward Lake Tiberias, unseen behind the eastern hills. At the foot of those hills, perhaps ten miles distant, was a village. It was as far as I would go this day, starting as late as I did.

As my horse picked its way down the path, I thought about what Esther had said about Jeshua. He must have changed a great deal in the last twenty-three years. I knew him as a precocious child, full of questions. Now, he apparently had all the answers. I wondered how he had learned so much.

I remembered our visit to the Valley of the Kings, the moon bathing the canyon in silver light. Jeshua spoke of souls awakening. I was moved then. But that was when I still believed.

The pain of loss returned. I shook it away. I did not want to be burdened by the past or fearful about the future on this spring day. I wanted to live in the present, to find happiness with the sun on my face and the hope of seeing a long-lost friend.

By nightfall, I reached the village I set my sights on earlier. Behind it, the land rose, then descended into Lake Tiberias, which was reportedly *lower* than the Green Sea!

"How can that be?" asked someone after dinner. "Wouldn't the ocean flow into it?"

A stocky man with thinning hair said, "The mountains bar it." His name was Esau, and he was an overseer at an estate near Cana, a town I had heard of somewhere. I spent a good part of the evening trying to recall where.

"So, if an earthquake cracks these mountains behind us," said another fellow, "then my house, which is on the shore in Magdala, will float away?"

"The way *you* built it, yes," said Esau.

Then I suddenly remembered where I had heard of Cana. It was from the man I met outside the theater in Sepphoris, the one who got so upset when I told him Jeshua might be dead. I wished I could tell him that Jeshua was unhurt. Then it occurred to me that Esau, being from Cana, might know the man and give him a message. But what was his name?

"Melchior," said Esau at that moment, "You said you know the Green Sea. Is there enough water in it to drown Peniel's house?"

"We'll start digging the canal as soon as may be," said another man with a long beard. He laughed in great explosions that reminded me of Balthazar.

"First work *you'll* ever do," said Peniel.

There was another round of laughter, followed by another round of drinks. In my usual way, I drank little and listened. I was thinking about the young man in Sepphoris whom I had alarmed with the dire news of Jeshua.

When our group broke up for bed, I followed Esau out to the courtyard, where we joined servants warming our hands at a fire. Esau took particular interest in their opium *narguileh*.

"Esau," I said. "You hail from Cana, correct?"

"Don't tell me you've been there," he said.

"No, but I met a fellow last night in Sepphoris who also hails from there."

"What was his name?"

"I cannot remember," I said. "He was thin and short, with curly hair that encircled his head like a laurel wreath." Esau furrowed his brow. "He seemed to know the Sepphoris Ethnarch."

Esau snapped his fingers. "The well digger!"

"Who?"

The servants finally noted Esau's interest in the water pipe and handed the wand to him. He took a long pull, then turned to me, exhaling luxuriously. "Naaman!"

"Yes!" I said. "But a well digger? He looked quite prosperous to me."

"He wasn't when I met him," said Esau. "He was just a hireling. He accused one of my laborers of stealing something from him, something he claimed to have buried on *my* property."

"Your *master's* property," I corrected.

"His in name, mine in use," said Esau, unperturbed. "Well, Naaman complained to the rabbi, but he wouldn't say what had been stolen. That being the case, the rabbi said there was nothing he could do. That's when Jeshua had a clever idea."

I knew Jeshua was a common name, so I did not react. I simply nodded for Esau to continue. Nevertheless, my heart began to gallop in my chest.

"Jeshua said if Naaman would help him finish the well, he'd pay him the value of whatever it was he'd lost, and if Naaman wasn't satisfied, Jeshua would submit to his judgment."

It *sounded* like something Jeshua would concoct. I looked up at the stars, once again surprised at the confluence of life's many rivers.

"After many days, they finally struck water," continued Esau. "It poured in fast, and Naaman got scared and pulled the rope down on his head. Jeshua climbed down and saved him." Esau paused. "I don't know if he's rich, but I've seen him with the Ethnarch, Neri."

"Is there not a man they call the Rabbi, whose name is also Jeshua?"

"One and the same," said Esau, reaching for another draw on the water pipe, then turning back. "A remarkable fellow."

"I knew him," I said. "In Alexandria."

Esau peered at me in the dim firelight. "You're the *magus*! Jeshua spoke of you. Tell me, can the Pharos really cast a light thirty miles out to sea?"

I laughed, surprised at the turn in conversation. "Yes, it can," I said.

"And the Library—is it as large as they say? Bigger than the Temple of Jerusalem?"

I nodded. "Have you seen Jeshua?"

"He used to stop by now and then, but with the army he has now, he must know I couldn't feed all of them. Haven't seen him in ages."

"Army?"

"Followers," said Esau. "Mostly poor folk, as well as a bunch of fisherman he hooked." He laughed. "I don't mean to mock, but Jeshua was always impractical. When he offered to pay the value of what Naaman had lost without even knowing what it was, I knew he was not cut out for commerce. He's a talented tekton, though—dug me a fine well."

"When did you see him last?"

"Not since Naaman's wedding, years ago. It was held at my estate." He paused. "Jeshua is more than a teacher, you know—he's a capable magician."

Perhaps the opium was starting to take effect. "Magician?" I asked.

"I didn't see it myself, but I believe it," said Esau, taking another pull from the opium wand. "Naaman turned out to be all right. He and Jeshua became friends. He had no family, so when he got married, Jeshua's mother—"

"Miriam?" I interjected.

"Yes, Miriam," said Esau. "Well, she volunteered to manage the wedding feast, and I said they could have it at my place. But she underestimated the number of guests, and they ran out of wine. Jeshua told her to fill six water jars from the well—the same well he and Naaman dug, by the way—and so they did. Then he told the servants to fill the guest's cups from the jars." He paused, as do all good storytellers, for effect.

"Yes," I said, feeling strangely resistant to this story.

"Now I knew nothing of this. I was with the guests. And when the wine finally came, I was surprised. It was wonderful! I clapped Naaman on the back, saying that most hosts serve the best wine first, and after everyone has drunk, *then* they bring out the poor stuff. But he had saved the best for last! I toasted him, but I should have toasted Jeshua!"

The opium had done its work. "You are saying Jeshua changed the water into wine."

"That's what I'm saying," said Esau.

"But you did not see him do it."

"No, but I tasted it."

"Did Naaman see him do it?"

"No," said Esau. "But he drank it too."

"So you all drank wine drawn from a well."

"No, we drank wine changed from water drawn from a well."

"You said you were all drunk."

"I said we *had* drunk," he snapped, "not that we *were* drunk." He frowned. "You don't know Jeshua at all, do you?"

"I know him well enough to know he would not play tricks on a bunch of drunken fools!"

Esau clenched his fists. "It was his friend's wedding!" he spat. "A friend who—unlike you—actually *knew* him!" And with that he stomped back inside the inn.

I watched him go, my heart thumping, having probably narrowly escaped a beating at Esau's hands. I turned to the servants, who were still standing around the fire, speechless at our dispute. One of them offered me the narguileh wand. I batted it away and walked into the darkness.

FORTY-SIX

The next morning I intended to ask Esau what *really* happened at the Cana wedding, but he had already left. Disappointed, I set off eastward. At the summit of the hills, a marvelous vista opened before me: a shallow basin containing a harp-shaped blue lake was surrounded by green hills. The lake was ten miles long and perhaps half as wide. Fishing boats plied its waters.

As the road descended to the lake, I passed farms surrounded by low stone walls. To the northeast, the snow-capped peak of Mt. Hermon glittered. Tiberias, the provincial capital, hugged the southwestern lakeshore. A fortress stood at the water's edge—the Tetrarch's palace, no doubt. I thought of turning toward the city, but Esther said Jeshua frequented a village at the northern end of the lake named Kepar Nahum—Nahum's Village.

So at the shore, I entered one of the many fishing villages on the lake. Magdala was no more than a few buildings and a dock, which was currently empty, all the boats out on the lake. Leaving my horse at the shore, I walked out onto the dock to stretch my legs. After a few minutes, I heard footsteps

A young man with side curls was approaching. "Shelama," he said.

"And unto you, peace," I said.

"We need help," he said, gesturing at a woman sitting on a low rock wall near my horse.

I turned away, disgusted. Beggars.

"Please, dominus, my wife is sick," he pleaded.

I glanced at her. She looked healthy enough, and so did he. "What do you want?"

"We are far from home," he said. "We're on our way to Jerusalem for Pesach."

"May your journey be safe," I said, turning away and ending the conversation.

I heard his footsteps recede. I turned and watched as he trudged along with slumped shoulders. *Beggars!* I thought. *Have they no pride at all?*

The youth helped the girl to her feet and shouldered a duffel. Theirs was an elaborate act, with the shuffling and bowed heads. I would rather he came up to me and boldly said, "Give me money!" than watch this obvious ruse.

But their posture, he with his arm around her, she with her hands folded across her stomach, was familiar. Then it struck me—she was pregnant. I cursed and strode down the pier, shouting, "Wait!" They turned. I held my money pouch aloft. "I will help you!"

As I approached, the boy lowered his head. "We weren't begging, sir."

"Then what do you want?"

"My wife needs medicine. She's pregnant."

"So you *were* begging," I said, some of my former resistance returning.

He shook his head. "I will work for whatever you give us. You looked wealthy, and I thought . . ."

I folded my arms. "What kind of work can you possibly do for me?"

"I know about horses," said the young man. "Yours is lame."

"She is just slow."

"She favors her left hind leg."

The horse was indeed standing with that hoof slightly raised. "What is your name, son?"

"Daniel."

"Well, Daniel, if you are right and you can help her, then I will pay you what is fair."

Daniel smiled and took his wife's hand. "This is Miriam."

I looked up, shaking my head. Miriam was a common name in Judea, but a striking coincidence just the same. I bowed and she lowered her head in response.

We found a stable in Magdala, and I bought what Daniel needed to care for the horse. I stood watching as he worked salve into the horse's hock and cannon. He raised the hoof and half closed his eyes, running his fingers across the underside. Then he showed me an infected crack in the soft tissue of the frog. I chided myself for not more carefully examining the mare when I bought her in Ptolemais. As Daniel treated the cut with a black gum, I asked about the horse's general health. He said it was fair, but I should not push her. "How far are you going?" he asked.

"I am not sure," I said, looking at Miriam, who was seated beneath a poplar tree in the dooryard, hands on her stomach. "You should not be traveling so close to her time," I said.

"If it's a boy, we must go to the Temple anyway," said Daniel. "To present him to Hashem."

I turned to the stable boy. "Fetch your master."

I followed the boy to the house, where I conferred with the stable master. When I returned, Daniel was in the dooryard helping Miriam to her feet. "I have something for you," I said. The boy appeared in the stable doorway, leading a donkey.

"For us?" said Miriam, her voice rising with emotion.

"For you," I said, nodding for the boy to hand Daniel the rope.

"You are too generous," said Daniel.

"Then perhaps it will make up for the times I have not been generous."

Miriam burst into tears. Daniel put his arm around her and looked up into my face. "You know him," he said with certainty.

"Know whom?" I asked, my chest suddenly tight.

"The Rabbi," said Miriam, raising her head from Daniel's chest.

I felt suddenly weak. I put my hand on the donkey to steady myself. "Jeshua?"

"I heard him teach," said Daniel. "North of here, where two hills form a valley at the lakeside. He spoke to thousands of people. He shared his logos."

"What is his logos?"

Daniel led Miriam back under the poplar, and she sat again. Daniel said, "He spoke to my heart. At times his words were like honey; at others, sharp like hunger. He spoke of being a light unto the world."

I thought of standing with Jeshua at the top of the Pharos.

"Then he spoke of the Law of Moshe."

"The commandments from Sinai," I said.

"He told us we were now bound by a higher law: As killing was wrong, so was being unjustly angry. As adultery was wrong, so was lust. As revenge was wrong, so was not forgiving those who injure us."

I was confused. According to Rabbi Mesha, the Law of Moshe was eternal, but Jeshua had swept it away, replacing it with new, impossible standards. I wondered how it was received by the crowd. My answer was in Daniel's eyes, which shone as he said, "Then he said, 'You have heard that you should love your neighbor and hate your enemy. But I say unto you, love your enemies, bless them that curse you, do good to them that hate you, and pray for them that persecute you.' " He stopped, tears welling. "I'm sorry," he said. "It was powerful."

"Go on," I said, feeling some of the same power.

"Then he commanded us to be *complete*, even as our Heavenly Father is complete."

"Heavenly Father?"

"Hashem," said Josef. "Jeshua said we are not Heavenly Father's servants but his children. And as children, he has promised to help us, if we ask."

I began to see the power and the peril of Jeshua's logos. His teachings were as far from Judaism as Judaism was from Serapism. Instead of a list of prohibitions, they were affirmative, designed not only to change behavior but desire as well. "This is very hard doctrine," I said.

Misunderstanding my statement as a criticism, Daniel said, "We should go." He led the donkey across the dooryard, followed by Miriam. Just before they passed through the gate, she whispered something to him. He shook his head, but she turned and walked slowly back to me.

"There is something I wish to tell you," she said. "What Daniel would not talk of, because he was asked not to by Jeshua, was that when he said he heard Jeshua teach, that was true. He *heard*, for Daniel has been blind since birth."

I remembered his sure touch and how, when he looked up at me, his eyes rarely met mine.

"He was so moved by the teachings," said Miriam, "that he asked Jeshua to heal him."

I could not help myself. "Were you there?"

She nodded. "Jeshua scooped dirt into his hand, spit into it, and kneaded it into mud. Then he rubbed the mud on Daniel's eyelids and told him to go wash in the lake."

I looked at Miriam. This was no drunken jokester at an inn; this was an honest woman. "From that moment on, Daniel could see," she said.

I did not know what to say.

"I tell you this because you are a believer," she whispered. Then she turned and joined her husband and they left my sight.

I sat down on the ground, all strength gone from my legs.

FORTY-SEVEN

As I rode north out of Magdala, I pondered Jeshua's radical doctrine. Love your enemies! It was ludicrous, and yet he no doubt meant it, for I knew him. I also knew Herod, Alexander, and Caesar—men who do not count the cost of the lives of others. How could the two worlds collide and Jeshua's logos survive?

I found the protected cove of which Daniel spoke, where the grassy hillside flowed down to the lakeshore. Had Jeshua truly given sight to him where I now stood?

In Alexandria, Hero built machines that fooled the gullible. In the Serapeum, a patron would ask a wooden bird a question. Then he would spin a wheel, forcing air through an unseen pipe, and the bird—nothing more than a flute, really—would "sing" if the answer was yes. But if the answer was no, a pontiff hiding behind the mechanism would disengage the pipe, and the bird would remain silent. Over the years, the device earned thousands of drachmas for the Serapeum.

Likewise, for Jeshua's miracles to be false, he would need accomplices who pretended to draw water from wells or to be blind. I never saw dishonesty in Jeshua, though honest boys can grow into dissembling men.

But I did not believe Jeshua's miracles involved chicanery. That left just one explanation: Jeshua was a sorcerer. Somehow he had obtained power from the Underworld. Perhaps he studied under a Persian necromancer. Perhaps he had mastered the mysteries of the Udjat, the Eye of Horus.

Or perhaps Hashem was the One True God, as the Jews claimed.

Perhaps all the other gods, including Serapis, were mere fictions and only Hashem existed.

Kepar Nahum was still hours away. As the sun westerned, I rode along the shore. My shadow stretched out before me, arriving at each point moments before I did. Was Jeshua such a shadow, preceding the arrival of this new god who would supplant the old ones? Would his "Heavenly Father" conquer the world with love?

I clucked my tongue. On my most credulous day I had never believed in such a world. That could mean only one thing: Jeshua was not only a sorcerer, he was also mad.

Nahum was located just west of the Jordan River, which flowed into Lake Tiberias. Though I arrived after sunset, men still sat on the docks, mending their nets by lamplight. Normally, I would seek an inn, but tonight I intended to find Jeshua's home, where I would be greeted with food and fellowship. Though the town was large, I knew how to find a Jew: ask a rabbi.

The synagogue was not far. The two-story building, with its triangular pediment and fluted columns, was Greek in design. I knocked on the double doors. One of them opened and a bearded man appeared, pulling his prayer shawl from his head.

"Shelama," I said.

"How may I help you?"

"I am looking for a man called the 'Teacher.' I have been told he lives in Nahum."

The rabbi shook his head.

"You know him?" I asked.

"I know him," he said, closing the door.

My age and station have generally required that I do with subtlety what younger men do with force. But I was growing impatient. I grabbed the door, preventing it from closing. The rabbi glared up at me, but said nothing. "Tell me where he lives," I said.

"He is not in Nahum."

"Do you know where he is?"

"No," said the rabbi. "Please leave."

I strengthened my hold on the door. "Do you read *Torah*?"

His face reddened. "What do you know of *Torah*?

"I know it commands kindness to strangers."

The rabbi folded his arms across his chest and glared at me.

"Do any of Jeshua's followers live here?"

"No," said the rabbi. "I have a very small congregation."

I peered beyond him at the carved pillars, marble floors, and golden candelabra. I whistled admiringly. "But a wealthy one."

"It was a gift," said the rabbi.

"From whom?"

"A Roman, like yourself," said the rabbi. "The centurion at the garrison. He's a friend of the Teacher. Ask *him* where he is!"

And with that he pulled the door from my grasp and slammed it shut. I turned and faced the street. I had met a few rabbis in my time, and no two were the same. This one seemed abnormally agitated about Jeshua. In addition, he had greatly offended me by calling me a Roman.

On the western bank of the Jordan was a garrison that policed the border between Galilee and Gaulanitis. Earthworks surrounded the camp and two soldiers guarded the entrance. I told them I had a message for their commander from the Nahum rabbi, and one of them went to alert the centurion. The soldier shortly returned and took me inside the palisade, directing me to the Praetorium at the edge of the parade ground.

Presently, the tent flap flew open, and the centurion appeared. He had brown eyes and wore woolen trousers, or *braccae*. His muscular chest was bare. He motioned for me to enter and sit, taking a seat across from me. The furnishings were spare: two chairs, a cot, a map table, and the legion standard—a gold eagle clutching a lightning bolt in its talons.

"So, then," said the centurion, placing his hands on his thighs. "The rabbi."

Seeing his serious manner, I had been thinking that my lie was foolhardy, but I was committed. "I just left him," I said, in the authoritative voice I affected at the Serapeum.

"How is old Dizahab?"

"He thanks you again for your generosity to the Synagogue."

The centurion waved it away.

"He recommends me to you. I am Melkorios Alexandreus, Vizier of Egyptian Prefect Cestius Galerius."

"Lucius Claudius Aquila, centurion of the Lion Cohort, Syrian province."

"Salve, centurion," I said.

"Look," he said, "I've got a full day tomorrow."

"I am seeking the man they call the 'Teacher,' Jeshua bar Josef, of Nazareth."

Aquila frowned. "What is it?"

"Dizahab said you might know his whereabouts," I said. I had determined to put as much truth into my lies as possible.

Aquila considered me. "You're far from Egypt. What brings you here?"

A chill slipped down my spine. Perhaps Dizahab had sent me to one of Jeshua's fiercest enemies. I gulped back my fear and ventured, "Is Jeshua here, under your . . . supervision?"

"I wish to Dis he *were*!" exclaimed Aquila, gesturing heavenward. "Here, I might be able to protect him. But out there," he said, nodding at the world beyond the tent flap, "he's got the Jews running in circles. Whatever they say, he says something better. Whatever they do, he outdoes them. Whatever they think up, he already thought it. And whatever they believe, he actually *lives* it."

"I see," I said. "It would be hard to protect such a man."

"But he doesn't stop there," said the centurion. "He performs miracles."

"Miracles?" I asked.

"Oh, let's see," said Aquila, ticking it off on a finger. "Not long ago, he fed a crowd of people with just a few fishes and couple of loaves of bread."

"How many were there?" I asked.

Aquila shrugged. "Far more than there was food for, that's certain."

"But you weren't there."

"No, but I've seen things with my own eyes as well."

"What things?"

Aquila's eyes took on a hard cast. "Who is Jeshua to you?"

"He is my friend," I said. "I knew him in Alexandria."

"Nonsense! He's never been out of the province!"

"His parents lived there when he was a child. They left many years ago, and I have come to see him again, before it is too late."

Aquila stiffened. "What have you heard? Is there a plot?"

"No," I said. "Too late for *me*."

The centurion leaned back, considering what I had said. "Servius!" he shouted suddenly, giving me a start. A young blonde man entered wearing a little bronze placard on a chain around his neck. "His name isn't really Servius," said Aquila. "It's some unpronounceable gibberish." He looked at Servius, who returned his gaze evenly. "He's the best slave I ever had, and I love him like a son. I've cared for him since we captured him in

Britannia. He was just a boy. I brought him back to Rome with me, had him schooled, and offered him his freedom years ago. But he won't accept it—says he'd rather be my slave than a free man."

I wondered what this had to do with Jeshua, but I didn't have to wait long. Aquila continued: "A while back, he got sick with a fever as hot as Pluto's furnace. He thrashed around, out of his mind, burning up. I sat at his bedside for three days, certain he was going to die. Doctors couldn't do a thing; all they wanted to do was let blood, smother him in poultices, and stink up the place with incense. Nothing was working." Aquila ran his hands through his hair.

"I'd heard of the Teacher," he continued. "I'm not a religious man. Do you see a family shrine here? No, you don't. But that doesn't mean I don't believe in the gods. I do. I've seen too many things not to not believe in something bigger than man because, by Janus, we *need* something bigger than man. Am I right?"

I thought that was arguably true, so I nodded.

"So I went to see Jeshua and got down on my knees. I told him I'd killed many men, some justifiably, some not. I told him I was not worthy of his help, but Servius was. I told him the boy was dearer to me than my own life. And I told him I'd do anything he asked, if he'd heal him. Then he lifted me to my feet and told me to lead the way. But I said no, he didn't have to come. I said I was a man of authority, and when I ordered something done, it was done. I said if he would just say the word, then I knew Servius would be healed."

Aquila got to his feet, wiping his eyes, for the story had overcome him. He put his hand on the youth's shoulder. "He said the word, and Servius was healed at that very moment."

For the second time that day, I was astonished beyond words.

Forty-eight

I lay in my tent, staring at the canvas ceiling for hours before finally fall-ing asleep. I could doubt Esau's water-to-wine tale as drunken hyper-bole, or Miriam's tale of Daniel's healing as youthful naiveté, but the centurion was as sober and serious as a skirmish line. He did not seem the sort of man who was easily deceived, nor did his tears feel false. My bones told me he was being truthful. Had the boy who threw rocks onto the Great Library roof grown up to be a miracle worker?

Reveille awoke me. I looked out my tent. Troops were mustering on the parade ground. I dressed and requested my horse. It had been fed and brushed, and I gratefully accepted help getting into the saddle.

Outside the garrison, the road was busy with travelers waiting to cross the river. I got in line and asked a man where everyone was going.

"To Jerusalem for Pesach. I go every year," he said proudly.

When my turn came and the ferry deposited me at Beth-Saida, I looked back across the river at Galilee. Puffy clouds sailed across the sky. Fishing boats dotted the lake. Nahum's market bustled. Tiberias glistened on the far shore. And beyond the green western hills lay Nazareth, where Jeshua had lived for twice as many years as he had lived in Alexandria, working with his father in their carpentry shop. I doubted he had ever gone back to school.

And yet, they called him "Teacher." How *had* he obtained the arcane knowledge he undoubtedly possessed? There *must* be an explanation.

I wished I had not burned his chart in Sinai. I longed to look it over again. I must have missed something when I predicted that he would reign as a king, when everything he was doing was taking him in the opposite direction: enraging the rabbis by working miracles outside the Jewish priesthood, aligning himself with the separationist Essenes, and nullifying the Law of Moshe. This was a strange path indeed for the heir to the Jewish throne.

He *must* have a plan that had escaped me, one that would take him to the halls of power by another route. I would ask him when we met. I spurred my horse southward along the eastern shoreline road. Seeing the number of people in transit, I realized where I would find Jeshua: in Jerusalem.

By late morning, dark clouds had gathered over the lake, and it began to rain. I took shelter under an oak tree to wait out the storm with a dozen other travelers. Standing near me, two women, one old and one much younger, were conversing. The younger woman pointed at the lake, which was obscured by driving rain. "It was just like this, and it arose just as quickly."

"I heard this before," said the older woman. "I didn't believe it then either."

"As you will," said the young woman, "But I do."

"I heard he only calmed the storm," said the elder. "I never heard he walked on water!"

"Shut up, you two!" scolded a bald man whom I took to be the young woman's husband.

She turned away from him. "He did both," she whispered, "just not at the same time."

"Of course not," whispered the older woman. "Why walk on water when it's pouring rain? Destroys the effect if no one can see you!"

"Milcah's brother-in-law was on that boat, and he swears it happened."

"Swears what happened?" asked the older woman.

"That he calmed the storm."

"But was he there when he walked on the water?"

"Yes, but that was another time."

"What's his name?"

"Matthew," said the younger woman.

"The publican?" snorted the older woman. "You believe *him*?"

"Milcah says Matthew is an honest man, even if he is a tax collector."

"I'll tax you both if you don't shut up!" said the husband. His wife was about to speak, then closed her mouth, looking vaguely past me toward the lake, gray behind the sheets of rain.

The older woman, aware I had been listening, turned to me. "Did *you* see Jeshua walk on water?"

I shook my head. Behind her, the bald man folded his arms and frowned.

The storm did not last long, and that evening I arrived at the village of Gergesa. There was no caravansary or public house, so along with many others, I rolled out my bedroll in a sodden pasture.

By noon the next day, I reached the southern end of the lake and entered the town of Kepar Semah. It was larger than Gergesa and boasted a paved *agora* where I bought flat bread and a poisonous wine, which, after sampling, I threw away. A Vestal temple faced the market, its wooden columns painted to look like marble. Through the doorway, I saw fire in the hearth, attended by two priestesses. Semah was a Greek town, and few Jews lived there.

There was a commotion behind me, and I turned. A young man was herding swine through the agora. I suddenly remembered that I had never performed an extispicy to confirm Jeshua's birth chart. Balthazar had chided me for it thirty years ago. Well, better late than never.

"Salve!" I called, walking over to the herdsman. "Any of these for sale?"

"All of them!" he said. "Five assarions each!"

That was less than half a day's wage hereabouts. "Five? You are sure?"

"All right," he said. "Two for five!"

"I only want one," I said. "What's wrong with them? Are they diseased?"

"No!" he said. "Look!" He turned a pig around, showing me. Indeed, it looked just fine. "These are the ones that survived the leap."

"The leap?"

"And there's no sign of possession."

I was startled. "They were possessed?"

He nodded. "I ate one, to see if the spirit would enter me, but it didn't."

He did not tear at his skin or try to bite himself as madmen often do. I leaned forward, sniffing for wine.

He pulled back. "I've not been drinking."

"What is this about, then? What 'spirit' are you talking about?"

He looked at my coin purse. I withdrew a mite, handing it to him.

"Follow me," he said. We were out of town before he would speak again. He let the swine graze near a brook. "I live up there, in Gadara," he said, pointing at the eastern hills. "A man was possessed of a spirit. He wouldn't let anybody cut his hair, so we called him Lasea, which means 'shaggy.' He lived in the cemetery and ate bugs and shouted in an unknown tongue. His legs and arms were bloody from sharpening stones on himself. At night, he would howl like a wolf. My father said we should put him out of his misery, but my uncle said calamity would befall us if we hurt him. So we asked the Apollo flamen, and he said the gods had cursed Lasea and that there was nothing we could do." He looked at my coin purse again. I gave him another mite. He stowed the money and said, "So we sent for the Teacher."

I dared not speak, but nodded for him to continue.

"He spoke to Lasea, and Lasea answered in words we could understand. 'What have I to do with you?' he cried. 'Torment me not!' We all quailed, for he looked like he might strike the Teacher. Then the Teacher said, 'What is your name?' And Lasea said in a low voice, 'Legion, for we are many.' "

I shuddered. I once tried to cure a demonic woman. We had luck for a time with blood lettings and restraints, but soon she was overcome again, clawing at her skin, screaming that she had to get out of it. In the end, we poisoned her to release her to the gods.

The swineherd continued: "Then the Teacher said, 'Come out of him,' and the spirits said, 'Don't take our home!' But the Teacher insisted, so they pointed at my pigs and said, 'Let us go into those.' I begged the Teacher not to do it, but he acted like he didn't hear me. He whispered to Lasea, who fell to the ground like he was dead. Just then, my swine galloped off down the hillside. Everyone stood staring, except me, because they were *mine*. I chased them down the slope. They ran straight off a cliff, like they were hoping to fly, and most drowned in the lake."

He knelt and ran his hand across the hair bristles on a swine's back. "But these are all right," he said. "They swam out. If you want one, it's only two assarions."

I did *not* want one of those swine. I began to back away.

"Any one you want," he said.

I shook my head.

"All right!" he said. "*One* assarion!"

But I turned and walked as fast as I could toward town.

Forty-nine

The next morning, I neared Philoteria, a crossroads town where one branch of the road continued west to Tiberias, the other turning south along the western bank of the Jordan River. Most people turned that way, but it meant another busy river crossing and it was well into evening before I reached Kepar Agon, a village in the west bank river bottoms. As before, there were no inns, and even if there had been, it was unlikely I would have found lodging, for the road was choked with people.

As I made a solitary camp a league past the village, I was overcome with melancholy. I missed my bed; I missed Thaesis and Athena; I even missed the Serapeum. My despair was heightened by a conversation I had had on the road with a man who declared that the world was flat and that the sun revolved around it. When I corrected him, he asked me from where I hailed.

"Alexandria," I said.

"What would a Spaniard know about astronomy?" he said.

I ignored his geographic ignorance and told him about Eratosthenes measuring the earth with a stick's shadow. When I finished, he called me a fool and rode on ahead.

At first I was angry, but then I realized he was right. I *was* a fool. I had believed in many foolish things: Serapis, Osiris, Apep, Jupiter . . .

But was I fool enough to believe these wild tales about Jeshua? The stories filled me with hope and fear, sometimes at the same moment. Jeshua had power—that much was certain—even if it was only to deceive the credulous. Yet, his teachings felt *right*, if impractical. Above all, they were dangerous to *him*. Multiply the hatred the Nahum rabbi had for Jeshua a hundred times, and you might approximate the hatred of Josef Caiaphas, the High Priest of Jerusalem. He would do more than close his ears to Jeshua's doctrine.

Jeshua may be more foolish than I, I thought, and despair overcame my melancholy. I sat on the riverbank, staring at the moving water, and wondered where I would end up if I fell in. The Jordan emptied into the Salt Sea, from which there was no outlet. The metaphor was plain: I could not escape my destiny, and even if I tried, I would still end up at a dead end.

"Shelama," came a voice in Aramaic.

I turned around. A long-haired man in a threadbare tunic stood behind me. I scrambled to my feet, grabbing my staff. "I have no money," I said, trying not to cower.

"That's unwise. Journeys are expensive, especially long ones like yours." He leaned against a tree trunk and folded his arms. "You are the Egyptian."

"Who are you?" I asked.

"I am Shimrith, which means 'Guardian.' "

"And whom do you guard?"

"Someone who has enemies."

"Well," I said, "whoever he is, he has no reason to fear me."

"Yet you inquire of him all along the Kinnereth Road," said Shimrith. He tucked a hand into his belt, just inside his cloak. I did not doubt he had a knife there.

I gripped my staff tighter. "Who are you talking about?"

Shimrith looked past me. "I served the Forerunner," he said, "but he is dead now."

I exhaled with relief. "Johanan," I said.

"One of your people killed him," said Shimrith flatly.

"*My* people?" I exclaimed. "The Tetrarch is a Jew, is he not?"

Shimrith shrugged. "He serves Rome. As do you."

"You know nothing of me," I said. "If you did, you would know I am a friend to both Johanan and his successor."

"He has no successor," said Shimrith, taking a step toward me. His hand came out of his cloak and, sure enough, it held a long, curved dagger.

I backed up, raising my staff. Who *was* this man? Who was he protecting if not—

"Jeshua is his master. It is he who sent Johanan to straighten the way."

I was confused. Were there *two* Jeshua's? No, Jeshua knew Johanan—they were cousins. Perhaps he *did* send Johanan. "All right," I said. "I meant no harm."

Shimrith was unconvinced. "What do you want with the Moshiach?"

"Nothing," I said, taking another step back, glancing over my shoulder. *I might yet find myself in the river*, I thought. "I am his follower, as you are!"

Shimrith shook his head. "For a Roman, you lie badly."

Something welled up inside me then, and I abandoned hope. I dropped my staff. "You are right," I said. "I am not his follower. I do not believe."

"That is obvious," said Shimrith.

"Yet, I have come in *search* of belief! If that is not enough reason to live, then . . ."

"Then what?" asked Shimrith.

I shook my head, knowing I sounded pathetic.

Shimrith must have thought so too, because he sheathed his knife and stooped, picking up my staff. "Without belief, your journey will be very hard," he said, looking out across the river. "Johanan baptized here."

"Baptized?" I asked.

"For the forgiveness of sins," said Shimrith.

What Serapis does with fire, I thought, *Adonai does with water*. Same difference.

"One day a man came to this very spot, asking to be baptized. I had never seen him before, but Johanan, who knew him, told him he had no need of forgiveness."

"You are speaking of Jeshua," I said tentatively, though I knew it for a certainty.

"I was confused by Johanan's words," continued Shimrith, "for do not all men sin?"

"All I have known," I said.

"But Jeshua insisted, saying all must be born again. So Johanan immersed him, and when he came out of the water, we gathered around, asking questions."

I had a few myself, but I dared not interrupt a zealot with fire in his eyes and my staff in his hand. I remained quiet.

"Then we heard a voice," said Shimrith, his eyes bright with memory, "which seemed to come from within our own breasts, though our ears heard it, and we looked to the heavens."

Shimrith was looking at the sky above the swift river, red now with sunset. "A dove descended from the sky," he continued. "And the voice said, 'This is my beloved son!' " He turned to me and his eyes were filled with certainty.

"*Whose* son?" I asked.

"Good fortune in your travels," said Shimrith, handing me my staff and walking away.

I was on a barque on a river under a starless sky. Everything glowed a pale, luminescent green. The barque was poled by faceless men and steered by falcon-headed Horus. Amidships, under a canopy, sat green-skinned Osiris on his throne, the flail and crook crossed on his lap, his tall, knobbed crown flanked by the two feathers of justice. Drums pounded and the smell of sulfur made my eyes water. I was in the Duat, and we sailed the Keku Samu, the River of Death. The shore was crowded with upright sarcophagi.

Suddenly there was a thrashing, and the stern was pulled hard to the left. I peered into the darkness behind us to see the source of the disturbance. Swells began to rock the barque. The polers struggled to keep us straight in the water. Soon, waves crested the gunwales as Horus struggled with the tiller. Osiris sat placidly on his throne, apparently unaware of the danger.

A wave breached the ship, soaking me. I grabbed onto Osiris's throne, fearing I would be washed overboard. The polers dug harder, their backs glistening in unearthly green light.

I heard a hiss as if from a great steam kettle, and the air was suddenly fetid and sour. Apep's giant head appeared above the boat's wake, its red eyes glowing, its tongue flicking out of a fanged maw. I shut my eyes and whispered, *Osiris, save me. Isis, save me. Horus, save me. Nephthys . . .*

When I opened my eyes, Apep still loomed high above, his cowl extended. Acid saliva dripped from his fangs, striking my bare shoulder. I screamed, clawing at my skin, which burned like fire.

Just then, the barque struck something, and I was hurled forward, slamming my head against Osiris's throne. Green stars burst brilliantly, then winked out.

When I awoke, I was on my back. I expected to see Apep looming above me, but he was gone. So were Horus and the polers. The barque slid swiftly along in the Keku Samu. Osiris sat like a statue on his throne, facing the front of the barque. I reached out to touch him. Suddenly, his head jerked back. I got to my feet slowly and peered over his shoulder. A serpent was coiled in his lap. Two dots on Osiris's chest dripped blood. Apep had struck the King of the Underworld!

I stumbled back, grabbing onto a canopy support. The serpent's head rose above Osiris's shoulder, and its eyes met mine. It was Apep, no less terrifying at this size than he had been before. A shriek died in my throat. My legs would not move. Apep slithered onto Osiris's immobile shoulder, his head bobbing slowly, preparing to strike again.

He reared back, and I screamed. Osiris's hand shot out, grabbing the serpent behind the head. Apep screeched, jerking from side to side. A great battle ensued, Apep snapping at Osiris and Osiris holding the snake at arm's length, squeezing. Finally, the red light of the serpent's eyes was extinguished, and Osiris dropped the lifeless serpent to the deck. He leaned back in his throne, exhausted.

I found myself at the tiller. In the greenish glow, I saw numberless sarcophagi on the shore as we passed. One by one, their lids opened, each cavity filling with white light. A mummy stirred, straining at its fetters. Another sat up. As we moved past the endless row of coffins, the dead came forth. Many stood upright, burial linens dropping off their bodies. Faces appeared—not those of a desiccated mummy, but the visages of living souls.

In the dark sky, a star appeared. Its fierce white light cast a shadow behind me. Then, in another part of the sky, another star appeared, casting a complementary shadow. Then another star, and still another, until a thousand distinct shadows were splayed out around my feet.

Then, suddenly, all the shadows were extinguished but one. Blinding light emanated from the golden throne. Osiris faced me, the flail on his lap and the crook in his hand. He no longer wore the Atef crown, but a different one: two ram's horns encompassing a sun disk.

Osiris had become Ra, the Sungod.

I heard singing. On the shore, countless people knelt, many still bound by burial linens, their hands raised as we passed, their voices lifted in praise. My own knees gave way, and I felt Osiris's eyes upon me. I dared not look at him. I raised my hands; I was unworthy. I shook my head; I was unclean. I lowered my face; I was an unbeliever. Then I felt the golden crook under my chin, gently raising it. I looked into the face of Osiris, expecting death. Instead, I received life.

It was Jeshua.

I came to myself on the riverbank, staring into river of stars above me. The trees shifted in the night breeze. I could not move. I was no longer a man but a vessel of love. The weakness that had been me was gone, burned away by the incandescence of Jeshua's logos. All that was left of me was love.

I was changed forever.

But then my hand moved, and tears filled my eyes, for I knew that though I would not forget the dream, the memory of the love in Jeshua's eyes would fade. My bones, which had been melted by his acceptance, were hardening again. My hands, warmed by his humility, were stiffening with cold. My heart, which had been filled with hope, was emptying. I let out a sob.

Not even the most powerful dream of my life would change me. Though I had seen eternity, I was still trapped inside myself.

FIFTY

In the morning, I arose listlessly and joined the pilgrims moving slowly south along the Jordan River. As my horse plodded along, I pondered my dream. Jeshua as Osiris? Osiris ruled in the Underworld. If Jeshua was Osiris, then an earthly kingship was impossible.

At midday it started to drizzle. I longed for Africa's cloudless skies. The rain continued into the night, and I crouched under a tree with my cloak over my head, shivering. When I awoke in the morning, clouds hung low, but the rain had stopped. I got to my feet, weeping tears of agony at the pain in my back. It took a long time to get on my horse. Dizzy with the effort, I guided her onto the muddy road, falling into step with the other travelers. It wasn't long before I dozed, my head bowed nearly to the horse's mane.

I awoke. A youth held the reins of my horse. "You almost fell off."

I looked around. "Where are we?"

"At the Beela ferry crossing," he said. "Where the Harod joins the Jordan."

I looked west. The cliffs bordering the valley had given way to an intersecting valley, the Jezreel. Farther south the land rose again to the Samarian highlands, now obscured by clouds.

After the crossing, the road skirted a number of shallow lakes. It was humid, and soon I was soaked with sweat. My stomach was empty, and my head ached. The only sound was the sucking of feet being pulled from mud—the river road had become a mire.

By afternoon, I started looking for a path branching away from the road. I would never get a dry bed if I remained with the multitude. And if I could get a decent meal, I would gladly die later in that bed. What was I thinking, an old man traipsing around this impoverished country in this abominable weather? If this was his kingdom, Jeshua was welcome to it.

Just before dark we came to an inn, a one-story building surrounded by stables. I dismounted and hobbled toward the door, which stood ajar. The crowded interior smelled of wet clothing and cooking food. Servants delivered cups of watery wine and bowls of steaming porridge to shouting patrons.

The proprietor yelled at everyone to shut up and wait their turn. I approached him and asked if there were any rooms. He shook his head and turned away. I opened my money pouch and tapped him on the shoulder. He turned, shouted at me in a strange tongue, and shoved me.

I fell sprawling onto the floor, my pouch knocked from my hand. Coins rang as they bounced across the flagstones. A maelstrom of shouting and grasping erupted. Someone kicked me in the head, and another stumbled across my legs. When I got to my feet, my money had been recovered, though not by me. I looked around. No one met my eyes, but I saw many fists closed around my money. The innkeeper smirked at me.

"You have effectively robbed me, sir," I said.

"Shut up, *mamser*," he said, then turned and shouldered his way through the crowd.

My jaw dropped. He had called me a bastard! I looked around in shock. Those whose eyes would meet mine glared hatefully at me. "I have been robbed!" I shouted, driving my staff into the stone floor, the metal tip ringing above the din.

Someone shouted, "Good!" and laughter erupted, all of it directed at me.

I left, using my staff to clear the way. It felt good to jab it into the back of a man who stood between me and the door. He turned, saw the fire in my eyes, and stepped aside.

Outside, stars peeked through gaps in the clouds. I mounted my horse and headed south. The road was empty, and I was glad; I was in no mood to see another person ever again.

After three miles, a narrow road branched off to the right and rose into the Samaritan hills. If I took it, I would be rid of the stink of the Jews. I thought about Jerusalem, which doubled in size during Pesach. I had a better chance of finding Jeshua in Alexandria. I looked into my money pouch. Still empty.

My back ached, and I had a lump on my head from where I'd been kicked. I was tired of bad food, inclement weather, and the arrogant Jews. I was done—I was going home.

I turned onto the spur and climbed into the foothills.

The steep trail was in poor condition, with many ruts and washouts. Clouds hung low; there was no moon. On my left were the dark outlines of boulders; on the right, nothing but darkness. My horse slowly picked its way along, head down. I feared she would stumble and throw me into the abyss, so I began looking for a place to make camp.

Where the road turned back on itself, I spied an evergreen with a carpet of needles under its low-hanging branches. I cleared a hole in the needles and built a small fire, warming my stiff hands. When the fire died, I curled up under my cloak and fell instantly asleep.

I awoke, my nostrils stinging with smoke. My fire was blazing—and so was the tree! Flaming debris was drifting down on me. I threw off my cloak and crawled out from under the tree. I limped to my horse, which was hobbled nearby. A great *crack!* startled me, and I turned. The tree exploded into flame. The horse shied, and I put my hand on her withers to calm her, then realized dully that my saddle and cloak were under the tree, which now burned like a torch.

I heard noise and turned. Two men were approaching on horseback. They stopped just beyond the firelight, dismounted, and walked toward me.

"We wondered where you were," said one.

"Thank you for the sign," said the other.

Now the fire lit their hard faces. I stepped back, stumbling over a rock. I lay on the ground, looking up at them, knowing it was useless to beg for mercy.

I did anyway.

Gratefully, I have little recollection of what happened, only of blows raining down on me and the iron taste of blood in my mouth. When I awoke, it was dark. I could open only one eye. I looked around. The tree smoldered, burned out. I was lying face down in the middle of the trail. My horse was gone. I rolled over, and the pain in my shoulder was so intense I fainted.

When I awoke again, it was day, and I was looking up at a brown sky moving slowly past me. A cloud of white flowers drifted by. Near the horizon, a shadow kept pace with me. I raised my head and saw, just before passing out again, a man walking upside down, his feet striding along the brown sky.

"Easy!" said a voice. "He's broken enough already."

Hands gripped my shoulders and feet, and my head was cradled. I was being carried.

"Is he dead?" asked a woman's voice.

I sighed with relief. Isis had met me at my death. Now she was taking me to the Keku Samu. I must have been unconscious when Anubis weighed my heart. No matter—I had emerged from the judgment justified. Ammit had not devoured my soul. They were carrying me aboard the Sektet boat where I would join Osiris on his journey through the Twelve Gates. And in the morning, I would join Thaesis and Athena in the Field of Reeds.

As I was lowered into a warm cloud, I smiled. I was home at last.

FIFTY-ONE

Are you alive?" asked a man's booming voice.

"If I am," I whispered, "blame Anubis."

The man laughed so hard I winced. I could not see; both my eyes were swollen shut. A hand grasped my shoulder. I imagined an enormous man standing over me. I pried my right eye open. Before me stood a giant. Gray hair hung to his shoulders and his beard, white near the chin and gray at the tips, was so long he could have tucked it into his braided belt. He leaned forward. "So you *can* see! Things are looking up for you!" His voice had an innate merriness to it, and my spirit could not help but be lifted. I tried to smile, but my lips cracked, and I tasted blood.

"Now don't get carried away," he said. "Time enough to curse Anubis. I'm Zebulon. I found you on the road near Aser."

"Melchior," I mumbled.

"What possessed you to travel at night?"

I recovered some wit. "*You* travel at night."

"Yes, but I'm a Samaritan," laughed Zebulon. "This is my country. You, on the other hand, are *not* a Samaritan—you've been doubly cursed!" He laughed again.

"My shoulder," I moaned.

"Separated," said Zebulon. "Deborah put it back in place and bound it."

I closed my eye. I did not speak for a time.

Then came the voice of Isis. "Is he awake?"

The bed moved as someone sat. I opened my eye and saw a beautiful woman with wavy black hair. Her green eyes shone behind long lashes.

She was not the cold and distant Isis; she was Diana, and she held a bowl of vegetable porridge. She leaned forward, "Can you eat?"

I had never before felt so ugly and old as when she spooned the porridge between my cracked lips. I could only guess at how bad I looked, but she gazed at me as if I were her own father. *Her grandfather*, I thought miserably, unable to look away from her emerald eyes.

"I've seen that look before," chuckled Zebulon.

"What look?" she asked.

"You know what look I mean."

"He's grateful, that's all," she said, dabbing at my mouth with a napkin.

"He certainly is," said Zebulon. "For many things."

I awoke again. It was night. An oil lamp burned at my bedside. I was in a room with a window opposite the bed. My tunic was on a chair, my sandals on top—all of my worldly possessions.

Yet, I *had* been lucky. Perhaps the gods had not abandoned me entirely. Or perhaps they were not done punishing me yet. I fell asleep again with that cheerful thought in my mind.

It was midmorning. I had been dozing. The swelling of my face had gone down, and I could now open my right eye. My left arm was bound tightly across my chest. I could wiggle my fingers, but not without pain. When I lifted the poultice over my left eye and felt underneath it, I made a horrifying discovery. There was a depression where my eye should have been. My heart filled with despair, and an agonized moan escaped my lips.

Deborah entered the room, followed by a young boy with a tray. "Melchior?" she whispered. "Can you eat?"

I opened my eye. Her hair was gathered loosely at her neck with an ivory comb, and her eyelids were shaded green with malachite. In Alexandria, she could have passed for a woman of wealth, but here in Judea, a woman who wore makeup and did not cover her head was probably a *lupa*—a prostitute. She gave me a morsel of bread. It tasted of cinnamon. I nodded weakly.

"He likes your bread, Mother," said the boy.

She gave me another bite and told me what had befallen me. Samaritan robbers keep watch for Jewish travelers straying from the Jordan road. Because of the enmity between the two people, the robbers saw themselves as righting past wrongs.

"Why the hatred?" I asked.

"The Jews destroyed our Temple," said Deborah. "And every time we rebuilt it, they came and destroyed it again. Some Samaritan men plot to destroy the Moriah Temple, but it is too well guarded." She paused. "But you are a Roman and don't care about these things."

"I am a citizen of the Empire," I said, "but I am Greek, not Roman. I live in Alexandria."

Deborah's eyes opened wide.

"Yes," I said, guessing her question. "The Pharos is as tall as they say."

She blushed, and I fell in love in that moment, though it was a father's love, for there was a sadness in her eyes that I knew had been etched there by men. Many men, I guessed.

"You are far from home," she said, then noticed her son looking anxiously at her, aware of what had passed between us. "It's all right," she said, shooing him away. He left reluctantly.

"He is protective of you," I said.

When Deborah looked back at me, some of the warmth had left her eyes. "With reason."

"A boy should care for his mother," I said. "You have other children?" She nodded.

"And they have different fathers," I said.

She looked out the window. It was late afternoon, and a golden light had settled on everything. She stood abruptly. "Can you feed yourself?"

She left, pulling the doorway curtain closed behind her.

The next morning another boy helped me to a seat outside in the sun. My left arm still ached, but the pain was lessening. A bird bath sat nearby on a tree stump. I bent over it and studied my reflection. A puffy red gash ran up my left cheek, disappearing under the bandage over my eye. I turned away in despair—I was permanently disfigured.

But my remaining eye still functioned, somewhat. I took in my surroundings. The inn was nestled in an olive orchard, which continued up the hillside behind it in neat terraces. Ruins filled the hill's summit, black from fire. This must be the temple Deborah spoke about.

Curious to see more, I motioned for the boy to help me, and together we walked to the front of the inn. Below us lay a good-sized town bounded by two hills.

"That's Sebaste," said the boy. He appeared to be twelve or thirteen years old.

" 'Sebaste' is Greek for 'Augustus,' " I answered. It was clearly a Greek city, as proved by the paved streets, the stadium, the amphitheater, and several columned temples.

The boy led me back to the rear of the inn, seating me on a bench in the garden. I was exhausted by our short tour and asked him for water. He returned with a pitcher and a cup. I sipped the water. "Where is your mother?" I asked.

He did not answer.

"Do you have a grandfather?"

He shook his head.

"Do you know what grandfathers are like?"

He shook his head again.

"Well, they would never harm a child's mother. Do you understand?"

He looked at me doubtfully.

"Ask you mother to come."

He went inside. I had not seen Deborah since the night before, when I had spoken out of turn about her personal life. All morning I had wondered how I would apologize. I finally decided to just blurt it out the same way I had blurted out my offense.

Deborah appeared in the doorway wearing a brown tunic. Her feet were bare and her hands were red from washing. She walked toward me, drying her hands on her apron.

"I want to apologize," I said. "You knew I was old. Now you know I am also a fool."

"You're the second stranger who has read my heart."

"Jeshua?" I ventured.

She looked at me in surprise. "Are you also a prophet?"

"No. But I knew him long ago. I have not seen him since he was a child."

"He came to Sebaste once, three years ago," said Deborah. "His friends went into town for food. I was drawing water at a well. He came and asked me draw water for him. I asked him if he knew I was a Samaritan. He said yes and asked me if I knew who *he* was." Deborah shook her head at the memory. "Then he said he would give me *living* water. I said,

'You have no bucket to draw with; how can you give *me* water?' And he said, 'If you drink of this well, you will thirst again, but the water *I* give is the water of everlasting life.' "

"So I drew him a bucket and he drank. Then I asked him for the living water, and he told me to bring my husband and he would give us both to drink." She hung her head.

"But you had no husband," I said.

"He told me I'd had five husbands, but the man I was with was not my husband." Tears stood in her eyes.

I wanted to reach out and comfort her, but I dared not. Her two sons stood in the inn doorway, out of earshot, watching for signs of trouble. Her back was to them. If they knew she was crying, they would come and take her from me. I waited, trying not to betray any emotion.

"I asked him who he was," said Deborah, her chin quivering. "He said he was the Moshiach and that he wanted to bless me!" She fell to her knees, burying her head in her hands, sobbing. Her boys started forward, but I raised my hand, and they stopped. After a time, Deborah looked up, tears in her eyes. "Me!" she whispered. "He wanted to bless *me!*"

I looked down at my hands, which were trembling. Deborah's life and mine were of a piece. We had both made poor choices, and yet we had met Jeshua, and he had changed us. Maybe he *was* the Moshiach. At the very least, he was a savior to *this* woman, for he had rescued her from hopelessness.

Watching her crying at my feet, my heart was softened. Maybe Jeshua could do for the hearts of his people what he had done for Deborah. Maybe, when I finally met him, he would do the same for me.

FIFTY-TWO

Deborah returned to her work, but I remained in the garden and pondered my life. From my vantage point as a lonely tower of self-loathing, I saw only my weaknesses. But Deborah had gained a better perspective. Humility showed her the truth of her life in a way regret had failed to show me the truth of mine. Obviously, regret alone does not change a heart. If it did, I would be perfect.

I thought of young, blind Daniel, who said Jeshua spoke of "finding yourself through losing yourself." Was that possible? Does the fish jump into the fisherman's boat? No, it seeks escape. Aren't the things we loathe about ourselves the very things that keep us alive?

Many an hour I had knelt in the Serapeum, aching to be pure, but knowing in my heart I never would be. My mind kept going back to Deborah, kneeling before me, brought low not by shame or regret, but by love. As she cried into her apron, I realized that Jeshua had planted a healing seed in her heart. It had germinated, grown, and flowered, and now she was free of regret. Her heart was new, liberated from her past. I wanted that freedom; I wanted to be a new man. My soul ached for it, knowing this was my last chance.

I realized I had changed my mind again: when I healed, I would go on to Jerusalem.

After dinner, Deborah helped me into bed. I thanked her for all she had done for me.

"It is a natural thing. Now." She smiled shyly.

"How can Jeshua afford such generosity? Does it not diminish him?"

"I don't think so. I've only sipped the living water, but it wells within me. I feel my soul expanding. You say you doubt, but it is not doubt that holds us back—it is fear. Jeshua's logos eradicates fear, and when it is gone, love can grow."

"Can it be that simple?" I asked. "That love conquers fear?"

"It might be. I'm testing it," she said. "I feel stronger . . . and kinder."

"Then it *is* working," I said, smiling. "Sometimes I think fear has driven all my choices."

"Isn't fear's greatest weapon the fear that we'll be nothing without it?"

"What will *I* be without it?" I wondered.

"You will be free," said Deborah.

After breakfast the next morning, as I sat outside, wondering how I would get to Jerusalem with no money, no transportation, a lame left arm, and one eye, the answer came striding out the door, shouting, "I'll disturb him if I want to!" I got to my feet as quickly as I could, leaning on my staff. "Melchior!" said Zebulon, "I understand you're going to Jerusalem."

"That is my intention," I said, "though I do not know when it will be."

"How about today? I'm going, and I will take you with me, if you wish."

"I have no money."

"Can you make conversation about something other than dice and women?"

"Yes, but I tend to be rather . . . morose," I said honestly.

"Hasn't Deborah cured you of that yet?"

"She has cured me of many things, but there is only one doctor for what truly ails me."

"Jeshua," said Zebulon, nodding.

"I should have guessed," I said, shaking my head. "You know him too."

"I met him years ago on the Jericho road, down from Jerusalem. He was building an addition on an inn. I'm proud to say we became friends."

"I would like to hear about that," I said.

"And I'd like to hear about the Pharos," said Zebulon. "Is it really as tall as they say?"

Deborah came over to me. "Find him, and you will find peace."

I did not know what to say, but it was of no matter. Speaking had already become unnecessary between us. We smiled at each other. Zebulon rounded the corner on his horse. "I will see you again," he said to Deborah. "I will remember you to Drusilla, and she will vex me for it!"

We started out, Zebulon on his gray horse and I on a brown donkey. Behind us were a dozen heavily laden donkeys and three handlers. I felt ridiculous, a bent man with an eye patch riding a donkey so small my feet grazed the ground. But I was riding, and that was good. I had recuperated under Deborah's nursing: My joints ached, but they always did in the morning. My cold was tapering off. My dislocated shoulder was healing. And though my eye socket drained yellow pus, the pain was not unbearable. As it was, I was doing better than I deserved.

Peace."

The trade route through Samaria was wide and paved with crushed granite. The donkey did its best under the burden I put upon it, as did I, for donkeys have saw-tooth backbones. Our caravan moved through stone-studded hills dotted with vineyards and groves, flocks of sheep and goats, and rushing streams. Flowers perfumed the air, and the clouds dappled the hillsides with shadow.

Zebulon kept me occupied with travel stories reaching from Tyre to Gaza. I told him about the Nile and the harvests that followed the inundations. He regaled me with tales of Petra. I told him about Alexandria and asked him about Babylon, which he had visited once.

"I have a Babylonian friend," I said. "Balthazar. By appearances, you could be brothers."

Zebulon smacked his knee with his crop. "Brothers!" he shouted. "I already have *five!*"

"Perhaps one fell from the cradle," I said.

"He rolled a long way, then!"

We ate well. Zebulon's merchandise was figs and dates, but two of his donkeys carried nothing but food for our journey. Meals were lavish. We devoured pigeon, lamb, and river fish. We ate hot bread and lentil stew and sampled wheels of cheese. For dessert, we relished spiced nuts and honey-baked locusts. He had two casks of wine. Most nights I lay under the stars, my belly full and my head pleasantly light, the pains of my journey fading like the miles behind us.

❧ ❧ ❧

After three days, we arrived at Gophna, a hillside village overlooking a valley. I heard birdsong and looked to the southwest. Zebulon smiled. "Naught there but good tidings, Melchior."

I nodded. "Old habit."

Zebulon regarded me. "You cried out in your sleep last night."

"I have nightmares," I said. "Omens from the Underworld."

"Where the Sungod dwells?"

"As well as his foes," said I. "He battles them nightly. Sometimes I am with him on his barque when he engages them."

"The Underworld, is it a terrible place?"

"Yes. Deborah would say my religion is based on fear."

"Yet for all that," said Zebulon, "your afterlife is one of hope, is it not?"

"Hope is woven into its fabric. But I doubt there is a weaver; it seems random to me."

"Hope is hard to find in the face of truth," said Zebulon.

I turned to him. We had been watching the servants water the stock at a brook. "But why is that?" I asked. "Socrates said truth is *the* noble virtue. Therefore it should *create* hope."

"Truth is not the problem," said Zebulon, "The problem is that we hope for that which is untrue."

I nodded. "I have hoped for untrue things: wealth, power, the praise of men—"

"To not have to change," said Zebulon.

"My greatest fear," I said, "is that if I change, I will cease to be me." I shook my head. "Which is amusing, because I hate myself."

"I think this is where Jeshua's logos comes in," said Zebulon. "His promise is that you will *not* cease to be you but that you will become the person you long to be. This is his living water. Deborah accepted it because she was thirsty. Her life was nothing like she wanted it to be. She was sincerely seeking truth. And she found it."

"What you are saying," I said flatly, "is that I am not thirsty."

"Not thirsty *enough*," said Zebulon.

"But I am!" I said, turning to him. "I am at the end! Everyone I have loved is gone. I have lost everything: my power, my prestige, my possessions, my health! Everything! I am brought low, begging for scraps of food from strangers! Why, then, is my heart still closed? Why do I look but not see? Why do I hear but not comprehend? Why do I desire change but do not change?" I lay back on the grass, despondent.

"Because you cannot change yourself," said Zebulon. "Oh, you can change your actions, but you cannot change your heart." We pondered that for a minute, then he whispered, "Jeshua must be a sorcerer."

I laughed ruefully. "I have considered that."

"But his magic is truth. He says the truth will set you free."

Now I laughed. "But first it will enrage you."

Zebulon laughed. "It certainly has a price, a sacrifice you are still unwilling to make."

"What sacrifice?"

"Yourself," said Zebulon. "You must, or leave your life unlived."

That is how I feel, I thought. *A life unlived. I am almost seventy years old, and I have not even been born yet.*

"Jeshua's magic shows you to yourself," said Zebulon. "And you will fear, not because he is fearsome, but what he asks you to do is."

"And what is that?"

"To die, that you might live."

FIFTY-THREE

e approached Jerusalem from the north. The Damascus Gate stood open, an archway under which five camels could pass abreast. Pilgrims were camped outside the wall, which meant there were no rooms in the city. No matter, I had only a single silver denarius and could not afford lodging in any case. I was no longer Melkorios Alexandreus, Supreme Pontiff of Serapis, Vizier to the Egyptian Prefect; I was a crippled old man riding a borrowed donkey.

Zebulon scanned the crowd for trouble as he helped me dismount. "As you know," he said, "Samaritans are not welcome in Jerusalem. I will be turning east, to Jericho." He dug into his pouch and removed a gold denarius worth twenty-five times the silver denarius Deborah had so generously given me. "Now don't argue," he said, placing the coin in my hand.

"But that is all we've *done* on our journey!" I said. "You shame me!"

"You shame yourself if you do not accept help when you need it. If you wish, you may repay me when we meet again."

"I will!" I affirmed. "But since you are being generous, I would impose further on you."

"From beggar to publican in an instant! How much more?"

I lifted my chin. "Another gold denarius."

Without a word, Zebulon began digging in his purse. I must tell you, I have never loved a man as much as I loved him in that moment. I had never known that kind of friendship before, nor have I since. He found the coin and handed it to me.

I gave it back. "Give this to Deborah. You pass through Ptolemais now and then, yes?"

Zebulon nodded.

"A friend of mine, a merchant seaman, docks at Ptolemais. His name is Honorius. He will deposit two gold denarii—with interest—in the Serapeum temple in Ptolemais in your name. Do you trust me?"

"Yes, I trust you. You must be wealthy indeed, Melkorios."

"The loss of your company will impoverish me."

"It is not lost," said Zebulon. "I will see that Deborah receives the money. And one day I will knock on Serapion's door in Alexandria."

"And he will answer it," I said, "but it will not be me. You will find me through Rabbi Apollos ben Mesha. He will know my whereabouts, in life or in death. But hurry in your visit, for I fear this pilgrimage to see the Moshiach is my last."

"I sense he is here and awaits you," said Zebulon. "Remember me to him."

"I surely will." I felt sadness at our parting and sadness for the days to come when I would not hear his hearty laughter. "Take care, my friend," I said.

Zebulon engulfed me. "Take care, my *brother*," he said, kissing me on both cheeks.

As I turned toward the Damascus Gate and was lost in the crowd, I felt a rare sensation—happiness.

The narrow street twisted past the Antonia Fortress, where the Roman cohort of six hundred soldiers was quartered. Legionnaires patrolled the towers, a reminder that though Temple sacrifices were being offered to Hashem, Rome was the effective god of this land.

Soon I was back in the trades quarter, where the stench of tanners and fullers leaked from ramshackle tenements. Rounding a corner, I saw the arches of the Temple viaduct spanning the shallow Tyropoeon Valley. Before ascending, I rinsed my feet in the mikvah. As I climbed the steps, I pulled up my cloak cowl to cover my head. Above me, an unbroken procession moved along the viaduct toward the Coponius Gate. *How shall I find him in this crowd?* I wondered. Yet, I knew if he were on the Mount, finding him would be easy—I would just look for a man amidst a multitude.

At the top of the steps, I paused to catch my breath. My empty eye socket ached, and my hands trembled. Steeling myself, I thrust myself into the crowd. People carried cages of doves or bore lambs in their arms. Soon, I was in the Great Court, astonished at the thousands of people. Animal vendors and moneychangers, usually confined to the perimeter porticoes, had spilled out onto the Court itself, some stalls even erected in the shadow of the Temple. The shouting of merchants and the bleating of sheep echoed in an almost unbearable din. But above it all, ecstatic cries of *Hosanna!* rose from the Temple itself, along with smoke and the tangy smell of blood.

At the Temple entrance, a dozen priests questioned patrons seeking admission. The doors of the Beautiful Gate were open. I looked through it and saw, in the innermost court, the rough-hewn altar blazing. Even at this distance, I could feel the heat as the meat exploded into flame. Behind the altar, the tall, blindingly white Sanctuary was barely visible through the boiling smoke.

I noticed one of the priests studying me and turned away, bumping into a man who was saying, "He's not here. Let's go."

"I am very sorry," I said in Aramaic.

"Salve," he said in Latin, then turned back to his friend.

"Salve, citizen," I responded in Latin.

He nodded curtly. Then the man to whom he had been speaking said, "Are you lost?"

"No," I said. "I am seeking someone."

"I am Nicodemus. This is my friend, Joel. We are also seeking someone, but as you can see, finding anyone here today is a challenge."

"I am Melkorios Alexandreus."

"Whom do you seek?" asked Joel coolly.

I noted that their cloaks bore a stripe of rank. If they served the Judean Prefect, I must be on my guard. "A friend from Galilee," I said vaguely. "A tekton," I added.

Nicodemus gestured to the colonnade. "Come." He guided us to the portico and turned. "Jeshua ben Josef?" he whispered.

I nodded warily.

He saw my reticence and said, "Shelama. We are friends of his."

Joel scowled. "We're just not sure *you* are."

"I knew his parents. In Alexandria."

Nicodemus grabbed his friend's arm in surprise. "The magus? *You're* the magus?"

I nodded, aware that with my ragged clothes and eye patch, I looked more like a beggar than a nobleman.

"Of course he is," mocked Joel.

Nicodemus studied me. "Yes. He is. Jeshua described him, and this man *is* very tall."

"All the better to see what you cannot," said Joel. "But I don't suppose he can do much harm in any case. All right, tell him."

Nicodemus smiled at me. "Joel and I are rulers in the Sanhedrin. Well met . . ."

"Melkorios," I said. "Call me Melchior."

"Melchior," said Nicodemus. "We too are looking for Jeshua, but finding him this late will be difficult. The Mount is about to get *very* crowded."

"It is not crowded now?" I asked, looking around.

"It is midday," said Joel. "The Seder meal begins at sunset, and there are a lot of sacrifices to be made before then."

"He will be here," said Nicodemus. "For the last three days, he has been on the Mount. The first day he spoke near Herod's Basilica." He pointed to the multi-storied building at the southern end of the Court. "Yesterday he taught at the soreg. His followers interfered with those entering and leaving the Temple. The kohens asked them to move, but they refused."

"Why would they not move?" I asked.

"They felt powerful because Jeshua entered the Mount through the Golden Gate," said Joel, pointing to an arch in the eastern portico not far from where we stood. "That gate is reserved solely for the Moshiach."

This was a prophecy Mesha had not told me about. I nodded for Joel to continue.

"The bridge to the gate is the Red Heifer bridge," said Joel.

"Are not its ashes used to purify those who come into contact with corpses?" I asked.

Nicodemus smiled. "See, Joel, you cannot judge a man by his cloak!"

I was still looking at Joel. "What is the significance of the red heifer?"

"The red heifer is sacrificed on the Mount of Olives, on the far side of the valley. There is a direct line of sight from the altar to the Sanctuary, *if* the Golden Gate is open, *which it never is*. The bridge was built to ensure that the ashes could be brought to the Temple without danger of coming into contact with a corpse."

"How often do they use the bridge?" I asked.

"Never!" said Joel. "Which is why Jeshua's use of it is so controversial."

"What does the red heifer signify?" I asked.

"The coming of the Moshiach," said Joel.

I grew bold. "Is Jeshua the Moshiach?"

Joel blew his cheeks out and turned away.

Nicodemus pursed his lips. "Many doubt it—like Joel here—but others believe he is."

"Do *you* believe he is the Moshiach?"

"Yes," said Nicodemus, straightening. "One can hardly meet Jeshua without considering it."

Joel harrumphed.

"Except Joel," said Nicodemus.

"I'm a Pharisee!" exclaimed Joel. "*All* the prophecies must be fulfilled!"

"What of his miracles?" asked Nicodemus gently. I could tell this was an argument they often had.

"The Adversary can conjure too! The problem is that Jeshua operates outside traditional priesthood authority. He has no synagogue, heals by touch—not prayer—and instead of beseeching Hashem for miracles, he *commands* the very elements. Many in the Sanhedrin believe he is a charlatan who leads the credulous into apostasy!"

"I was told he cast demons into a herd of swine in Gadara."

"Yes, we heard about that," said Joel. "But what concerns me is that the demons knew his *name*."

"So?"

"Whose name but the Adversary's would a demon know?"

"But explain how," I said, "he walked on water."

Joel looked at me as if I had just proven his point.

"He has raised the dead," said Nicodemus, looking at his friend.

I stared at him. "What?"

Nicodemus nodded. "A man from Bethany."

"Bethany!" crowed Joel. "A den of thieves and lepers."

"Was it Zechariah?" I asked. "Or Johanan?"

Nicodemus shrugged. "I don't know his name, only that he lived there."

"It doesn't matter," said Joel.

"Why?" I asked. "You do not find miracles compelling?"

Joel grabbed the hem of my cloak. "As an Egyptian, perhaps you can tell us whether Jeshua learned sorcery and exorcism in *your* country, from pagan priests?"

I was cut to the quick, for I *was* such a priest. "He is a devout Jew."

"A devout Jew who is trained in the dark arts, or he could not do what he does."

"So you don't doubt his miracles?" asked Nicodemus.

"No!" answered Joel. "I simply doubt that they emanate from Hashem!"

"I believe they do," said Nicodemus.

"Then why did he curse the Temple—Hashem's earthly footstool?"

I looked at Nicodemus for rebuttal, but he was silent.

"What did he say?" I asked.

"He said he would destroy the Temple and in three days raise it again," said Joel.

"You didn't hear him say this," said Nicodemus.

"I heard it from one of his disciples," countered Joel. "Cursing the Temple is blasphemy."

"But it is a prophecy capable of *proof*," I said. "If it does not come to pass, he is a false prophet. And if the Temple indeed falls, who will then oppose him?"

"The kohens fear him more for his miracles than his prophecies," said Joel. "They would wink at the prophecy if it helped them convict him of sorcery."

"Which means death by stoning," said Nicodemus.

"But you believe him," I said, looking at Nicodemus. "Are there not more in the Sanhedrin who also believe?"

"Many," said Nicodemus. "But they fear losing their power."

"I am not one of those," said Joel. "But I fear for my life, as Jeshua should. The chief kohens—Sadducees, all—will maintain the balance of power over the Pharisees at all costs. But we both value the Temple, and if Jeshua has cast a spell on it, all will be united against him."

"But what if he really *is* the Moshiach?" I asked. "Will they not unite *behind* him?"

"*If* he's the Moshiach," said Nicodemus. "But many think he's a magician or an illusionist. Regardless, he has made this much clear: he has no plans to overthrow Roman rule in Judea, which would be supported by everyone: Pharisee, Sadducee, Samaritan, and pagan alike."

Joel nodded darkly. "Short of that, he will be destroyed by the kohens."

"Short of that?" I said, horrified. "Listen: I know something of the Empire. Suppose Jeshua succeeds in ousting the Prefect and his cohort of six hundred legionnaires. What happens when Rome returns with sixty thousand? Will he defeat them?" I lowered my voice because several merchants were looking over at us. "Face facts: your province will never be free, not even if Jeshua were Hashem himself!"

Joel lifted his chin defiantly but said nothing.

"Besides," I said, "his logos is not war! It is peace!"

"Then he is not the Moshiach," said Joel, turning and walking away.

FIFTY-FOUR

We watched Joel thread his way through the crowd. He did not look back. Nicodemus took me to the least crowded corner of the Mount, directly under the Antonia, near the animal pens. The smell of the pens and our closeness to the pagan Fortress guaranteed us a small measure of privacy.

"For one who espouses peace, your words are violent," said Nicodemus.

"I am sorry," I said. "But I *know* Jeshua, or at least I knew him many years ago. Over the last few weeks, I have traveled from Gaza to Ptolemais to Kinnereth to Samaria. I have heard much about him. His teachings are not violent, and his miracles are not evil. He restores sight, feeds the hungry, and casts out demons! He is no necromancer; he is a holy man."

"I agree," said Nicodemus. "On one occasion, I came to him by night, fearing what would happen if I were seen with him by day. I asked what I must do to obtain eternal life. His answer was cryptic: I must be *born again*. I asked, 'Can a man enter his mother's womb a second time?' and he said, 'You must be born of water and the spirit, or you cannot enter the kingdom of God.'"

"What does that mean?" I asked.

"I do not know, except that I believe his message is about *inner* change, not armed revolution. His miracles, as Joel rightly pointed out, do not convince. But his teachings *do*." His eyes glistened with emotion. "But he makes enemies as well as friends. As you pointed out," he said, gesturing at the soldiers patrolling the parapets above us, "we are Roman slaves, a weak people in a weak province, yet how she squeezes and harries us! Her prefects vex us with burdensome taxes, and her emperors defile our temples!"

I thought of how the Jews themselves defiled a Samaritan temple, but said nothing.

"Moshiachs come regular as spring," said Nicodemus. "Most are petty charlatans who attract a few malcontents and end up dead in a ditch. Almost two hundred years ago the Maccabees stirred up a real revolution. Twenty-five years ago, the Zealots revolted, and Augustus practically burned Galilee to the ground in response. Now, the Essenes talk of revolution. Some say Jeshua is an Essene. And Rome watches with great interest . . ." He again gestured to the surrounding parapets, where scores of red-cloaked legionnaires stood at attention, their metal-tipped spears glinting in the sun.

"They have nothing to fear from Jeshua," I said.

"Truth has never prevented fear," said Nicodemus. "That is why I am here today. There have been heated discussions in the Sanhedrin about Jeshua. When he entered the Mount through the Golden Gate five days ago, riding a donkey colt—another prophecy!—the crowd swept the way with palm fronds! When he returned the next day, there was violence."

"Against him?"

"*By* him," said Nicodemus. "He took umbrage at the rates of the moneychangers and upended their tables. He whipped several and drove them back under the porticoes."

"They *are* very near the Temple," I said.

"And so was he," said Nicodemus. "He taught at the soreg, as we told you. His listeners gathered around, blocking the Temple entrance—and thus the sacrifices—which are the largest portion of the Kohen Gadol's income. And then yesterday, he came again. This time, he marched right into the Temple complex, along with hundreds of his followers, who held the priests at bay with their numbers. Jeshua strode into the Court of the Israelites, then climbed over the low wall and entered the Court of the Priests."

"He is of a priestly family," I said. "Zechariah—"

"He stood on the steps of the Sanctuary, and he is *not* a Levite!"

"What *is* his tribe?"

"Judah. His followers also jumped the wall and filled the Priests' Court, also a violation of the Law. Then he spoke."

"What did he say?"

"Ironically, he spoke of accommodation. Someone—whether it was a kohen or a follower is unclear—asked him if Jews should pay taxes to Rome."

"Nonpayment of taxes is treason," I said. "He was trying to trick him."

Nicodemus nodded. "Jeshua held up a Roman coin and a Temple coin and said, 'Render unto Caesar what is Caesar's and unto Hashem what is Hashem's.'"

"That is sound logic," I said. "Who can argue with that?"

"The Kohen Gadol can," said Nicodemus. "The kohens quietly foment hatred for Rome. They want the people to be angry. Discontent turns men religious, and sacrifice means more money for Caiaphas." He looked at the Temple. "I'm ashamed to say this, especially to a non-Jew."

"I am—or *was*—a pontiff of Serapis," I said. "Compared to my cult, Judaism is spotless."

"Not spotless enough," said Nicodemus. "So you see, no matter what Jeshua says, he is doomed! Simply bringing a Roman coin into the Temple was considered a great sin by many. Beyond that, if he preaches peace and the people follow, the priests and rulers will stir up trouble, for they fear his growing power. If he preaches rebellion and Rome hears of it, then all of Judea suffers."

"He is no fool," I said. "He must be aware of this."

"Certainly," said Nicodemus. "But apparently, he does not care." Nicodemus stroked his long beard. "And there is more to fear than Rome. The Sanhedrin is sharply divided on this matter. Many believe in Jeshua as I do, but many are skeptical as Joel is. But most would just as soon see him gone. Which is why I came here today, to warn him."

"He might be in Bethany," I said. "He once had family there."

"He certainly is not here," said Nicodemus, looking around at the crowded Mount. "And I cannot leave the city and return before sunset, when the Seder starts."

"I will go," I said. "I will take your warning to him in Bethany, if he is there. If he remains in Jerusalem, I trust you will discover his whereabouts and warn him yourself."

"I see the wisdom of your counsel," said Nicodemus. "Go to Bethany. I will search here. We will both try to warn Jeshua of the danger, though he is a hard man to dissuade from his purpose. In any case, when you return, come to my home in the Upper City, where I will hear your tidings and you will find a hot meal and a comfortable bed."

"I will," I said, turning to go.

"One more thing," said Nicodemus. "It will be dark when you arrive in Bethany. No doors will open for you. If that happens, just tell them you're Eliyahu."

"Who is that?"

"A Seder guest for whom they always leave an empty chair."

"And when they find out I'm *not* Eliyahu?" I asked.

"How do you know you're not him?" asked Nicodemus. "Eliyahu is prophesied to return before the great and terrible day of Hashem." He took my hand firmly, his dark eyes boring into mine. "If this isn't that day, when is it?"

FIFTY-FIVE

I found a stable in the Kidron Valley, east of the Mount, but they would not sell me a horse. They would, however, *rent* me one for the same price. I cursed and paid, then headed to Bethany. As I rode along, I wondered what had come over Jeshua. Challenging the priests on the Sanctuary steps! No wonder the High Priest was angry. I comforted myself with the thought that if the world Jeshua promised ever came to fruition, no one could stop him. Twenty legions could not put down a peaceful rebellion; the soldiers themselves would rebel. And then how would Rome rule the world? Would not her very reason for being—to bring peace and order—be vitiated by Jeshua's logos?

But there was one article of faith that even Jeshua could not overthrow: *The powerful do not willingly abdicate power.* And even though he did not directly challenge Rome or the Jewish priests, he was still a threat to them, and they would know it. I had known many Jews; they were all proud. And I knew from seven hundred years of history the pride of Rome. When pride clashed with pride, the outcome was certain: I despaired for the safety of Jeshua bar Josef.

❦   ❦   ❦

Within a short time, the horse began to limp, forcing me to dismount and walk the rest of the way. I stewed with anger at being cheated because I was a foreigner. Well, foreigners get lost in strange lands—I just might forget where I rented the horse.

I arrived in Bethany in the late afternoon. People were camping on the outskirts of town and in the square. I inquired of a man about Jeshua. He said he'd seen the Rabbi whip the moneychangers at the Temple several days ago and had returned each succeeding day in hopes of seeing it again. He had a cloudy right eye, and I took him for mad until he winked. "He's here. That way." He pointed down a narrow alley.

I gave him a mite and walked down two blocks to a drab mud-brick house behind a flaking plaster wall. Through an open door, I saw men moving tables into the courtyard. I stood in the doorway. "Shelama!" I called out. No one paid me any mind. "Shelama!"

A child yelled, "Mother!"

A matron appeared. Her hair was pulled back from her broad forehead and she wore a blue head kerchief. "What do you want?" she asked brusquely.

"I am seeking Jeshua bar Josef," I said, bowing. "I am a friend of his parents, Josef and Miriam." The woman squinted at me. "And Zechariah," I added.

"You knew Zechariah? And his wife?"

"Elisheba," I said. The names were a test. I added another: "And their son Johanan."

"I am Martha. Shelama." She pointed at another woman who was placing a cloth over a table. "That is Miriam, my sister. Somewhere inside the house is my brother Eleazar." She gestured for me to enter, and the hubbub around us resumed.

Miriam approached us. "Why do you seek Jeshua in Bethany?"

"Long ago, his aunt and uncle lived here. I thought he might still have family in town."

"You are a Roman, and Jeshua has no dealings with Romans," said Martha, frowning. "Truthfully, now, how do you know him?"

I was so weary of being interrogated that testiness crept into my voice. "I heard him cry on his mother's lap more than thirty years ago. I am Melkorios Alexandreus, and I took Jeshua and his family to Egypt with me, where I was a welcome guest in their home."

"You're the magus!" said Miriam, dropping to her knees. Martha knelt too. I suddenly felt guilty for my imperious outburst.

"What's this?" came a voice. A slender man of middle age strode toward us. "Get up! Get up!" he commanded the women. To me: "Who are you?"

"The m-magus," said Martha, still on her knees.

"The *who*?" asked the man, gesturing for the women to rise. They did not.

"Melkorios Alexandreus," I said. "I am seeking Jeshua bar Josef."

"He is not here," said the man. "Be gone!"

"Then I am wondering," I said, looking down at the two women, "if you might tell me where I might find Zechariah, father of Johanan the prophet."

The man frowned. "In his tomb."

"Then it was not he who was raised from the dead?"

"What have you heard?" he asked.

"I was told Jeshua raised a man of Bethany from the dead."

Miriam got to her feet. "The man of whom you speak stands before you. This is Eleazar."

Eleazar gestured for Martha to stand. "I am he," he said, taking me by the forearm in the Roman manner. "I apologize; there are many who come to see me as a curiosity and a few because they wish to harm Jeshua. We did not know in which camp you resided."

"Neither," I said.

Eleazar led me to a low table, and we sat on cushions on the ground. A number of men joined us. Martha busied herself inside the house, but Miriam sat next to me, gazing up at me as if I were Jeshua himself. It was uncomfortable to go from disdain to honor so quickly.

"I gather you want to hear the story," said Eleazar.

"I have no time," I said. "I bring word of a plot against Jeshua."

"Who's word?" asked Eleazar.

"A member of the Sanhedrin."

A man across from me spat on the ground. "Jeshua has few friends in the Sanhedrin."

"Or the Temple," said another.

"Or the government," said a third.

"What was his name?" asked Eleazar.

"Nicodemus."

"I do not know him."

"After what has happened on the Mount recently, he fears for Jeshua's safety."

"Jeshua is not in Bethany," said Eleazar.

"Then I must return to Jerusalem!" I started to get up.

Eleazar put a hand on my arm. "Calm yourself, Melchior. Hear my story, and you will see why we do not fear for Jeshua's safety."

His manner was confident. I realized that if Jeshua was not in Bethany, he would be in Jerusalem. If he wished to be found, Nicodemus would find him. I nodded at Eleazar to continue.

"For obvious reasons," said Eleazar, "I cannot tell the story. Miriam?"

"We have known Jeshua for many years," began Miriam. "He is like family. When Eleazar fell sick, Jeshua was in Perea, to the east, across the Jordan. Martha sent word, begging him to come speedily."

At this point, Martha appeared, leading servants bearing plates and pitchers. She saw us at the table and said, "You will all have to make way, for the Seder is nearly upon us."

Eleazar took her hand and said, "Martha, sit and be at peace. There is time."

Martha sighed and patted her brother on the arm. "And if Eliyahu arrives and we have not made him a place at the table, will you explain to him why that is?"

Eleazar smiled and moved over, giving her a place on the cushion next to him. She sat, and I saw her demeanor slowly change from harried matron to loving sister. Eleazar nodded at Miriam, who continued: "But Jeshua did not come for two days, and Eleazar grew worse. We feared he would die, and he did."

All eyes turned to Eleazar, who gazed into the distance. After a time, Miriam spoke again. "We anointed his body, put him in the sepulcher, and sealed it. And still Jeshua had not arrived." Tears filled her eyes. "He finally came after Eleazar had been in the grave four days."

"I was angry," interjected Martha, "because if Jeshua had been here, Eleazar would not have died, and I told him so when he arrived." There were nods around the table. Only Martha, it seemed, was not intimidated by Jeshua.

"But then you said," continued Miriam, "that you *knew* that whatever Jeshua asked of Hashem would be done."

Martha shrugged. I could not help but smile. Here was a woman who had no need of faith, for she *knew*. I envied her.

Miriam continued, "Jeshua said, 'I am the resurrection and the life; he that believes in me, though he were dead, yet shall he live.' He asked us to take him to the tomb. We all stood before it and wept, including Jeshua." There was a pause as Miriam collected herself. She wiped away a tear and said, "After a while, he said, 'Take away the stone!' And we said—"

"*I* said," interrupted Martha. "I said we dared not, for he had been dead four days."

"But he insisted, and so we did," said Miriam. "We stared into the tomb, afraid. Then Jeshua bade us all to kneel, and then he prayed."

"That was the first thing I remember," interjected Eleazar, and a hush fell upon us. The children were silent, the animals in their stalls were still as stones, and the evening breeze did not rustle a leaf. "I heard him say, 'Eleazar, come forth!' and I stood and walked to the entrance, the kerchief still over my face." He pulled off his head kerchief and showed it to me. "*This* kerchief." He placed his hand over his heart. "I witness that Jeshua of Nazareth is the Moshiach."

My heart pounded, and I passed a hand across my eyes, overcome.

Eleazar looked steadily at me. "That is why we do not fear for Jeshua."

FIFTY-SIX

Martha said that though Jeshua had returned to Bethany on each of the preceding four nights, he had not returned that day. She assured me he was celebrating Pesach in Jerusalem, and she invited me to partake of the Seder with them.

I declined. Notwithstanding Eleazar's astonishing story, I was still anxious about Jeshua. I asked Eleazar to loan me a horse so I could get back to Jerusalem, describing the merchant who had cheated me. "I will reckon with him," said Eleazar. I respected this quiet man more and more, though I was not certain if I believed his remarkable tale.

I had so many questions: Had he seen the Sektet boat on the Keku Samu? Was Osiris there? What about Apep? Was there a Field of Reeds? *Had he seen Thaesis and Athena?*

But I did not ask them because I knew no answer would be convincing. I was destined to doubt even the restoration of life. As the story unfolded, my heart had leapt within me, but moments later the inevitable questions arose: Were they telling the truth? Had they been tricked? Had he really been dead? Was this simply a joke they played on strangers?

Was Jeshua a sorcerer?

That was the key question. If Jeshua was the Moshiach, then he was Hashem's emissary (or Hashem himself, as some believed), and Eleazar's story had to be true. But if witchcraft was involved, then Jeshua possessed a dark power and could trick the credulous. I knew something about darkness; I had served the fraudulent fiction of Serapis, to whom many wonders and miracles had also been attributed.

Eleazar must have seen the doubt in my eyes. He took my elbow and led me out into the cobblestone street, where we were alone. It was after sunset, and darkness surrounded us. "You doubt," he said simply.

I said nothing and busied myself with the horse's harness.

"I too have struggled with doubt," said Eleazar. "Perhaps that is why Jeshua blessed me in this way—to remove my doubts once and for all. Perhaps he will do the same for you—though I hope in your case death is not involved." He smiled.

"May it be so," I said. "But he had better hurry, for I have not much time left. I made this journey hoping to find him on his throne. *That* alone would go a long way to assuaging my doubts."

"He *is* on his throne," said Eleazar. "And the earth is his footstool."

Eleazar's horse had me back in Jerusalem in under an hour. All along the road were encampments, where families were participating in the Seder, celebrating their forefathers' exodus from Egypt more than a thousand years ago. Or so they say.

I entered through the Damascus Gate. Though the main street was lit with torches, every window was shuttered, and no one was outdoors. I led my horse toward the Upper City, where the wealthy live in walled compounds. As I walked, I often heard singing—dirge-like melodies that incorporated the "shee-shee" and "ha-ha" sounds of Hebrew. I heard bits of the same song over and over as I walked, the horse's hooves clicking on the cobblestones. As I crossed the Tyropoeon Valley, I looked up at the Mount. The Antonia was dark, its narrow windows black. No soldiers patrolled the parapets; they were dining as well and afterward would attend to their own rituals of knucklebones and dice.

Just past the viaduct, I passed the Hasmonean Palace. Porch braziers splayed column shadows down the steps. The Palace commemorated Jewish independence from the Seleucid Empire. Two hundred years ago, King Mithridates slaughtered a swine on the Temple altar and ordered the priests to eat it. When they refused, he cut out their tongues, chopped off their hands and feet, scalped them, and burned them alive on the altar.

Judah Maccabee and his brothers led a guerilla war against Mithridates, whom Hashem killed (so said the Jews) as he marched on Jerusalem. Thereafter, the Jews enjoyed self-rule for a hundred years until Roman general Pompey conquered Jerusalem. When Augustus Caesar made Herod the vassal king, Herod built his own fortress in the Upper City, the Citadel, where the Roman prefects now dwell, including the current resident, Pontius Pilatus, when he is not debauching in his seaside resort Caesaria Maritima.

Nicodemus said the Hasmonean Palace was normally empty, except when Herod's sons Philip or Antipas visited Jerusalem. On that night there were lights in many windows. Nicodemus had given me directions to his home from this point.

The crumbling old north city wall ran parallel to the street connecting the Mount to the Joppa Gate. The Upper City lay south of this street. To the west rose the three Citadel towers, which I knew all too well from my encounters with Herod thirty years in the past and with Pontius Pilatus just a few weeks ago.

A block before reaching the Citadel, I turned left. I found Nicodemus's villa and listened at the door. Inside, voices were lifted in song. I did not want to disturb their Seder, but I needed to know if he had located Jeshua. I knocked, and the singing stopped. I brushed the dust off my cloak and adjusted my eye patch. Nicodemus opened the door, wearing a head kerchief.

"Salve—"

He pulled me inside, shutting the door and slamming the bolt home. "What news?"

"Nothing," I said. "You?"

"Jeshua's disciple, Simeon bar Jonah, was seen in Mount Zion just before sunset."

"Then let us go!" I said.

"Mount Zion covers the entire southwest city—he could be anywhere! Did you leave a message for Jeshua at Bethany?"

"Yes," I said. "With the very man he raised from the dead."

Nicodemus's mouth tightened. "So it is true. And the man shows no signs of . . ."

"Of dying again?" I asked. "No more than the rest of us. He is compelling evidence of Jeshua's power. And he has no fear for Jeshua. After listening to him, my own concerns were somewhat allayed."

"You're saying a man who can raise the dead is in no danger of dying himself?"

I shrugged.

"Regardless," said Nicodemus, "I do not want to see that hope tested."

"Nor do I," I said. "I am still determined to find him."

Nicodemus took my cloak. Before us was a courtyard surrounded by a portico. "There is nothing more we can do tonight," said Nicodemus, leading the way. "We'll find him tomorrow. Tonight he is celebrating Pesach, as we are."

We had crossed the courtyard and now stood under the portico before two doors. Nicodemus pulled them open. Inside, a table was crowded with food and people. "My family," said Nicodemus.

"Is that Eliyahu?" asked a boy in a tremulous voice.

"No," I said. "I am Melkorios of Alexandria."

"An Egyptian!" said a young girl.

Nicodemus lifted his hand for quiet. He turned to me. "I insist you join us."

"I am very tired," I said. "I have been on the road since early morning. I wish only a bite of porridge, a cup of wine if you have it, and a soft bed."

"You shall have all three," said Nicodemus, "but first you will celebrate Pesach with us." The force of his voice told me I had no choice. An open place was made for me alongside Nicodemus. I nodded my greetings and sat. There were a dozen adults and twice as many children, and it appeared that they were well into the dinner. Nicodemus turned to a boy and asked, "Jonah, do you remember what I said about strangers when I lifted the dish of matzo?"

Jonah pursed his lips and thought. The other children tittered, and Nicodemus's wife Adina shushed them. Jonah raised his chin and quoted: "All who are in distress, come and celebrate Pesach." He smiled proudly at a younger brother, who stuck his tongue out at him.

Nicodemus pretended not to notice. "Very good. Now, where were we?"

Hands went up. Nicodemus looked at another boy. "Taavi?"

"You were reading about the Destroying Angel," said Taavi, glancing at me.

"Just so," said Nicodemus, and he opened a large scroll and began to read: "And the Egyptians ill-treated us and laid heavy bondage upon us. And they set taskmasters over us, to afflict us with burdens, and we built cities for Pharaoh: Pithom, and Rameses. And we cried unto Hashem, and Hashem heard our voice, saw our affliction, our sorrow, and our oppression. And Hashem brought us forth from Egypt: not by means of an angel, nor by means of a seraph, nor by means of a messenger; but the most Holy, blessed be He, in His own glory, as it is said, 'I will pass through the land of Egypt this night, and I will smite every first-born in the land of Egypt, both man and beast; and on all the gods of Egypt I will execute judgment. I, the Eternal.' "

I had been listening, my hands in my lap, looking at the plate before me, which was filled with an odd assortment of food: a stick of celery, a hard-boiled egg, herbs, a roasted lamb shank, and a finely chopped salad of apples, nuts, and cinnamon. There was a goblet of wine, which I was aching to drain, but I dared not do so until the others drank.

I felt eyes upon me and looked up. Nicodemus was looking down at the scroll on his lap, his eyes moving from line to line. He looked up, and when he saw no reaction on my face, he continued reading: "How many abundant favors hath the Omnipresent performed upon us? If He had brought us forth from Egypt and had not inflicted judgment upon the Egyptians, it would have been sufficient. If He had inflicted justice on them and had not executed judgment upon their gods, it would have been sufficient. If he had executed judgment upon their gods and had not slain their first-born, it would have been sufficient . . ."

Again he stopped, and I understood why, for now I was listening. The children were looking at me fearfully. Here was an Egyptian at their very own table, and their father was reading about Egypt's many sins! They were wondering when I would explode. I cleared my throat and focused on the goblet before me. Had I drunk a few of these before entering his home tonight, nothing Nicodemus could have read would have offended me. But, parched of throat and clear of mind, anger welled in my chest. I wanted to shout, "I am *not* an Egyptian—I am a Greek!" but I knew such distinctions were lost there. To them, everyone who was not a Jew was an oppressor. I calmed myself. The events cited in the ritual, if they took place at all, occurred more than a millennium ago. Why should I take offense? So I said nothing and avoided the stares of the children.

Nicodemus continued, but his voice quavered, for he must have felt my anger. "He brought us forth from Egypt, executed judgment upon the Egyptians and their gods, slew their first-born, gave us their wealth, divided the sea for us, caused us to pass through its midst on dry land, supplied us with everything during forty years, fed us with manna, gave us the Sabbath, led us to Mount Sinai, gave us the Law, brought us to the land of Israel, and built the Holy Temple for us to atone for our iniquities." Then he raised his cup and said, "Therefore, we are bound to thank, praise, laud, glorify, extol, honor, bless, exalt, and reverence Him who performed for our fathers, and for us, all these miracles. He brought us from slavery to freedom, from sorrow to joy, from mourning to festivity, and from servitude to redemption. Let us therefore sing a new song in His presence. Hallelujah!"

"Hallelujah!" said everyone at the table, lifting their goblets.

Nicodemus sipped from his goblet. I grabbed mine, sloshing wine over the rim, and drained it in one long gulp. Everyone else had merely sipped from their cups. I looked around. The adults did not meet my eyes, but the children did, more out of curiosity than hatred.

"I feel ill," I said. "I beg your pardon." I got up and left.

Outside, I strode angrily across the courtyard. *I did not enslave their fathers!* I thought. *I did not force them to build the pyramids! I did not order the death of their first-born! I had nothing to do with it!*

Then why are you angry? my heart asked. *No one said* you *did these things.*

"Melkorios!" I turned. Nicodemus had followed me.

I raised my hand. "It is just a troubled stomach. I needed some fresh air."

Nicodemus said, "If you had stayed, you would have heard this: 'Blessed art thou, King of the Universe, who feeds the whole world with goodness, grace, kindness, and mercy, who gives food unto every creature. Thy mercy endures forever.' " Sincerity lit his eyes. "The Seder merely reminds us of the past," he said. "It is not an indictment of anyone."

"You are wrong," I said. "It is an indictment of *everyone.*"

I turned and walked out of the front door, closing it behind me.

Fifty-seven

It was cold, and my breath fogged. A rain shower had wet the streets. In my hurry, I had left without my cloak. I rubbed my arms as I walked, hating Jews, Egyptians, Romans, and myself. I limped along, hoping to find a place to eat where I would not have to hear about age-old grudges. But nothing was open.

Then I saw a man emerging from a side street. His hood was up, shadowing his face. He carried something in his arms and was looking back over his shoulder.

"Salve, citizen," I said, stepping into the light of a nearby torch sconce.

He stopped, startled. "Salve," he said, taking a step backward.

"Do you speak Latin?"

He shook his head. Another step.

"Aramaic?"

He nodded, looking around. He adjusted the bundle he held. It seemed heavy.

"I have lost my way," I said. "I am staying with Nicodemus."

He pulled his hood back, revealing a brown beard and side curls and dark, troubled eyes. "Nicodemus of the Sanhedrin?"

I nodded.

"Are they still in meeting?"

"I do not know. I am Melkorios—"

"Tell them," he said quickly, "tell them I cannot do it. I cannot. I just left him, and I cannot do it. Tell them." His eyes were red, but whether from tears or drink I could not tell. He took a step forward, holding the bundle out to me, which I saw was a leather sack. "They have not seen him in his glory, but I have! I cannot do it!" He shook the sack at me. Coins rattled.

"You know Jeshua bar Josef?" I asked.

He nodded miserably, then dropped the sack. The coins hitting the ground were so loud I expected every cutpurse in the city to be instantly upon us. I knelt to pick it up. The man turned away. "Stop!" I called, but he shook his head, raising his hood. "I am not in the Sanhedrin!"

He turned back and hauled me to my feet. "Who are you, then?"

"No one," I said, terrified. His grip was powerful, and rage filled his eyes.

He snatched the coin sack from me and shoved it inside his cloak. "Do you know the Kohen Gadol?" he barked. "Caiaphas?"

"No, but I know who he is."

He shoved me, and I fell to the ground, landing on my staff, breaking it. Pain shot up my leg. The man ran off, looking around as if he expected the very walls to lunge for him.

I called after him. "Where is Jeshua?"

At his name, the man broke into a run. I limped forward, but soon stopped. He was young and spurred by fear; I was old and tired. I also knew—though I did not know how—that going back to Jeshua was the last place he would go tonight.

It was after midnight before I found my way back to Nicodemus's home. I had to go back to the Citadel and retrace my steps. Finally, however, I stood before the heavy wooden door, knocking. There were footsteps, and a slide opened. An old man held up a lamp. I did not recognize him.

"I am Melkorios. I was at the Seder," I said.

"I was not," said the old man. "I was with *my* family."

I sighed. "I am the Egyptian."

"Oh!" he said, opening the door. "I heard about that."

"Where is Nicodemus?"

"At council."

"Do they often meet at midnight?"

The old fellow shrugged.

"Is the mistress of the house awake?"

"No," said the old man. "Everyone's asleep except me. I don't sleep much."

"When do you expect Nicodemus to return?"

"When he does," said the old fellow, leading me to an upper room. A meeting of the Jewish elders at midnight could have no other purpose than to consider the turmoil stirred up by Jeshua bar Josef. I hesitated on the stairs, thinking I should find out where they met and go there, but when I saw the soft mattress and plump pillows in the sleeping chamber, I forgot the urgency.

As you know, I am a weak man. The moment my head touched the pillow, I was asleep.

FIFTY-EIGHT

Nicodemus jostled me awake. "Wake up!" he hissed. "Melkorios! Wake *up*!"

I struggled to focus. I fumbled for my eye patch, but Nicodemus grabbed it from me. "They have him!" he said. "They have Jeshua!"

He helped me sit. I was still very tired. My eye socket throbbed and my back ached. Nicodemus removed a metal basin of water from a chair and placed it in my lap.

"Where were you last night?" I asked as I doused my face. The cold water made my head pound. I moaned and buried my head in my hands.

"An emergency meeting of the Sanhedrin was called, so I went to the Temple, where we usually meet. What I didn't know was that the Kohen Gadol was holding a secret tribunal at his home at the same time. Those of us he guessed would oppose him stood milling around the Inner Court like the fools we are. Damn him!"

"I also heard his name last night," I said. "A man with a bag of—"

"Get dressed," interrupted Nicodemus. "Quickly!"

I moved as fast as I could, but every joint ached. "When did they take him?"

"After his Seder with his followers." Nicodemus shook his head. "They ate not two blocks from here—and I did not know where he was!" He sat down, dismayed.

"I imagine that was on purpose," I said. "Jeshua undoubtedly wanted privacy, and the fewer who knew, the better. Not even his friends in Bethany knew where he was."

"After the Seder, Jeshua and his disciples went to Gat Shemen, an oil press in the Kidron. Caiaphas had a spy in their midst and knew their plan. He sent the Temple guard to arrest him."

"How do you know this?" I asked.

"Joel," said Nicodemus, shaking his head ruefully. "His fence-sitting paid off. Unlike me, he was invited to the tribunal, but when he opposed their decision, they ejected him."

"What decision?" I asked, my stomach churning.

Nicodemus looked flatly at me. Then he said, "The guard found Jeshua sitting under an olive tree, as if he were waiting for them. Joel watched from a distance as they tied Jeshua's hands and took him away." He buried his head in his hands.

I put my hand on Nicodemus's shoulder. "What then?"

Nicodemus looked up. "Joel followed them back to the Kohen Gadol's, then ran and fetched me. I was just returning from the Mount, fit to be tied. We went to Caiaphas's house and demanded entrance. The guards barred the way, but I started shouting and the neighbors began coming out of their homes. They finally let us inside."

I stood, ready to go, but Nicodemus still sat, running his hands through his long beard, distracted. I sat again.

"You should have seen it! I've never seen such a miscarriage of justice!" He pointed to himself. "We are daylight judges, not midnight executioners! For hours, they brought false witness against Jeshua, twisting his words. We voiced our objections, but Caiaphas overruled us. Finally, near dawn, he was convicted."

"Of what?" I asked.

"Blasphemy."

"Blasphemy? How so?"

"Caiaphas asked Jeshua if he truly *was* the Moshiach, as several witnesses had sworn. Now, mind you, Jeshua has never said he was the Moshiach— all the witnesses said was that they had heard others say he was."

"We call that 'hearsay,' " I said.

"I call it a travesty!" said Nicodemus. "Then Jeshua said, 'You have said it,' and Caiaphas tore his gown and shouted, 'You have heard it!' "

"What did they do?"

"They put a kerchief over his head and struck him, asking him to prophesy who it was who had hit him. I tried to stop them, but they threw me out."

"What happened then?"

"I waited in the shadows. Joel joined me later, after the tribunal finished. They knew the charges against Jeshua were weak. They also knew if they killed him, the people would riot. They argued for a long time, and finally Caiaphas said they had righteously condemned Jeshua as a sorcerer. The only thing that remained was to carry out the execution."

I sighed with relief. "Fortunately, blasphemy is not a capital crime."

"It is if the blasphemy threatens Rome."

"How could it?" I asked. "It is a religious matter. They would have to prove *maiestas*—treason—to execute him."

"Yes, and maiestas would be found if they convince Pilatus that Jeshua has cast a spell on the Emperor."

"Jeshua does not cast spells," I sputtered.

"No, but he casts out evil spirits," said Nicodemus. "And thus has knowledge of the Adversary. To many of my fellow rulers, Jeshua's miracles are magic because he does them outside of the authority of the Temple kohens. But most of all, raising that man from the dead just days ago is susceptible to the charge of necromancy."

"Nonsense," I said. "Why would the devil raise the dead?"

"To deceive us!" said Nicodemus.

"So you are saying you don't know the difference between miracles and magic."

Nicodemus met my gaze determinedly. "Do you?"

Silence stretched out between us. I knew he was right; I just hated the question.

"They took him to Pilatus, at the Antonia," said Nicodemus, finally.

"I thought he was at the Citadel."

"During festivals, he stays at the Antonia Fortress in case of trouble. We followed as they took Jeshua to the forecourt just before dawn. Pilatus came out on the porch in his bedclothes and invited us all inside."

"You went in?" I asked. "I am surprised you escaped with—"

"The Sadducees—Caiaphas and the chief kohens—went in. No Pharisee would defile himself by entering a Roman stronghold." He shivered.

"So you refused to go in and help Jeshua because of *purity* laws?" I was aghast.

Nicodemus hung his head. "I came back here to fetch you. You're a magistrate. You know Roman law. You can help Jeshua!" He hauled me to my feet. "Let's go!"

❦ ❦ ❦

The day was no more than an hour old when Nicodemus bustled me onto the street. We passed the High Priest's stately home with its tall walls and sharply pitched red roofs. A group of Sanhedrin members stood outside the entrance. As we passed, one of them engaged Nicodemus in a whispered conversation. I did not slow; if Jeshua was not here, I had no interest in this place. Nicodemus shortly caught up to me again. "What is the word?" I asked.

"Confusion," he said. "No one knows where he is."

We turned eastward along the old city wall. At the far end, south of the viaduct, the twin towers of the Hasmonean palace rose, their golden cupolas catching the morning sun. I moved slowly. When I fell last night, breaking my staff, I badly bruised my thigh. I was hobbling even more than usual. Nicodemus got under my arm to speed me up. As we turned down the street fronting the palace, he pointed. "Look!"

A crowd spilled from the porch onto the marble steps. Many present wore the Sanhedrin cloak with the gold border. As we scaled the steps, I said, "Pilatus is no fool."

"What do you mean?"

"You left before Caiaphas and the others emerged from the Antonia, but I can guess how it turned out," I said. "The High Priest accused Jeshua of blasphemy. Pilatus shrugged; what does he care about such things? But Caiaphas was adamant: Jeshua is a sorcerer who is leading the people into apostasy. Again, Pilatus shrugged. He knew very well who Jeshua threatened: just a few days ago, he led a crowd of cheering people into the Temple. So Pilatus was not inclined to do anything about Jeshua—he likes the idea of a challenge to Caiaphas, his enemy. This gives him power over the High Priest."

"Pilatus will need it," said Nicodemus. "His handling of the aqueduct riots has made his relationship with the kohens precarious."

"What riots?" I asked.

"A few months ago, Pilatus ran out of money for an aqueduct. He sent soldiers to the Temple and 'requisitioned' funds to cover the shortfall. The kohens demonstrated in front of the Antonia. Pilatus sent soldiers into the crowd dressed as Jews, and on his command they clubbed and stabbed the ringleaders. Caiaphas was outraged. As things stand now, he and Pilatus are avowed enemies."

"That is promising," I said. "If there is true enmity between them,

Pilate will oppose whatever Caiaphas wishes."

"I pray that is the case," said Nicodemus.

"But beware," I said, stopping. We were just a few steps below the crowd on the porch and I did not want anyone else to hear what I was about to say. "Both the Prefect and the High Priest are politicians, and politicians are nothing if not *pragmatic*. Their opposition may be mere theater. On the other hand, it may be real, and Pilatus may yet see Jeshua as an opportunity to mend fences with Caiaphas, who is wealthy and powerful. It would appear Pilatus has debts, and Caiaphas has money. Ergo."

"But why do you say Pilatus is no fool?" asked Nicodemus.

"Antipas is here, in the Hasmonean Palace, is he not?" I asked.

"How can you be sure?"

"Because Antipas rules Galilee, and Jeshua is a Galilean," I said. "Pilatus is engaging in Rome's most infamous political maneuver: in having a subordinate make a difficult decision, he thus insulates himself from possible negative consequences."

Nicodemus looked at me with newfound respect. He went up a few steps and spoke to another man, then returned. "You're right. Jeshua is inside. But I fear more for him here than I did at the Antonia. Antipas killed Johanan ben Zechariah."

"Yes, but Antipas grew up in Rome; he knows precisely why Pilatus sent Jeshua to him. If he is half as smart as his father, he will not take the bait."

"Here things get complex," said Nicodemus. "Antipas is a *tetrarch*, a local ruler, and part Jewish. He knows if he releases Jeshua, Caiaphas and the kohens will be angry with *him*, not at Pilatus. But if he kills Jeshua, the people will rebel, and by the time he gets back to Tiberias, his own life may be forfeit. Jeshua is, after all, the most important Galilean since Zadduk."

"The answer is before us," I said, pointing.

There was movement on the porch. We caught a glimpse of a dark-haired man in a purple robe, surrounded by Temple guards. A tall man in a blue turban and cloak followed: Caiaphas. The guards shuffled the captive along the porch toward the viaduct. The crowd started moving along the steps in the same direction. Nicodemus turned to me, confused.

"Apparently, Antipas did not take the bait," I said.

Fifty-nine

The procession passed under the arches of the Tyropoeon viaduct, picking up interested onlookers on the way. We fell behind because of my lame leg. Nicodemus was distressed at my slow pace but said nothing. Sure enough, we were headed back to the Antonia Fortress, where red banners on its ramparts fluttered in the morning breeze. More people joined the crowd, pushing us even further behind. Ahead, there were shouts as people recognized Jeshua.

If possible, an even greater number of people were entering the Temple Mount. I asked Nicodemus why that was, if the Seder was the previous night. Wasn't Pesach over?

"No," he said. "At noon, in the Temple, an unblemished lamb will be sacrificed in remembrance of the blood the Israelites painted on their door posts in Egypt so the Angel of Death would pass over that household."

I looked at Nicodemus to see if he saw the irony, but there was nothing on his face to indicate that he did. I hoped I was wrong.

A block from the Antonia, the procession stopped. Temple guards had set up a barricade where the street narrowed. Nicodemus elbowed our way forward, shouting that he was a member of the Sanhedrin. As we neared the barrier, we heard an echoing voice shout, "The Praefectus Iudaea! Salve Romani!" The street was empty beyond the barrier; the forecourt of the Antonia was around the corner to our right, out of our line of sight.

We exchanged worried looks and redoubled our efforts. Hope was kindled when two rulers of the Sanhedrin were allowed past the blockade. They disappeared around the corner.

Finally, our progress was halted by the throng. No one in front of us would move aside, no matter how much Nicodemus shouted. The Temple guards stood shoulder to shoulder behind the barrier.

"Go ahead," I said.

"I'll tell them to admit you," he said, shoving the man in front of him bodily out of the way. In a short time he was speaking to the guards, pointing at me. They let him pass. He waved me forward, then disappeared around the corner. I pushed as best I could, but it was some time before I faced a guard. "I am with Nicodemus. May I pass?"

He ignored me, shouting at the crowd. "Quit shoving back there!"

"I am a magistrate," I said. "I am expected at the hearing."

He finally looked at me. I did not look very magisterial, and his sneer told me so. He cocked his head. "Magistrate, huh? What court?"

"Requests," I said, hoping he did not probe further.

He did not, but he did say, "This is a capital case. I doubt they need your expertise."

"Nevertheless," I said, "I suggest you not impede me, or I shall see you flogged." I said it so flatly, so matter-of-fact, that the crowd around me fell silent. The guard too was taken aback. "What's your name?"

"Melkorios Alexandreus," I said. "Vizier to the Prefect of Egypt."

The guard started at the mention of Egypt. It seemed he too had attended a Seder last night. "You're here for the Prefect?" he asked tentatively.

He was asking if I was there to help Pilatus condemn Jeshua. Hating myself for lying, I nodded. The guard stepped aside. "Pass."

I crawled over the wooden barricade and limped down the street. As I turned the corner, I noted that all the men in the forecourt before me wore either the gold-bordered cloak of the Sanhedrin or the white robe of the Temple priests. Down an intersecting street was another barrier manned by guards holding an even larger crowd at bay. The mob glared at me as I crossed their field of view.

I turned to the fortress. A columned porch shaded two iron doors above many marble steps. Legionnaires filled the broad porch, scanning the hundred or so men in the forecourt. I could not pick out Nicodemus as everyone faced away from me.

Then the soldiers snapped to attention, striking their shields three times with the hafts of their gladii. Pilatus appeared in a white toga with a single red stripe trimming it. He looked out over the crowd. At the foot of the steps, Caiaphas rose from his seat in his sedan chair.

Pilatus snapped his fingers. Two soldiers appeared with a man held between them. His face was dirty, and one eye was swollen shut. His mouth was set, whether from resolve or anger, I knew not. His hair was matted, and he wore a shapeless tunic under a mocking purple gown. There was no doubt that this grim, weary man had once been the boy I had taken to the top of the Pharos lighthouse. His eyes were veiled in shadow, but I could feel the piercing power of his gaze as it moved across the silent men in the forecourt. A priest visibly blanched when Jeshua's eyes fell upon him. A member of the Sanhedrin made a hex sign and looked away. All around me men were glassy-eyed with fear, too afraid to shout their hatred and too weak-kneed to flee.

Jeshua's posture was regal but relaxed. His hands were clasped loosely before him. I marveled. If I ever found myself before a crowd of accusers such as this, I would not be meeting their hateful stares with his quiet dignity.

When his eyes finally found mine, they hesitated, as if he could not place me. And in that instant, my life focused as light through a prism, reaching pinpoint clarity. Evidence was presented, considered dispassionately, and my heart rendered the inarguable, just judgment: I was a coward. Like everyone else, I looked away.

Pilatus spoke. "You have brought this man before me as one who has threatened your Temple. I find no fault in him."

Someone shouted, "He is a sorcerer!"

"He may very well be," said Pilatus, "but he is harmless. Your charge of *maleficium*—harmful magic—cannot stand if he represents no danger to you, your people, or your temple."

Caiaphas pointed at Pilatus. "What about danger to *Rome*?"

Pilatus addressed the crowd as if he had not heard the question: "The custom during Passover is to free a prisoner, a remembrance of when the Hebrews were freed from Egypt. I was going to free the murderer Bar-Abbas, who killed a soldier during the aqueduct riots. In the spirit of reconciliation, I shall give you a choice." His benevolent gaze rested upon Caiaphas. "I will release either Jeshua of Nazareth, the sorcerer, or Bar-Abbas, the murderer."

A large man, his eyes peering out from under a mop of black hair, was brought forward. His hands and feet were bound with chains. He seemed disoriented, squinting at the crowd. The guards turned him to face the Prefect.

The priests began to chant, "Bar-Abbas! Release Bar-Abbas!" The words echoed off the fortress walls. "Release Bar-Abbas! Release him!"

I knew from the look on Pilatus's face that Caiaphas was feigning surprise at the choice.

Pilatus raised his hands, quieting the crowd. "As you wish," he said. "I will release Bar-Abbas. But what of Jeshua of Nazareth? What shall I do with him?"

Again, the priests, joined after a time by most of the Sanhedrin, began to chant: "Crucify him! Crucify him!"

It was at that moment that I finally spotted Nicodemus. He was near the front and was trying to reason with one of the shouting priests.

Pilatus raised his hands again and the men fell quiet. "I will not crucify him, for I've found in him no cause of death," he said. "But if it pleases you, I will chastise him, and then let him go." There were more shouts and fists raised. Spittle flew and hatred was hurled toward the Prefect.

Pilatus surveyed the crowd, frowning. "And even if it does *not* please you," he said, turning and leaving the porch, nodding at the soldiers to bring Jeshua along. The massive fortress doors shut behind them.

Bar-Abbas remained, blinking in the sun, surrounded by soldiers. The crowd began to converse, and I made my way to Nicodemus near the steps. He looked around in dismay.

"How will Pilatus chastise Jeshua?" I asked.

Nicodemus shook his head.

I started forward. I felt stares on my back as I limped up the steps. The legionnaires above me watched with amusement. "Centurion!" I shouted.

An officer appeared from behind the phalanx of soldiers. He found me sufficiently Roman to say, "What is your business, citizen?"

"I have evidence for the Prefect," I said. "I am Vizier to the Praefectus Alexandriae."

"You're a long way from home, dominus," said the centurion. He leaned forward and whispered, "Best to stay clear of this thing."

"I know the accused! I have come to give evidence on his behalf."

"Got all the evidence we need."

"An innocent man's life is at stake," I said, fixing him with my sternest gaze.

He gave me a humorless smile. "No one is innocent." He turned away.

I started forward, but the guards closed ranks. I glared at them, but they did not move. I finally turned and walked down the steps. As I descended, I met Caiaphas's eyes and saw a glimmer of recognition in them. I continued down the steps until I stood before him. "You are an evil man," I growled. "Jeshua is innocent."

"Ah," said Caiaphas, surprising me with a smile. "How fortunate you are here!" He turned to his fellow priests. "This is the Egyptian sorcerer who instructed Jeshua in the maleficium of which he has been found guilty!"

I looked at Caiaphas. "*You* are the sorcerer, transmuting lies into truth." I raised my voice, looking around. "Jeshua is innocent, and you all know it!"

A couple of younger priests reached out for me, but Caiaphas raised his hand. He leaned forward and whispered, "We could not prove an Egyptian connection until this moment. Thank you for settling the matter." He turned away, dismissing me.

I felt a hand on my arm and Nicodemus pulled me to one side. "It is too late," he said, leading me back to the rear of the assembly. Just then the fortress doors opened. The Prefect walked out onto the porch. The crowd went silent.

"He is innocent!" I shouted. Someone struck me from behind, almost knocking me off my feet. I turned and met the hateful stare of a priest.

Pilatus looked out across the crowd in a feeble attempt to engage each man as Jeshua had done so masterfully minutes before. The eyes that greeted him were sullen and uncompromising. He lifted his chin. "Behold the man!" he said.

Two soldiers dragged Jeshua forward. On his head was a crown of thorns that had been pressed down so hard that blood streamed down his face. As they turned him around for display, the audience gasped at the bloody welts on the backs of his legs. He had been beaten with bundled iron rods, a favored punishment in the legions. Nicodemus gasped in horror, but the men around us stood in stony silence.

Pilatus allowed himself a smile. "I have humbled him. I now release him to you."

"Crucify him!" shouted a Sanhedrin ruler. "He says he is the Son of God!"

Raising his hand for quiet, Pilatus turned and spoke to Jeshua, low yet clear enough for everyone to hear. "Is that true? Are you the Son of God?"

Jeshua raised his head and blinked blood from his eyes.

"I have power over you," said Pilatus. "I can crucify you, or I can release you." From his tone, he clearly preferred the latter, if only Jeshua would cooperate.

I noticed that Pilatus's hands trembled as he spoke. A glimmer of hope lodged in my heart. Pilatus was afraid of what Jeshua would do if he really *were* a sorcerer.

Jeshua raised his head and looked at Pilatus as if seeing him for the first time. "You have no power but what Adonai gives you," he said through broken teeth. It was an orator's voice, enlarged from speaking to thousands, yet gentled by private prayer.

A shiver ran up my spine. If Jeshua truly were the Moshiach, he would reveal himself now. I grabbed Nicodemus's arm. He nodded, also aware that this was the moment of truth.

But Jeshua did not call down angels to smite his accusers. Instead, he said to Pilatus, "Your soul is in jeopardy, yet the one who delivered me to you has the greater sin." He looked at Caiaphas.

Caiaphas spit on the ground, all pretense of dispassion gone. "Crucify him!" he raged, his teeth and fists clenched. The crowd repeated the words with increasing volume until our ears rang with the echoes in the confined courtyard.

Then, from the unseen crowd held at bay down the narrow streets, we heard, "Jeshua! Jeshua! Hosanna to God! Jeshua!" The priests and rulers, hearing the competing chorus, redoubled their efforts, drowning out Jeshua's supporters, shouting, "Crucify him! Crucify him!"

The Prefect's face went slack at the uncooperative captive at his side and the bloodthirsty mob at his feet. "Shall I crucify your king, then?" he said, one last appeal to vanity.

Caiaphas raised his hand and the crowd quieted. He glared coldly at Pilatus. "He said he is the King of the Jews. This is maiestas—sedition against the Emperor! He must die!"

"So he *is* your king, then," said Pilatus.

Caiaphas shouted, "*We have no king but Caesar!*"

I groaned. Jeshua's miracles and the charge of sedition were a murderous mix. The miracles meant he was either a sorcerer or a prophet. If he was a sorcerer, he could cast a spell upon anyone, including the priests and rulers. They were understandably afraid of him.

But in the Prefect's eyes, I saw nascent *belief.* After meeting Jeshua and sensing his power, Pilatus had shuffled him off to Antipas to avoid taking a stand against the Galilean. He knew Antipas would not kill Jeshua either. They had both hoped the priests and rulers would tire of this nonsense and let Jeshua go.

But now, with the men shouting for blood, Pilatus had to make a choice that might doom not only him but the Empire as well, if Jeshua's cursing power extended to Tiberias Caesar. So he had done the only thing he could think of to save his own life: he had humiliated and beaten Jeshua to incite him to demonstrate his power. Pilatus looked like a man waiting for a lightning strike, eyes squinted and hands clenched. The end was near.

But Jeshua just hung limply between the two soldiers, looking at Caiaphas, as blood dripped from his chin.

Relief entered the Prefect's eyes, and I groaned. Jeshua was not the Moshiach. He was not a sorcerer but merely an illusionist. He was not going to smite his accusers or light the sky on fire. He was just a foolish man out of his depth. He had tempted Rome's power and would now suffer.

Pilatus placed his palms on Jeshua's bloody cheeks and then held them up before us. The crowd, incited by the blood, roared even louder. "Crucify him! *Crucify him!*"

The unseen crowd behind the barricades, shocked by the murderous blood lust of the priests and rulers, fell suddenly silent.

Pilatus thrust his hands into a basin of water. "I am innocent of the blood of this man!"

"His blood be upon us and our children!" howled Caiaphas.

"So be it!" shouted Pilatus. He barked an order at the centurion and went back inside the Antonia. The doors closed solidly behind him.

The soldiers dragged Jeshua down the steps. The crowd, already pressed for space in the small forecourt, gave back but little. Nicodemus and I were pushed against a wall. Nicodemus, being much shorter than I, could not see. "What are they doing?"

"They are binding him to a post," I said. They pulled off Jeshua's robe and tore his tunic down the back. His hands were secured to two iron rings atop the post. When the soldiers released him, he fell to his knees.

Caiaphas turned and walked away, leaving his sedan chair behind. Two more soldiers came down the steps, stripping off their armor and baring their chests. One had a *flagrum*, a leather whip with tips embedded with lead balls, sharp bone, and glass shards. The other circled the post, showing his gladius to the crowd, warning them to move back.

All around me, I saw faces filled with hatred. Caiaphas left the forecourt, leaving his chief priests behind to oversee the brutality.

When the first stroke landed on Jeshua's back, an audible cry went up from the crowd despite their bloodlust. Nicodemus turned away. The whip fell again, and when I looked, Jeshua was shuddering with pain, blood dripping from his chin. His back bore two scarlet lines where the flagrum had opened deep gashes. I gasped, my stomach reeling. I looked back at Nicodemus. He had disappeared.

Above us, tattered clouds obscured the sun. My mouth tasted of ash. My fists were knotted so tightly my neck muscles ached. The whip fell again and again, making blood fly. Jeshua clutched the post, his skin flayed. I recoiled at the stink of anger and fear emanating from the men around me. I looked up, saw the sky roll back into darkness, and knew no more.

Sixty

I still looked up at the sky, but it was now dense with gray clouds.

"Shelama," said a voice. A young man's face came into view.

"Shelama," I repeated weakly.

"Do not move," said the youth, who had dark hair and a sparse beard. His tunic was drab, but his eyes were bright. I lifted my head and felt a stabbing pain in my neck. He cradled my head in his lap. "Careful, grandfather," he said. "You're injured."

I touched my face. My eye patch was gone. I blinked. The sun was painful in my eye as I looked around. We were alone in the forecourt. "What happened?"

"I don't know," said the young man. "I squeezed past the barricade and got here just as they finished scourging him. I saw you lying here. You must have fainted or been struck."

"Fainted," I said, grimacing at the pain in my empty eye socket. "What happened to him?"

"They've taken him away. To Golgotha."

All was lost. "They will crucify him," I groaned.

"Not unless he allows it," said the youth.

I looked at him. "What is your name, son?"

"My birth name is Arah, but Jeshua calls me Philip."

"You are his follower?"

Philip nodded. "I grew up in Cana, not far from Nazareth."

"Philip," I said, "what did you mean, 'not unless he allows it'?"

Philip gave me a knowing smile. "I have been with him since the first. I have seen what others have only heard rumors of. I saw him walk on the water."

"And Eleazar?" I asked. "When he arose from the dead?"

He nodded.

I slowly got to my feet and put my hand on Philip's shoulder to steady myself. I could barely turn my head for the pain in my neck.

"You should rest," he said.

"Later," I said, fumbling in my coin purse for a prutah with which to reward him.

Philip shook his head. "Jeshua says doing good is its own reward."

For the good he had done, Jeshua was about to be murdered. But I did not have the heart to point this out to the kind young man. "Thank you, Philip. Now go. Find your master."

"Will you be all right?"

"No," I said, "but that is no concern of yours. Go now."

Philip turned and in an instant was gone.

I hobbled down the cobblestone street. I had no trouble knowing where to go, for the weeping of women echoed in the narrow, winding streets. The procession must have passed this way not long ago, because many people still stood in the lane, women's faces buried in their aprons, men staring stoically at the ground, children standing blank-faced at their weeping mothers' sides.

As I left the city, wind whipped my chiton around my knees, raising a dust storm. I could barely see and stumbled along, hands out before me like the blind man I was. But I did not need to see where I was going—the keening lament of mourning women still led me. Others were on the road, but no one spoke. All eyes were lifted to the horizon. Before us was a barren, rocky hill with a garbage dump at its foot. A path led up the flank.

I stopped to catch my breath and looked around at the crowd gathered at the base of the hill, their kerchiefs raised to fend off the smell, their eyes raised to the summit. Some wore Sanhedrin cloaks or the robes of Temple priests. Nicodemus was not among them. A knot of legionnaires stood nearby, their hands on the hafts of their swords.

At the summit were three tall *gibbet* posts set into the ground. On the farthest gibbet, a man had been roped and nailed to a *patibulum*, or crossbeam. He was sobbing, clenching his fists in horrible agony. His wails came and went on the chill breeze, and I caught my breath, steeling myself for the horror I was about to witness.

A small group of people, not soldiers, stood to one side. A half-dozen red-cloaked legionnaires knelt on the ground near the first gibbet. Another man—possibly Jeshua—lay waiting to be nailed to his cross. I heard the ring of iron and a blood-curdling scream.

I began my ascent. The path was steep, and I concentrated on my footing. I was almost to the summit when I slipped on something wet, going down hard on one knee. I examined my bloody knee, but I was uninjured—someone else's blood had pooled on the stone. I got slowly to my feet and continued climbing upward.

Several legionnaires were kneeling around a man in front of the nearest gibbet. Others stood behind the post, holding ropes that went through an iron ring at the top of the post and down to the crossbeam on the ground. On command, the soldiers heaved, raising the patibulum. The victim shrieked. I wanted to cry out to them to be careful, but they grimly hoisted him up like a sack of grain. He moaned, then his shoulders dislocated, and for a terrible moment there was silence, then he screamed in such agony that the witnesses covered their ears in horror.

The crossbeam settled into its notch. The ropes were tied off. Soldiers bent the man's legs up under him and drove the ankle spike home. His scream cut off in the middle as his vocal cords tore, and thereafter his heart-rending cries were muffled.

Jeshua lay in front of the middle gibbet, his wrists already tied to the crossbeam. He was naked and his face was a bloody, pulpy mess. He still bore the thorn crown. In the group of people at his feet, I saw several women and two men, one of whom was Philip. He had an arm around a sobbing woman. As I stepped onto the summit, our eyes met. His were full of despair. Clouds brooded above us, turning everything gray except the blood and the soldiers' cloaks.

Soldiers knelt around Jeshua, two holding him fast, another raising a heavy maul. I heard a grunt, the sharp report of iron on iron, and a sickening melon-like sound, accompanied by a weak cry. Though Jeshua's face was blocked from view, his feet were not, and they twitched in agony, stilling only for the instant it took to drive in another spike. The soldier wielding the maul leaned back, armed sweat from his brow, and looked at me impassively. He turned and raised the maul again. I stumbled backward as it fell. Jeshua let out a hoarse cry.

Philip and the woman he comforted had turned away. A strikingly beautiful and grave woman with dark red hair braved the violence, her fists clenched in anger. A blond man had his arm around a third woman, whose face was invisible under her kerchief.

I heard a voice behind me. "Get up there!"

I turned and saw the Antonia centurion herding several Temple priests up the path. I stood aside as they summited. The centurion gestured at the crosses, and they walked over and huddled behind the middle gibbet. The working soldiers looked at the centurion, a question in their eyes.

"Pilatus says if they want him dead, then they can raise him up," he said. "See how they like *human* blood on their hands."

A ladder was set against the middle gibbet. A soldier threaded two ropes through the ring, then lowered them to another soldier. In short order, the ropes were tied to Jeshua's patibulum.

"Go ahead!" shouted the centurion, pointing at the rope. "Haul him up!"

The priests reluctantly picked up the rope and took up the slack. When they started pulling it taut, Jeshua cried out. The priests dropped the rope and backed away.

The soldier with the maul cursed and started toward them. They grabbed the rope again and began pulling Jeshua up onto the gibbet. The terrible creaking of stretching rope mingled with Jeshua's cries as he was lifted from the ground. The priests hauled the crossbeam up until it came to a rest in its notch, leaving Jeshua dangling in agony.

I started forward, but a soldier lifted his shield and struck me across the chest with it. I fell, stunned. As I got up, I heard a gasp and turned. Miriam stood behind me, her hands covering her mouth, her eyes wide in disbelief. We stared at each other across decades of years and hundreds of miles, finally brought together at this terrible time and place.

I reached out for her, but a hand gripped my shoulder, whirling me around. The centurion stood before me, his face chalked with dust and grime. "I remember you."

Behind him, two soldiers lifted and centered Jeshua's ankles on the gibbet. The soldier with the maul strode toward the cross, holding a long iron spike in his fist.

"You're the Egyptian vizier," said the centurion.

I could not take my eyes off Jeshua. The soldier drove the spike through Jeshua's ankles. He cried out. The women behind me screamed;

one voice was Miriam's. Anger flooded my heart; no mother should have to witness this horror.

The centurion moved to block my view. "You must be lettered," he said, thrusting a wax tablet into my hands. "Pilatus wrote the Latin," he said. "His scribe copied it in Hebrew. But we need someone who knows Greek."

"I am Greek," I admitted. The irony of my long-standing boast was not lost on me, even here, in Hades itself.

"Good," said the centurion, placing a stylus in my hand. "Copy it, then."

I looked down at the tablet. In Latin, it read:

IESVS NAZARENVS REX IVDÆORVM

Below it, scrawled in shaky Hebrew letters, was:

ישוע נצרט מלך היהודים

My Hebrew was poor and it was hard, in any case, to make sense of a language that did not use vowels, but something was wrong. I shook my head.

"What is it? asked the centurion. "Don't they say the same thing?"

"Yes," I said. "But that might be a problem."

"What does it say?" asked one of the priests from behind the cross.

"Both the Latin *and* the Hebrew say that this man"—I looked up at Jeshua shuddering on the cross, blood dripping from the spike through his ankles—"*is* the King of the Jews. Is that what Pilatus wrote?"

The centurion shrugged.

"It says *what?*" said one of the priests, coming over, carefully skirting the cross. I held up the titulus and he studied it, shaking his head slowly. "It's supposed to say, '*He said*, "I am the King of the Jews," ' not '*The* King of the Jews,' " said the priest. "It's wrong."

"Tell it to the Prefect," said the centurion, shoving the priest away. "Now you," he said, pointing at me, "copy it into Greek."

I looked up at Jeshua. He was gazing mournfully at the knot of people behind me. A crow settled on the iron ring above his head. A soldier batted it away with his spear, shouting, "Not yet!" and giving a bark-like laugh.

"Just write it," said the centurion, nudging me with his gladius.

I placed the tablet on my lap. Sweat dripped off my nose, puddling onto the wax. I pressed the stylus and wrote in a shaking hand:

ΙΗΣΟΥΣ Ο ΝΑΖΩΡΑΙΟΣ Ο ΒΑΣΙΛΕΥΣ ΤΩΝ ΙΟΥΔΑΙΩΝ

The centurion took the tablet and examined it. "No tricks, right?"

"I copied it word for word," I said, looking at the priests, who scowled at me in return.

One of the soldiers laughed. "Centurion, you can't even read *Latin*!"

"It doesn't matter," said the centurion. "Everyone knows who he is." He walked over to the priests and shoved the tablet into the hands of the one who had complained. "Now put it up!" he shouted. The priest did not move until the centurion started to withdraw his gladius, then he quickly mounted the ladder leaning against the gibbet and placed the placard above Jeshua's head.

I felt a hand on my shoulder and turned. Philip stood before me, and with him was Miriam, tears filling her eyes. "It *is* you," she said, clutching my hand in hers. "Melchior!"

I kissed her hands, but no words came. Then Jeshua spoke, but not to us. He was looking at the priests. "Abba," he croaked, "forgive them, for they know not what they do."

The priests blanched and turned away, hurrying down the path.

A soldier held up Jeshua's purple robe. "Wait! Don't you want a chance to win this?"

The soldiers laughed. One produced a pair of dice and the legionnaires gathered around.

I turned to Miriam. "You should not be here."

"Where else should I be? He is my son."

The wind shifted, and from the foot of the hill we heard the priests, now safely at a distance, shout, "You saved others, Jeshua, but you cannot save yourself! If you're the King of the Jews, come down from the cross— then we'll believe!"

Miriam ignored their jibes and looked up at me. "Why are you here?"

"It had been so many years," I said. "I had hoped to see Jeshua on his throne, but it has all come to nothing . . ."

"You have changed much," said Miriam, nodding at the puffy red scar across my face.

I shook my head. "How I wish that were true."

I looked at Jeshua again, and now he was looking at me. I limped over to the cross. A rivulet of blood dripped from his feet, tracking down the gibbet. "Jeshua!" I moaned. In his eyes I saw numberless worlds where love reigned—but not on this one. If they would kill a man such as he, then this world was lost. "Please," I said, looking up at him desperately. "You can stop this! You cannot end this way!" Unable to speak, he just looked down at me as blood dripped from his chin. I collapsed to my knees. Philip and the other man picked me up, turning me toward Miriam.

"Do not despair, Melchior," said Miriam, her eyes nonetheless wet with tears. "We don't understand why, but he said it must be so."

"Why must it?" I said. "His death will change nothing! Rome rolls on unimpeded. He will be forgotten! Where are his disciples? Where are his throngs of followers? Where are the legions of angels they say he commands? He is a *man*, Miriam," I shouted, "and he is going to *die*!"

Miriam blinked at me, shocked by my outburst. I bent toward her. "I am sorry. I brought myrrh from Egypt as a gift, just as I did so many years ago, to celebrate his kingship. But I was robbed in Samaria, and now I have nothing." I dug into my belt and withdrew the gold denarius Zebulon gave me. "Except this," I whispered, pressing it into her palm. "For his burial."

"I used your myrrh after his birth," said Miriam, considering the coin. "I will use this for his death. It will buy olive oil, aloe, and myrrh, and we will anoint his body." She looked up at me. "He knew you, Melchior," she said, "but I wonder if you ever really knew *him*."

Sixty-one

I stumbled down the hill, took a spill, and came to a stop in front of a group of priests. Seeing how dirty I was compared to their own white robes, they did not help me up.

"Don't *you* die today," said one, giving me a wide berth.

"He will soon enough, from the looks of him," said another.

"Sons of Dis!" I spat. This brought only laughter. "Hades take you!"

"As he's taken you!" shouted one.

Just then, a black dog darted between us. The priests jumped back, alarmed. I pointed at them. "Bloody rain!" I shouted. "Poxed entrails! Barren wombs!"

My curses shook the humor from them. They made signs, muttering counter-incantations. "Kohens!" I shouted. "As you said: his blood shall be on you and your children!"

Just then a blinding knife of lightning blasted the summit of the Mount of Olives, accompanied by bone-rattling thunder. I shook my fist at the priests and limped off.

By the time I reached the city gate, day had drained away. Torches on both sides of the arch had been lit but sputtered weakly in the wind, giving almost no light. Clouds hung low, and a mist had arisen. I could see no more than a few feet in front of me. Inside the city, I passed people looking heavenward, making warding-off gestures. Though it was after noontide, it was midnight-dark. Now and then light flashed in the east, and a moment later, thunderclaps too near for comfort put my heart in my throat.

I intended to return to Nicodemus's home in the Upper City, but when I saw the pale walls of the Temple Mount, I felt compelled to turn toward them. I was wearier than I had ever been in my life. I imagined that when my feet finally stopped moving, so would the blood in my veins. The darkness reminded me of my nightmare of the River of Death. At any moment, I expected to see the solar barque gliding out of the fog with Horus at the tiller and Osiris upon his golden throne.

After several wrong turns, I finally found the steps of the Tyropoeon viaduct. I expected to see a multitude—they were sacrificing the Pesach lamb today.

They already did, came a voice from within.

As I scaled the steps, I looked up, trying to distinguish the sacrificial smoke from the glowering clouds but could not. At the summit, the bridge was nearly empty, and everyone that emerged from the dark fog was leaving the Mount. Perhaps they were closing the Mount because of the darkness. I groped my way along the viaduct, squinting into the dank mist.

Finally, the Coponius Gate appeared. The twin doors stood ajar, unattended. I passed under the arch and felt rather than saw the expanse of the Great Court before me. Though the Temple complex hulked directly in front of me, I could not see it. I listened for voices but heard nothing aside from the wind's moan.

I found the low stone balustrade and felt my way along it, finally coming to a corner, and followed it to the Temple entrance. There were no priests, no guards, and no patrons. I sniffed at the air; the fog had cleansed it of all smell.

Suddenly, light exploded in the darkness, and every drop of suspended water glistened like a diamond. I was thrown to the ground. Thunder boomed, and I covered my head, expecting a rain of debris. When none came, I got to my feet, my eye throbbing from the flash, an image of the Temple seared into it: the gold and white Sanctuary looming above me.

I groped past the balustrade and up the first set of steps, finally stubbing my toe on the steps of the Beautiful Gate. The doors stood open, framing an even deeper darkness. I collapsed wearily on the top step, leaning against the doorpost. I could not see the balustrade, though it was only a few paces away. I pressed the heels of my palms into my weary eye sockets. My neck ached dully, my left knee throbbed, my nose was running, and my head was stuffy.

"Hello!" shouted someone, as if from a great distance.

I saw no one, but heard the shuffling of feet. "Over here," I said. Soon a burly man in a striped cloak appeared. He carried a torch that gave off little light. His cowl was thrown back revealing a bald head above dark eyes and a black beard. "Where is everyone?" He took a step closer. "What are you doing inside the soreg? Where are the guards?"

I shrugged and began to rise, but he gestured at me to stay seated. He tossed his useless torch aside and sat down heavily on the step. "Doesn't matter. Nothing matters." He stared into the darkness, which had drawn so close around us I could barely make out his features.

"To tell the truth," I said, "I am surprised no one is here."

"After last night, nothing will ever surprise me again," he said. His hair was wild, and his eyes were red. He seemed distant even from himself as he gazed blankly into the darkness.

"You are a Galilean?" I asked, noting an accent I with which I had become familiar. He shot me an uneasy glance. "I hail from Egypt," I said. "Came all this way for nothing."

He nodded in a way that made me think he too had come a long way for nothing. I was about to speak when he said, "It is not nothing. And that is my greatest fear."

"That it is *not* nothing?

He nodded.

I almost laughed. I had been thinking that I had would have traded *everything* for the hope of *anything*. The emptiness of a world that would kill a man like Jeshua left me hollowed out; now this man said there was something even worse. "What is it you fear?"

"He called me Cephas," he said, shaking his head.

"That's 'rock' in Greek," I said. "A compliment?"

"I thought so," he said. "But perhaps he meant dense as a stone. I'll never know."

"Why not?"

The man regarded me, his gaze settling on my empty eye. "Because they've killed him."

"Jeshua," I said, no longer surprised at these coincidental meetings. "You knew him?"

He did not answer for a long time. "No," he said finally. "But I denied him—just as he said I would." Looking at him was like looking into a mirror, for in his eyes I saw my own emptiness. "They took him to the Kohen Gadol's. Johanan went in with him, but I was afraid."

I said nothing. It seemed everyone I met had a story about Jeshua they needed to tell.

"I tried to prevent his arrest," said the man, pulling a short sword from his belt that still had blood on the blade. "I cut off a kohen's ear. Jeshua reprimanded me, saying those who live by the sword will die by it. If only that were true!" He dropped the blade and it rang on the stone. "As I waited in the courtyard, three times I was asked if I knew Jeshua, but each time I said no."

"What is your name?" I asked.

"You will hear it soon enough," said the man. "I will be remembered as the disciple who denied the Moshiach."

"*Is* he the Moshiach?" I asked.

"He could have been. But they crucified him. I was too ashamed to even watch." He smote himself on the breast. "I should have stopped it, but I was afraid!"

Lightning struck again, and for an instant the eastern portico cast a garish shadow across the Court. The storm was moving our way. "At least you knew him," I said. "I came all the way from Egypt and never got to speak to him until I was at the foot of the cross. By then all he could do was look at me. His eyes . . ." I could not continue.

"After I denied him the third time," said my companion, "they brought him out of the Kohen Gadol's house. He looked at me. I was ashamed and ran away—I have been hiding ever since. I've come here to cast myself off the Temple pinnacle, but I'm too much of a coward."

"Strength in numbers," I said. "I may join you." I extended my hand. "Melkorios."

He took my bony hand in his broad one. "Simeon."

We sat staring at nothing. "Hurry, darkness," I said, quoting Homer. "Cover our sins."

Simeon nodded.

Suddenly, the hair on my neck tingled. The earth began to shake. We were tossed off the steps and thrown, sprawling, onto the flagstones. A roaring filled my ears. The earth beneath me shrieked, and I scrabbled away as a fissure opened up where I had been lying. Chunks of marble paving tilted and fell into the darkness below.

A great *crack!* rattled my teeth, and I looked behind me. The steps of the Beautiful Gate were jarred loose and fell in succession into an immense fissure. The doorjambs shook, and the great golden doors, now unhinged, toppled into the ever-widening crevasse. From inside the courtyard came a succession of *booms!* as marble columns fell, followed by the *whoosh!* of air carrying choking marble dust. The ground rose and fell like the deck of a storm-tossed ship. The Temple walls shook like curtains, tearing asunder, great stone blocks toppling to the ground with deafening *thuds*.

After more than a minute, the earthquake stopped. Simeon helped me to my feet. The impenetrable darkness had receded a bit, and a weak, gray light allowed us to make out the basic shape of the Temple complex for the first time. The exterior walls lay in great heaps of broken stone. "Can you see the Sanctuary?" I asked, my eye smarting at the fuming stone dust.

Simeon pulled me forward, helping me skirt the crevasse that had swallowed the Beautiful Gate. We climbed over a pile of stone and ducked under the broken lintel.

The pavilions at each corner of the Women's Court had been reduced to piles of rubble; broken columns were scattered about like jackstraws. We threaded our way over and around them, slowly making our way to the Nicanor Gate. The steps leading up to it were split cleanly in half, the chasm running further into the darkness. The doorway lintel was broken and sagging almost to the ground. We crawled under it and entered the narrow Men's Court. I peered into the darkness, unable to see the Sanctuary, though I felt its looming presence.

To our left, the altar had literally exploded, its immense stones hurled across the Court. One of the four giant horns, caked with years of dried blood, lay shattered on the pavement, blood sizzling on its white-hot surface. The bronze brazier had been cleaved in two as if by a giant's sword stroke. Coals glowed red underfoot. The butchering tables and animal pens were piles of broken stone, splintered wood, and bloody carcasses.

Simeon picked up a stick of wood and thrust it into some coals. It caught fire and he held it high. We saw two slashes of red in the distance—the bronze Sanctuary porch columns. One lay across the stone steps. The other leaned against the Sanctuary wall. The jagged tear in the earth ran up the steps. The enormous golden Sanctuary doors had been smashed into kindling, and the entrance was a black rectangle out of which roiling smoke billowed. Simeon made his way across the courtyard and up the broken steps. He finally stood on the Sanctuary porch, a tiny figure holding a faint flame.

I slowly picked my way forward, shouting at Simeon, but getting no response. After an interminable time, I found the steps and began crawling upward, feeling the broken stone shift under my weight, expecting at any moment to fall into the apparently bottomless crevasse.

Simeon was staring into the darkness of the Sanctuary when I finally reached him. His torch had gone out, and he was flagging smoke with his cloak. I peered into the antechamber, which was lit by a flaming carpet that had been ignited by an overturned candelabrum. The antechamber was *tau*-shaped, the narrow stem ending at twelve broad steps, above which hung a tall curtain of indigo, scarlet, and purple. The chasm—the same one that rent the Beautiful Gate—zigzagged across the room and up the steps, disappearing under the veil into the *Kodesh Hakodashim*—the Holy of Holies.

As I watched, a tapestry fell off a wall, toppling a brazier and hurling blazing oil onto a wooden chest. The coverlet burst into flame, engulfing several loaves of bread that had been stacked on the chest. For a brief moment, the aroma of baking bread filled the room, then the loaves were consumed in a flash of broken light.

The fire raced up the steps from one pool of lamp oil to another until it reached the veil. In seconds, the Sanctuary was filled with light as the flames licked up the thick curtain. In the smoky darkness high above, something snapped, and half of the veil wafted to the ground, soon engulfed in flame and firing carpets, tapestries, and furniture.

"Adonai!" shouted Simeon, tugging his cloak over his head and running into the Sanctuary. I followed but was turned aside when another tapestry fell, throwing up a wall of flame before me. Through the fire and smoke, I saw Simeon take the Kodesh Hakodashim steps three at a time. Shreds of burning veil drifted downward, landing unnoticed on his head and shoulders. I sidestepped the flames and climbed the steps, drawing alongside Simeon at the entrance of Judaism's most sacred precinct. I squinted into the darkness. Simeon's eyes were bulging with astonishment.

"What is it?" I asked.

"There's nothing here!"

Piles of burning veil behind us threw our shadows into the inner chamber. It was indeed empty. Simeon turned to me, his pupils reflecting the flames. "He said he would destroy the Temple and raise it in three days!"

I looked around. Everything was on fire. The tapestries were veritable torches. Acrid smoke bubbled along the ceiling, dropping ever lower. "We will be suffocated!" I shouted, coughing.

Simeon shucked his cloak and threw it over me. Then he grabbed me roughly, slung me over his shoulder, and picked his way down the steps. I found it hard to breathe, hauled, as I was, like a sack of grain. After an interminable time, he laid me down and pulled off the cloak. We were outside, at the foot of the Sanctuary steps. He lugged me over to the *laver*, a water-filled basin balanced on the backs of twelve stone oxen, and scooped water into my face. I came to, coughing. He leaned toward me, shouting, but I could not hear him.

He picked me up again and carried me out of the Temple, not setting me down until we were outside the balustrade, where I collapsed in another coughing fit. Without a word, he ran off toward the Coponius Gate at a sprint, disappearing into the gray mist. I looked back at the Temple. Red and yellow flames leapt into the sky above the Sanctuary.

I felt a hand on my shoulder. A young priest knelt next to me, his eyes reflecting the fiery horror. He gripped my shoulder so tightly I cried out in pain. He let go, rose, and walked stiffly toward the Beautiful Gate. As he scaled the broken steps, he was silhouetted by a wall of fire.

Sixty-Two

I must have fainted again, because when I awoke, there were many priests running in and out of the Temple, retrieving bundles of charred fabrics and armloads of golden tableware.

As I rounded the fallen walls, flames from the Sanctuary inferno threw my shadow before me. If not for their hellish light, I would have fallen into the chasm where the Tyropoeon viaduct had once stood.

The bridge was gone, reduced to a tumble of stone far below. Only portions of the arches remained. I heard screaming and crying. I held on to the gatepost, my heart racing. Had Simeon hurled himself off this precipice in despair, or had he inadvertently fallen to his death as he raced out the gate?

I felt my way southward through the Great Court toward the Huldah Gate, where Balthazar and I had first entered the Mount all those years ago. After what seemed like an hour, I finally stood before the tunnel entrance. The darkness before me was terrifying. I turned. Far across the Court, the Sanctuary fire was burning itself out. Now only a faint hellish glow rose above the ragged walls.

I turned back to the tunnel and fear gripped me. The ramp sloped steeply downward, disappearing into utter blackness. As I stepped forward, the temperature dropped suddenly. Sweat that sheened my brow quickly turned to ice, and my heart froze. I touched the wall and took a step forward, then another, and another. I was moving slowly, but I was moving. Then I touched something hot and recoiled, stumbling backward, holding my hands up before me, crying, "Hashem! Hashem!"

I looked behind me. The tunnel's downward slope had removed the Temple glow from sight, and the archway was only incrementally less dark than the tunnel itself. I rubbed my elbow, feeling wetness there, knowing it was blood.

Tentatively, I reached out again, closing my eyes against the horror, and touched the wall. This time, I felt warm metal. I heaved a sigh of relief. A sconce. The first time I had touched the torch head, which had been blown out by the earthquake, I supposed, which was why it was still hot. I pulled the torch from its holder, wishing I had flint. I did not, but at least now I had a club.

I took another tentative step. Only a thousand to go.

Eventually I found Nicodemus's home. It was very late. Most of Jerusalem was asleep; the earthquake's damage seemed to have localized on the Mount. Here and there, I saw cracks in a façade or a tumbled wall but no wholesale destruction. Normal darkness had returned, offering familiar shades of black. The sun had set, and with it, the blinding darkness that prohibited me from seeing my hand in front of my face. Jeshua's death had turned the world inside out—night had become brighter than day. I seriously wondered if the sun would rise in the morning. Perhaps Amun-Ra himself had been destroyed along with Hashem's temple.

Nicodemus's servant let me in. His master had not returned. His wife and children were asleep, worn out by worrying and fear. I climbed the stairs to my room and huddled under a blanket, staring out the window, scanning the sky for stars.

There were none.

In the morning, I awoke, faintly surprised to see the sun peaking over the Temple Mount. The Sanctuary, normally rising majestically above the parapets and visible from any point in Jerusalem, was gone. Smoke coiled heavenward from where it once stood.

Nicodemus had returned shortly after I did the night before. He sat in his courtyard, a blanket pulled tight around his shoulders and head, lost in thought in the chill morning air. I carried with me a small bundle of possessions I had managed to hold onto during my travels.

"You are going," said Nicodemus flatly.

I nodded.

"I was waylaid," he said, pulling the blanket back to reveal a puffy eye, turning purple. "The kohens attacked me." He touched the swollen flesh and winced. "Now I'm like you," he said, attempting a sad joke.

I did not want to talk. I turned toward the door.

"Melkorios?" asked Nicodemus.

I turned.

"When I arrived at Golgotha, he was dead."

I nodded.

"Then the quake, and we all fell to the earth. I cowered in the refuse heap for hours as the city shook itself asunder. I was afraid."

"I was too," I said.

"Was it Hashem?" asked Nicodemus. "Punishing us?"

"If it was, he was angry at more than Jeshua's murder—he destroyed his own Temple."

Nicodemus nodded. "I saw it, late last night. Split right down the middle, the Kodesh Hakodashim is now open to the heavens. I guess Jeshua meant what he said—that he would destroy the Temple."

I remembered Simeon saying the same thing. "But why?" I asked.

Nicodemus shrugged. "I thought he meant something else."

"What other temple could he have meant?"

"Himself," said Nicodemus.

"Well," I said, turning away, "in either case, he succeeded."

I considered just walking west out of Jerusalem until I reached Alexandria. In my state of shock, it seemed a credible plan. But I still had Eleazar's horse and knew I should return it to him. They were not rich, and a horse was a valuable commodity. I retrieved it from the stable near Nicodemus's home and headed down the Tyropoeon Valley, exiting Jerusalem at the foot of the City of David. I followed the road as it turned up the Kidron Valley and remembered searching a bazaar here with Caspar and Balthazar for a gift to give the newborn Moshiach.

On my left was the Necropolis, climbing up the Moriah hill, its rocky terraces terminating just under the pinnacle, a sheer stone wall a hundred cubits tall. There were people going and coming, carrying shrouded bodies. I wondered if they had found Simeon's broken corpse this morning, just a few feet from the other dead. Or perhaps one of those shrouds covered Jeshua's body. In addition to him, apparently many others had died in the cataclysm yesterday. I wondered why he would take so many others to Hades with him. Whose logos was *that?*

Ahead were the remains of the Red Heifer Bridge. Constructed of wood, it too had collapsed, and the timbers were now being scavenged by people whose homes had no doubt been destroyed in the earthquake. A large portion of the bridge had fallen across the road, blocking it, so I took a path to the right, which climbed up the Olive Mount.

Soon I was a good way up, surrounded by terraced orchards, when I saw Gat Shemen, the press where Jeshua took his followers after their Seder meal and where Nicodemus said he was arrested. What significance was there in an olive press? I thought about Esther, the woman in Nazareth, who also owned a press. What was it she had said to me? "Jeshua will teach you to be unafraid."

I looked back at the Mount. Under the leaden sky, the charred, tumbled Temple walls mocked the very idea. Smoke rose above the Sanctuary—a new kind of sacrifice.

"Teach me to be unafraid?" I muttered. "No. He taught me to fear *everything.*"

When I arrived at Eleazar's home in Bethany, the door was shut. From inside, women's voices were raised in a sorrowful lament:

> *May his great name be exalted and sanctified*
> *In the world which will be renewed*
> *And where he will give life to the dead*
> *And raise them to eternal life*
> *And may his salvation blossom and his Anointed be near*
> *During your lifetime and during your days*
> *And during the lifetimes of all the house of Israel*
> *Speedily and very soon!*

Then a man's voice, which I recognized as Eleazar's, in a clear tenor:

> *May his great name be blessed forever*
> *And to all eternity!*

I knew this song; it was the Mourner's Kaddish. I had heard it sung outside Mesha ben Huz's sepulcher in the Alexandria necropolis. I was loath to knock at the door, for I feared they had Jeshua's body inside, and I would have to face it—and them—with all my pain and anger.

I turned away and bumped into a woman in a black mourning cloak. She was veiled and carried a water jar on her hip. I backed up, thinking she was a servant. "I do not wish to disturb them," I said, nodding at the door. "But this is Eleazar's horse." I held out the reins.

She put the amphora down and lifted her veil. It was the same beautiful red-haired woman I had seen on Golgotha, whose hands clenched with anger as she watched them crucify Jeshua.

"You are the magus," she said.

"I am no one," I said. "Here." I held out the reins.

"Won't you come in?" she asked, reaching for the door latch.

I closed my hand over hers. "I cannot. Please understand."

"We are saying Kaddish," she said. "Will you not join us?"

The voices inside continued singing:

May he who makes peace in his high places
Grant peace for us
And for all Israel

I shook my head. "I cannot."

"Is it because the Kaddish mentions the Anointed One?"

I shook my head. "It is because I cannot bear to see his body."

Inexplicably, she smiled. "He is not here," she said. "We placed him in the tomb last night. Miriam bought salves and oil with the money you gave her. I know she will want to thank you." She reached out for the latch again.

I did not try to prevent her. I just dropped the reins and walked past her, up the street. Beyond the wall, the mourners were singing:

May the prayers and supplications of all Israel
Be accepted by their father who is in heaven

"Wait!"

I kept walking. Soon a hand grasped my sleeve. I turned. She looked up at me and was surprised to see tears in my eyes. She took my hand, and I looked around, knowing such a thing, especially during mourning, was strictly prohibited in her religion.

"You loved him," she said, her eyes gleaming.

I looked away.

She squeezed my hand in both of hers. "I did too." Her eyes met mine, and I was reminded of Deborah, whose beauty I thought could never be eclipsed, but I was mistaken. "He is," she said in Aramaic.

I caught the double meaning. "He is" was a form of the verb "to be." The first person form, "I am," is what Adonai called himself on the Sinai mountaintop as he spoke to Moshe from the burning bush. It was also an affirmation that Jeshua was not dead.

"But he *is* dead," I said flatly.

She let go of my hand. I turned away again.

"He promised us eternal life," she said.

I raised my hand as a precursor to speaking, then dropped it. Reasoning with these people was futile. I walked on a few paces, then stopped and turned. She still stood there, her hands out before her, radiant in her hope, yet tears streamed down her face.

"If you believe, then why do you cry?" I asked.

She shook her head.

I took a step closer. "Why?"

"I cry for you," she said. "Because you do not believe."

I nodded.

"You cannot," she said. "Not as I do."

My shoulders went slack, and I bowed my head. I was going to hear about another miracle.

She came toward me. "You cannot believe because you have not seen. And I cannot show you. But I *saw*. He opened my heart and filled it." My look begged the question. "With love," she finished, reaching out for my hand.

"There is no such thing," I said, pulling back.

"Your wife would not say that."

"I have no wife," I countered, tears welling.

"Yes you do," she said. "The Spirit whispers that you will see her again."

"Stop!" I shouted, raising my hand and turning away in grief. "No more lies!"

She grasped my hand and held it to her cheek. No one had held my hand in fifteen years. I wanted to pull it away, to scream that she had no right to remind me of what I had lost, but I did not. I recoiled and rejoiced at the same time in the warmth of her touch. After a time, she let go, and

I leaned against a nearby wall, exhausted from the inner conflict.

It began to rain. I looked up in dismay. Insult to injury.

But she turned her face up, closing her eyes, smiling.

"Why do you smile?" I asked.

Her eyes remained closed as the rain washed her face. "The spring rain brings life. He will awaken."

I remembered what young Jeshua said to me in the Valley of the Kings about the dead awakening to everlasting life.

She opened her eyes and said, "Then, he will awaken *you*." She turned to go.

"What is your name?" I asked.

She stopped and raised her hood. "Miriam," she said, "of Magdala." She continued toward the door, gathering the horse reins and picking up the water jar.

I turned away. In Aramaic, Magdala meant "magnificent."

$\mathcal{S}$IXTY-THREE

The stable master grimaced at my singed hair. "Where have you been, grandfather?"

"Hades," I replied flatly.

Unlike most of the other stable masters I had met on my journeys, he was a kind soul, and when he saw I had no provisions for the Sinai and no money left after buying the camel, he had his wife pack me some flatbread, cheese, and dried mutton, and he gave me a full water skin.

On the Via Maris, dunes rising to my right and a blistering hot wind blowing incessantly from my left, I rode along listlessly, not caring when or if I arrived home. I ate none of the food I had been given; I had no appetite. My remaining eye had been scorched in the Temple fire and it pained me to open it. What little I could see was cloudy, so I tore a strip of fabric from my chiton and made a blindfold. Thus I passed through the desert, blind in eye and dead in heart.

Occasionally a caravan would approach, and I would lift the blindfold to watch as the indistinct shapes passed. I looked near death; most people would take my appearance as punishment from the gods and avoid me. That was the only part of my trip that pleased me.

I lost track of time. I dozed as the camel trudged along. For a few days, I drank when thirsty, but my thirst eventually ceased. When the camel stopped, I dismounted and slept, leaning against its slowly moving rib cage. I had no dreams; my mind was scoured like the Sinai itself. When the camel stirred in the morning, I would grope my way onto it again and hope the coming day would be my last. I knew I was close to death because I neither feared nor welcomed it.

Then one afternoon, the camel's gait changed. I pulled up my blind-fold. We had left the main road and were heading toward the southern mountains, which rose like gray steps toward the white sky. I pulled my blindfold back down and returned to the thoughtless darkness.

When I awoke, we had stopped. I squinted into the fading light. Before me, burnished crags jutted upward, their peaks blazing red in the setting sun. I faced an alcove, the entrance framed by limestone boulders. Inside, two stunted palms bent over a shallow pool of muddy water. There was a fire pit of blackened stones. A shock of recognition jolted me. I had been here before: once thirty-odd years ago, and again just three months ago.

I dismounted and limped over to the fire ring. I first met Apep here and took his appearance as a sign to return to Judea. There I found Josef and Miriam and their newborn son and took them with me to Egypt, beginning the pointless journey I was now finally ending.

I looked around, perversely satisfied. It was fitting that I die where my flesh would feed scavengers and my bones would feed the earth. As far as my *ba*—if I possessed one—was concerned, I cared not whether it was condemned to the emptiness of Tartarus, to endless coma in the Underworld, or eat dirt forever in Gehenna. I concurred with Epicurus, who was famously droll about death. He said when a man is alive, he does not feel the pain of death because he is not experiencing death. And when he dies, he does not feel the pain of death because he is dead, and since death is annihilation, he feels nothing.

I preferred annihilation because I could not bear to ponder the fantastic failure of Jeshua's self-destruction. Why did he attack the priests in their own temple? When Antipas asked him about his miracles, why did he not answer? Why was he rude to the Prefect, who, it was clear to me, *wanted* to set him free? In short, why did he not render unto Caesar what was Caesar's, as he had counseled others to do just the day before?

Hubris. He overestimated his abilities, and his arrogance killed him. He would be forgotten—the latest in a long line of failed messiahs. Yet he was not entirely to blame; the root cause of his hubris flowed in his blood: the Jews could not work within any system but their own. The Gauls, recently conquered, already had men in the Senate, yet the Jews had been Roman subjects for a hundred years and still had no one in the halls of power!

It was Adonai's fault—he was an absurdly jealous god. That, and their barbarous self-mutilation and ridiculous dietary laws, stood the Jews apart from all others. "And when you stand apart, you stand alone," my father used to say.

I kicked at a blackened ring stone. It rolled out of its socket and into the pit, raising a puff of ash. Something glimmered in the stirred ash—a gold coin? I picked it up. My Serapis amulet. I frowned at it, then hurled it over the trees. I did not see where it landed, nor did I hear it *clink* as it bounced off stone. I brushed my hands together, glad to be rid of the twin curses of religion and lucre. In the end, religion, which gives man hope, and money, which gives him power, were no more real than man, and all would return to the same dust.

A thunderclap awoke me. I got up on my elbows, grimacing at the stiffness in my back. Lightning lit distant peaks as thunder tumbled across the mountains. The wind swirled sand around me, stinging my eye. I pulled my cloak over my head and huddled against the camel.

When I awoke, the dust storm had passed. I shook sand from my cloak. Directly above me, a circle of empty sky had been carved from the blanket of clouds, the crescent moon centered within it. The clouds slowly circled the moon like foamy water around a drain. I marveled at the strange sight. Suddenly, the moon burst into light, illuminating everything around me for a split second, then shrinking back on itself, becoming a tiny, brilliant sun. The light pulsed momentarily, then elongated, forming a column, which slowly descended toward me.

In the impossibly bright light, I could not move. A distant part of my mind informed me that the light had come to take me. My heart rate slowed, I unclenched my fists, and waited with the first hope I could remember in days.

Soon, the light stood directly over me, pulsing slowly, a myriad of colors shimmering within it like sunlight on calm water. The colors coalesced into shapes. Four legs and two heads resolved for each of three figures. I soon recognized Balthazar's purple turban. Behind him rode Caspar, and on the third camel was a man with a prominent nose and a proud chin. Behind them all the sky was crowded with singing stars.

Like smoke, the caravan wafted away, replaced by shepherds on a hillside curled in their cloaks under the same stars. A pillar of light descended toward them. They awoke and shielded their eyes. A voice bid them to fear not, "For unto you is born this day a Savior."

The hillside dissolved, but the constant stars remained. In the foreground, Herod sat on his golden throne, surrounded by men with knives. He shouted at them, and as they left, I heard women shrieking and sobbing at the death of their children.

Herod vanished and against the same stars, I saw myself crouching at the edge of a fire ring, eyes wide with fear. I had just awoken from the Apep nightmare. My younger self scrabbled backward, searching the ground for invisible serpents. Then realization lit my eyes, and I jumped to my feet. I was going back to Jerusalem.

A cascade of images, then, all against the same singing stars: A full moon cast blue light upon the barren slopes of the Valley of the Kings. Jeshua and I standing on the Pharos balcony, watching as a sail disappeared below the horizon far out to sea. We were in the Museum, examining Philo's solar clock. We were laughing during a meal at Josef's home. Jeshua was wheeling Athena's chair around the courtyard, the merry madness of children's laughter filling the air. We were embracing on the Alexandria docks, saying good-bye.

Then images I had not witnessed: Josef setting up a workbench outside a mud brick house in Nazareth. Young Jeshua at the Temple, responding to the priests' questions. An older Jeshua, planing a piece of wood, his arms muscled, his face browned by the sun. Jeshua again, a grown man now, standing before a whitewashed stone, his arm around his weeping mother. Jeshua emerging from the Jordan as a voice declared, "This is my beloved son."

And the stars sang a melody that was both fire and ice in my heart.

Then the light pillar descended further, enveloping me. I was no longer in the Sinai desert; I was seated with many others on a grassy Galilean hillside, the lake shining below us. Just offshore, Jeshua stood on the prow of a boat, his hands lifted.

"Blessed are the meek," he said, and I blanched at my boundless pride.

"Blessed are the poor," he said, and I felt the folds of my silk chiton against my skin.

"Blessed are the merciful," he said, and I heard my many harsh judgments.

"Blessed are those who are persecuted for my name's sake," he said, and I saw Simeon seated at the boat's tiller, his eyes shining, unaware of his future failings.

"Blessed are they who weep," he said, and I saw the tortured man on the dark Jerusalem street, clutching the sack of coins to his chest.

"Blessed are those who mourn," he said, and I saw the death masks of Thaesis and Athena.

"Blessed are they who believe in me," he said, and I saw Daniel, also in the crowd. In a few hours, a young man who had never seen light would be filled with it.

Now I was on a gravel parade ground. The faith-filled centurion burst from his tent, shouting with joy. Soldiers came running and gasped as a young man stepped weakly from the tent, healed by a word.

Far out on a placid lake, a fishing boat made its way. The wind rose and clouds filled the sky. I was in the boat, desperately clutching the gunwales as immense waves buffeted us. Jeshua slept in the bow, his cloak a pillow. The sails snapped and tore. Men shouted, others cursed, and still others prayed. Philip awakened Jeshua. "Master," he cried, "we perish!"

Lightning forked into the water, and thunder boomed. Jeshua stood and lifted his hands. "Peace, be still." The howling winds died and the mountainous waves subsided. Soon slanting sunlight dappled the calm water. As we stared at him in disbelief, he looked at me and said, "Where is your faith?"

The sun moved across the sky, and it was a different day. We were again out on the lake. Jeshua was walking toward us on the water. Simeon eagerly stepped out of the boat, taking three impossible steps before sinking. Jeshua grasped his hand, lifting him into the boat, where Simeon collapsed in shame. But pride lit Jeshua's eyes. Simeon, the man who denied him three times, had also taken three steps on the water.

We were in Bethany. A funeral procession moved slowly along, lamps lifted against the darkness. Jeshua stood at the tomb entrance. "Eleazar, come forth!" he said, and a man bound in burial linen emerged from the sepulcher. Jeshua took him in his arms, crying with joy.

I stood on a barren hill before the cross. Jeshua looked heavenward. "Abba," he whispered, "into your hands I commend my spirit." The earth shook, and I fell to the ground. Jeshua's head hung limply, his chin on his unmoving chest.

When I came to myself, the light was gone. I lay on the ground by my camel. I thought there were no stars until I remembered I was mostly blind. "Why?" I croaked. "Why send a messiah to die?"

I listened but heard nothing. It was a dream—what of it? What were dreams? Did they mean anything? No. But people *believed* they did—I had made a career interpreting dreams for credulous fools. Maybe dreams were our minds trying to make sense of a senseless world. Or maybe they were our minds protecting us, but from *what*?

From the truth, I thought sadly.

The greatest truth of all: the stars are not gods. The universe is nothing but bits of matter—atoms—careening senselessly through space. Everything that occurs is the result of atoms colliding—there is no purpose behind their random motion. A human is nothing more than a jumble of atoms; therefore, life has no purpose. There are no gods to judge, reward, or punish us. We live by accident and die the same way.

I lowered my blindfold, rolled over on my side, and bid the darkness come.

Sixty-four

I was in a garden. The morning sun peeked through the trees. The air was fragrant; it had rained the night before. I heard voices and turned. Through the trees, I saw a rocky slope with tombs cut into it. One stood open, a wheel of stone rolled to the side. A blinding light issued from the cavity. I covered my eyes. Hearing a voice, I looked again. A man in white stood outside the tomb, his back to me. A red-haired woman knelt before him, her face radiant.

The man must have heard my approach, but before he could turn, I found myself in a dark room. Men were seated on cushions around a low table, dipping bread into a pot and conversing quietly. Simeon, called Cephas, paced the room, hands clasped behind his back, head down, lost in thought. The room began to brighten, and suddenly Jeshua stood among them, materializing out of the air itself.

The men cowered in fear. Jeshua's face was bright as lightning. He said, "Why are you troubled? It is I. Touch me and see." He held out his hands, which bore the nail holes in the wrists. Simeon touched Jeshua's ankles, which had been pierced by the spike. "You are now my witnesses," said Jeshua, leaning forward and breathing on each man in turn. "Receive the Spirit."

Now I stood just outside the firelight on a lakeshore under a sliver of moon. Jeshua sat with his friends around the blazing fire, sharing their dinner of roast sprat and millet cake. He turned to Simeon and asked, "Simeon, do you love me?"

"You know I love you."

Jeshua repeated his question: "Simeon, do you love me?"

Simeon met Jeshua's eyes squarely. "You know I love you, Rabbi."

Jeshua put his hand on Simeon's shoulder. "Simeon, do you love me?"

Simeon's eyes were full of tears. His life was multiples of three. He had taken three tentative steps on the water. A few days ago he fearfully denied Jeshua three times. Now he confirmed his love a third time: "You know I love you!"

Jeshua nodded. "Feed my sheep."

I stood inside the balustrade of the Temple. The earthquake's scar had been filled in and paved with new granite flagstones. Smoke rose from the altar and billowed above the repaired Sanctuary. The Great Court was crowded. Simeon and the blond disciple, Johanan, made their way through the gap in the balustrade, striding toward the Temple. A lame man sat on the curving steps of the Gate Beautiful, his begging cup raised but his eyes lowered. Simeon stopped in front of the man. "Look on us," he commanded.

The man looked up hopefully, lifting his cup higher.

Simeon considered the man for a moment, then said, "Silver and gold have I none, but such as I have I give to you: in the name of Jeshua of Nazareth, rise up and walk." He took the beggar's hand and lifted him to his feet. The man stared down in shock, then grabbed Simeon, shouting, "Praise Hashem! Praise his Son!" He threw his begging cup away and ran leaping into the Temple.

Again, Simeon, his beard gray and his face lined with age, stood on the steps of the Temple of Saturn in Rome, boldly addressing a crowd. Though his listeners were mostly poor, a number of prosperous men in silk togas also gave him their attention. Suddenly a platoon of Praetorian guards shouldered their way through the crowd and grabbed him, took him before the magistrate, and saw him condemned. He was crucified, head-down. His last words were an assertion that he was unworthy to die as his master had died.

On a barren island in a turquoise sea, I saw Simeon's fellow disciple Johanan in the entrance of a cave. He turned and seated himself at a rough table. By the light of a single candle, he bent over a manuscript and dipped a quill, recording Jeshua's words and deeds.

In a dark room, a scribe copied Johanan's words onto a scroll. Nearby, a dozen similar vellum rolls waited to be filled.

In their Temple meeting place, a Sanhedrin ruler railed against Jeshua's followers. In a tiny upstairs room in the Upper City, I saw a small group of men meeting in secret, the doors and windows shut tight. A man read Johanan's words from a scroll. His listeners were of every race and creed. The words of Jeshua filled the room in Aramaic, Hebrew, Latin, and, much to my surprise, Greek. I saw Roman soldiers burst into the room, arresting them. They were imprisoned, tortured, and some were murdered.

Nevertheless, Jeshua's witnesses shared his logos to the nations bordering the Green Sea. In Rome, I watched in surprise as an aged Emperor declared Jeshua's teachings to be the official religion of the Empire.

I stood at the foot of the Serapeum steps in Alexandria. It had become a meeting place for the followers of Jeshua, who called themselves "Christians," a word derived from the Greek for Moshiach: Christós. Looking up, I was surprised to see a cross topping the pediment. I shuddered, wondering if the Christians themselves chose the terrible symbol or if it was imposed upon them by others. Looking about, I saw crosses topping the roofs of the Paneum, the Vestia Temple, and even Jupiter Capitolinus itself.

I scaled the steps, noting that the bronze sacrificial brazier was missing from the porch. Inside, the giant statue of Serapis was gone. Amidst the forest of columns, a group of Christians sat in a circle around a low table, sharing a meal of wine and bread. A man stood and held up a simple wooden cup, bowing his head. He was obviously their leader, but wore no priestly garb or golden diadem.

"Jesus said, 'This is my blood,' " the man said, taking a sip from the wine cup. " 'Do this in remembrance of me.' "

He then repeated the ritual with a loaf of bread, saying, "Jesus said, 'This is my body' " as he tore it and distributed it to the others. The ritual seemed akin to blood sacrifice, but sacrifice of a different sort: of pride, possessions, and position.

I stood on the banks of the Nile in flood, watching the flotsam of the years flow past. A room of men in heavy, hooded robes carefully copied Jeshua's words from tattered scrolls onto illuminated codices. Behind them were shelves filled to bursting with identical books.

I watched in utter delight as the screw on a contraption as singular as one of Hero's inventions was turned, pressing a platen against a sheet of paper, copying an entire written page in a moment. All around the machine were stacks of drying pages. They were then bound together between leather covers bearing the words der heilige Bibel—"biblion" being Greek for "book."

I saw flamens, priests, and pontiffs reading from the book to audiences in ornate buildings with soaring arches and colored glass windows depicting episodes from Jeshua's life: his birth in a cave, his baptism, his healings, his calming of the storm, his crucifixion, and even his resurrection.

Standing on the banks of the River of Time, I realized how limited my vantage point had been. Yet now, I was receiving the greatest gift of all: Adonai's unique view of our tiny planet, rotating on its tilted axis like a top, orbiting our small sun, the entire affair speeding through space, carefully guided by Hashem himself.

Like me, the world awakened slowly. In the muddy waters flowing past me I saw fire destroy the Great Library and Museum. Geminus's remarkable solar clock lay at the bottom of the Green Sea. The Pharos was shaken into a pile of rubble by an earthquake.

For many years thereafter, the river flowed empty and dark. Science retreated to whispers. Great thinkers were ignored or untrained. Tyrants ruled and armies plundered. Men forgot not only the earth's planned place in the cosmos but their own place as well.

Even Jeshua's words were lost to all but a few, who read them in secret and prohibited others from seeing them at all. Soon his logos was distorted and reduced to fanciful myths for children but ignored by the powerful, those who needed them most.

Then I saw a man nailing a placard to the door of a Christian temple. In his eyes was the fire of a reformer. A priest—now familiarly vested in purple and gold—angrily tore the page off the door, but the man remained defiant and many followed him. After a millennia of darkness, the Biblion was read once more, and people learned of Jeshua's wonderful works and words.

Light began to fill the world. Knowledge was reborn. Strange glass lenses allowed astronomers to view details on the moon. The true understanding of the solar system was restored. Archimedes, Aristarchus, and Eratosthenes were vindicated. Jeshua's logos spread. People of every color heard his words and, emulating him, were baptized as he was, emerging as reborn souls, committed to following their new master.

Technology that would astonish Hero aided their efforts. Wagons without horses raced along iron rails. Silver birds with living people in their bellies soared through the sky. A man spoke into a box and, a world away, another man answered. Across the nations, Christian temples were built, topped by the cross, which had become a symbol not of Jeshua's dreadful death, but of his remarkable resurrection. Like Jeshua's favored fisherman Simeon centuries before, his followers continued to heal the sick, cast out demons, feed the poor, and comfort the dying.

Jeshua's logos had indeed survived. Simeon's name was blessed, not accursed as he feared. His momentary lapse in faith had been eclipsed by a lifetime of loving labor, and millions had followed his extraordinary example.

From my vantage point on the bank of time's river, I witnessed Adonai's gentle hand upon the earth, caressing and caring for all who dwelt thereon, his influence invisible to most, but easily seen by those with spiritual sight. I wept with gratitude that I had been permitted to see these things, my soul blindness finally healed.

I awoke, surprised to find it night, for it seemed I had been traveling through time for days. Yet, it was still hours before dawn. Orion was setting in the west.

I looked into the heavens. Whereas before I saw the stars as an indictment of the absurdity of human hope, now each one was a testament to the order of Adonai's vast universe. They were not distant, fiery stones. They were Adonai's fingertips, touching every point in a universe crowded with his works. Jeshua had not come to earth to be murdered; he came to show mankind the way home. Through the centuries that followed his death, mistaken men had confused much of his teachings, but as long as people read the words, "Blessed are . . . ," no one was confused about how to conduct themselves. His logos was a perfect prescription for joy. Everyone, from beggar to emperor, knew what their purpose was—it was written in their hearts by Adonai himself.

How had it escaped me for so long? How had I lived for so many years without understanding the world and my place in it, when it had been right before me all the time? It was in the eyes of my beloved Thaesis and in the lisp of my tiny Athena: *Love*. Love was all, and it radiated from Adonai, through his emissary, Jeshua of Nazareth.

Now fully awake, I saw a plain stretching out under a starry sky. A multitude filled the plain, their upturned faces radiant with expectation. The promised day had arrived—Jeshua was returning to the earth. These were the souls who had his name written in their hearts. These were the sheep Jeshua asked Simeon to feed. These were his people, chosen not by race, creed, or color, but by the purity of their hearts.

I moved among them like a ghost, looking for my own face, which I could not find. I began to fear. Was I still unworthy to be present on this joyous occasion? I stopped, my heart desperate with despair. It seemed I had been chosen as a witness but not as a participant. I was beyond forgiveness. Hot tears spilled down my cheeks.

"Melkorios."

I turned, and there was Thaesis. And at her side, *standing*, was Athena, smiling up at me. I enveloped Thaesis in my arms. She hugged me, whispering, "Will you not join us?"

"I am with you," I said, drinking in the scent of her hair and skin.

She pulled back and fixed me with her gray eyes. "No, you are not."

My shoulders went slack. "It is hard for me not to doubt."

"Yes," she said. "For you, it is the hardest thing."

Athena tugged at my cloak. I knelt and took her in my arms. Her warmth melted my soul. "Father," she whispered, "I love you."

My heart dissolved into joy.

"You are not far," said Thaesis, kneeling before me.

"No?" I sobbed, clutching Athena tightly to me. "I fear I will never see you again!"

"It is not courage that overcomes fear, but love," she said, touching my cheek. "Fill your heart with love, and we will be reunited."

SIXTY-FIVE

❧

I came to myself. A faint white line on the eastern horizon promised dawn. Once upon a time, I greeted the sunrise with hands raised, celebrating Ra's defeat of darkness.

That morning, I looked down at my hands. In my dreams and visions of the night, I had enjoyed the blessing of two eyes. Now, only the cloudy vision in my right eye remained. I rose and went to the fire ring and sat on a blackened stone, staring into the pit, sobered by a new realization: life was indisputably meaningful and I must face that fact or I would lose Thaesis and Athena—and myself—forever.

I no longer had the luxury of disbelief, for truth now ran in my veins like blood. I saw its golden thread woven through my days. The weaver was Adonai, and he had long worked the loom of my life: My lineage as an astrologer, which taught me to study the night sky; my initiation into the cult of Serapis, where I learned to honor the Infinite; my casting of natal charts, which apprised me of Jeshua's birth; my superstitious fears of Apep, which stirred me to protect Josef and Miriam and their tiny child; my late marriage to Thaesis, which was a crucible for healing my lifelong selfishness; the blessing of crippled Athena, who destroyed my hardened heart and gifted me with a new one; my discovery of the Serapis lie, which freed me from unquestioning belief; the loss of Thaesis, which filled me with despair and planted the seed of humility; and my second journey to Judea, which introduced me to Jeshua's life-changing logos.

In addition, Adonai had skillfully woven many people into my life: The faithful magi, Balthazar and Caspar; the steadfast priest Zechariah and his blessed wife Elisheba; the loving tekton Josef and his soulful sweetheart Miriam, earthly mother of Jeshua; the visionary Daniel and his lovely bride Miriam; the faithful centurion Lucius Aquila; the fierce disciple Shimrith; the humble inn mistress Deborah; the jolly Samaritan Zebulon; the courageous Pharisee Nicodemus; the compassionate disciple Philip; the weak yet unmatched Simeon Cephas; the magnificent Miriam of Magdala—my poor life would have been immeasurably poorer without each and every one of them. I fell to my knees, closed my eyes, and gave thanks for them all.

When I opened my eyes, I saw a star on the western horizon. It was not Mercury or Venus, for they followed the sun. It was not a comet, for it had no tail. It was not Mars or Saturn or Jupiter, for they were in their appointed places elsewhere in the sky. It was a new star. And this time, I did not doubt the miracle, because I knew it had been specifically woven into *my* tapestry. I looked at it and whispered, "What do you wish, Adonai?"

Believe.

"I believe," I whispered. "Help my unbelief."

Belief is action—it is what we do.

"But Adonai," I said, "I am old, lame, and blind. What can *I* do?"

Fill your heart with love.

"I will try," I said. "Will you help me?"

I always have.

"Long ago," I whispered to the star, "I followed another star. Now I will follow *you*. I will falter, and I will stumble . . . but I will follow."

ACKNOWLEDGMENTS

When writing historical fiction, the author is expected to get the history right as well as the made-up stuff. Because a listing of all my sources would be impossible, I will mention only the most memorable books I consulted: *Life in Egypt Under Roman Rule* by Naphtali Lewis; *The Rise and Fall of Alexandria* by Pollard and Reid; *The Greco-Roman World* by James Jeffers; *Josephus: The Essential Writings* translated by Paul Maier; *Knowledge for the Afterlife* by Abt and Hornung; *Cities of the Biblical World* by LaMoine DeVries; *Rabbi Jesus* by Bruce Chilton; *The Mummy* by Wallis Budge; *The Bible Atlas* by Aharoni and Avi-Yonah; and *Charting the New Testament* by Welch and Hall. Though not one percent of the valuable information in these and other brilliant books made it into *The Wise Man Returns*, all of it made it into *me*, and thus I thank the authors.

After research comes writing, and for that I am solely responsible. Because of the contributions of so many, this writing experience was a uniquely illuminating and satisfying one. The first person viewpoint is always a challenge, especially when writing about events about which almost everyone has knowledge *and* an opinion. I hope my entry into these well-known waters will be received with patience and forbearance by my readers.

After writing comes reaction, and I was blessed with a number of thoughtful friends who reviewed the manuscript and offered wise counsel: Natalie Reed, Marilyn Brown, Jack Welch, Douglas Page, Cheri Gittins, Bonnie Sheets, Pat Kennedy, and Virginia Kemp.

Reid Later did the first massive review, ensuring that the manuscript would be accepted by Shersta Gatica at Cedar Fort Publishers, which put talented editor Megan Welton on the case. Heather Holm and Michelle Stoll did a final clean-up, and then it went to designer Angela Olsen, who produced a book cover that beautifully captures my highest hopes for Melchior's story.

Marketing was overseen by Adam Thomas, who authored the alchemy which finally resulted in the book finding its way into your hands. Bookselling is an art, and so I would like to thank the many people who have recommended or reviewed this book. Hundreds of thousands of books are published each year in America, and shelf space is steadily shrinking, so the fact that you have found and then chosen to read my book is nothing short of a miracle.

So I thank you, dear reader, most of all. I believe everyone has a story to tell, and I have been blessed to have received, over the course of my life, encouragement sufficient to believe my stories were worth sharing. I have always been fascinated by belief and sometimes even my own belief seems balanced on the most tenuous of evidence. Nevertheless, those of us who see the Infinite in the night sky have a great advantage over those who do not: we can, in good faith, wish upon a star. And, as Melchior discovered, the Clockmaker is wonderfully generous: there are stars we don't have wishes for.

—KENNY KEMP

APPENDIX A

HISTORICAL FIGURES

ALEXANDER THE GREAT *(356–323 bc)*

Alexander inherited Macedon, a state in the northeastern region of Greece, from his father, Phillip II, before he was twenty. By the age of thirty, he had created one of the largest empires in history, stretching from Greece to the Himalaya, but died at age thirty-three in Babylon, presumably of poisoning. Tutored by Aristotle himself, Alexander had in mind an empire covering the known world, and to that end he built eponymous cities everywhere he went, including the famed Alexandria in Egypt. In the years following his death, his empire was rocked by a civil war waged between his own generals. One of these, the clever Ptolemy I, kidnapped Alexander's corpse from Babylon and took it to Egypt, where he placed it in a crystal sarcophagus in Alexandria.

ANAXIMANDER OF MILETUS *(610–534 bc)*

Ionian scientist and perhaps the first person to conduct an experiment, Anaximander examined the shadow cast by a vertical stick and thus accurately determined the length of the year and the seasons. He invented the sundial, a map of the world, and a celestial globe with constellations. He also proposed human evolution from lower animals.

ARCHIMEDES OF SYRACUSE *(c. 287–212 bc)*

Greek mathematician, physicist, engineer, astronomer and philosopher, Archimedes exceeded all other mathematicians prior to the Renaissance. In a civilization with an awkward numeral system and a language in which "myriad" (literally "ten thousand") meant "infinity," he invented a positional numeral system and used it to write numbers up to 10^{64}. He invented the water-lifting screw, levers, hydrostatics, odometers, the compound pulley, siege engines, water-timers, catapults, and was the first to identify the concept of center of gravity. Archimedes and his contemporaries constituted the peak of Greek mathematical rigor. During the Middle Ages, mathematicians who could understand Archimedes' work were few and far between. Many of his works were lost when the Library of Alexandria burned, surviving only in Latin or Arabic translations. As a result, his mechanical methods were lost until around 1900, after arithmetization analysis had been carried out successfully. We can only speculate about the effect that his method would have had on the development of calculus had it been known in the 16th and 17th centuries.

ARISTARCHUS OF SAMOS *(310–225 bc)*

Greek mathematician and librarian at Alexandria. From the size of the earth's shadow on the moon during a lunar eclipse, Aristarchus deduced that the sun had to be much larger than the earth, as well as very far away, which led to the question: why would a much larger body like the sun revolve around a smaller one, like the earth? Unable to answer his question, he invented the heliocentric ("sun-centered") theory of the solar system and went on to postulate that the earth rotates on its axis once a day and circles the sun once a year. But his theory was rejected by most of his contemporaries because of the religious implications of a non-earth-centered universe. Some credit him with the discovery of precession, the top-like wobbling of the earth on its axis, which results in the Grand Circle of 26,000 years in which the earth's pole moves in a circle, passing through, as it does today, the star Polaris (currently the pole star).

ARISTOTLE *(384–322 bc)*

Aristotle was the Greek student of Plato and teacher of Alexander the Great and possibly Ptolemy I as well. He wrote on many subjects, including physics, poetry, zoology, logic, rhetoric, government, and biology. Along with Plato and Socrates, he is considered one of the most influential Greek philosophers. Aristotle is known for being one of the few figures in history who studied almost every subject possible at the time. In science, Aristotle studied anatomy, astronomy, economics, embryology, geography, geology, meteorology, physics, and zoology. In philosophy,

Aristotle wrote on aesthetics, ethics, government, metaphysics, politics, psychology, rhetoric, and theology. He also dealt with education, foreign customs, literature, and poetry. His combined works practically constitute an encyclopedia of Greek knowledge.

AUGUSTUS OCTAVIAN CAESAR *(63 bc– ad 14)*

Augustus Caesar was the first emperor of the Roman Empire, which he ruled from 27 BC until his death. Born Gaius Octavius Thurinus, he was adopted by his great-uncle Julius Caesar via his will. When he took power, the Senate awarded him the honorific title Augustus ("revered one"). After Julius Caesar was assassinated in 44 BC, young Octavius joined forces with Mark Antony and Marcus Lepidus in a military dictatorship known as the Second Triumvirate, which was eventually torn apart due to the competing ambitions of its members. Lepidus went into exile, and Antony committed suicide following his defeat at Actium in 31 BC. Under Augustus's rule, Rome remained a republic in name only, as he wielded near-total autocratic power bequeathed to him for life by the Senate because of his substantial wealth, his special ties to the military, and the acclaim of the people. His rule through patronage, military power, and accumulation of the offices of the defunct Republic became the model for all later imperial governments. Augustus enlarged the Empire dramatically, annexing Egypt, Dalmatia, Pannonia, and Raetia; expanded possessions in Africa; and completed the conquest of Hispania. Upon his death, he was declared a god by the Senate and was worshipped as such. His names Augustus and Caesar were adopted by subsequent emperors, and the month of Sextilis was renamed "Augustus" (now August) in his honor. He was succeeded by his adopted son, Tiberius.

DEMETRIUS OF PHALERUM *(c. 350–280 bc)*

Demetrius was an Athenian orator and a student of Aristotle. In Egypt, he met Ptolemy I, and tradition has it that his suggestion resulted in the creation of the Library of Alexandria.

DEMOCRITUS OF ABDERA *(460–360 bc)*

Ionian scientist who said that the simplest forms of life arose from primeval ooze, Democritus invented the word *atom*, Greek for "unable to be cut." He believed the Milky Way was composed mainly of unresolved stars and did not believe in the gods or in the immortal soul.

DINOCRATES OF RHODES *(c. 330 bc)*

Greek architect and technical adviser to Alexander the Great, who appointed him director of surveying and urban planning work for the proposed Egyptian city of Alexandria. He also worked on, among other things, a funerary monument for King Phillip of Macedonia, Alexander's grandfather.

ERATOSTHENES OF CYRENE *(276–194 bc)*

Hellenistic astronomer, mathematician, geographer, literary critic, and librarian at Alexandria, Eratosthenes was called "Beta" because he was the second best in the world in many subjects. He invented the armillary sphere, which was used to demonstrate the movements of the heliocentric solar system and is credited with calculating the earth's circumference using trigonometry and knowledge of the angle of elevation of the sun at noon in Alexandria and at a well at Elephantine Island near modern Aswan. His calculations were accurate within two hundred miles. Eratosthenes created a leap year calendar, which was later adopted by Rome, becoming the "Julian" calendar, the predecessor to our current Gregorian calendar. He created a star catalog with constellations and mythology and, using the angle of the earth's tilt, explained the seasons. He believed it was possible to reach India by sailing west from Spain.

EUCLID *(c. 325–265 bc)*

Euclid was a mathematician who lived in Alexandria during the reign of Ptolemy I. Considered the "father of geometry," his most popular work is *Elements*, which is considered to be one of the most successful textbooks in the history of mathematics. Euclid also wrote works on perspective, conic sections, spherical geometry, and possibly quadric surfaces.

GEMINUS OF RHODES *(c. 110–40 bc)*

Greek astronomer and mathematician, Geminus was a Stoic philosopher and scholar. During his career he wrote introductory works in mathematics and astronomy, and is typically credited with the construction of the Antikythera Mechanism (*see* Appendix B). His astronomical observations noted that the length of a day varied in different parts of the world. His mathematical work divided the field into pure and applied mathematics. Pure mathematics included number theory and the various properties of numbers. In applied mathematics he included surveying, musical harmony, optics, astronomy, mechanics, and accounting.

HEROD "ANTIPAS" ANTIPATROS *(c. 20 bc–c. ad 39)*

The most famous of Herod the Great's many sons, Antipas was named tetrarch ("ruler of a fourth") of Galilee and Perea in his father's will. Like his father, he was a notable builder, re-constructing Sepphoris after a great fire and building his capital Tiberias on the western shore of the Sea of Galilee, which he named in honor of his patron, the Roman emperor Tiberius. Antipas divorced his first wife Phasaelis and married Herodias, who had been married to his brother, Herod Philip. John the Baptist condemned this arrangement, and Antipas had him arrested, eventually putting him to death at the behest of Herodias. In 39 AD, Antipas was accused by his nephew Agrippa of conspiracy against the new Emperor Caligula, who exiled him to Gaul, where he died.

HEROD ARCHELAUS *(23 bc–c. ad 30)*

Second son of Herod the Great and fourth wife Malthace, Archelaus was gifted the tetrarchy of Samaria, Judea, and Idumea in his father's will. Prior to traveling to Rome to confirm his appointment, he quelled a Pharisee uprising, killing nearly three thousand people. He later divorced his first wife and married his brother Alexander's widow in violation of Mosaic Law. This act and his astonishing cruelty enraged the Jews, who complained to Augustus Caesar, who deposed Archelaus in 6 AD, banishing him to Gaul and turning his tetrarchy into the Roman province of Judea, ending the Herodian reign in Samaria, Judea, and Idumea.

HEROD PHILIP *(c. 30 bc– ad 34)*

Better known as Philip the Tetrarch, Philip was son of Herod the Great and his fifth wife Cleopatra of Jerusalem, and half-brother of Herod Antipas and Herod Archelaus. He inherited the northeast part of his father's kingdom, marrying his niece Salome, daughter of Herodias, who both appear in the Bible in connection with the execution of John the Baptist. Philip named the capital of his tetrarchy near the source of the Jordan River Caesarea Philippi, to distinguish it from his father's coastal city, Caesarea. When he died without a male heir, his realm was annexed to the Roman province of Syria.

HEROD THE GREAT *(c. 74–4 bc)*

Herod was the second son of Antipater, a high-ranking official under the Palestinian ethnarch Hyrcanus II. He was appointed governor of the Galilee region at twenty-five years old. His elder brother Phasael was governor of Jerusalem. Antipater was poisoned in 43 BC because of his support of Caesar's murderers. Herod, also under suspicion, asserted to Mark Antony and Octavian that Antipater was forced to help the murderers. Convinced, they named Herod tetrarch of Galilee. He was later elected "King of the Jews" by the Roman Senate around 40 BC. Married ten times, Herod often executed wives and even children in his ongoing efforts to retain power in Judea. Upon his death, his will split his realm between three of his sons: Philip, Antipas, and Archelaus.

HERODOTUS *(484–425 bc)*

Called by Cicero the "father of history," Herodotus wrote *The Histories*, a collection of stories on different places and people he encountered in his travels. The word he used, *historie*, which previously meant simply "inquiry," passed into Latin and took on its modern connotation.

HERON (HERO) OF ALEXANDRIA *(ad 10–70)*

Egyptian engineer, geometer, and teacher at the Museum, Hero's most famous invention was the first documented steam engine, the *aeolipile*. Most of his writings appear to be lecture notes for courses in mathematics, mechanics, physics, and pneumatics.

HIPPARCHUS *(c. 190–120 bc)*

Turkish astronomer, geographer, and mathematician, Hipparchus was considered the greatest astronomical observer of antiquity. Using the observations accumulated over centuries by the Chaldeans in Babylonia, he developed accurate motion models of the sun and moon and was the first to develop a reliable method of predicting solar eclipses. He also may have discovered precession (the wobbling of the earth on its axis), compiled the first star catalog in the western world, and is credited with inventing the astrolabe.

HIPPOCRATES OF CHIOS *(c. 470–410 bc)*

Greek mathematician and astronomer, Hippocrates tried to explain the phenomena of comets and the Milky Way. His ideas have not been handed down very clearly, but he probably thought both were optical illusions resulting from the refraction of solar light by moisture that was exhaled by, respectively, a supposed planet near the sun and the stars. The fact that Hippocrates thought that light rays originated in our eyes, instead of in the object that is seen, adds to the unfamiliar character of his ideas, which belong to the realm of speculative philosophy.

HIPPOCRATES OF COS *(460–380 bc)*

Greek physician called the "father of medicine," Hippocrates rejected superstition and magic and laid the foundations of medicine as a branch of science. He is attributed with saying, "He who does not understand astrology is not a doctor but a fool," and, "There are in fact, two things: science and opinion; the former begets knowledge, the latter ignorance."

HOMER *(c. 750 bc)*

Greek poet and tragedian who wrote *The Iliad* and most believe *The Odyssey* as well. Homer (whose name means "hostage") was possibly an amalgam of other writers. Reputed to be blind, his work has had an unparalleled impact on Western literature.

LUCIUS VITELLIUS *(c. 5 bc– ad 51)*

Vitellius was named consul in AD 34 and governor of Syria a year later. A year after that, he deposed Pontius Pilate after the Samaritans complained about his cruelty. Vitellius was consul two more times under Emperor Claudius's reign and even governed Rome when Claudius left to subjugate Britain.

MANETHO *(c. 300 bc)*

Egyptian priest and historian during the reigns of Ptolemy I and Ptolemy II, Manetho is said to have been involved in the creation of the cult of Serapis. He wrote the three-volume *Aegyptiaca*, which divided Egyptian history into thirty dynasties, divisions which are still in use today.

PHILO OF ALEXANDRIA *(20 bc– ad 40)*

Philo was a Hellenized Jewish philosopher born in Alexandria to a wealthy and highly influential family. He was educated in Greek and philosophy and was convinced that Plato and Moses said essentially the same things. He believed Judaism was a universal religion and attempted to insinuate his philosophy into the Greco-Roman culture by asserting that all the good to be found therein in fact stemmed from Judaism. The universal nature of his beliefs resulted in his enthusiastic reception by early Christians.

PLATO *(c. 427–347 bc)*

Student of Socrates and founder of the Academy in Athens where Aristotle studied, Plato wrote on philosophical issues, dealing especially in politics, ethics, metaphysics and epistemology. His most important writings are his *Dialogues*, in which Socrates is often a character. How much of the content and argument of any given dialogue is Socrates's point of view and how much of it is Plato's is heavily disputed, since Socrates himself did not record his teachings. However, Plato was doubtless strongly influenced by Socrates's teachings, thus many of the ideas presented, at least in his early works, were likely borrowed.

PONTIUS PILATUS *(c. ad 5–after ad 37)*

Prefect of the Roman province of Judea from AD 26–36 who acted as judge at Jesus's trial, authorizing his crucifixion. He was described as greedy, vindictive, and cruel. Breaking with the practice of prior prefects, Pilatus scorned Jewish customs and did little to build a relationship between the Jews and Rome. An example of this is the story of Pilatus allowing Roman soldiers to carry their standards under the cover of night into Jerusalem, a violation of Mosaic Law because of the images of the Emperor on them. The next day, when the population discovered the standards flying atop the ramparts surrounding the Temple, great mobs besieged Pilatus in his coastal capital of Caesarea and did not allow him to leave until the standards were removed.

PTOLEMY *(367 bc– c. 283 bc)*

Macedonian general under Alexander the Great (and possibly his half-brother) who became ruler of Egypt and founder of the Ptolemaic Dynasty, which lasted three hundred years until the death of Cleopatra in

30 BC. One of Alexander's most trusted generals, he was also one of Alexander's seven trusted bodyguards. Following Alexander's death, Ptolemy took his body to Egypt to solidify his role as successor and then engaged in a series of wars (the Diadochi Wars) against various enemies as well as the other generals he had once served with. When he died at 84, he left a well-ordered realm and a reputation for liberality and shrewd governance, including the creation of the Greek/Egyptian cult of Serapis, which subdued Egyptian natives and allowed his rule to prevail.

PYTHAGORAS *(560–500 bc)*

Ionian/Greek geometer, born on the island of Samos in the Aegean, Pythagoras is considered the "father of numbers." He deduced that the earth is a sphere by noting that when ships disappear over the horizon, their sails disappear last. He was author of the famous theorem: "the sum of the squares of the shorter sides of a right triangle equals the square of the longer side" ($a^2 + b^2 = c^2$). Pythagoras invented the word *cosmos* to explain a well-ordered and harmonious universe. He postulated that the planets orbit the sun in perfectly circular orbits, not ellipses, which was an impediment to Kepler, centuries later.

SOCRATES *(469–399 bc)*

Athenian philosopher and teacher, none of whose writings have survived. Plato, following Greek tradition, appears to have attributed his own ideas, theories, and possibly personal traits, to his mentor. Socrates was said to have run a school famous for the "Socratic Method," in which key moral concepts such as *good* and *justice*—terms constantly used without any real definition—were defined through a series of questions designed to force the student to examine his own beliefs and the validity thereof. The Socratic Method eliminates faulty hypotheses by steadily identifying and eliminating those which lead to contradictions. Thus, Socrates is regarded as the father of political philosophy and ethics.

STRABO *(64 bc– ad 24)*

Greek historian, geographer, and philosopher, Strabo made extensive travels to Egypt. He is mostly remembered for his 17-volume *Geographika*, which presented a descriptive history of people and places from different regions of the known world.

THALES OF MILETUS *(625–550 bc)*

Considered the founder of natural philosophy, Thales was the Ionian astronomer who predicted solar eclipses. He measured the height of a pyramid from the length of its shadow and the angle of the sun above the horizon and comparing it to a stick placed into the ground nearby, of which he knew the height. He proved geometric theorems of the sort codified by Euclid three centuries later. He sought to explain the world without resorting to supernatural explanations, believed water to be the fundamental element, affirmed the ecliptic, and calculated the size of the sun.

TITUS LIVIUS (LIVY) *(59 bc– ad 17)*

Roman historian whose 142-book *History* spans the time from the end of the Trojan War to AD 17. He foresaw the decline of the Empire due to its lasciviousness and immorality. Livy believed Rome was a mighty nation, but its history was in many ways squalid and brutal. He felt that no nation grows great without great virtues, and it was those virtues—fair dealing, integrity, the fear of God, political competence, and, above all, a devoted patriotism, which resulted in Roman dominance and power.

ZENODOTUS *(c. 280 bc)*

Greek grammarian and literary critic, Zenodotus was first librarian of the Library of Alexandria. He was responsible for the division of Homer's epic poems into twenty-four books each and was possibly the author of the calculation of the days of the *Iliad* in the *Tabula Iliaca*.

APPENDIX B

THE ANTIKYTHERA MECHANISM

In Chapter XXII, Melkorios is invited by Josef to a presentation at the Museum, where Philo shows the astonished crowd a large box with many dials. This was the world's first computer, and it actually existed during Jesus's time. Historians posit that a storm sunk the ship carrying it near the Greek island of Antikythera. For the purposes of my story, I had it survive the storm and stop in Egypt on its way to Rome.

In October 1900, a team of Greek sponge divers were diving near the island of Antikythera, northeast of Crete, when they came upon a shipwreck about sixty meters deep. Among the bronze and stone statues, they recovered a chunk of rock that had a gear wheel embedded in it. This mechanism is now considered the world's oldest computer and has been dated to about 100 BC. The degree of its technological sophistication and complexity did not reappear until the 14th century.

About the size and shape of a large shoebox, the mechanism contains seventy-two intermeshed gears and may have originated in Corinth, which implies a connection with Archimedes. When stood on end, a crank on the side enters a date, and the mechanism calculates the position of the sun, moon, stars, and planets. The box has three main dials, one on the front and two on the back.

The front dial has two concentric scales, the outer marked with the 365-day Egyptian calendar. The inner scale is marked with the Greek signs of the Zodiac and is divided into degrees. Three hands show the date and the positions of the sun and the moon, including adjustments for anomalies in their orbits. The dial includes a spherical model of the moon that displays lunar phases. The front also includes an almanac that marks the rising and setting of specific stars, which are identified by Greek characters.

The upper back dial forms a spiral with forty-seven divisions per turn. It displays the 235 months of the Metonic Cycle, an almost perfect multiple of the solar year and the lunar month. NASA still uses this nineteen-year cycle today when analyzing launch windows for lunar missions. It is also the basis for the Hebrew calendar.

The lower back dial is also in the form of a spiral with 223 divisions showing the Saros Cycle, which predicts eclipses of the sun and moon. Ancient Babylonian astronomers, the *magi*, are credited with the discovery of this cycle.

Scientists first speculated that the Antikythera Mechanism was a clock or astrolabe, but after recent 3-D X-ray tomographic scans revealed all its hidden wonders, the consensus now is that the mechanism is an astronomical device used to predict the seasons, the movement of stars and planets, eclipses, and even to fix the date of the Olympic Games.

Over the years, many copies of the device have been constructed. A 2006 model was built in London by Imperial College professor Michael Wright. Reproductions of the Antikythera Mechanism and moving CG renditions thereof can be found online at *www.kennykemp.com*.

APPENDIX C

HE MAGI

Although the magi are an integral part of the nativity story, most of what we believe about them is apocryphal. Greek historian Herodotus said the magi were priests of Zoroaster, a Persian monotheistic religious leader, and thus experts in astronomy and magic. The three men who visited Judea to celebrate the birth of Christ were also known as "kings" because it was the custom back then for philosophers and wise men to be rulers.

The scriptures state that these notable men came from the east, the three most likely places being Persia, Babylon, and the desert regions of Judea. They were probably Gentiles because they are portrayed as referring to the Jews as a foreign people and showing no knowledge of Jewish scripture. The traditional view is that there were three magi because there were three gifts given to the child. Alternate traditions have as few as two and as many as twelve visiting Jesus.

Their traditional names in Western Christianity are Caspar, Melchior, and Balthazar. Ethiopian Christians call them Karsudan, Hor, and Basanater. Armenians have Kagpha, Badadakharids, and Badadilma. Syrian Christians call them Larvandad, Hormisdas, and Gushnasaph.

The magi first visited Herod, asking him where the newborn King could be found. Herod, showing his knowledge of prophecy, sent them to Bethlehem, and asked that they return when they had found him (Matt. 2:1–8). There they appeared before the infant Jesus, noting that they observed the Star of Bethlehem *rising in the east* (another possible translation: his star was in the ascendant, an astrological term denoting coming greatness), and offered him gifts of gold, frankincense, and myrrh. The magi were warned in a dream not to go back to Herod and so returned home by another route. This infuriated Herod and resulted in his massacre of the innocents.

Their gifts were notable. Gold was given because it was a traditional offering symbolizing kingship and virtue. Frankincense is a whitish resin derived from the bark of the Boswellia tree and is burned in homage to deity, the smoke rising heavenward like the prayers of the faithful. Myrrh is an aromatic gum resin that oozes from cuts in the bark of the dindin tree, which then hardens into tear-drop shaped chunks that are ground into powder or made into ointments or perfumes.

Myrrh has many medicinal uses, including the cleaning of wounds and sores, treatment for worms, coughs, colds, sore throats, and indigestion. Myrrh was also used as a painkiller, such as when Christ was offered "wine mingled with myrrh" on the cross (Mark 15:23). In addition, myrrh was often used in the embalming or anointing of the dead and thus came to represent mortality, suffering, and sorrow. Nicodemus bought a mixture of myrrh and aloes to prepare Jesus's body for burial (John 19:39). In liquid form, it was used as anointing oil or to perfume men's beards. The psalmist portrays Christ as a king upon his wedding day being clothed in garments scented with myrrh and aloes and cassia (Ps. 45:8).

APPENDIX D

The Star of Bethlehem

> Now when Jesus was born in Bethlehem of Judea in the days of Herod the king, behold, wise men from the east came to Jerusalem, saying, "Where is he who has been born king of the Jews? For we saw his star in the east and have come to worship him."
>
> —Matthew 2:1–2

Matthew's account indicates that the magi knew from the star—even before they arrived in Jerusalem—that a Jewish king had been born. And though Luke says Jesus was born in a stable, Matthew notes that the magi found Jesus with his mother in a house and he was by then a "young child" (Matt. 2:11) as opposed to a "babe" as indicated in Luke 2:16. Further indication of time passing is seen when Herod had every Jewish child under the age of two killed, so it may have taken the magi up to two years to arrive in Judea after the birth.

Luke reports that a census ordered by Augustus Caesar was under way when Jesus was born. Roman records reveal censuses in 28 BC, 8 BC, and AD 14. In an empire as large as Rome's, the census would take years to complete. Roman historical records place the death of Herod the Great in the year 4 BC. Taking into account the dating of Herod's slaughter of the innocents (above), it is likely that Jesus was born around 6 BC, which begs the question: What astronomical events occurred during that time?

The word *planet* is Greek for "wandering star" because of the atypical transits of some planets across the night sky, sometimes slowing down, stationing, or speeding up. The ancients were as familiar with the movements of heavenly bodies as we are with tonight's television program line-up. Any changes or variations on the endlessly repeating parade of celestial objects would have been cause for interest or even alarm, as was the case of comets, which were considered bad omens. Therefore, if the Star of Bethlehem was an actual object in the night sky, it is hard to imagine the entire population of the Levant not making the journey to Bethlehem to witness the birth of the Savior. But this was not the case, as we know of only a few nearby shepherds witnessing the world-changing event. The magi appeared months, maybe years later, also led by a "star." By now it is reasonable to wonder if the Star of Bethlehem was an astronomical event or an astrological one.

It may have been both. In order for an astronomical event to go unnoticed by everyone in Judea, it would have to be somehow obscured. Because the sun hides the starry sky during the day, the "star" of Bethlehem may have been an astronomical event that was found on star charts yet invisible to the naked eye.

In astrology, the planet Jupiter (the Romanized version of Zeus, king of the Greek gods) bears special significance, and a lunar conjunction with Jupiter is held as one condition for a king's birth. In such cases, the heavenly bodies appear as one to the naked eye—that is, if they are not obscured by the sun.

On April 17, 6 BC, such a conjunction took place. At dawn on that spring morning, Jupiter rose behind the sun in close proximity to the moon and Saturn in the constellation Aries, which ancient stargazers associated with the Jews because of the story of Abraham and the ram in the thicket (Gen. 22:13). The conjunction of the sun, moon, Jupiter, and Saturn was a portentous event to ancient astronomers, as the greatness of a ruler depended upon the number of regal astrological events at the time of birth. The Jews did not practice astrology because it was considered pagan, and so they would not have recognized the significance of the conjunction or its presence in the Aries constellation, even if they could have seen it.

The conditions of that day never repeated again perfectly, but the core elements have a period of about sixty years. This is a short time, but it was very long for ancient times—a once-in-a-lifetime occurrence.

A spring date for the birth also corresponds with Luke's account in which shepherds were watching their flocks by night. As opposed to other seasons when flocks were generally gathered inside the walled family compound for protection against thieves and predators, in the spring shepherds tended their flocks in the pastures at night as the ewes gave birth.

Later that same year, Jupiter reversed direction on August 23 and would have stationed again on December 19, which could suggest that the magi arrived at or after that time. The interval of eight months since the birth could reasonably accommodate a journey by the magi to see the newborn king.

APPENDIX E

Jesus and Astrology

This is a delicate subject for believers who were brought up, as I was, to be more than skeptical of astrology—indeed, most Christians flatly dismiss the idea of distant planets exercising some sort of influence on our personalities and lives.

People like us glance at the horoscope in the paper and think, *Well, of course this applies to me. So does the forecast for Gemini on certain days and Libra on others. Since we're all multi-faceted, any of these predictions can be true at any given time. That doesn't mean it's factual.*

There are other dismissive arguments: Twelve houses means 500 million people share the same basic personalities. Why is the crucial astrological moment birth and not conception? Uranus, Neptune, and Pluto were discovered in 1781, 1846, and 1930 respectively, so how could they fit into a paradigm thousands of years old? Isn't astrology a form of bigotry, judgment based on an accident of birth? Why are planets the prime source of influence and not stars or comets? Finally, astrology simply *doesn't work*—its predictions bear no more accuracy than blind chance.

Yes, yes, and *yes*. But still, when confronted with the idea that God wished to inform the world of the Advent, wouldn't he use the system believed in by the majority of people of the time? After all, astrology began not as a way to plan your Tuesday but as a study of the "wandering stars" which sped ahead, slowed down, or stationed against the stolid, predictable march of the starry background. These inexplicable movements excited humanity's pattern-seeking tendency—there *had* to be an explanation for their erratic transits.

This motion is called "apparent retrograde," and, like a faster car on a highway, when the earth overtakes an outer planet's slower orbit, it appears to stop, reverse motion and move backward for a time, then resume its forward motion as we pass it. The inner planets Venus and Mercury also retrograde, but because of their closer orbits to the sun, their retrograde cycles are less noticeable.

As I've shown in Appendix D, a good candidate for the date of Jesus's birth is April 17, 6 BC, due to a conjunction of the known planets, sun, and moon at dawn in the Aries constellation, a once-in-a-lifetime event for the people of that time. It only remained to create a birth chart of the sort Melkorios would have drawn to confirm that a king of the Jews had been born.

Modern astrologers use software programmed with astronomical data to locate the position of celestial objects. The Antikythera Mechanism explained in Appendix B is an example of the clockwork nature of our universe: just turn a crank, and the planets move through their predictable positions. Astrologers then apply traditional understandings of the objects' relations with one another to "cast" horoscopes. Thus it is a simple thing to turn back time and look at the sky at the moment of Jesus's birth and cast his natal chart.

More on that anon, but first you'll need a short introduction to astrology so when you see the chart you will be able to make sense of it.

The *zodiac* (Greek for "circle of animals") was codified as early as 2,600 BC for the benefit of seafarers seeking a celestial mapping system. Twelve constellations are found in the ecliptic (the planets' orbital path), which determine the twelve "houses" of energy that are believed to influence our lives: self, money, communication, home, creativity, service, partnership, shared resources, education, reputation, friends, and secrets.

The birth chart is a wheel divided into twelve pie-shaped houses with celestial objects (planets, sun, moon) placed thereon according to their actual location in the sky at that time and place. The newborn's first breath indicates the time of day used to calculate the chart, as does the location of the birth.

The objects on the chart change significance according to the house in which they appear. For example, the presence of the sun in a house makes the characteristic of that house your predominant characteristic. The sun sign is further categorized according to energy (male or female), quality (proactive, stubborn, or flexible), and element (kind of energy, practicality, intellect and social I.Q., sensitivity).

Each of the twelve signs rises over the horizon for two hours every day. The sun sign that rises at the moment of your birth represents what you show to the world. Except those born precisely at dawn, we all wear "masks" different from our true selves as determined by the house in which the sun sign is found.

The planets denote mental and emotional energies, as well as the people in our lives. (For this purpose, the sun and moon are also planets.) When a planet is present in a house, it rules that house, otherwise the following is the case: the sun, moon, Mercury, Venus, and Mars govern personal energies, Jupiter and Saturn affect social relationships, and Uranus, Neptune, and Pluto are involved in trans-personal aspects, including intuition, idealism, the subconscious, spirituality, power, and transformation.

If you believe that astrology doesn't affect you, think again. We have seven days of the week because that was the number of planets known to the ancients: Sunday (sun), Monday (moon), Tuesday (French: *Mardi*, in reference to Mars), Wednesday (French: *Mercredi*, in reference to Mercury), Thursday (French: *Jeudi*, in reference to Jupiter), Friday (French: *Vendredi*, in reference to Venus), Saturday (Saturn).

There are a great number of other elements on a chart, including angles, aspects, signatures, and so forth, but what we really want to know is how accurate Jesus's birth chart was.

A simplified chart appears at the end of this entry. You will immediately note that the chart is extremely lopsided. All the known planets of the time (along with the moon) are found in close proximity to the sun, which is the conjunction noted in astronomical charts as well.

The rising sign (the sun) is in Aries (denoting new beginnings) and reveals major personality traits, which in this case are dynamism, a confident personality, and tremendous leadership potential. The sun in the 12th house denotes a powerful instinctual response to life that results in an occasional need to withdraw to meditate. Drawn to the helping professions, the subject empathizes with others' difficulties, but is also idealistic and highly imaginative, even visionary. The sun rising at the moment of birth means the subject wears no mask before the world; he has no hidden agenda or falseness about him.

The moon represents secondary traits, the past, and instinct resulting in deep emotional needs. The moon in Taurus means the subject is stable and loyal, slow to anger, but dangerous when aroused. Its presence in the 1st house (see the inner numbered dial) denotes moodiness and impulsiveness, which are balanced by powerful instincts. The moon in conjunction with the sun denotes a tension between will and emotion, but that tension sparks great achievement. Tension also exists between the subject's parents (Mary and stepfather Joseph?). Mercury's conjunction denotes a conflict between rational thought and emotional responses (cursing the unripe fig tree?). Mars's conjunction with the moon means sensitivity and intense emotions.

Mercury is the planet of communication. Its presence in Taurus denotes a measured voice that is attractive to others. Its presence in the 1st house yields talkativeness and an ability to gather and share information. Nearby Mars indicates certainty, an ability to trust intuition. Uranus's soft aspect to Mercury results in little patience with opposing viewpoints and a willingness to upset apple carts in the name of progress (cleansing the Temple?).

Venus is the planet of relationships. The subject is compassionate and loving, with strong empathic abilities, giving without limits, and seeing others for who they truly are. The subject also has a great attraction to those with special needs (healing of the sick?), but must be on guard about developing unrealistic expectations of himself and others ("Could ye not watch with me one hour?"). Poetry, art, and music hold special appeal. Earthly concerns such as money hold little interest ("Behold the lilies of the field . . ."). Venus in the 12th house denotes an extraordinary ability to instantly "know" other people ("I will make you fishers of men . . ."). The subject may experience at least one affair of the heart that they choose to keep to themselves.

Mars is a chart-ruler and connotes impressions made on others. It is a planet of action and indicates where energy is placed. Its presence in Taurus denotes determination and endurance bordering on fanaticism and thus supports the craftsman/artisan profession choice (Jesus was a *tekton*, Greek for "artisan"). Mars's presence in the 1st house means the subject is active, impulsive, and has a strong sense of survival with a strong physical constitution.

Jupiter is the planet of expansion and taking things beyond normal limits, representing faith, spiritual beliefs, and ideals. Its presence in Aries means success in life will be a direct result of the subject's ability to initiate action. An excess of energy, assertiveness, and optimism are present in this life, but overextension of abilities sometimes occurs. Jupiter in the

12th house means the presence of spiritual protection (comforting angels in Gethsemane?). Other people will not be able to undermine the subject's goals; eventually he will triumph ("Thou couldest have no power against me, except it were given from above . . ."). Meditation and time alone is beneficial for the subject and will result in spiritual experiences (forty days in the wilderness).

Saturn is disciplinary, showing inadequacies in order to guide the subject toward perfection. It also represents life lessons, trials, and tests. Its presence in Pisces indicates issues from past lives that must be resolved ("Here am I, send me . . ."). Life lessons include forgiveness, humility, and altruism. The subject has the ability to combine spiritual realizations with earthly existence, and to do so he must help his fellow man without thought of reward. A tendency to undervalue one's contribution to mankind must be fought (considered the "least of all"). Special care of feet must be given (the washing of the disciples' feet?). Saturn in the 12th house means altruism is a priority. The subject emphasizes with others' feelings of hopelessness and despair because he has either experienced these emotions himself or has memories of past lives to draw upon.

Though the three outer planets were unknown in Jesus's time, they are included here for reasons that will become apparent:

Uranus is the planet of individuality and the unexpected. Its presence in Pisces for seven years places the subject in a large group of people sharing fundamental characteristics of compassion and idealism. An unusual approach to spirituality, including utopian ideals, is the solution ("Ye have heard . . . but I say unto you . . ."). Uranus in the 11th house yields a genius for creating radical or wide-scale social changes through working cooperatively with others who share the same goals ("Go ye therefore, and teach all nations . . ."). Unusual relationships are the norm, and those formed within the subject's group may have a detached quality ("Who is my mother or my brethren?"). Pluto's relationship with Uranus promises a revolution; the subject is a freedom fighter that will leave the world very different from the one he entered.

Neptune dissolves boundaries and is the realm of imagination and spirit. Neptune in the 7th house encourages the subject to see people as they are, not in idealistic fashion. Self-doubt will be reflected back through unreliable others (Simon Peter or perhaps Judas?). Pluto's relationship to Neptune yields a low tolerance for bigotry and narrow thinking (Jesus spoke to the Samaritan woman at the well) and an ability to see the big picture. The subject's spirituality will be transformed beyond recognition after a period of chaos and confusion (the Crucifixion followed by the Resurrection?). Neptune in retrograde means that the subject finds it difficult to share his real pain with others ("And he went away . . . and prayed . . ."), but also reveals a desire to heal the entire world, which begins by forgiving himself.

Pluto transforms and, due to its slow movement across the ecliptic, exerts generational influence. Pluto in Virgo places the subject in a generation whose prime characteristic is radical change in all aspects of life. Its presence in the 5th house reveals an all or nothing approach to love, and its retrograde status connotes a tremendous inner upheaval followed by inner rejuvenation.

As I read the birth chart overview (the complete version is at *www.kenny kemp.com*), I found it difficult to think of anyone *except* Jesus. Gainsayers will dismiss the attributes as universal, and that may be true to some extent, but I found the chart interesting not so much as a prediction of Jesus's life and personality, but as a birth announcement to those who had "eyes to see"—the magi—which prompted them to travel great distances to Jerusalem to pay homage to the newborn as a fulfillment of the Messianic prophecies of the Old Testament.

But it's also interesting in that the birth chart *is* remarkably evocative of the personality of Jesus as revealed in the scriptures: his powerful sense of mission, his boundless empathy and love, his occasional incandescent anger, and above all, the aching loneliness and sadness that built inexorably as he moved toward the incredible suffering at the end of his life.

Plus, as every astrologer will tell you, the planets do not *cause* things to happen, they're mere barometers indicating the energies occurring on earth at a particular time and place. Perhaps the conjunction of the planets in the sky behind the sun that spring dawn of 6 BC were not the only energies being felt upon the earth at that moment. I like to think that God's love in sending Jesus to us was the most powerful celestial influence felt that day and all days thereafter.

BIRTH CHART FOR JESUS OF NAZARETH

Date 17 April 6 B.C.
Time 5:33 A.M. (dawn)
Location Bethlehem, Israel
Coordinates 31 N 43 35 E 12

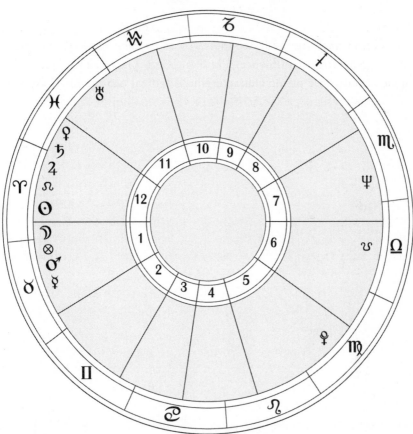

ZODIAC SIGNS	HOUSES	PLANET SYMBOLS
♈ Aries	1. Physical Self, Personality, Early Childhood	☉ Sun
♉ Taurus	2. Possessions, Earning Abilities, Self-Esteem	☽ Moon
♊ Gemini	3. Knowledge, Siblings, Environment	☿ Mercury
♋ Cancer	4. Home and Family, Foundation of Life	♀ Venus
♌ Leo	5. Creativity, Fun, Romance, Risk, Children	⊕ Earth
♍ Virgo	6. Personal Responsibilities, Health, Service	♂ Mars
♎ Libra	7. Primary Relationships, Partnerships	♃ Jupiter
♏ Scorpio	8. Joint Resources, Sex, Death, Rebirth	♄ Saturn
♐ Sagittarius	9. Education, Philosophy, Religion, Travel, Law	♅ Uranus
♑ Capricorn	10. Reputation, Career, Social Responsibilities	♆ Neptune
♒ Aquarius	11. Goals, Groups, Friends	♀ Pluto
♓ Pisces	12. Subconscious, Privacy, Past Karma	☊ North Node
		☋ South Node